Stone Heart

by

Kitty Shields

The Stone Heart Series

Stone Heart

Cover Art by *Kristian Norris*

The Wild Rose Press, Inc.
PO Box 708
Adams Basin, NY 14410-0708
Visit us at www.thewildrosepress.com

Publishing History
First Edition, 2023
Trade Paperback ISBN 978-1-5092-5045-5
Digital ISBN 978-1-5092-5046-2

The Stone Heart Series
Published in the United States of America

"You have plenty of wealth, and you better take it and run, Roma, for I will come for you. Now, let the boy go and let us be done with this business."

"Give me the gem," the man demanded.

"No."

"I will kill him," the robber said, shoving the gun back into Tilton's throat.

Edward looked from the Roma to Tilton and back again. He wanted to kill, Edward realized. There was hatred in his eyes. He hated them, and they had never met. Edward took the handkerchief from his pocket, rubbed the stone clean, and then folded the handkerchief neatly into squares. He tucked it inside his front vest pocket as he bent down and added the stone to the pile. A spasm of pain crossed his face as he carefully set it down, one he could not subdue or hide.

"There," he said standing and stepping back. "I have nothing left."

A wild joy overtook the Roma's eyes. He grinned, pointed the gun at Edward, and shot.

Prologue

August 4, 1789
Dockside, London

The stone heart was gaining in weight. So much so that every step now was difficult for Edward. The tiny satchel under his shirt, half the size of a fist, weighed more than the duffel bag on his back. The leather thong containing the heart pulled at his neck like an inverted noose, dragging him down into Hell. Edward grunted. That's certainly where he belonged.

The stone heart had gained weight every day since he'd found out what it was, not by much, an ounce or two perhaps, but enough. Enough now that it felt like carrying around a toddler. Who knew a heart could be so heavy? Or at least half of one. Half of Phoebe's heart—the woman he had cast aside.

Edward closed his eyes and felt the familiar rush of self-loathing that rose every time he remembered that night. When he opened them again, he was faced with the harsh reality of Dockside. He stared at the weathered, soot-stained docks on the Thames and wondered if this was what Perseus felt bearing the goddess Hera across the river on his back. Certainly, if Edward set one step off the riverbank, he would sink under the water and into the sludge and not be able to gain the air again.

What would the The Daily Rag read then? he thought. *English lord murdered by barrel of fish. Lord Edward Fitzwilliam Pierce, Marquess of Winchester, was knocked off the docks on his way to ship and never resurfaced. Harbor master uncaring, says he should have learned to swim before stepping onto docks. Women's groups complain that filth in harbor is responsible, and call for cleanup or at least perfumed water!*

Without realizing it, a grim smile overtook Edward's features transforming his face from striking to terrifying. Even the Dockside sailors, men whose lives were defined by violence and risk, looked at him warily, noting that this man was not one to vex. Wisely, they danced along the edge of the docks to give him a wide berth. Edward did not pay much attention. He'd not the time for recriminations and wallowing. He could sink into misery after he saved Phoebe's life. For now, he needed to locate his quarry: *The Golden Apple.*

With an inelegant snort, Edward shook his head. He had somehow stepped into a myth, and the golden apple was the prize. If his business manager had not already insisted that this ship was the only one leaving for the Continent this week, Edward would have refused. But he had little time as it was to waffle over stories.

He paused right before the floating dock, wondering if the rotting wood could bear the weight of the stone heart or if the docks would indeed collapse and he would fall to the muddy waters below. The Thames was far filthier than its shores. There was a certainty at the base of his gut, as if some long forgotten instinct already understood that should he fall into the river with the stone heart around his neck, he would not be able to break the surface again. And Phoebe would die.

With a grim shake of his head, Edward cast aside his fear. There was no other way of reaching the Continent. Sucking air in through his nose, filling his lungs as if the oxygen could make him lighter, Edward took the figurative leap of faith. The weight his step introduced made the entire length of the floating dock descend a good foot or so into the murk-ridden harbor water. Several people cried out or paused in their busy comings and goings to regain their balance. They all cast suspicious eyes about or up at the sky for explanation.

Edward tried his best to hunch into his own body and weaved amongst the sailors and couriers toward *The Golden Apple.* One misstep or accidental bump and Edward knew he would fall into the harbor's bosom. A tight, bitter smile touched his lips as he climbed the gangway up onto the front deck. The ship dipped with him, but these sailors took the shift in their sea stride.

A man came down from the foredeck wearing the largest hat Edward had ever seen. The appalling headwear was the color of evergreens, with no less than three ostrich feathers dyed blue, and a silk sash of faded ebony tied around. It was horrific, offensive to anyone with fashion sense, and Edward was certain that most of the ton would faint dead at the sight of it. He had found his quarry.

"Sir," Edward called, "would you be the captain?"

"Aye, that be me," the captain agreed, running his permanent squint over Edward.

Whatever he saw, the captain grunted and came to

the rail. There, he thumped out the ash from his pipe. With the precision of a practiced smoker, the captain stuffed the elegant mahogany piece with new tobacco. The smell of the weed, even unlit, somehow overpowered the stench of centuries' dead fish and detritus reeking from the harbor, a testament to its quality. Briefly, Edward wondered if the pipe, a beautiful piece of craftsmanship sculpted into an ornate eagle's talon, was stolen or earned. But it mattered little. He was not here to police a pirate.

"What business do ye bring to me ship?" the old sea dog asked, bringing Edward out of his thoughts.

Edward noted the flinty glint in the captain's eyes, his mean stance, and the blazing white streak in his dusty black hair where he'd been touched by the Devil. He was beardless, a strange decision for one in his profession, and his teeth were weathered like the wooden planks underfoot. There was a scar at the right corner of his mouth, jerking it wide and up into a grimacing skeleton's grin. He was a schemer this one. Edward made a note to keep strict check on his possessions.

"I need passage to Hamburg," Edward answered. The captain nodded as if such a journey was a spit's distance away. To a man born by the waves and the pull of tides, the distance between London and Hamburg probably was.

"I'll no bargain with ye," the captain said. "Passage costs twenty-six pounds up front."

"Thirteen now," Edward told him, "thirteen on arrival."

"I said I won't bargain," the captain growled.

"Well, sir, I suggest you do not argue either,"

Edward said. "I've no interest in haggling down your price, merely surviving the passage. It would be wise not to cause a ruckus over fair payment terms. Do you agree?"

The captain squinted at Edward once more, either trying to decide whether he told the truth or if it was worth causing the ruckus, Edward could not tell. Finally, the captain nodded, and Edward paid him the thirteen pounds, making sure to conceal the true amount of money he possessed on his person.

"T'aint yer first journey overseas, aye?" the captain asked.

"No," Edward assured him.

The captain nodded. "Ye've the smell of a traveled man. Where have ye been?"

"Abroad," Edward said shortly.

The captain eyed Edward again, then shrugged. He called out his first mate's name.

"Dig, here, will take ye down to yer room. We ain't get many passengers. There's only two others below, a young gentle like yerself and his tutor. Na doubt ye'll meet them at eating time. Stay out of the way of me crew until we cast off."

With a curt nod, Edward followed Dig down below to the closet they called a room. Once alone, Edward looked around and reflected his closet at home was, in fact, larger. Sighing, he set his bag down and sat on the bed, staring out the tiny window toward the sky. He took the satchel with the stone heart from around his neck and slid the object onto his hand, enjoying the press of it into his palm.

It was a rough, uncut red diamond that weighed like a ton of gold. One side was jagged and uneven where the stone had broken in half. The other side was smoother, as if worn down by a hundred thousand tender kisses. It was warm as well, not too warm. Not warm enough by half. Not warm enough for life. And if it went perfectly cold… Edward shook his head. He did not want to consider the implications of that. Instead, he studied it, noting the flickers in the depths of the stone, wondering if the woman whose heart he held could feel his hand around it. Did Phoebe sense him?

Edward once again looked out the window, so like the windows in the haunted tower from the opera. The opera where Nancy Storace had died by fire on stage in front of him. And that, of course, had led him here.

Part One

Chapter One

July 21, 1789
The Royale Theater, Drury Lane

It was immediately agreed by the ton that the new
Drury Lane Theater was an improvement on the old
opera house. And this night was a double bonus. Not
only was the new theater now open, but they were
presenting an English opera. Traditionally, operas came
from the Continent and were translated into English in
the ballad style. Not this season. *The Haunted Tower*
was an opera written by Stephen Storace, a London boy
born and raised in the parish of St. Marylebone, and
everyone tittered with excitement.

Except Edward. Edward was prepared for a night
of dull drama and misspent song. He found the idea of
English opera more than a little tawdry and was about
to say so when he glanced at his mother. As the carriage
drew up, she leaned toward the window with happy
engagement, pointing something out to Miss Ann
Gordon, the other occupant in the carriage. Edward held
his tongue, reminding himself that he was not here for
his own reasons. His father had never missed a show in
whatever city they resided. Edward would not either.

And so Edward disembarked from the carriage and
wiped sweat from his brow. Why his countrymen
insisted on wearing anything heavier than linen in this

sort of humid, July heat escaped him. The Indians knew how to dress for the heat. The English, Edward reflected not for the first time, were stark raving mad. He couldn't imagine how the women were holding up in as many layers as they wore.

Stuffing his handkerchief back into his pocket, he held his hand out to Miss Gordon, eldest daughter of the Earl of Huntly, and aided her down from the carriage. The gossip rags took careful note, scribbling about the perfect couple. Miss Gordon gazed demurely at him as she came down, ever aware of an audience. Edward hardly noticed. He held out a hand for his mother next, the Dowager Marchioness, whom his father had affectionately called Lady Trueheart. Thinking of his father made Edward sigh without even realizing it.

"So heavy a sigh, my son," Lady Winchester said.

Edward grimaced, thought about blaming it on the weather. He hoped the new theater had fans. "Perhaps the opera was a poor idea after all, Mother," he said. *I should have gone to the countryside,* he thought. *Or to the Continent. Denmark is nice this time of year, much cooler.* But every time he thought of leaving London, his mother refused to go with him, and that ended the discussion. He would not leave her, and she would not return to the country manor that only held memories of her dead husband.

"It is the grand opening of the Theater Royale," his mother rebuked, "and we are patrons. We must show our support. Besides, you promised Miss Gordon."

Edward nodded once and arranged his features into a grim smile, offering his arm to Miss Gordon, who'd politely awaited just aside while mother and son spoke.

Of late, the only smile Edward could offer was a grim one. Most other peers of the realm had taken to avoiding him for such an expression, saying that he'd surpassed his father's hawk-nosed fierceness in both caliber and intensity and he lacked his father's good humor. Well, Edward couldn't argue with that. Miss Gordon did not allow such dour expressions to frighten her. Lord Winchester would make a fine husband, once he was turned around. And she had plans for the turning.

"Do you like the opera, my Lord Marquess?" she asked.

They were still getting to know one another, the courting in its infancy so, no, she did not have permission to use his given name. It was true that even "courting" was a heavy word, for it was mostly one-sided. However, if this upset her, Miss Gordon did not showcase it in any way but maintained a perfect level of gentility throughout all their interactions.

She must know the rumors about him. That he was suffering from a broken heart. He had no doubt that his mother had already assured Miss Gordon he would only need time and patience to bring back to the proper direction and fulfill the duty of his rank. Obviously, she considered herself up to the task. And why should she not? As the eldest daughter of the Earl of Huntly, and with a substantial dowery in her favor, their coupling made a sensible match.

Edward did not want a sensible match. But, over the last six months, he'd come to the conclusion that Fate did not intend to give him what he wanted. And he still had a duty to his title to fulfill.

"The opera is passable entertainment," Edward

replied to her question. "My father was quite passionate about supporting the arts. Hence, when Sheridan came looking for patrons for his grand new theater, it seemed an appropriate way to honor my father's memory."

"Of course," Miss Gordon murmured. "This is much larger than the old theater," she said. "And quite fashionable."

While Miss Gordon admired the stunning facade, all ornate gilt, tall Corinthians, and thousands of iron lanterns lighting the front, Edward studied her. Privately, he admitted to himself that she was rather fetching. Miss Gordon was a slight woman of eighteen with the paleness of a true Englishwoman. Her waist was tiny, her dress cinching in to a narrow V and then billowing out in ruffles of pink, embroidered satin at the hips. And yet, he could not help but internally criticize her. The color of Miss Gordon's hair was too yellow, like polished gold, not nearly enough strawberry in it. The curve of her breasts too voluptuous. The size of her hands petite, easily crushed within his callused fingers.

She had one obvious flaw—freckles across her cheeks that she determinedly hid with egregious amounts of powder and vainly tried to disperse with lemon juice. Not even her French perfume could hide the citrusy smell. Edward found her freckles the most appealing feature about her for they were genuine. Despite them, she carried herself like a pureblooded royal and acted like a proper woman that would make a proper wife for any Englishman. She was a pretty doll with views that never compromised her family or their good name. He should want her.

But Edward longed for clever fingers that were skilled at piano and chess and strong enough to deliver a ringing blow. He wanted what he'd given up. And because he could not have what he really wanted, instead he just wanted to let go of Miss Gordon and bow his way out of the opulent room with its pomp and peacocked gentry. To retreat back to his study, his self-appointed work of translating the folk stories of the North. There he could at least forget. However, he promised his mother he would make an effort to be more sociable. So here he was. Socializing.

In the lobby, the Viscount Hereford approached with his wife on hand. He was generally a happy, well-intentioned man and often a great boon at card games as he took very little personally. Edward liked the Viscount Hereford. Or he used to. Tonight, Edward found the viscount's generous, jolly mood mildly offensive. Why must the man always be so damn happy?

"My Lord Marquess, how nice to see you and your mother out and about the ton," Hereford said.

Edward nodded politely, reining in his temper, and in doing so, he forgot to introduce Miss Gordon. His mother stepped in.

"Viscount Hereford, I am sure you know Miss Gordon, daughter of the Earl of Huntly," she said.

"Of course." The viscount bowed, and his wife and Miss Gordon curtsied. "Your father is a man I admire greatly. Excellent in the hunt," he said and then chuckled at his own joke.

Miss Gordon flashed him a smile without any rebuke but full of perfectly feigned amusement and charm. Edward noted it never reached her eyes, but then it did not need to. It simply needed to convince. The viscount chatted happily, and Miss Gordon obliged while Edward stood, a statue void of emotion. She would make a fine wife. She could play all the gentry's games and provide him with children—provide his mother with the grandchildren she so desperately longed for.

His mother nudged Edward into action. He had been silent too long. Withholding a grimace, Edward asked after the Hereford's fortunes.

"Because of the War in America, we lost a large plantation," Hereford said, serious for the first time. "We rely on our holdings in Barbados now, but I'm expanding in the Continent. It's safer. They understand our way of life unlike the Americans. My son Edward"—he smiled at Edward and winked, as if them sharing a name was a secret—"just bought an estate outside Berlin, and from there we shall look into other avenues. We are not as unlucky as some others who lost more in the Rebellion, but I will not risk our legacy."

"Of course," Dowager Winchester put in. "Securing the future for our families is of the utmost importance." Her gaze moved between Edward and Miss Gordon. Again Edward reminded himself of how sensible their match was.

"Thank the Lord, we are not French," Lady Hereford added, flapping her fan in both fear and disgust. News of the assault on the Bastille had just come across the Channel, and it was on most everyone's lips.

The viscount grunted, all trace of cheer gone. "Serves them right for supporting the colonies."

Edward could only agree. His father had died in the war, and his feelings regarding the rebels were strong. Despite good trade with the Americans now, a trade that profited England greatly, Edward had a difficult time seeing the rebels as anything but savage. Phoebe, of course, had disagreed with him heartily on the subject. It was one of the few, and one of the last, arguments they had fought before she quit London. It was then that he had realized he loved her—that they could disagree so strongly and yet he still cared for her. She could always drive him out of his silences and withdrawals. She'd been so very good at it.

"Are you ill, My Lord Marquess?" Miss Gordon asked.

Edward snapped back to the moment and stared at her, not understanding the question.

"You are pale, Edward," his mother said, laying a hand on his forearm in concern.

Clearing his throat, Edward begged for their pardon. Before he could lie an excuse, a groom came around and encouraged them to their seats. After bidding Hereford and his wife farewell, the footman showed up to lead Edward and his guests to their box.

"Is that the Duke of Brey over there?" Miss Gordon asked, nodding across the theater. "I heard he was also a patron, but that he was out of town."

Directly across from their box, in an outrageously bright blue silk suit that matched his wife's dress, sat Rhys, the Duke of Brey. He chatted with his wife, his easy smile flashing across the theater. Edward frowned at Rhys's easiness. They'd been close friends, brothers even, up until last year. The loss of Rhys, Edward admitted, had been almost as difficult as the loss of Phoebe. But some words spoken could not be forgiven afterward.

"No doubt we will see him at the intermission,"

Lady Winchester said, glancing with concern at her son.

I should have stayed in my study, Edward thought.

The dowager patted his arm. Before she could say anything to divert Edward's mood, however, the footman arrived with refreshments. The small group took up chairs while the footman served the champagne, before bowing his way out. Edward turned his back on the theater to avoid looking at his old friend until the lights dimmed and the heavy gold-tasseled curtains on stage drew back.

Pausing in the act of settling into the cushions, Edward watched as a woman glided out to center stage. She looked so like his Phoebe, he had to stare hard from this distance to pick out the tiniest differences. Edward admonished himself. He could no longer consider her "his Phoebe" any more than he could consider his dead father the Marquess of Winchester. Yet, some things were difficult to change in the mind, even if in reality, they changed all too quickly.

The opening aria began, but Edward didn't hear a word of it. He was busy cataloging the actress's looks. Her eyes were of the purest cornflower blue. They could pierce the back of the theater, no doubt. But Phoebe's were a mix of green and gold, like autumn leaves. The actress's neck was longer and her bosom not quite as full. Her height, Edward guessed, was also not quite as tall as his Phoebe. But if he squinted his eyes and let them fall slightly out of focus…

"Who is she?" he whispered.

"Nancy Storace," Miss Gordon whispered back. "She's the rising star of Drury Lane." Edward blinked, having not realized he had asked out loud. "She is married, I believe," Miss Gordon added, her voice noticeably neutral on that last bit.

With a flush of shame, Edward leaned back into his chair away from the stage and cast a quick, irritated look at Miss Gordon. Then he reprimanded himself. He had been practically salivating at the sight of the woman, and he had arrived with Miss Gordon. Her thoughts were clearly misguided, but he could not fault her for reacting to his behavior. Edward had no interest in Mrs. Storace, he was just…fascinated by her likeness.

Shaking these dark thoughts away, Edward returned to his inspection of the actress as the story unfolded onstage. *The Haunted Tower* was no great drama but a beauty and the beast love story where a trapped ghost falls for a local maiden. The opera would be gauche if not for its star. And Nancy Storace was a star. She set the scene, walking through the lonely forest of wooden backdrops in front of a great rundown tower with tiny round windows and a white covered head peeking out, convincing the audience of her loneliness, her fears, her needs. Behind her, the ghost watched and longed, singing a counter-song of his own.

When the curtain touched the wooden stage, bringing an undeniable close to his imperfect musings, Edward realized he'd been completely sucked in. The light touch on his arm made him flinch. There was a pause as he glanced up to see Miss Gordon's somewhat startled reaction. Her face smoothed instantly, obtaining the sort of perfected nonchalance of a marble statue. She inquired if he wanted to go for a drink during the intermission. Reluctantly, Edward pulled himself to his feet and joined her in leaving the box.

In the lobby, women in wide-hooped dresses

mingled with men in finely tailored suits. Edward allowed his companions to weave their way through the throng, as he brought up the tail end. A waiter brought round drinks, and Edward gratefully took a glass of scotch. Through the crowd, the Duke of Brey appeared and bowed over the dowager's hand.

"Lady Winchester," he greeted, genuine affection in his voice.

"Oh, Rhys, Jane," she replied, with a smile.

The Duchess of Brey, resplendent in her blue satin, came over to kiss the dowager on the cheek.

"Edward," Rhys greeted. His voice was cool, his eyes losing their warmth and tuning down to curt. His expression, however, was questioning.

It was the first time they'd met in months, and Edward was surprised at the sharp pain in his chest at the sight of his former friend. It tightened like a cage around his lungs. But just as quickly as the pain arrived, so too did the anger, firing up in his stomach.

"Rhys," Edward said, matching him tone for tone.

He certainly was not going to be the first one to lay down the olive branch. He couldn't fault Rhys for his concern over Phoebe. They were blood. And yet Rhys was as a brother to him. Did that mean nothing? Did those years spent together, the shared grief when they mourned their fathers, the womanizing, the fights, the fun, all of it bear down to nothing? Edward could not abide the words Rhys had said that night. The very memory deepened his anger, and Edward could not keep it out of his eyes.

There was a tightening around Rhys's own eyes that said he saw this, but he was too well-bred to comment on it. He simply moved on to Miss Gordon.

Edward, not distracted this time, introduced them in a cold voice, all the while observing Rhys's behavior toward his companion.

Brey was polite to the point, his bow at the correct degree and his smile, not unlike Miss Gordon's, arranged to display welcome without meaning it. If Miss Gordon noticed, she did not react. Perhaps she did not mind, or perhaps, like Edward, she did not feel any need to be more than polite to the duke.

The duke. Edward shook his head. Rhys had come into his inheritance at the same time as Edward himself. Both their fathers had been killed in the same battle, and news had reached them the same week. It had been that tragedy, that shared grief, that had made their initial bond of friendship so strong. And now it lay in tatters along with Edward's patience.

"—to a ball?"

They were all looking at him.

"Pardon me, what was that?" Edward asked, not hiding the fact that he hadn't bothered to keep track of the conversation. Instead of being annoyed, Rhys seemed faintly smug.

"I was just saying how much you love to dance," Rhys said, "and Miss Gordon replied that you have yet to attend a ball with her. I am indeed shocked," he said, though his eyes lacked surprise.

"I have spent much of the summer concentrating on my work," Edward said tightly.

"Indeed," Rhys said, taking a sip from his glass. "No time at all for dancing? What a shame."

For the first time, Miss Gordon frowned, her beautiful facade broken by the duke's implications. Edward was torn between relief at seeing a genuine emotion, and irritation that it was Rhys who had conjured it. He too frowned with annoyance, and he could see that Rhys took some pleasure in it.

"Well, Edward has come out to show support for this new show," Lady Winchester stepped in.

"Yes, of course, we'd heard that you had become patrons," the duchess said, also trying to put the conversation back on track. She put her arm on her husband's as a restraining gesture. "There is so much excitement surrounding this new style of opera."

"Edward hates English opera," Rhys said flatly. "He finds it vulgar."

All three women paused at that, then looked to Edward. Miss Gordon's eyes took on a calculating glint, while Lady Winchester and the duchess exchanged helpless looks.

"I prefer Italian opera," Edward said. "But I suppose anyone with class does."

The women laughed nervously.

"I have not seen you at the tracks either," the duke pressed on, ignoring the tension in the group. "No more horse races, Edward?" he asked, an eyebrow cocked arrogantly.

"There are more important things than gambling, Brey," Edward replied.

"Ah." Rhys nodded, and his smile was bitter. The deliberate jab using his title instead of his name was clear to everyone that even if Rhys didn't consider the tie severed, Edward did.

Before the conversation could continue, the gong sounded announcing the end of intermission.

"Enjoy the rest of the opera," Edward said with a bare nod in the direction of the duchess as he offered his arm to Miss Gordon. She took it quietly, head high with dignity, and with Lady Winchester in tow, they turned to head back toward their box.

Once seated, Miss Gordon smoothed out her skirts and said, "Well, the duke seems very rash."

She smiled at Edward, no doubt trying to gain his favor by dismissing the encounter, but Edward only glanced at her. He heard his mother follow up with a comment but could not concentrate on the conversation for all the fury burning in his chest.

Of course, Rhys would still be fighting with him as if the last six months had not occurred. He was so damned stubborn! He couldn't see how badly matched Phoebe and Edward had been, and time hadn't changed his mind. Why must he continue this conflict?

Across the theater, the Breys reached their box, and Edward could feel Rhys's eyes on him, pressing into him. Edward unconsciously clenched his fists, and he was glad when the house lights dimmed. He was too angry to pretend to socialize. He considered leaving. Perhaps sneaking away in the dark was a better course of action. He could send the carriage back for Miss Gordon and his mother after it had dropped him off. He did not want to be around people. And then the curtains drew back, and Nancy Storace stepped up again and began to sing. And Edward's need to escape was forgotten in the presence of that face.

The story was silly really. The first act categorized the ghost in the tower falling in love with Nancy's poor village girl character. The second act detailed their impossible romance as the ghost tried to catch Nancy's attention and then win her heart. Edward glanced at the playbill which said it was a comic opera. He wanted to snort, but the singing brought his eyes back to the stage. Again, he saw Phoebe. Despite not wanting to, he became sucked into the story. It was a terrible opera. Phoebe would have adored it.

Without thought, Edward leaned forward, looking for the features in the actress that reminded him of Phoebe. This was torture, he knew, a self-inflicted torture as well. This was not Phoebe, but a simulacrum, a fake. The woman on stage only served to remind him of the loss, and worse, the betrayal. And yet he could no more stop himself from watching her than he could work up the calm to restore his friendship with Rhys. Some ties were severed and could not be sewn together again. Edward had held the scissors himself. Nancy finished her aria and exited stage right to give way for the other players in this story.

A male actor, the rival, Edward didn't even know his name, came out swinging a wooden sword and singing out a challenge to the ghost. His voice was quite good, but Edward hardly cared. He waited impatiently for the moment when Nancy Storace came back out on stage.

When Nancy reappeared and joined in a duet with the rival, the ghost watched them from his tower, miserable and lonely. *I am the ghost,* Edward thought. *I tried to win her affection, and she already loved another.* Nancy's voice rose steadily, as if agreeing with his assessment. Then she traveled down the octave effortlessly, declaring her confusion and indecision for the two males seeking her heart. It was in the middle of this soul-searching moment that her song broke in a horrible choked gasp.

The theater was already silent, enraptured by the

opera, but the silence took on a shocked, thick feel at this overt mistake. For a moment, Edward thought she was going to recover. Then Nancy Storace's eyes widened, her skin faded to a gray-white so quickly it looked like she'd dipped herself in stage makeup, and she staggered forward, reaching out as if she could see a real ghost before her eyes.

A round of gasps echoed around the hall. The orchestra's music abruptly cut off as those closest to the stage jumped to their feet as if to catch the stumbling actress. And then Nancy's sickly expression transformed to horror. Her body straightened violently until she was standing on her toes, her spine arching. Throwing back her head, Nancy Storace screamed a sound of pure animal agony.

She was a trained singer, a well-practiced talent, and so when that awful sound tore out of her body, it lasted minutes. Minutes that trapped the audience and her fellow players who stood rapt, confused, and frightened. The scream ended in a dry, wracking coughing fit, which sent Nancy to her knees. The spell broken, players and ushers converged on the stage. The ghost himself ran out from behind the so-called haunted tower to her side as Nancy convulsed.

It was a testament to the confusion that no one thought to draw the curtains. And so the ton, as well as the actors, all saw what happened next. Clouds of black smoke erupted from the Nancy's mouth as she writhed under the hands of the others who were crying for doctors and trying to hold her down. Then one of the actors shrieked in pain and snapped his hand. More people retracted their hands or fell back as Nancy's hair burst into flames. She cried out in pain and horror, helpless to whatever evil had overcome her. Her skin went from ashen gray to an ugly red and blistered and blackened in large patches as some internal heat burned her from the inside out. Smoke poured from her mouth, nose, and ears. Her eyes swelled impossibly large. Then Nancy screamed again, weakly this time, blood tears streaming down her face. She gasped one last word, before her entire body was consumed by fire and she burnt there on the stage into a heap of smoldering flesh leaving the theater in stunned, disbelieving silence.

Chapter Two

July 25, 1789
Bedlam Hospital

Four days later, Edward looked up at Bedlam and immediately regretted volunteering for this errand. His mother had insisted, as patrons of Drury Lane, on coming to visit and offer comfort to the late Nancy Storace's husband. The man was presently institutionalized after the tragic event a few nights ago. Upon hearing her intentions at the breakfast table, Edward had convinced his mother to allow him to go in her stead.

He did not regret putting her off from this task, for Bethlem Royal Hospital, or Bedlam as it was commonly known, was no place for a lady of her stature. Still, he had no desire to spend more than the smallest necessary amount of time here. Nor did he want any reminder of that awful night. He could not escape that ghastly scene in his dreams. He had no wish to add to the nightmare with details of this foul place.

As he walked up the front path, Edward took in the exterior. The hospital building had once been the height of refinement and science—a testament to the Enlightenment. Now the wings stretched out wide over a vast estate of dying grass like the Angel of Death's wings unfolding. There was a feeling of foreboding, of intimidation here. Between the soot-stained stone and the frayed edges of the dome, it was clear Bedlam was decaying. The place was damned to be sure. The clouds overhead threatening rain, and adding to the humidity didn't make it any better.

The interior was as ghastly as the exterior facade, with dark hallways painted in faded olive and walls bearing the marks of time and madness. Some of the walls appeared to be buckling while the floors were uneven and stained. Edward began to doubt their charity. Perhaps he should have sent Mr. Halkerstone, his business manager, in his stead.

Steeling himself, Edward entered, and a nun guided him to the office of the physician in charge. Dr. Lewis was an ordinary-looking man with little to call attention to outside of a neat appearance and well-tied cravat.

"My Lord Marquess." Dr. Lewis bowed properly. The use of Edward's title indicated the man was familiar with high society and well-trained. Edward revised his opinion.

"Dr. Lewis, how do you do?" Edward greeted. "I've come on behalf of my mother, the Lady Winchester. She wishes to check on the condition of a recently admitted patient."

Dr. Lewis gestured for Edward to sit, which he did, and inquired after the patient. Edward gave the name. The expression it pulled from Dr. Lewis was emphatic and pitying.

"That poor man," he said. "I fear he is quite suicidal. The circumstances surrounding his wife's death are astounding."

There was an eagerness to his voice that Edward did not like, and he, once more, revised his opinion.

"I would characterize it more as tragic, Doctor," Edward said sharply.

"Of course," Dr. Lewis agreed, nodding. The eagerness did not abate. "You must understand, my lord, that for a man in my position, the opportunity to inspect the body of a person whose cause of death was spontaneous combustion is truly a rare one."

"Is that the official cause, then?"

Dr. Lewis nodded. "There can be no doubt. Mrs. Storace was, by all accounts, nowhere near the stage lights, nor, I'm afraid, was her clothing found to be doused in any sort of flammable material. Evidence from the autopsy indicates the flames started *within* her body. It is very…" He hesitated at Edward's dark expression. "Well, it is certainly intriguing."

"And her husband?" Edward asked.

"As I said, a bit delusional and quite suicidal, I'm afraid. The man claims that her death is his fault. Something to do with a fairy-tale heart."

Edward considered this. Perhaps he should not see the patient, after all. Perhaps it was best to simply leave some funds for his care and be done with it. He inquired along this line of thought.

"That is, of course, up to you, my lord," Dr. Lewis said. "Mr. Storace is fully cognizant and capable of conversation. It is just that he has convinced himself so thoroughly of this fairy tale, you see, that he can no longer reason on his own. The death of his wife on the same night their home burnt down was simply too much for his mind to endure. He has retreated into this story. Visiting such disturbed people can have an ill effect on some. Best that your mother did not attend. Do you want to proceed in seeing him?"

Not in the least, Edward thought. But if he did not, his mother would insist on coming back with or without him.

"I had better," he said. "To pay my respects."

Dr. Lewis nodded and guided Edward through some hallways until they stopped at a tiny room. Here, Edward lingered in the doorway, while Dr. Lewis stepped inside to check on the patient. The doctor returned a moment later and bade him enter, saying Mr. Storace was conscious although withdrawn. Edward paused again, reflecting that he had come all this way. And still, the look of Mrs. Storace, so like his Phoebe, coupled with the nightmares, made him hesitate. *Perhaps hearing about a woman unlike Phoebe will put this to rest,* he thought, and stepped inside. The doctor withdrew, allowing them some privacy.

Mr. Storace was a short blond man with what must have once been a sweet, childish face now droopy with despair. His arms hung at his sides like the limp, gray-green hospital gown he wore and the shadows under his eyes. He hunched in his chair, facing the narrow windows which let out onto the dying lawn, but he saw none of it. Edward had an inkling of what the man saw. It took three tries to arouse his attention, and even then, Edward flinched back at the blank horror in the man's face.

He cleared his throat and tried again.

"Mr. Storace…I am Lord Marquess of Winchester, a patron of the Drury Lane theatrical group."

Mr. Storace stared.

"I have come to relay my deepest sympathies on your late wife's passing," Edward said. Mr. Storace blinked slowly, and his brown eyes seemed to darken the shadows around them somehow. Edward lacked inspiration on what to say to that expression of such soul-rending pain. "My heart aches for your loss," he said, knowing how pathetically inadequate that statement sounded. "This was a mistake."

He stood, but Mr. Storace cleared his throat. "A patron?" he asked. "Were you there opening night?"

Edward stopped. He did not want to answer that question, fearing the inevitable follow-up, yet compelled out of respect for the dead to do so. He nodded.

"Did you see her fall?" Mr. Storace asked quietly.

"I did," Edward said just as quietly.

Mr. Storace's expression didn't change save that tears welled up in his eyes. "I loved her so much," he said. Edward could only nod helplessly. "They say smoke came out of her mouth when she fell." He didn't seem to want a confirmation, but Edward hung his head in acknowledgment, feeling ever more a fool for re-stoking this man's pain. "That was my fault. I did not protect her, like I promised."

"Mr. Storace, the fire was not your fault," Edward said. "The doctors said it was spontaneous combustion. No one could have—"

"You do not understand," he said and covered his eyes with his hand, his face drawn and pale.

Edward sat back down. He should not. Good manners and breeding dictated that he make his regrets known and leave the poor man to whatever life remained. And yet Edward could not turn away from this wretched soul. The doctor had said the man was stuck in a delusion. Edward was no medical professional. If anything, Mr. Storace needed a priest.

And yet, his father had always said there were times when men must exorcise demons simply by talking them out. Edward had never been particularly good at this. Rhys would have known what to say. Rhys always knew what to say, until he didn't. Still, Edward asked.

"What do I not understand?" he asked gently.

Mr. Storace dropped his hand, and it hit his lap with a mild *thwack*, lifeless and dull. He looked at Edward. The man simply stared for a moment, his eyes seeing other visions.

"I hid it in a box," Mr. Storace said after a moment. Edward blinked. What did a box have to do with Mrs. Storace's death? "I bought it on Oxford Street after we were married. Nancy proposed to me, you know." He smiled weakly at the memory. Then shook his head to clear it away, his face once more taking up the repose of doom. "She was a wild, free lass. My brothers teased me marrying a thespian, but I cared none. I loved her. God, I loved her so."

He was silent a moment, wiping moisture from his face and pulling at the sleeve of his robes.

"I never thought she would marry me, to be honest," he admitted. "Theater groups travel and whatnot. I am a simple grocer. The money is steady, but not romantic." He glanced at Edward. "Thing was, Nancy loved to come around and buy cherries from my stand when they were in season. She loved all sorts of fruit, but cherries were her favorite, and she said I sold the best.

"I'd give her a discount, on account she was so pretty, and she'd stay and talk to me some. We got to walking out after a while. I went to see her in *Macbeth*. Did you ever see her in *Macbeth*?" Edward shook his head.

"She was marvelous scary," Mr. Storace said. " 'Out damned spot' and all that. No reason to love me, but she did. She said I was the only honest man in London. She said she liked that I was so stable. She had been raised good, and she knew she could not be acting forever. She wanted a life for afterward."

Mr. Storace paused to collect his thoughts.

"One day, I got in a pineapple. It was a tiny thing. A trial one from one of the gardens in Richmond. My friend is a gardener there, and the lord did not want it, on account it not being big enough for his table. My friend offered it to me, and I just knew, just knew, I had to eat it with Nancy.

"So I invited her over. She had been sick all week with a high fever and a dark rash on her chest. I sent her some oranges as they was in season. Once she was better, I had her come over for a proper dinner. I told her she needed her strength for her next show, and we had a grand old time." Mr. Storace smiled. "I've never been so happy 'til that night, laughing with her. She used to tell the best stories, she did. For dessert, I rolled the pineapple out. She was so excited, and we cut it open. I know you lords just put them on display and whatnot. But we ate the whole thing. It was so sweet and delicious.

"She said, 'I have a surprise for you, too.' She got real bashful then. Nancy never gets bashful. From the pocket of her dress, she pulled out a stone, a diamond, really. Uncut, the size of her tiny little fist." Edward felt his stomach tighten. He had seen a similar stone. He had been given a similar stone. "A red diamond," Mr. Storace repeated. "You can imagine my surprise at the…the wealth of it. I was afraid she had stolen it, but she shook her head. She said, 'I grew it, out of my love for you. I grew it right here,' and she pointed to her chest."

Dread filled Edward. The nightmare flashed in his mind along with Phoebe's face. She had been laid low by a high fever as well. Her maid had mentioned a rash, he thought, but it had been gone by the time he saw her next. And the stone she had given him—an uncut gem, red. Red was the rarest diamond. Mr. Storace failed to notice Edward's color. He was crying again, and when he leaned in, his expression became pleading.

"It was her heart," he said, lowering his voice. Edward felt the words like a slap on the face. "I know that sounds crazy, but it was *her heart*." He hissed the last words.

Edward sat back, rattled. Phoebe had said the same thing. But it was impossible. It was crazy, ludicrous. What a story. Edward cleared his throat. "Perhaps it was a representation of her heart, her love for you, Mr. Storace."

"No," Mr. Storace said, gripping Edward's arm. "It was her actual heart. When she was sick, she had grown it out through her chest. That was why we could not cut it or sell it. It would kill her. She told me, she said some families were special. She said I was her beloved," he choked and began to sob.

Phoebe and Mrs. Storace had a keen likeness. Could they have been distantly related? Or was this simply coincidence? There was evidence in Edward's office buried in a chest that he refused to look at for the last six months. Mr. Storace continued to blubber.

"She asked me to marry her. She said if I accepted,

I had to protect her heart. To keep it safe or she would get hurt. I promised her. I promised I would keep it safe forever."

Edward felt his stomach heave. Surprising both of them, he stood swiftly and ran to the nearest bowl, promptly sicking up into it. He hovered over the bowl for a moment, stunned beyond thought.

"You seen one before," Mr. Storace said as Edward straightened.

Edward's hands were shaking as he pulled out his handkerchief and wiped his mouth. He was at a loss for words.

"You know what I speak of," Mr. Storace pressed. Edward looked at him, and there was a sad recognition in his eyes. What was he to say?

"I think I do," he said cautiously.

Mr. Storace nodded slowly and settled back down. His blubbering had ceased, and some of the despair had gone from his face. He seemed calmer now. Edward realized the demons were exorcised. Mr. Storace had found someone to believe him. But the demon had leapt from one man to another and currently sat on Edward's shoulders.

"So you understand," Mr. Storace said. "I killed her."

"You loved her," Edward protested.

"I kept it underneath the floorboards in the living room like a fool. Thought thieves were the only thing I had to worry about. I never thought…"

Tears welled up again in Mr. Storace's eyes, and he shook his head.

"If you know what I'm talking about, then you need to protect that heart. You protect it from the mean world, milord. Make sure no one damages it," Mr. Storace said, his face desperate, as if Edward could somehow redeem him. "No water, no fire, no cutting the stone. Do you understand?"

Edward nodded dully. He could not bring himself to confess the truth, that he had already broken Phoebe's heart. He could only nod. The nurse that arrived seconds later to usher him out was a savior, for Edward couldn't bear the look of hope in Mr. Storace's eyes. He was a damn liar to a man whose entire world was torn away from him. But the story couldn't be true.

Edward walked down the halls blindly following the nurse. Dr. Lewis waited for him back in his office.

"Damn sad, isn't it?" he asked, seeing Edward's face. Edward cleared his throat, tried to work moisture back into it. He nodded once.

"Doctor, was there anything strange about Mrs. Storace's organs?" he asked.

"You mean did she have a heart?" he asked with amusement.

"I meant was there anything about her organs, her stomach perhaps, perhaps something she ate, that could have contributed to her demise," Edward said coldly.

His tone ran the smile off the doctor's face, and the man shifted uncomfortably.

"Not that we could see," he said, shrugging. "There was so much damage to the internal organs, most of them were ash when we opened her up." He caught Edward's expression. "I've no doubt the heart was in there, my lord, simply it was destroyed. The only odd thing we found was shards of a gem melted into the skin of her chest and neck, no doubt from a necklace."

"Mrs. Storace was not wearing a necklace that

night," Edward said with certainty.

The doctor hesitated, but Edward remembered clearly that Mrs. Storace's assets had been on full display without impediment. "It must have been hidden in her bodice, then," the doctor said.

Edward realized he could not refute that one way or another. He agreed out loud and then thanked the man. It was a relief to leave Bedlam behind. Climbing into his carriage, Edward welcomed the dark interior. His thoughts certainly suited the shadows.

None of it was possible. Mrs. Storace had had a heart. Dr. Lewis had confirmed it. And yet, the nightmarish image of Phoebe sprang to mind, immediately followed by the vision of Mrs. Storace aflame. Edward failed to dismiss these visions. And if any of it was even remotely possible, he might have killed the woman he once wanted to marry.

Chapter Three

July 25, 1789
Winchester London Townhouse

Upon returning to his home, Edward heard female voices in the parlor. He did not want to socialize, but his mother spotted him before he could make good his escape.

"Dear," she called.

Tightening his jaw, Edward reached for calm and entered the parlor. Miss Gordon was there, of course. She took every opportunity to visit their home. He was beginning to wonder who was chasing whom. There were a few other women surrounding his mother, as well, all of whom he knew: neighbors and family friends. He bowed accordingly.

"How did it go, darling?" his mother asked. "You look dreadful."

"Bethlem is an unwelcoming sort of place," he said. "Mr. Storace, unfortunately, has suffered a great deal."

"Indeed, to lose one's wife in such a way," Lady Howe said. "It's simply horrible."

"On top of it all, he lost his house on the same night," Edward said grimly.

A round of gasps went up at this news. They all agreed this was the worst sort of luck.

"I heard that was not the only bit of news from that night," Duchess Ravensworth put in slyly. "A young peer was caught kissing a staff member in his box during the performance." There was another round of gasps. "But that is not all. The staff member was another man."

Before the women could dive into this juicy bit of gossip, Edward cleared his throat warningly.

"With all due respect, Duchess, I daresay the inappropriate behavior of a peer is hardly comparable to the death and tragedy that passed that night. Have some respect for the dead, if you will."

"Edward," his mother clucked disapprovingly at him.

Edward glanced at his mother's face and then back to the flushed and angry duchess. He bowed shortly and gave his excuses, but he did not apologize. He would hear of it later, no doubt, but he did not care.

As he climbed the stairs, Edward told himself he just needed rest. A good bit of sleep and a scotch and he would be right again. Yet, his feet carried him to his study, to stand at the door staring at the chest that had stayed closed for six months. He stared at it accusingly. Silently reprimanding it for keeping secrets because he could not think to reprimand himself. Its iron latches and salt-bleached wood had not changed in any discernible fashion since he had last opened it. Yet, it seemed to mock him, to question both his sanity and his courage.

Growling, Edward stalked across the room and opened the damn chest. He tore everything out of it, all his silks and figurines from India, his clothes from Denmark, all the important keepsakes from his family's travels that he'd not let the servants place in storage. Like a whirling dervish, it all came out until he reached the bottom corner where the lapis lazuli box lay. With shaking hands, he picked it up, noting its incredible weight, and cradled it in his lap.

On that fateful night he sent the letter ending their association, the butler had said Phoebe demanded to wait in Edward's study for him to return. He'd been at his club, deep in his cups already, but no one else had known that. The next day, he found the stone on the floor, the box haphazard, as if in her haste to get away, Phoebe had dropped it. She'd left a small chunk of her heart behind.

At the time, Edward thought she'd smashed the stone in her anger toward him, though he'd no idea with what or how, and he'd been too hungover to puzzle it out. Heart aching, he could not bring himself to get rid of the diamond, damaged as it was. Instead, he put it back into the lapis lazuli box and stuffed it deep in the chest to be forgotten along with his feelings for Phoebe.

Six months the box had remained hidden and untouched. He stared at the box, tracing the lapis lazuli design carved on top, delaying for several minutes, afraid of what he might see should he be brave enough to open it. Would the stone now be in more pieces? Would it be dust? What happened to a stone heart once it was broken? The fact that she had come to retrieve the heart meant she had survived his callous disengagement. The butler had mentioned Phoebe seemed ill at the time she'd come to take the heart. Edward remembered that specifically. He had been too angry to care. Had the shock of his cruel words killed her later on?

Realizing he could not bear to wait any longer to know, Edward lifted the lid. Inside, nestled amongst the black velvet folds was the diamond. It was as he remembered, an uncut gem larger than a walnut, with stripes of deep mauve. One edge was jagged where it had broken off from the larger stone. Tentatively, Edward traced that edge, recalling Phoebe's secretive smile when he asked her what sort of stone it was. It was a specific sort of smile, one she saved only for their most intimate moments. A slight tug at the corner of her bow shaped lips, really. Edward missed that smile.

"Sir." Percy's voice cut through Edward's memories. The marquess looked up. He hadn't heard his valet enter at all. Percy took in the mess, and Edward abruptly realized with embarrassment how manic the mess appeared.

"Percy," he said standing, trying to smooth the lines he knew must show on his face. Again, he was surprised at the weight of so small an object in his hand. It made standing a chore.

"Are you all right, sir?" Percy asked uncertainly. He stepped forward and began folding some of the clothes on the floor. "Is there anything I can assist you with?"

"No…" Edward paused. "No, I don't think you can."

Chapter Four

July 26, 1789
The Rookery of St. Giles

For the rest of the night and into the next day, Edward devoted himself to serious brooding. He sat at his desk with the box open, his studies and work forgotten. Instead, consumed with Mr. Storace's tale and the corroborating words of a woman he'd thrown away, Edward studied the uncut diamond for hours. As he did, he conducted a thorough argument over the validity of the story and his own sanity in even considering it as truth until the sixth time Percy had come into the room with a worried expression. At which point, Percy had asked if he should call a doctor.

Abruptly, Edward realized he needed to go outside. He needed to leave. And without much thought, he locked the lapis lazuli box and put it in the corner of his desk. Despite the fact that there was no way any of it could be real, he insisted that the carriage driver take him to Drury Lane to speak with the theater manager, where he obtained the Storaces' address.

From there, he directed his carriage to one of the poorer rookeries in London. On the way, Edward wrestled with the conflicting stories. It was unbelievable that in God's kingdom such people should exist, that a diamond could be spiritually or metaphysically connected to a body. Edward reprimanded himself for even considering the notion. It was Devil's work. But then Mr. Storace's face would float into his vision, followed by Phoebe's face, delicate and glowing as she presented the gem to him. He banished the ghosts with an angry flick of his head and glanced around at the street corner his carriage pulled up to.

"Are you sure you don't want me to wait for you, my lord?" the carriage driver asked.

With a stern shake of his head, Edward reread the address on the piece of paper he held. He got his bearings and strode off. He would prove to himself that this was all his mind playing a dark turn. His confusion and upset at Phoebe's betrayal could no longer be held at bay and were merely manifesting because of Nancy Storace's close appearance to his former paramour. To disprove all this nonsense, Edward determined that he approach the investigation as a scientist and put this horrible, horrible nightmare to rest.

Rest. For a second, Edward swayed on his feet. He had not slept well at all since the opera and not a wink the night before. His dreams were infected. Surely, this was folly, but Edward could no more turn his steps away than he could deny the Lord Himself, even as his feet carried him through the Seven Dials and into St. Giles, one of the worst rookeries in London.

Ignoring the swaths of poor and neglected, the cat calls of the prostitutes, and keeping a firm hand on the wallet inside his coat, Edward made his way to the address the theater manager had provided. He had to know. He had to prove this was all myth, and then he could sleep again, safe in the knowledge that what he'd done six months ago, that putting Phoebe off had been the correct and right decision.

It did not take long to locate the building. Even if Edward had not known the house the Storaces resided in had been burned, he would have felt it. It drew him like a lodestone. The building was merely a husk now, a burnt and black thing, creaking in the uneven rain. If it had been a thunderstorm, Edward would have expected the misshapen body to be struck by lightning. Alas, it was only London rain—dreary, gray, and penetrating to even the best waterproof wool.

The remains of the building sat smushed between the other buildings on this crowded street. Smoke had damaged its neighbors, though Edward saw that did not stop residents on either side. He ducked through the hollowed-out doorway and passed into the charred front hall. The fire had not stopped the original tenants returning either. St. Giles had a reputation for cramming as many bodies into a building, families into a room, as they needed. Despite the unsteadiness and creaking of the timbers, despite the fire and the smell, occupants had moved back into the building. Someone had hung ragged strips of cloth to replace burnt walls or cover holes wrought from the intense heat. The building seemed to house four apartments on the first floor. Even with the cloth walls, Edward could hear the tenants: mothers with their children, hungry babies, elders, all seeking any sort of shelter they could find.

One glance at the address on the paper showed him the Storaces' apartment was on the second floor. No one dared approach or even question him as he mounted the stairs. It was an undertaking. Some were so damaged as not to hold his weight, and he was cautious in placing one foot in front of the other. He cursed more than once as he almost fell through, and he wondered that he did not bring rope with him. At last, he made it to the second floor landing, or what was left of it. It was barely a strip a foot wide of uneven plank.

The tenants kept to the first floor, it seemed, for the second and, one glance above told him, the third floors were simply unstable. Like a tightrope walker, Edward hurried across the landing, casting his arms out for balance. His heavy coat did not help, and he considered casting it off. Then he imagined the riffraff below fighting over it like dogs.

Mr. Storace had not been specific in his tale, only that he'd hidden the box under the living room floor. Edward found their apartment and entered the living room. The sight before him was disheartening. Much of the floor was gone, a hole that could fit a horse gaping to the room below. Edward spied a mother nursing an ill child below him and felt a faint embarrassment at stumbling on the scene. She glanced up once, to see what made the ceiling creak, and then away quickly when she realized it was a toff.

Sighing, Edward was ready to admit defeat. He stared at the hole and concluded the box Mr. Storace had described must have been lost in the fire, or worse, picked away by the thieves and vultures after the smoke cleared. But he had come all this way.

Setting his teeth, he walked around the hole, careful to test each step lest he end up in the woman's care below quite accidentally. He circled, looking for what he did not know, evidence of the thing. There was, indeed, a gap in between the ceiling of the room below and the floor of this room. 'Twas perhaps six inches, not large by any means, enough space for the cross beams to run between the levels.

He almost completed his circuit, his steps falling close to a disintegrated lump that must have once been a receiving sofa, when he caught a glint. There, across from him, nearer to the door, something remained in the depths of the space between floors. Edward quickened his steps, throwing caution away until one heel struck a weak spot and collapsed through the floor. He cried out in pain and anger, cursing like an American, before wrenching his heel out of the wood.

Splinters had pierced the leather boot, and he could feel blood seeping into his stocking. He swore again and pulled a large hunk of wood from his boot. It seemed as though the leather had saved him from serious injury, though it hurt like hell. Closing his eyes, he waited until the worst of the pain passed, before opening them again.

"Are you...are you all right, milord?" a female voice asked hesitantly.

The woman below was gazing up at him with uncertain concern.

"Well, enough, madam," he said. "I will attempt not to fall into your...uh, home."

The woman clearly did not know what to say to this, and so she did not respond. Edward tested his weight against the injury. Pain shot up his calf, and he winced, but the leg held. It would do.

Edward took the last two steps to the edge about where he saw the glint and tested the floorboards. He maneuvered until he felt secure, and then knelt, grateful to take weight off the injury. Hanging slightly over the hole, he groped in between the ceiling and floor until his fingers brushed a dirty edge. It was just out of reach. Carefully, ever so carefully, he lay on his chest, trying to ignore the embarrassment of lying across such a place, half hanging out over the poor woman and her child below, who despite the paleness of cheek, was watching him with bated curiosity, as he reached his entire arm into the space to grasp at the corner of the box.

With barely a hold, he pulled it forth and finally recovered it from its hiding place. Placing it beside him, Edward shimmied back, away from the edge, and then drew the box to himself, out of sight of the witnesses below. He so badly wanted to open it then and there but realized the danger. The woman and her child weren't the only people loitering in this place, and he was injured.

Pulling a few coins from his wallet, he walked back up to the edge.

"I'd be pleased for your discretion, madam," he said quietly and dropped the coins down. He didn't wait for a reply, hoping that it was enough to buy her silence for him to get away. He needed to retreat. Tucking the box under his coat, Edward stood and grimaced again with pain. Hobbling, he made his way down the stairs and out the door without hindrance or challenge.

Once out onto the street, Edward glanced around sternly, warning more than a few braver pickpockets away with his stare. Then he limped his way out of St. Giles, toward a busier street where he caught a hackney and headed home.

Chapter Five

July 27, 1789
Winchester London Townhouse

At home, Edward went straight to his study despite Mr. Nevin's protests about his limp. Edward collapsed gratefully in his chair, desperately aching for a drink but unwilling to move to get one from the sideboard. There was a knock, and Percy entered inquiring if there was anything Edward needed. He asked for a scotch and then, deciding it was best to get the injury attended to before it got worse, for some fresh water and bandages.

Quick boy that he was, Percy fetched the alcohol first. Then he fetched the housekeeper, who doubled as something of a nurse. The wound was not as bad as Edward feared. The leather had saved him for the most part. There was a small gash where the wood had pierced him, and a few splinters left which were removed. The heel was swollen, but the housekeeper applied a balm and then wrapped it tight. Meanwhile, Percy fetched Edward's slippers.

"It's really the placement of the cut," the housekeeper told him. "Sensitive, you know. Not unlike Achilles, milord."

Edward grimaced. "Achilles was an arrogant and cruel man," he said. "I hope to God I am not like him."

The housekeeper did not know how to respond to that, and so she bowed out gracefully. Edward asked Percy to bring him another drink and then dismissed him. Now that his injury was attended to, he could hardly wait any longer. With the door safely closed behind his staff, Edward pulled the box from his coat.

The box had once been beautiful. Perhaps not in a way that a man of his wealth or position would have bought. Yet, as Edward traced the delicate grains on the intact side, he saw that real craftsmanship went into its making. One wall had burst from heat, and so the contents inside had been open to the fire. This, if Mr. Storace could be believed, was the doom of his wife, Nancy Storace.

The lid had become disfigured from the heat and did not sit right. Its tiny hinges had melted in the flames, and Edward had to wrench it off to get a clear view of the inside. It might have been lined in velvet at one point. Guiltily, Edward glanced at his own velvet-lined box with its lapis lazuli details. The box that he had placed on the corner of his desk after his talk with Mr. Storace. The box that held the remnant of his red diamond.

Turning his attention back to the burnt box, with a shaking hand, he touched the inside fragments. The heat had made the diamond explode, or implode, Edward couldn't tell. All that was left were tiny, pale red shards that twinkled in the candlelight.

Edward sat back. In this part of his story, at least, Mr. Storace had been truthful.

"Damn," Edward muttered. How he wanted the man to be insane. How he wanted to cast away this hateful story as nonsense and not waste another thought on it. His gaze pulled with magnetic force to the lapis lazuli box. How he could no longer dismiss it out of hand.

"I am a scholar and a man of reason," he told the box. "Mr. Storace's story might have been factual in its contents on this box, but that does not mean you are a heart."

The box did not reply. Edward grimaced. He was speaking to a stone.

A quiet, efficient rap at the door caused Edward to start, but he bade them enter. The butler stepped inside.

"My lord, tea is being served in the library this afternoon," the butler said. "Shall I have some brought up here?"

"No, send fresh wash water to my rooms and have Percy lay out a new suit," he said. "Tell my mother I will be but a few moments."

"Very good, my lord," Mr. Nevin said. "Miss Gordon sent a note around," he added, handing a cream envelope to Edward that smelled faintly of rose water.

Irritation rose up in Edward's chest as he took the note. Opening it hastily, he ripped the edge in his impatience. Sighing, he scanned the contents. An invitation to dinner. They were having a singer that night accompanied by a famous violinist. Edward did not have the patience or the politeness to entertain. He stopped the butler from exiting with a quick call of his name.

"On second thought, have Percy prepare me a clean suit and tell my mother I have an appointment to attend. No, I will tell her on my way out."

Whatever the butler's thoughts on Edward ducking out of tea and leaving with an injured foot, the man showed none of it on his face. He merely acquiesced to Edward's command with a nod before exiting. Edward penned a response to Miss Gordon's note and covered it in dust to dry. Then he stuffed it into an envelope, uncaring of his own haste. He sealed it with a few drops of wax and the crest on his ring.

That done, he once more studied the damaged box and its contents. He needed to know more. He needed to know everything. He would find out. And then... Edward's heart sputtered at where his thoughts tread, and he halted them. Inhaling deeply, he told himself he did not know enough yet. He needed answers before giving in to his fears. He stood and hobbled determinedly to his bedroom. He had an appointment to make.

Chapter Six

July 27, 1789
British Museum at Montagu Mansion

The British Museum was smaller than Edward recalled, but he had not attended since he first got back to England with his mother seven years prior. He hobbled the halls, boots clicking unevenly on the polished floors. Sunlight streamed in through tiny windows at both ends of the hallway. The museum had inherited both Sir Sloan's collection of natural history items, as well as the Royal Library from King George.

He passed by documents and manuscripts, displays of insects, animals, and bones. Usually his quick, inquisitive mind would stop to consider the displays and seek out any new ones, but today he did not see them. Today, he sought a scholar, and Edward prayed the man was up to the task.

The docent in front of him led Edward, albeit slowly as Edward limped, to a wing he'd never been in before. At last, they stopped outside a small room with a nameplate that read Dr. Allistair Eyre. The docent bowed and left as Edward knocked twice and let himself in.

Dr. Eyre sat behind a desk with a pair of magnification glasses atop his head that stuck out at odd angles like metallic horns. The tiny room was neat and organized, with one wall of shelves hosting a number of labeled jars and their chemical contents and another hosting a large chalkboard with calculations. Underneath, a metal table with scientific equipment, flasks and tubes and brass and flames. There was also quite a collection of crystals and stones. The desk was organized by stacks of paper, and Dr. Eyre sat hunched over the middle one, in the midst of drawing up notes.

"May I help you?" the man asked. He was perhaps forty, with sandy-colored hair and pale eyes and hands gnarled from years of digging.

"Dr. Eyre?" Edward asked. At a quick, nodded response, Edward continued. "My name is Edward Pierce. I am the Marquess of Winchester." He handed over his card. Dr. Eyre's eyes widened slightly as he read it, and he bowed in a sloppy, ill-practiced manner. Edward shut the door behind him.

"I am in need of your particular expertise," Edward said. He jingled a bag of money. "I am in a hurry and require discretion as well."

Dr. Eyre blinked at that. Clearly, he was not accustomed to such a notion, but he nodded once, slowly.

"What can I help you with, my lord?"

Edward pulled a large velvet bag which he'd had tucked under his arm and set it on the table. Opening it, he revealed the burnt box. He removed the lid.

"This gem was caught in a fire," he said. "I require to know what kind of stone it was and if you can tell me its origins."

Dr. Eyre took the box and inspected it curiously. Edward watched him impatiently. His heel was throbbing, and there was no other chair than the one Dr.

Eyre occupied. He was about to snap at the man that the box was not the subject of this investigation, when the doctor began muttering to himself about the wood.

"Mahogany, West Indian," he said. "Straight grain, durable, no visible flaws. Mahogany bursts at between approximately 300 and 343 degrees Celsius depending on the gasses in the area. That coupled with the crystalline structure, the heat must have been extreme…" He puttered off into a quiet mutter that Edward could not discern as he turned his back.

Putting the box down on his work table, Eyre used a pair of tongs to extract a fragment of the stone. Placing it under a microscope, he began turning dials until he had a fine picture, at which point the doctor became silent. He removed the slide and made another with another fragment. And another. And a fourth even, until Edward was practically vibrating with impatience behind him.

"Well?" he demanded.

"This is a red diamond," Dr. Eyre explained. "Very rare. I am not sure why you brought this to me and not a jeweler." Dr. Eyre looked up to study Edward.

"As I said, to find out its origins," Edward said.

Dr. Eyre went back to the microscope. "It could have come from anywhere. Unless you have a certificate, one cannot precisely place a jewel such as this, my lord, especially one so damaged." He stood. "If you are trying to find its origins, finding out which jeweler handled the transaction would be your best route. It is such a rare color I do not doubt you would be able to discover its origins."

"I already tried that," Edward snapped. Dr. Eyre stared at him quizzically. Edward sighed. Obviously, there was nothing the man could tell him. It was just a diamond. Edward closed his eyes and calmed himself. "Is there anything you can tell me about the stone? Anything at all?"

Dr. Eyre bent over the microscope again. He removed the slide and took another fragment. He examined it. Then he examined another, and another. He made a curious humming sound at the back of his throat.

"What is it?" Edward asked.

"Well," Dr. Eyre said, tapping his lower lip thoughtfully. "The structure of this diamond is odd."

"How so?"

"This diamond appears to have a uniform deformation."

"Explain in plain terms, Doctor," Edward ordered.

The doctor shrugged. "Diamonds form over thousands of years with pressure from the earth. It is that pressure which forces the stone to take on a certain composition, my lord, like stacking and aligning books properly, but even pressure cannot prevent a few flaws or inclusions as they are called, like stacking books of different sizes together—it's never perfectly even. This diamond, however, seems to have what they call a fingerprint inclusion." The doctor looked around for support. "I've never seen it in a diamond. It's usually found in rubies, but this is clearly *not* a ruby."

"What can cause a fingerprint?" Edward asked.

The doctor shrugged. "We do not know," he said. "We simply do not know enough about how long it takes to create a diamond or all the factors that go into it. It's almost as if—"

He cut himself off.

"What?" Edward demanded.

The doctor hesitated again and then shrugged to himself. "I knew a man, once, that posited with the right equipment, a diamond could be grown. I feel as if that is what I'm seeing," the doctor said. "It's as if it were grown. Which is impossible of course." He glanced at Edward who was doing his best to remain stoic.

Edward's heart thundered in his chest. He took a silent, steadying breath and cleared his throat. "Is the color significant?" he asked.

The doctor shrugged again. "Without testing I cannot be sure what is creating the color. Iron, magnesium, aluminum, different things can make the color."

"But if you had to hazard a guess," Edward pressed.

Dr. Eyre frowned. He took another piece out of the box and examined it. "Iron, manganese, bromine. Any of these might affect the color."

"Are any of these found in the human body?" Edward asked.

At this, Dr. Eyre really did look at him. Edward did not shift under that stare.

"The diamond might have been smuggled inside a corpse," he lied.

"How ghastly," Dr. Eyre said, glancing back at the box with a frown.

"Hence my investigation on where it came from," Edward added, realizing his story was making him look bad. "It was a gift, and now I fear it came to me in a nefarious manner." Good Lord, he sounded like he was in a penny dreadful.

Dr. Eyre nodded. "And then it was destroyed. Sounds like a penny dreadful to me," the doctor said with a shake of his head, echoing Edward's thoughts. "I can understand your desire for caution then, my lord. All the elements I listed with the exception of bromine are in the body. However, if this diamond were smuggled in a body, it was red before it got there. The smuggling would not affect its color."

Somehow, Edward did not feel better.

"Thank you, Doctor," Edward said, throwing money on the desk. He gathered up the box back into its bag.

"Don't you want me to run tests on it?" Dr. Eyre asked.

"No," Edward said. He walked over with such quickness that Dr. Eyre flinched back. Edward ignored him, taking the slides with the samples and dumping them in the bag too. He would leave no evidence behind. Edward left then, ignoring the stuttered protests of the academic in his wake.

Chapter Seven

July 27, 1789
Earl of Huntly's London Townhouse

That afternoon, Ann Gordon waited patiently in the drawing room for Edward's answer. She sat by the open window, allowing the inconstant breeze to relieve some of the heat while she embroidered a pillow. When Edward's answer finally arrived, it was a terse note of banal regret, barely registering emotion. He had been so distracted of late. Not that he had ever been particularly attentive to her. Still, Ann tore the note up in frustration. Edward was *straying.* He needed to be brought back in line.

Standing, Ann glided up the stairs. There was one person who would know what to do: Auntie Eleanor.

The woman was the pinnacle of womanhood. Intelligent, driven, beautiful, and always polite, Aunt Eleanor had survived the uprising in France. She had made her way from her French chateau through the torn and chaotic countryside filled with terrible, murderous peasants and taken ship by herself back to England. Her husband, Lukas, unfortunately had not survived. The chateau was burned too, along with their Paris town house. Yet, all of Auntie Eleanor's fortune had been successfully transferred from a French bank to an English one before the riots and revolution took hold. It was as if she could read the future. Either way, Aunt Eleanor had waltzed her way back into the ton an aristocratic heroine, the men admiring her foresight and the women her courage in the face of so much tragedy.

Of course, it had been her suggestion last winter that led Ann to catch Edward's eye. At the time, he'd been infatuated with some Austrian widow. That had ended quickly, just as Aunt Eleanor promised it would, and after a due amount of time for Edward to recover his wits, and with Aunt Eleanor's careful maneuverings to make sure that Ann was invited to all the important events, finally she had caught his eye.

Now that he was straying, Ann knew that Aunt Eleanor would know what to do. At her aunt's door, Ann knocked twice and heard a clear, light voice bid her enter.

"Auntie Eleanor?" Ann let herself in.

The older woman turned toward her niece. Lady Eleanor Argent was stately, with silky hair the color of dark mahogany and eyes the blue of a virgin morning. Her face was nearly unlined despite her two and forty years. Her dress of cornflower blue emphasized her straight-backed posture and lithe curves to their most appealing while the mother-of-pearl beading around her décolleté drew attention to her womanly attributes.

"As much as I love to be admired, child, I would like to know why you are interrupting my morning prayers more," Lady Eleanor said.

"It is Edward," Ann said solemnly.

The name brought a sharpness to Lady Eleanor's gaze, and she gestured for Ann to sit. Ann explained the situation quickly.

"So like his father," Lady Eleanor said with a slight

sneer.

There was history there, a history that neither Auntie Eleanor nor Miss Gordon's mother, the Lady Huntly, would speak of. Not for the first time, Ann ran through the list of people who might inform her of that history as she studied her aunt.

"What shall I do to bring him back to the fold?" Ann asked, bringing the subject back.

The ugliness on Auntie Eleanor's face melted instantly into a reassuring smile. "No worries, my darling child. We shall make sure the good marquess is yours. You continue to pay his"—her mouth twisted involuntarily—"mother more visits and keep up your attentions. Half of a good marriage is winning over your mother-in-law! I will discover what is distracting our young friend and make the necessary corrections."

Privately, Ann continued to wonder what it was that had her aunt so focused on the Marquess of Winchester. He *was* a sensible match, but as long as she married well, Ann was not too concerned over which suitor it was. She determined to find out her aunt's stake in this. On the surface, she sighed with relief and smiled demurely. "Thank you, auntie darling."

Chapter Eight

July 27, 1789
Winchester London Townhouse

After the museum, Edward went home. He did not drink; he did not sleep. He stared at the firelight as it played off the fragments of one diamond and the broken edges of the other. He had gone to two jewelers and the museum yesterday, and all he'd found was more evidence that Mr. Storace was telling the truth.

Of course, none of the men he had spoken to yesterday could completely confirm the existence of a person that could *grow* a diamond heart. But, then, nothing they'd told him had really denied it either. And despite all his attempts to rationalize and ignore the situation, the more Edward stared at the two boxes, the more convinced he became of the truth behind Mr. Storace's story. Which meant that Phoebe had done more than give him a beautiful, if odd, gift that day last winter.

His reverie was interrupted by Percy's knock and entrance. Edward sat up from his slumped position at his desk and realized that the morning light was straining against the drawn and thick drapes.

"My lord," Percy said, "are you well?"

His valet carried around an air of perturbation so fuzzy it inspired a headache in Edward. Then Percy drew the drapes back, flooding the room with light. Edward cried out and covered his eyes. Now it was a full-blown headache.

"Damnation, Percy!" Edward complained.

"Sorry, milord." Percy dropped the drapes back in place while Edward rubbed his eyes. "Did you want me to bring you barley water? Or some willow bark tea?"

"No," Edward said. He doubted all the usual remedies for a hangover were going to help him now.

"Shall I help you dress then, my lord?" Percy asked hesitantly.

The headache spiked. Despite it, Edward considered Percy's question. He wanted to go to bed. He wanted to wake in a world where the possibility of him killing a woman merely by breaking things off with her did not exist. He wanted to be exonerated of a crime when the evidence was sitting on his desk. Who was he to turn to?

"Send my card around to Duke Brey's," he said softly. Percy's eyes widened dramatically, and Edward belatedly remembered he was not speaking to Rhys. He swore under his breath, then cleared his throat. "Tell him…tell him it's damn important. And lay out the blue suit."

As Percy headed toward the door, Edward massaged the bridge of his nose and called out to stop him. "Also, send a message to Mr. Halkerstone's office as well. I'll need him available this afternoon."

Linus Halkerstone was Edward's solicitor and business manager. If Edward was going to the Continent, and he could not believe he was even considering it, he would need to alert Mr. Halkerstone to send letters of credit ahead of him.

After the door closed, Edward stood and groaned against the stiffness in his body and his skull. He stretched his back trying to loosen muscles tight from inaction. The pain in his foot gradually lessened as he walked; he limped as blood flowed back into the heel. It did not dissipate entirely, but by the time Edward got to his bedroom, he found he could walk, more or less, normally. All the same he felt like a lame stallion pushed into the yard for fresh air.

Percy was laying out the suit when he got there. After Edward washed, Percy assisted him in dressing. Ever the forethinker, Percy had also summoned the housekeeper who arrived shortly after with clean bandages. She unwrapped his tender foot. It looked better. Though it was still swollen, it was slightly more yellow and less blue. The scab was gorgeous. Rhys would have loved it, but the housekeeper appreciated it less so. She grunted and gave him tea with willow bark for the pain and swelling, then told him he would heal faster if he stopped gallivanting, to which Edward took some offense. He did not gallivant.

He strutted occasionally, promenaded when necessary, and, perhaps, on special occasions, he took a jaunt, but he did *not* gallivant. He did not mention this, however, because of the women in his life not worth picking a fight with, his housekeeper ranked number two—only below his mother.

At breakfast, Lady Winchester expressed some concern at his appearance. He tried to wave her off, but she was persistent, lowering her voice so the servants wouldn't hear.

"Edward," she said. "You look as bad as last winter. I will not watch you suffer through more doldrums. I am calling the doctor."

"No, Mother," he said firmly. "You are not. I am going to see Rhys today."

Lady Winchester's expression changed to surprise. "As pleased as I am that you are going to renew your friendship with Duke Brey, if it's going to send you back into this...state, I confess more concern than before."

Before he could respond, however, the butler came in with a note and offered it to Edward on a silver plate. Edward took it and scanned the contents. Rhys had responded, agreeing to meet Edward, though his tone, even on paper, was terse.

"What does he say?" Lady Winchester asked.

"He will see me," Edward said. He stood and winced at the pain in his foot, but it held. Lady Winchester called his name to bring him back.

"I will be fine," he said and kissed her cheek as he passed. Then he left to face his former friend, clutching the curt response in his hand. It reminded him of all the angry words that had passed between them.

Chapter Nine

March 7, 1789 - Five months ago
Winchester London Townhouse

"Edward." Rhys flew into the office as if chased by a hive of bees. "I have heard a disturbing rumor."

Edward faced the windows, watching snow drift lazily as he drank his scotch. He did not meet his friend's eyes.

"And by the looks of it, it is true," Rhys said, slowing to a halt in front of Edward's desk, taking in the nearly empty decanter of scotch and the flush over Edward's cheeks. Rhys sat in the only other chair. "Did you cast Phoebe off?"

"Yes," Edward said.

"By the Lord in Heaven, why?" Rhys demanded.

"She was a liar, Rhys," Edward said. He poured himself another drink and then one for Rhys. Rhys took the glass but put it down on the desk without drinking.

"Explain to me what happened," Rhys said.

Edward opened a drawer and pulled out a stack of letters. He pushed them at Rhys who took up first one, then another, scanning the flourishing handwriting on the first and the neat, boxy letters on the second.

"These are letters between Phoebe and her husband," Rhys stated.

"They are," Edward agreed. "He called her 'Bright

Star' because of Keats's poem. He sent her love notes and poetry when he traveled."

"So?" Rhys said, still mystified. "Where did you get these, Edward? And why do they matter at all? It's none of your business!"

"Because she loved him back," Edward said softly. He picked up one of the letters in the flourished handwriting. "She wrote him back in kind.

O my Luve is like a red, red rose
That's newly sprung in June;
O my Luve is like the melody
That's sweetly played in tune.

"She was quoting Burns for godsakes! She even composed a verse or two of her own for him," Edward added, slurring slightly at the end.

When he was done, Rhys stared at him in consternation. "Just because Phoebe loved her first husband does not mean she does not love you."

Edward shook his head. "Does it not?" he asked. "I know my view on love and marriage is a bit more traditional than most, but when you say you love a man, you should mean it. You know as well as I, there is only one match for a person in their lifetime, one soul mate. You found yours, Rhys. Do you really think if God Almighty took Cecilia from your side, that you could find someone else?"

Rhys shook his head and stood. "Edward, I know you take your parents' marriage to be a sacred sort of example, but there are exceptions—"

"No, Rhys, there are not," Edward said. "A man and a woman in holy matrimony. It is a sacrament. God knows too many of our peers marry for money or social standing, and if that is how they want to live, so be it. I want what you have, what my parents had. I want *that* kind of love. Not…secondhand affection."

Rhys saw the hurt and agony on Edward's face.

"She looked at me, Rhys, and told me she loved me. What's worse? That she could have lied to me, or she could have lied so well to the last man she married? Because she lied to one of us."

"Or she loved him in a different way, and now she loves you," Rhys snapped, unable to contain his temper. "I know she loves you, Edward. She has told me herself."

"I am sorry, my friend," Edward said, pouring himself another glass. "I know you have a close bond as brother and sister and you grew up together, but I cannot believe her lies any longer."

"So you were okay with the notion that she was a widow if she did not love her husband?" Rhys asked. "It was okay when she married the first time for social standing or money—"

"She married him at her parents' direction," Edward snapped defensively, slamming his glass down and sloshing the contents all over his desk. Edward let it go in annoyance, shook the excess off his hand, and then threw back what was left in the glass.

"Edward, you are throwing away love," Rhys pleaded.

"IT'S NOT REAL." Edward threw the glass tumbler into the fire and faced his friend.

Rhys narrowed his eyes and went pale with anger. "Do not scream at me," Rhys said heatedly. "And do not assume to know what love is."

"What are you saying?" Edward demanded.

"I am saying that if you knew what this was, you

would not be acting like a fool."

Edward straightened, his fist tightening with the urge to strike his dear friend. "You go too far, Rhys."

"And you are far too in your cups to continue this conversation," Rhys said. "You may call when you are prepared to speak rationally on the matter."

"Do not order me about like one of your servants," Edward said. "Or dare to give me permission to call. You forget, I am your peer, Rhys. My name is as good as yours."

"I have forgotten nothing," Rhys said. "You, on the other hand, have forgotten all good sense. Look at you." He waved in disgust. "You are drunk and miserable because you have thrown away a woman that you love and who loves you back with all her heart. It is the worst kind of sin I can think of."

"Do not preach to me, Rhys," Edward said.

Rhys made a noise of disgust in the back of his throat and shook his head. The things he wanted to voice he dared not. Instead, he headed to the door. Before he opened it, he looked back at Edward. "I expect an apology when you come by next," he said.

"You will burn in Hell before I apologize," Edward snapped.

"So that is it? You are willing to throw away our friendship as callously as you threw Phoebe away? And for what? Your pride? I wonder, Edward, which one of us will burn in Hell. Good day, sir."

Chapter Ten

July 27, 1789
Brey House, London

Edward was not the only one reflecting on that
dreadful night. Rhys stared into the cold, soot-stained
fireplace reliving the fight. There was no reason for the
fire in the summer heat, but he suddenly wished for
one. The soothing pops of wood and cheery light might
lift his black mood. Rhys finished off his drink,
wondering what was so damn important that Edward
had asked for an audience. His behavior at the opera
had made it clear to all parties that Edward considered
their friendship a dead thing. That had been the final
straw for Rhys, who had hoped that time apart might
ease the tension between them. They'd gone through
spring and most of the summer without a word.

Since his return to London, Edward had not called
on Rhys, who still hoped that upon seeing each other at
the opera, they might begin rebuilding their torn
friendship. Those hopes dashed, Rhys had decided to
put the foolish Marquess of Winchester out of his mind
permanently and avoid him ever afterward. It hurt more
than he wanted to admit, but Edward had become
unreasonable. If he wanted to act like an ass, that was
now solely his own affair.

When the butler presented the Marquess of

Kitty Shields

Winchester's card this morning, Rhys was surprised. His surprise doubled when Edward followed through and came to present himself. It was on the tip of Rhys's tongue to send him away out of spite, but Edward's note had said it was of paramount concern. For all his flaws, Edward was not one to exaggerate. *Except about love and betrayal,* Rhys thought bitterly. After a moment's hesitation, Rhys gestured to his butler let the Marquess of Winchester in.

The Duke of Brey's character was not laced with spite. Still, he believed in justice. Therefore, he would hear whatever the Marquess of Winchester had to say and then be done with the man. He felt there was an apology owed for their argument last winter and, again, for Edward's behavior at the theater. Certainly, a man may disagree with a friend, but Edward had said things that could not be dismissed. Rhys determined to make his feelings on the topic known, and also to treat Edward as distantly as he had been so treated. See? Justice. His determination firmed until Edward actually walked into the room.

The man appeared nearly disheveled. Not so much to the untrained eye, of course. His valet was top rate. His cravat was perfect, his clothes well brushed and attended, even his boots shined. But Edward's gait was stiff, almost a limp. His eyes were haunted, and he was sweating. Edward rarely sweated—he'd spent most of his childhood in India, and the heat didn't get to him. There was an air about him that Rhys had never witnessed before: feverish. It reminded Rhys of the Redcoats returned from the war—the guise of men who have seen or done awful atrocities. It caused the Duke of Brey to rise to his feet and all thoughts of distancing

66

himself to evaporate.

"Edward, are you well?" he asked, coming around his desk.

"Quite well, thank you," he said, though clearly it was a lie. Edward's eyes twitched to the left, where the butler stood just out of sight near the door.

"Thank you, Humphries," Rhys said, dismissing his butler. "You may go."

The butler bowed and closed the door behind him.

"Now will you tell me why you look so…stricken," Rhys said. "I thought we were not speaking," he added, dryly.

Edward's eyes snapped to his. His posture straightened. His countenance went noticeably pale. He opened his mouth and shifted uncomfortably. Rhys waited. Clearing his throat, Edward said, "It has come to my attention, recently, that…" He trailed off and cleared his throat again. He met Rhys's gaze and inhaled deeply.

"There were many things said… I was in a state of extreme agitation." He clenched his jaw. "Many of them were in poor taste which I regret." Edward sighed and tried again. "I do not like how our friendship floundered."

For his part, Rhys watched his friend struggle. He had known Edward for six years, since their fathers had been killed within the same month during the Colonies Rebellion. He was a proud, intractable man, too hard by half, Rhys had thought. But then, much of that hardness had come from the loss of his father. Whatever tempering Edward might have undergone in his bachelor years with his father as a guide had been swept away by that deprivation. Edward was unyielding because that was what he imagined his father had been. Never around Rhys, of course. There had always been a strong bond, an intimate understanding of loss and grief between them, true, but real affection as well.

More than one peer had commented upon Edward's rigid nature to Rhys. Before six months ago, Rhys had always laughed such notions off. Of course, Edward was standoffish, even remote to others. What did it matter to him? They were brothers. And then Phoebe had come, and Edward had softened. He'd become lighter, happier. And then those damn letters and the end of the world it seemed. Rhys still wondered how Edward had come across the letters, but he'd never the opportunity to ask.

He had required an apology from Edward but never expected it. *Perhaps that makes me the intractable one,* Rhys thought. Though it was not a quality apology, Rhys understood his friend well enough to know that this was what Edward could offer. Without a word, Rhys stood and went over to a liquor cabinet which he unlocked.

"Rhys?" Edward asked.

"Well," his friend said, "if we are to be friends again, we are going to need to drink on it. Scotch seems entirely too...prosaic. I have some excellent cognac here."

It was more than excellent. It was a century old, and the expense could buy a few of the ton out. That's why it was locked away, reserved for appropriate and dignified occasions. *Like regaining one's best friend back,* Rhys thought. He poured two glasses, handing one off to Edward.

"I appreciate your words," Rhys said carefully.

Edward's entire being seemed to unwind a notch, like piano cord pulled too tight and out of tune. It appeased Rhys to know that perhaps Edward had suffered as much as he by their falling out. Also, he noted, the fact that Edward was not holding a grudge or expecting something of the same from Rhys spoke to the man's unsettled state of mind. Edward had been driven here. Rhys clinked their glasses together, and Edward raised his in salute, but only took a sip out of politeness. Rhys took more than a sip. It was excellent cognac.

"Your note implied there was another matter of import," Rhys prompted.

"Is Phoebe still alive?" Edward asked. He asked the question with such unease in his eyes that it caught Rhys off guard.

"Why would she not be?" Rhys asked. Then his eyes widened. "Did you think she took her own life?"

"No," Edward said, waving his hand. "God above, no. She is far too proud for that. Yet, she lives," he pressed.

"Yes," Rhys said. "Yes, of course."

"When did you last hear news of her? Is she quite well?"

"Edward," Rhys said, patiently, taking another sip to steel himself for whatever was coming next. "Forgive me for not bowing under this barrage of questions about a woman you made very clear with whom you wanted no connection, to the lengths that you ended our friendship, but I am still astounded and confused you are even asking. I require an explanation."

"I, I do not know even how to explain," Edward said, gesturing wildly with the tumbler without drinking.

"Perhaps by explaining why you thought Phoebe might be dead," Rhys suggested.

"No, that would not make any sense," Edward replied, shaking his head. Rhys's eyebrows shot up, but Edward did not notice. He put down the tumbler on the corner of the desk. It was a testament to how distracted he was that he was not drinking.

For a moment, Rhys wondered if Edward was already in his cups, but he did not appear so. "I am afraid you will think me quite mad," Edward admitted.

"You are too grounded to be mad, Edward," Rhys said. "And not nearly creative enough," he teased. Edward blinked and looked up at that. Rhys was wearing his half smile though, and Edward unwound a little more. "Start at the beginning."

Nodding as if steeling himself, Edward finally reached for the cognac. He downed it like a sailor, making Rhys wince.

"It's not a beer," he protested.

Edward nodded again. "The actress, Nancy Storace," he said, ignoring Rhys's protest entirely.

"The poor woman who died on stage?" Rhys asked, finding his chair and sinking into it.

"I went to see her husband," Edward said. From Rhys's expression, this alone baffled him. "My mother insisted that because we were patrons, we should check in on the man."

Rhys made a noise of understanding. In some ways, the Marchioness Winchester was more formidable than her son.

"She wanted to go to Bedlam." Rhys pulled a face at the very idea.

Edward acknowledged the face with, "Exactly. I convinced her to let me go in her stead. There I spoke with Mr. Storace, who told me their house caught fire the same night as Mrs. Storace's death."

"Good God," Rhys said. "The devil's luck."

"No," Edward said, shaking his head. "Perhaps 'ill-fated' is a better word. Mr. Storace arrived home to the tenant building already aflame. He was taken to Bedlam because he was trying to run into the burning building. It took three men to restrain him as the building burnt down. He kept screaming, 'I have to save her. I have to get her heart.' "

Edward paused collecting his thoughts. "This prompted a memory in me of something Phoebe once told me, of which I will explain momentarily." Then, perhaps afraid of losing his nerve, Edward plunged into his account with Mr. Storace and the stone heart.

After he was done, Edward stared at the empty glass forlornly, though for once Rhys did not think it had to do with lack of liquor.

Finally, Rhys said, "You think this business about the stone heart is real and Phoebe may…have one?"

"Worse," Edward said. "I think she gave it to me."

Chapter Eleven

February 6, 1789 - Six months ago
Sterling Country Estate

The freezing weather kept the entire party indoors. Edward had suffered through an afternoon of cards and polite discussion on a range of topics. He did not dislike Lord Sterling. The man was a stout Tory and the soul of aristocracy, but Edward was desperate to see his love.

Phoebe had taken ill the week before with a high fever and a strange rash. The doctor had quarantined her in one room in the north wing and stayed every night to make sure she was well. Of course, that made sense with Lord Sterling's oldest daughter and Phoebe's cousin, seven months pregnant with her first child, also staying at the manor. But the doctor had not simply denied a pregnant lady; he had denied any visitors from seeing Phoebe. Only her maid and the doctor himself had been in to see her, and after a week, Edward was chafing.

Outside, the weather reminded Edward how much he missed sun-bathed India, or any country that featured the sun more than two months of the year. Sleet *plinked* against the wavy glass of the manor, and the clouds were a deep, desolate gray. There was no going out hunting or even ice-fishing in this weather.

He folded another hand at cards, ignoring the way

Rhys cocked an amused eye at him, and the other men continued with their small talk. Edward wasn't even aware of his sighing until Lord Sterling chuckled.

"You are severely lovesick, Winchester," he said.

Edward did not deny it. It had been a week, and he missed Phoebe desperately.

"All right, go see what the doctor says today," Lord Sterling said, taking pity on the younger man. Edward glanced at the clock, noting it was about the time the doctor came down for tea. He considered how he would react if the damn man said he couldn't see Phoebe again today and realized the hope that he might was enough to get him moving.

With a nod at the other players, he stood and wandered into the main hall. As if by Fate, the doctor was coming down the stairs.

"Ah, my lord," he said as if he'd been hoping to catch Edward.

Edward immediately perked up, holding his breath.

"Lady Phoebe would like to see you," the doctor said. "She's finally past the worst of it."

Without even waiting to hear the rest of the diagnosis, Edward took the stairs two at a time with a relief immeasurable. Through the twisting halls of the large manor home, he practically ran until he came to a nice corner room. Outside of the door, he paused, straightened his vest and jacket, ran a hand through his hair. He hadn't a mirror to check his cravat, but it would have to be enough. It had been a week.

With a gentle knock, he waited until given permission to enter. Phoebe was, thankfully, alone, save for her lady's maid who was embroidering a pillow in the corner. Edward glanced at the girl, whose name was

Mary. He liked her well enough for she seemed respectful and efficient in her work. Yet, he wished there was some excuse or reason for her to leave that would not damage Phoebe's reputation in any way.

Turning his attention to Phoebe, he knelt down by the bed and clasped her hand.

"My darling," he greeted, kissing the back of her palm gently.

Phoebe looked stunning with her strawberry blonde hair fanned out in gentle waves around the pillows, her skin paler than cream, and her eyes sparkling. He could see the effects of the ailment. There was a feeling of exhaustion to her, and the usual blush in her cheeks was all but gone. There was no rash to speak of, but Edward assumed that the doctor would not allow visitors if there was. Still, she radiated beauty with her pert little nose and pointed chin and full lips. And he told her so.

"My Lord Marquess, you could sweeten the berry off the vine," she said.

"Oh, Phoebe, are we back to this?" he asked, teasing her. It had taken him nearly two weeks to convince her to call him by his first name. She was bold in all other things, it seemed, but that level of intimacy brought out her shyness.

"Pardon me," she said. "Edward."

He hummed approval and kissed the back of her hand again, which was scandalous with Mary so close by, but Edward did not care.

"I have a gift for you," Phoebe said.

"What? Have you been sewing while you were supposed to be resting?" Edward asked.

"No," she said. She gestured at a stunning lapis lazuli box on the side table. Curious, Edward picked it up and opened it. Inside was a raw, uncut gemstone, a ruby, he guessed, from the color. It was a deep red and warm, and there was a strange quality to it, almost as if something stirred in its depths. It was easily the size of Phoebe's fist and absolutely priceless. It was a gift fit for kings. And there had been rumors Phoebe was chasing Edward for his money!

"I am truly speechless," he said. "But what is this for?"

"For you," she said, and there was an odd touch of pride in her voice, which Edward did not understand. "It is my heart, Edward, and it is yours."

"Phoebe," he said, putting it back into its box and on the table. "You do not need to buy me gifts like this. Who is courting whom?" he teased. She smiled secretively, though, and he could see she was getting sleepy.

"I will explain later," she said. "Perhaps after we are married. Promise me you will not cut it, though. Promise me you will keep it safe, exactly as it is."

"For you, I would do anything," he said and kissed her forehead. "Sleep, darling. Rest so that we may get you out of this dark and dismal room soon."

Phoebe nodded and drifted off to sleep. Edward picked up the box in wonderment, tucked it safely under his arm, and left.

Chapter Twelve

July 27, 1789
Brey House, London

Rhys sat back in his chair drumming his fingers across the tabletop. Outside the sun was nearing its zenith, heat and light at the house in waves. Edward, who loved the heat, felt dizzy as the memory cleared from his mind's eye. For the first time, it occurred to him that if the story was true that Phoebe really did grow this jewel and she was cousins with Rhys…

Edward cleared his throat. "Rhys, you do not—"

"I buy my diamonds, Edward, I do not grow them," the duke said wryly, throwing up a hand to stop that line of thinking. "But you can ask Cecilia if it will ease your mind."

Edward flushed. "Then I am mad," he said sadly.

"No." Rhys shook his head. "Phoebe's father is my cousin. A bit of a bastard really. Her mother, however." Rhys squinted. It was something he did while he reviewed information in that shrewd brain of his. The Duke of Brey was fierce, and it wasn't just the title, Edward knew. Years of being his friend had shown Edward that Rhys seemed to know everything about everyone. While Edward's education had been about diplomacy, trade, cultures, and history, Rhys's had been deeply schooled in politics, scandals, and secrets.

Edward would not be surprised if the king himself came to Rhys with questions.

Oddly, it was one of the things that made their friendship work. For while everyone else in the ton seemed to want to speak with Rhys about politics, Edward did not give a fig. He could afford not to, of course, but he rarely paid attention. Rhys had commented more than once that he found this trait in Edward extremely restful.

"Her mother's side is strange," Rhys admitted. "Sort of quiet people, but there have ever been rumors about that family. Of course, Breys rarely take into account myths while choosing brides, so I doubt Phoebe's father paid much attention to the stories when he married. After all, Phoebe's mother is quite lovely."

"You believe this story could be true then?" Edward asked.

"Have you ever dreamed of your father?" Rhys asked, changing the subject so abruptly Edward blinked in surprise. He shook his head in answer.

Rhys leaned forward, folding his hands in front of him and studying the fine grains of pale oak in the desktop. "Before we received notice of my father's passing, I dreamed of him. He was already dead, you see, but I saw him. Four nights running I dreamed. We were in a forest, other spirits around us, and he was trying to speak to me."

"What did he say?" Edward asked, fascinated despite himself.

"To take care of my mother and sister, and that he was sorry." Rhys frowned. "He did not say he was dead, but I knew. I knew."

"Why didn't you tell me?" Edward asked

heartbroken for his friend.

Rhys looked at him directly. "I did not know you yet, Edward. By the time we became friends, the dreams were done. I cannot say with any real certainty what is possible or impossible in this world. And since I cannot say, I am therefore willing to take possibilities however improbable under due consideration. Now, we shall need an expert to consult."

"I have gone to an expert, Rhys," Edward said, relieved Rhys did not think he was mad. More relieved that he was not alone in this anymore. "Several. I went to two jewelers who said they have not heard talk of any discoveries of red diamonds legal or otherwise, and then I went to a geologist, a person who studies rocks if you can believe such a thing exists, at the British Museum."

"What did the last one say?" Rhys asked curiously. He was more curious as to whether Edward had searched for a reason not to believe or to believe in the story. Then a thought occurred to him. "You did not give him Phoebe's stone?" Rhys did not quite believe the story, but he was not one to test fate either.

Edward shook his head quickly. "Fragments of Mrs. Stor—of the stone I recovered from the Storaces' apartment," he amended. "He said that the diamond was, indeed, odd. He believed it almost seemed as if it had been grown. His words, without my prompting."

Rhys drummed his fingers again. "Interesting," he said. "Well, I meant a different sort of expert. There is a man recently escaped the Revolution in France. He claims to be a count although if he is one, then I am a fisherman," Rhys said derisively. "That said, I have seen him perform in a seance."

"Lord in Heaven, why?"

"Well," Rhys said, "because Cecilia was curious and you and I were not speaking."

Edward had no reply to that.

"I have found myself exploring a number of…unusual entertainments since we last spoke. Whatever his social origin or name, I believe the count may have some knowledge or expertise in this arena. Certainly more than either of us."

"Do you think he will see us?" Edward asked.

"I know he will," Rhys said, pouring himself another drink. "For a price."

Chapter Thirteen

July 28, 1789
Earl Aylseford London House

Count Alessandro Cagliostro was a short man with a fat face and an unimpressive demeanor, although he tried very hard at it. He wore a silk suit of the deepest red, fine stockings in gold, and a cape lined with golden fur. He wore kohl about his eyes and had gemstones in the shape of the all-seeing eye on his chest like a house crest. He also carried the air of the indolent nobleman, reclining upon the fainting sofa while he smoked. The scent of his leaf was spicy and exotic and made Edward's eyes water.

The count's host, the Earl of Aylseford, had furnished his parlor with thick drapes and furniture in the latest style. The drapes were drawn against the strong afternoon light, and the room was lit by a flourish of candles. It was rumored that Cagliostro had charmed the earl's wife, one Lady Edith, and that they studied more than the night sky after the popular seances she held.

When Edward entered with Rhys at his side, the count smiled and stood, waving his arms about as he greeted them in a far-too-friendly fashion.

"My lords," he purred and then bowed not quite low enough. "How good of you to come see me."

As if this was a social call. Edward immediately disliked the man. He was reminded of a mottled eel common in Indian marketplaces. The image was only reinforced by the fact that although the count's face was heavily powdered, it could not quite hide a pimpled skin condition. The eel produced a vast amount of mucous, and as the man spoke, he produced an overabundance of saliva. Yes, this man reminded Edward of a mottled eel.

Rhys must have seen Edward's expression for he took immediate charge.

"Count," Rhys said with a head nod, before introducing Edward. Rhys glanced around at the footman waiting near the door. "Perhaps we can have some privacy?"

"Of course," the count said. "Did you want any refreshments before I send the boy away? The earl's cook is quite skilled. He makes a delicious apricot and fig tart."

Both men declined, and the count waved the footman out. Then the three arranged themselves on the various furnishings, Edward putting as much distance between himself and the eel as politely possible.

"Duke Brey said this was an urgent matter," the count said, eying Edward.

On any other occasion, Edward would simply have scowled at the man, watched in satisfaction as he paled, and left. But this was not any other occasion. And it was not about Edward's disgust or even his feelings. It was about Phoebe's life. So, swallowing hard his own disgust, he produced the jewel. The count took it and plucked a monocle from his vest to study it, his eyes glimmering with interest.

"Well, this is quite a lovely gem," he purred. "So very…" His voice faltered as he studied the depths of the stone. After a moment, his eyes widened. "Where did you get this?" he asked.

Edward and Rhys exchanged glances again.

"The source is hardly important," Rhys said. "Do you know what this is?"

The count glanced between the two men and nodded slowly, his oily persona suddenly gone, slithering off him like a second skin. Now, he seemed to Edward just a slightly fat, normal man and was instantly more likable. "This is a Hrungnir's heart," he said.

"A what?" Rhys asked.

"Hrungnir's heart," the count repeated. Edward frowned. The story sparked a memory in him, but he could not place it before the conversation brought his attention back.

When both peers continued to be mystified, the count explained.

"It's a Viking legend." He gestured at the diamond. "Hrungnir was a stone giant."

That seemed to ignite Edward's memory. "He made a wager with Odin, did he not?"

The count seemed unaccountably pleased that Edward knew.

"A scholar," he purred impressed. Even Rhys looked impressed.

"I have lived in a number of places with a number of nannies telling stories," Edward said dryly.

"Not to mention your translations," Rhys added. Edward managed to look momentarily embarrassed by this and cleared his throat.

"Truly impressive, my lord," Cagliostro said. "Hrungnir did, indeed, lay a wager with Odin. But that is not the legend we are speaking of. There is another story.

"According to the myths, the stone giants went to war with the gods. After the giants lost a great battle, they were banished from the realm. The legends are a bit murky as to where they were banished. Some claim to another place entirely, like Hell, but some say the giants were banished to live here amongst men.

"Hrungnir was one of these giants and was said to have a particular talent with his heart. He could remove it at will. When he took it out of his chest, it took the shape of a diamond. A red diamond. Removing the heart made Hrungnir invincible in battle for even if the enemy struck him, he would not die. You see, he could not die for his heart remained intact somewhere else."

"What does this have to do with the stone in your hand?" Rhys asked.

"The legends say only Hrungnir and his progeny can make these jewels." The count looked again at both men. "You cannot dig this stone up from the ground, gentlemen, unless you are digging up a grave."

Edward sat back, ruminating on this story. He was not certain whether to feel vindicated or horrified to hear more evidence that the story was true. There was a relief knowing he was not as mad as a hatter, but that was very short-lived. Fleeting in fact. Now he had the consequences to contend with.

The count frowned. "This heart is still warm, and yet it is broken," he said. He studied Edward carefully. "Has the owner recently, uh, passed on?"

Rhys shook his head, although his face was a

frown and his eyes riveted to the stone. "And herein lies our reason for coming to see you," he said quietly.

"How do I repair it? It is a mystical object broken by unconventional means. Is there a…magic paste of some sort to apply to it?" Edward asked, wiggling his fingers demonstrably.

Count Cagliostro had the good grace to look astonished. "Are you implying the owner of this heart is still amongst the living?"

Neither Rhys nor Edward replied, but the count received his answer nonetheless. It took the count a moment to gather himself before he continued.

"I am not certain that you can repair it," he said, handling it very carefully as he passed it back to Edward. "This is not a subject I am well-versed in. And I only know some because of a Roma with whom I had the occasion to share a jail cell in France." Both gentlemen gave him a look, and the count shrugged. "We were exchanging professional information." He made a face and shook the memory away. "I think, however, that you do not have much time."

"Why is that?" Edward asked, suddenly on high alert.

"It is a heart, if you believe the legends," Cagliostro said. "If a heart grows too cold, it is not a heart anymore."

"It's not very warm now," Edward said with concern.

The count stood and went over to the door. He called out to the footman to fetch his quill and paper, then closed the door again. "You need a master of the arcane arts for this."

"Do you know of anyone?" Rhys asked.

The count nodded. When the footman returned, the count dismissed him again. He took the quill, paper, and ink provided and wrote down a name and address.

"I suggest you bring something of great value to barter," he said handing it over. Rhys read it over Edward's shoulder and frowned.

"This man is dead," Rhys stated. "He died in Altona six or seven years ago, as I recall."

The count glanced at the door conspiratorially and lowered his voice. "The Comte de Saint Germaine has taken many steps to appear deceased. He will not be happy about my disclosing his little secret or disposed toward helping you, I fear. That is why I suggest whatever payment you prepare be of *great* value."

Edward nodded grimly. He took out a money bag filled generously and handed it over.

"For your information, and your discretion," he said, eying the count.

"Of course, my Lord Marquess," he said. "Good luck. I fear you will need it."

Part Two
Chapter Fourteen

August 7, 1789
Sailing down the River Thames

The sea was calm, and London was three days behind them, but internally, Edward felt unsettled and stormy. He had not had a good night's repose since the night Nancy Storace had died on stage. Nightmares in a variety of shapes and forms, from watching Phoebe die, to haunted messages from his deceased father, chased him. Sometimes he remembered the dreams; sometimes he did not. He recalled Rhys's comments about his late father in his dreams, but Edward thought these were more of a response to hearing about it rather than real. They didn't feel real. They felt like stress. Last night had been a particular dreadful night, the rocking of the boat making him uncharacteristically seasick, along with the vision of Phoebe dying in the snow.

The sea offered very little in terms of company save for harsh winds and an unbroken, blue-gray color. Edward was grateful for this too as he wanted no other company nor generosity nor cheer.

"Good morning, Winchester." The Honorable Tilton joined him.

The youth was abominably happy. In response, Edward barely withheld a roll of his eyes, which would be poor manners and quite vulgar but only just. Edward had met the Honorable Tilton on the second day at breakfast. Edward seated himself quietly at one of the empty tables a bit late in the morning, for the very purpose of avoiding company. He was eating in blissful and contemplative silence when an unearthly happy voice broke the peaceful solitude of his meal.

That voice was followed by a young dandy in full ton costume. His cravat was large and ruffly, almost covering his unbearded chin with delicate lace. His cuffs were similarly adorned. He wore a pale, yellow silk suit with white stockings and fine, English shoes. His hair was long and gathered at the nape in a simple tail.

The dandy could have been no more than eighteen with a slight build, high arching eyebrows, and a broad smile. He was pretty and slightly dashing, though he would need to fill out to fulfill that descriptor more aptly. His hair was a nice caramel color, the eyes blue. The hands were callused, Edward noted idly, but probably from an instrument. Violin or oboe or something akin was his guess.

"Ah, you must be the Marquess Winchester," the dandy greeted, sketching a perfect if somewhat lower than necessary bow. *I must have rank on him,* Edward thought. "I am Walter Tilton, son of the Viscount Marsey, at your service."

Edward nodded at him politely, hoping that would fulfill their social obligation and his silence would drive the dandy away. It worked for most of the ton. He was incorrect on this score.

"My friends call me Tilton," the dandy informed him.

Blinking at that, Edward was not sure why the dandy was offering such an intimate level of friendship so soon. It spoke volumes of a rash and naïve character. He went back to his bowl of watery stew, this time deliberately giving Tilton the cold shoulder. Tilton did not notice.

"My good man!" Tilton waved at the cook. "Libations and sustenance, if you please." The cook, uneducated and unused to hearing words with more than two syllables, stared at the dandy in confusion. *Or perhaps it's the yellow silk blinding him,* Edward thought. Tilton, however, didn't wait for verification of his orders but sat gingerly across from Edward.

"This is exciting," he said. "To be on the open sea! Traveling! I, myself, have not had the occasion to leave England. As you can probably tell, this will be my Grand Tour!"

Of course, it will, Edward thought. The Grand Tour, a tradition amongst English gentility. When a man reaches his adulthood, he takes a tour of the continent to become "worldly." Edward had never needed a Grand Tour, having spent most of his life abroad. Tilton did not seem to need a response, or indeed, any sort of encouragement. He happily continued the conversation anyway.

"I'm starting with Hamburg and then moving on to Cologne," Tilton said. "From there, Zurich, Milan. Well, all of Italy really. Rome, of course, and then perhaps Greece. My tutor, that is George Welfries, I'll introduce you later, says we have to take into account the time and expense."

The cook, having guessed that since the dandy had taken a seat he wanted food, delivered a portion of stew, some bread, and a mug of ale to the table. Edward wondered what the dandy would do with such food, but

Tilton managed to take it in stride.

"Such an adventure," he exclaimed after his first bite.

Edward reflected the shine of adventure would wear thin quite quickly as the food would not change or improve. He didn't impart these thoughts, however. He finished his meal and stood.

"Where are you going?" the lordling asked, surprised.

"Back to my room," Edward said shortly. And that had ended their first conversation.

Edward had hoped, prayed even to remain aloof. He wrapped himself in his dark silence and spent a good deal of his time at the bow, brooding at the sea for the last few days. The crew, at least, was wise enough to leave well enough alone. Tilton, however, seemed either immune or purposefully ignorant of Edward's continuing dismal mood and dislike of him.

On this particular day, Edward had once again taken up residence in his favorite spot to watch the water. They had broken free of the mainland only last night. England was lost somewhere behind them in a thick fog, and before them the unchanging flatness of the water spread out like a silk, silver carpet. That's where Edward was, pondering the count's words on luck, ruminating on his guilt, and praying this famed Saint Germaine could provide the key to this mystical puzzle before Phoebe's heart went cold. Edward's stomach clenched to think on what would happen should it grow cold. He unconsciously fished the leather thong out of his shirt and, with a quick glance to make sure no one was watching, slid the stone heart out. It was warm, but perhaps less so than yesterday.

Edward swore. He would never be able to forgive himself if Phoebe died for his cruelty. Did she know that her time was limited? Is that why she had left England so soon afterward, to make peace with her impending doom? Before he could further think on these things, that's when Tilton appeared.

"Ah, this is perfect, beautiful English weather for you," Tilton exclaimed, glancing about the dour sky with what could only be described as a grand smile.

Edward looked at the younger man wondering what, or if anything, actually filled that head of his besides ludicrous and exaggerated statements. So he was doubly stunned when, after his customary silent response, Tilton said, "Another day of fine brooding planned out?"

This direct, if accurate, observation shocked Edward out of his reverie. He stared at Tilton with some surprise. Tilton laughed. "You're so much like my brother. I wonder if you know how to smile, Winchester."

He was teasing, but on an altogether far too familiar way for Edward's comfort.

"What my thoughts are, are not any of your concern or business," he snapped. "Do not patronize me, sir."

Now, it was Tilton's turn to be surprised. His eyes widened, and he stuttered an apology. He was saved from further embarrassment by the arrival of his tutor, Welfries, an altogether awkward human being with an uneven mustache and fading hairline.

"Young master," he said, "let us begin your lessons."

Tilton glanced at Edward. "Somewhere away from

the marquess so as not to disturb him," Tilton replied. Edward glanced to see if Tilton was mocking him again, but there was only a slight hurt and worry in those usually bright eyes.

"Of course, of course," Welfries said with a slight bow to Edward.

They moved off down the railing, toward the mid deck. Edward could only hear snippets of their conversation when the wind turned their voices his way. He concentrated on what he was doing and abruptly realized Tilton was right. He was brooding. Not that he had much else to do on this journey.

He spent some time staring off into the sea, playing over in his mind how things might go with Phoebe. Would she be happy to see him? Angry? Surely there would be tears. And then he wondered how he, himself, would react. How would he react when he saw her once again? As Edward stared out to sea, he realized he honestly did not know.

He wished Rhys were here. He missed the times before marriage and courtship when it was the two of them getting into scrapes and fights. When they relied on each other. When the best part of his day was waiting to see what plot Rhys had cooked up for him. He missed the steady comfort of that friendship. And he wondered if he'd blundered again at their most recent goodbye.

Rhys had come to see him off the night before his departure. They shared a quiet drink, and Rhys had smiled warmly at him, wishing him luck. It was nice to see Rhys's smile. Edward realized he had truly missed it. He had so few real friends, many of them back in India or scattered about the Empire from obligations to family and Crown. Since returning to England, Edward had made few friends and realized, sitting there with Rhys, that maybe it was his own fault. It made him realize that he did not want to lose any more friends.

"Thank you, Rhys," he said, meaning it. "When I return, we will need to spend some proper time catching up."

"I look forward to it," Rhys said. "Phoebe really does love you. She will take you back. You may want to practice groveling on the journey though."

At that, Edward gave him a confused look. He had no intention of asking for Phoebe to take him back and said as much. Rhys's face was aghast.

"Then why are you making this journey?" he asked.

"Because Phoebe's life is on the line," Edward said. "I cared about her very much. But it doesn't change what happened. She loved her husband, Rhys. She is not my match."

"The diamond—" Rhys started.

"We do not know enough about the diamond to know anything for sure," Edward said. He shook his head. "I know you think we were meant to be, but I do not."

Rhys's expression was swift in changing many times over, and he looked toward the fire. Edward saw his mouth tighten and feared for a moment he had spoiled the re-found friendship. Then Rhys sighed.

"Good luck, Edward," he said, this time his tone different. Edward was not sure what to take from that. Surely his friend was disappointed, but Rhys could not understand. Rhys had found his love early and easily. Love was meant to be like a blossom, beautiful and perfect in its first shapening. The tragedy at hand only proved that what he and Phoebe had might have been wonderful, but this was certainly not *true* love.

Edward wondered if that kind of love would ever be in his life. He had closed his feelings off for Phoebe after finding out about her feelings for her first husband. He was willing to admit, now, that he'd handled the situation badly and he'd been cruel. It had hurt more than he wanted to admit realizing that she had loved another. But the last six months of misery had taught Edward he *did* care for Phoebe a great deal. He couldn't deny it, and he would do everything in his power to see her restored. She deserved that.

Staring at the horizon, Edward wondered if that's what real love was: an illusion. The illusion of sky meeting sea in some great distance. The horizon was a place that could never be reached. Was that really what true love was? Out of reach?

He sighed and thought of his parents. Their romance had been so perfect, so true. Not love at first sight, or any of that nonsense, but genuine nevertheless. One need only have looked at the way they spoke with their eyes, teased each other, danced together to know that the former marquess and his Lady Trueheart were a love match.

"I don't understand at all." Tilton's voice carried with the wind interrupted Edward's brooding.

Lady Trueheart would scold Edward for treating Tilton in the manner he'd been treating him. The thought made Edward grimace. He glanced over at the two men huddled against the strong wind. His mother, he thought, would encourage him to make friends with the only other peer within miles and do his family proud in acting honorably. Edward missed her desperately as well.

She had been understanding of his leaving even though he'd given only vague reasons. She had been mystified when he had asked her to keep his journey a secret, but she respected his privacy. Were *she* here, Lady Trueheart would be making friends with everyone on board despite their status. Edward smiled to think of how she'd won over the hardened sea dogs on the voyage from Denmark back home. She had had them all drinking tea and playing cards on their off hours. His father had been both amused and amazed. She convinced them all to teach her how to play dice and then laughed in good humor when she lost. Edward was fairly certain the entire crew had been in love with her by the time they disembarked.

Though he hated leaving her alone, knowing how she was with people, how people fell for her, Edward was reassured she would be protected. Besides, he had made sure to tell Halkerstone to check in on her. Still, some of his guilt was leaving her to the social piranhas and rumors that would surely spring up in his absence. The ton was not forgiving. If anything, it fed on heresy and rumor. If the ton got wind of how Edward had treated Tilton, not that Edward would care, but given their difference in rank, Tilton might actually suffer from such slight.

Edward realized he'd been more than rude to Tilton. They were, after all, the only peers on board. Of course, he had no one else to talk to but his tutor who was a hired hand. It made sense for Tilton to try and make friends with the only other person of his class. It might be easier if the captain was a man of substance and held dinner with the officers like a proper navy man, but the captain was more pirate than naught and took his meals by himself.

The journey to Hamburg would be short, and Edward should make the most of it. He glanced over again, wondering how to broach the subject. Welfries was holding a map of the Indian subcontinent and pointing during his lecture. Tilton looked bored. Rhys would like Tilton. Rhys had a more easy-going nature about him, and Tilton's lustful enthusiasm for life would amuse Rhys, not in a calloused way, of course, but in a delighted, mischievous way.

Just then, another snatch of conversation came his way with the wind.

"You see India is divided into states that are ruled by royal families, much like England," Welfries said. "Of course their governments are not as sophisticated as ours."

"Not necessarily," Edward said, striding over. His voice carried despite the wind, and Tilton, who was nearly asleep on his feet, suddenly became alert.

"What do you mean?" he asked.

Welfries, the tutor, seemed torn between arguing with a lord who was so much above his class, and being right. Edward sighed. Why had he interrupted? But it was better than thinking about Rhys's voice at the goodbye. Or Phoebe. And he should make up for his behavior.

"Many Indian prince states actually have governments set up alongside the monarchies," Edward said, moving closer. "I can think of about fifteen off the top of my head, although I think there are more. There are many more states simply ruled by monarchies, of course, but even that, on some level, is a sham. The Crown controls most of the Indian continent."

"Really?" Tilton asked. He sighed. "I would love to see India."

"It is beautiful," Edward said with a nod. "But hot. Ungodly hot. Still, there are sights there found nowhere else in the world. Beasts that rival fairy tales, and the food." Edward smiled. "Well, unlike anything England has ever boasted, I assure you."

"You've been there?" Tilton asked. He seemed to accept Edward's change of mood without harboring any ill will. Or perhaps he really was that bored. Edward made a noise of assent.

"My father was sent there for a decade or so as a governor of one of the coastal states," Edward said. "I spent a great deal of time there in my childhood."

"Where else have you been?" Tilton asked, leaning against the rail next to Edward.

"We stopped in different ports on the way to and from," Edward said with a shrug. "Spent a few years in Denmark before returning to England. My father was recalled to fight the Americans."

Tilton nodded. "My brother as well," he said. "He died there."

Edward felt a great swell of sympathy all of a sudden. He nodded again, as if to say he understood. He did not voice what happened to his father, but Tilton seemed to understand all the same. For a moment, they were on equal footing.

"Well, young master, we should continue your lessons," Welfries interrupted.

Tilton looked less than thrilled. As Edward moved off, Tilton said, "Perhaps, you would not mind me asking you more about India later?" Tilton's voice was so hopeful, even Edward could not deny him. He nodded, and Tilton grinned. If there was a touch of triumph in that smile, Edward chose not to see it.

He left the two to their lesson and went down below. He was exhausted. Perhaps, at last, he would sleep. In his room, Edward lay down in his tiny bunk and took out the stone heart. He stared into its depths, seeing the tiniest flicker of movement. Phoebe was still alive. But for how long?

Chapter Fifteen

July 31, 1789
Earl of Huntley London Townhouse

"The Count Alessandro Cagliostro," the butler announced.

In walked an unimpressive baby-faced man in a ridiculous cape with moons and stars sewn into it. A peasant, no doubt, whatever his claims. Lady Eleanor kept her thoughts off her face as she took in all the details, already predicting how this would go. People were so obvious in their motivations. She gestured at the count to take a seat.

"Lady Argent," he said, bowing over her hand first.

Lady Eleanor worked not to wipe the feel of the peasant's lips off her flawless skin.

"Count," she greeted putting just enough warmth in her smile to pass for flirtatious. "Would you like some tea?"

"I would be honored," he agreed, glancing around. "I was under the impression that I was here for a seance, your ladyship."

Lady Eleanor nodded at the maid in the corner to serve the tea.

"I hear you have other talents," she said. "Palm reading, tarot cards. I was hoping for something a little more private." She put some heat into her voice and saw the disgusting man smile seductively.

"But, of course," he said taking a sip, his voice a tad smug. "My knowledge of the arcane, indeed of many subjects, is quite broad. We may…investigate and explore many avenues until you are quite satisfied."

Lady Eleanor smiled and with a small flick of her wrist dismissed the maid. Count Cagliostro saw, and his smile grew more smug. Now he resembled a possum. She idly wondered what in the Devil's Hell the man thought he had to be so smug about. He was fat, ugly, clearly a peasant. She doubted any carnal prowess made up for all that.

"Such a beautiful woman, if I may say," he said. Well, at least he was not stupid.

Behind him, coming in as the maid left, was a bulky, muscular man named Cliff. Lady Eleanor was not sure if that was truly the thug's real name but had been told it was a nickname more to do with how he handled problems. The door closed with a faint click. She sipped her tea and wondered if there were any cliffs close enough or if he came from a part of the country on a higher elevation.

"Where shall we start?" he asked, still unaware of Cliff's presence. He leaned back into the couch and spread his legs a bit in obvious invitation. Did the man expect her to climb onto his lap like some loose barmaid?

So tacky and predictable, she thought unamused. "We shall begin with what you told the Marquess of Winchester and the Duke of Brey several days ago," she said.

Count Cagliostro's smiled slipped and then reappeared a second later. The smugness did not return with it which was gratifying. If anything, he seemed nervous.

"Your ladyship, such consultations are private and confidential," he said. "I would be happy to read your future, though."

Cliff came up behind the count and placed a hand on his shoulder. The little man squeaked and jumped but did not go anywhere. Lady Eleanor was pleased at the wince Cliff elicited when his massive hand squeezed.

"In a moment, my associate is going to break your collarbone," Lady Eleanor said. "That is, unless you tell me what transpired between yourself and the marquess."

"N-nothing," the count stammered. "He came in for a reading about some long-lost love. I read the cards for him. I told him it was over and to search for new prospects."

Lady Eleanor hummed to herself and took another sip of tea. It was an excellent Assam. Then she set the cup down and flicked a wrist at Cliff. There was a clean crunch, and the count screamed.

"I dislike being lied to," Lady Eleanor said, flicking invisible lint off her skirt. "The future happiness of my dear niece is at stake, you see, so I am afraid we will have to begin again. Now, what did you and the marquess talk about?"

A little while later after the count had stopped whimpering and been dismissed, Lady Eleanor busied herself writing letters. One to an acquaintance in Vienna and one to her business manager hiding just inside the German border from the French peasants. As she finished putting drying powder on the correspondence, Cliff returned.

"Has the foolish moron been delivered back to the Earl of Aylesford's home?" she asked.

"Yes, my lady," he replied. He was an excellent man, was Cliff. Bright enough to follow orders but not creative enough to misinterpret them. And his propensity for violence was most gratifying.

"Good, you'll be going to Hamburg presently. You are to discourage the Marquess Winchester at every opportunity. I will provide you with plenty of coin. Hire whomever you deem necessary," she said.

"Yes, my lady," he said.

"Discourage him only, Cliff," she stressed and was amused by the grimace on her man's face. "After all, we need him alive for Ann. Meanwhile, I'll send someone to finish off this chit von Croy."

Cliff cocked his head curiously, unperturbed by talk of murder and such. "She musta dun something right terrible to git you so mad at 'er," he observed.

Lady Eleanor blinked. *That's right,* she thought. *Cliff had been the one to steal the letters and deliver them to Winchester's house for me.* She frowned. He may have been smarter than he appeared. Maybe a raise was required to keep him loyal then.

"Not at all," Lady Eleanor said. "She is merely an obstacle. The marquess is my main target. His father…" She twirled her pearls around her finger. "Well, let's just say that our families were supposed to join years ago, and the fool man got turned around. I'm sparing his son the pain of a poor match. Ann is perfect. Her rise in society will help us all. I had thought forwarding that chit's letters to the marquess would be enough to stop this idiocy, but the von Croy woman got her hooks in deep. When she's dead, the marquess will come running back to Ann and all will be well again. So, as I said, Cliff, discourage only."

"I'll do my best, my lady," he promised.

Chapter Sixteen

August 8, 1789
On the Open Sea

Edward had not slept well during the day nor
during the night. He had forced himself to stay awake,
reading by the light of a candle a few books his
business manager, Mr. Halkerstone, had managed to
procure for him before his journey. Halkerstone was
solid, and Edward was confident in his ability to not
only run things in his absence, but check in on his
mother. The late Lord Winchester had expressed trust
in Halkerstone, and so did Edward.

So when Edward had asked for books that the
Count Cagliostro had recommended might be of some
use, Edward had gone to Halkerstone who had not so
much as raised an eyebrow. The first book was
Probierstein, an alchemical tome written by a German
alchemist. Halkerstone had also included a German
workbook for Edward, for which he was grateful. His
German was rusty, and the translating helped not only
prepare him for the journey ahead, but kept his mind
active on the task at hand.

The second book was in French, and it was a
collection of folk tales, which included several of the
stories regarding Viking myths. Edward's French was
much better than his German, though the book did not

contain much else to help.

It talked but little of Hrungnir, the stone giant, only about the bet he made with the god Odin. Edward had hoped his research would force him into a dreamless state, but it did the opposite. The alchemy book with its recipes for making gold and rites to call spirits fueled Edward's dark imagination. Now each iteration of Phoebe's death was worse than before.

He woke in the morning in a foul mood. And such was less than bright when Tilton found him at Edward's customary fast breaking time.

"Winchester," the young lordling greeted.

Despite Edward's affirmation to be kinder to the young dandy, he could not handle the sun beams shining from that smile.

"Give over, Tilton," he snapped. "Why are you so damn happy all the time?"

Rather than be offended, Tilton shrugged. "Perhaps because you are so gloomy all the time. One must balance out the ship, or we will tip over," Tilton said.

Edward stared at him, and Tilton's smile slipped. He glanced around with a slight furrow to his brow, obviously worried his teasing was having an ill effect once more. Instead, Edward grunted and turned back to his breakfast. After waving the cook over for food, Tilton slammed the tabletop hard making Edward jump.

"I know what you need," Tilton said loudly. "A bit of sport. How about after breakfast we practice some fencing."

For his part, Edward was stunned Tilton even knew how to hold a sword, let alone handle one. It was on his lips to say "no" when he realized he had nothing else to do. Besides, it was a distraction.

"Very well," Edward said.

Tilton grinned again and bent into his food enthusiastically.

"This would not, I take it, interfere in your other studies?" Edward asked.

Tilton did not reply but only winked.

So it was after breakfast Edward went to his room to fetch his sword. He did not have a fencing foil, but a real sleek blade. Still, he supposed he could get cork or some such from the cook and stifle the point. He told himself, as he climbed the stairs, not to go too hard on the dandy. Or take too much pleasure in winning.

Ten minutes later, Edward found himself promptly knocked on his arse. It startled a laugh from him. Tilton lowered his sword, a beautiful piece of craftsmanship Edward had noticed, and peered at him. "Why, Winchester, you have a very nice laugh," he said.

Edward narrowed his eyes at Tilton as he picked himself off the mid deck.

"Be honest," he said. "Did you challenge me to this to make me feel better, or yourself?"

"Both," Tilton said, circling him. "I find a nice bit of exercise in the morning makes the day shine longer."

"Tilton, you were born with an inordinate amount of optimism," Edward said. "It's unnatural, really. Englishmen are supposed to be grim."

Tilton's eyes widened. "My Lord Marquess, was that a joke?"

"A truer statement as I have ever spoken," Edward said saluting him. And then went back to fencing.

Tilton was an expert swordsman. Under all those foppish clothes, the dandy had a keen sense of balance that even the rocking of the ship could not throw. He was muscled, and the calluses on his hands earned. Edward found his opinion of Tilton risen considerably by noon.

When they stopped for lunch, Tilton asked him about his travels. Edward found telling him about his travels easy talk, even if his father was featured in those stories. Tilton knew about loss.

"Where was your brother killed?" Edward asked after a natural lull in the conversation.

"The Battle of Princeton," Tilton said. "He was a good man, Robert was. More English than I if your definition stands." At Edward's look, Tilton said, "Grim. No, rather he was a serious fellow. Of course, my father and mother wept bitterly at the loss."

There was a tone in his voice Edward had yet to hear and a passing of sourness in Tilton's own face. Then it was gone.

"The spare becoming the heir," Edward said. It was an awful if pragmatic way of looking at children. Always have an heir and a spare. In Tilton's case, he was needed to fill his brother's vacancy.

Tilton nodded. "I was not prepared to be the heir," he admitted. "I am not sure I will ever be…enough."

Edward understood that sentiment. "It is a burden we all bear," he said. "My father was a great man. I do not think I can ever really live up to his name."

"How do you live with it?" Tilton asked.

"By being the best man I can be," Edward said. "Always striving, always testing, always vigilant."

Tilton studied Edward from the corner of his eyes. "That sounds exhausting," he said and broke into a smile. "No wonder you are so stony. Come now, is that why you are on this boat? Striving for perfection?"

"Perfection is only in God's realm," Edward said softly. "And, no, my purpose is not toward perfection. Quite the opposite."

"You are striving toward imperfection? Inferiority? Inefficiency?" Tilton mock gasped.

At this, Edward scowled fiercely. "Redemption," he said shortly.

Tilton's smile slipped. He knew well enough not to tease about that. He stared at the Marquess of Winchester curiously, wondering what a man like this could possibly need redemption for. Before he could pry, though, Welfries interrupted.

"I think it is best you do not practice anymore in this harsh sun, young master," Welfries said. "Shall we continue our discussion on India belowdecks?"

Tilton sighed. "Tomorrow then?" he asked. Edward nodded assent and watched Tilton disappear down the stairs. He had not meant to reveal that much, and now that he had, he cringed at his own foolishness. He would need to come up with a better story by tomorrow, for Tilton would ask. Tilton would surely ask.

****

Edward managed to avoid Tilton the rest of the day, a feat considering the limited options on places to go. He had never been particularly good at subterfuge, and he viewed lying as a cowardly act. Still, he did not want to attempt to explain his errand to the younger peer, not just because it sounded like grounds for admittance to Bedlam, but also because it was a point of shame. He had caused a great deal of pain and put someone he cared for in danger.

Edward's fear for Phoebe's life drove him, but it

also kept him awake. For days, he went over and over in his mind how he could have handled the situation differently. How could he have let her off? He had wanted to hurt her, he admitted. He had been so hurt himself, and angry. And that childish gesture might very well bring Phoebe to her end.

Which is what plagued Edward, yet again, as he stood at the bow of the ship, this time in the middle of the night. One ship's lantern burned, and the moon hung half full, lighting the ship like a stage. Edward hated the reminder. The night crew moved like ghosts about their tasks. Edward stood and felt more than saw the ocean pass around him as the ship cut a sharp line through the surface. He took out the stone heart, testing its warmth. He couldn't tell if it had changed or not. With a sigh, he put it away. He wished he could put his nightmares away so easily.

"Quiet night, aye?" The captain came beside Edward, leaning on the rail only as a rogue can lean— the qualities of danger and mastery etched in his stance.

"Yes, quiet," Edward agreed, although he was scarcely pleased with it. The mutterings and curses of the sailors had long ago faded into the background of Edward's thoughts leaving him with the lapping of the waves and the inconsistent, yet eerie keening of the west wind. Edward longed for noise, longed for the devilish banter of merchants and prostitutes in London's dingier districts, for the clacking of horse's hooves against the cobblestones of the dressier streets, even the echoes in the London fog. Anything loud enough to distract him from his current course.

"Been watching ye for nearly a week, tryin' to figure what makes yer eyes so black and yer presence like thunder. There's a curse on ye, sir, as sure as there's a curse on every sailor ta ride the sea," the captain told him. There was no response Edward could form to redress this observation, so he let it pass. "Aye, a man's business be his own," the captain continued.

"It is indeed," Edward replied, letting the thunder, as he called it, leak into his voice.

"'Tis indeed." The captain nodded, unaffected. *Perhaps he is deaf,* Edward thought with no small amount of sarcasm. Annoyance brimmed and burned Edward's throat at his impudent ignorance of his need to be left alone.

"I think I will go below," Edward said.

"Best stay above if yer seasick," the captain suggested. "A weather eye on the horizon fixes most ailments," he said wisely.

"Not this one," Edward muttered.

"Eh? Ye think yer the only man who suffers?"

"Excuse me, sir," Edward returned coldly, now allowing all the biting anger aimed toward himself into his voice, "but I doubt we speak of the same subject. Good night—"

But the captain was a hardened sea dog, and he caught Edward's arm as the other man meant to storm past. Turning to wrench his limb from his hold, Edward's eyes caught the captain's, and Edward saw what he truly was.

The captain was like a whale, both of the sea and not, constantly having to resurface for air only to dive down to unimaginable fathoms below, guarding all sorts of secrets. He was an ancient creature in his own right, but with a fortitude and unbending will he carried on until that day when the old ocean gods would sweep him from his vessel into the inky depths. It would be a fitting death and one, Edward thought staring into those squinting eyes, the captain was beginning to long for. Perhaps that's why he stopped Edward. A young seaman would care little for the troubles of other men for they only looked for their mermaids and pearls on the crests of ocean waves. But a man such as this one, well, like all old men, he wanted to be heard, to warn the young of folly and foolishness.

"Ye didna speak of ailments of the body, aye?" he asked, stunning the angry admonishments from Edward's tongue. "Nor me," the captain said and unhanded the lord.

A moment hung between them as Edward weighed the benefits of listening to the old whale speak his peace or storming down below with naught but icy thoughts for company. The idea, however, of another night drenched with nothing more than self-loathing caused a violent shudder to ripple through Edward's body. *A distraction,* Edward told himself. *That is what this man offers. You have nothing to lose*.

Whilst Edward debated his course of action, the captain tapped out ash from his mahogany pipe and reloaded it like one does a pistol. For a moment, Edward imagined it was a pistol he loaded, but it gave him pause to consider whose name was marked on the musket ball inside.

"Ye seem right pathetic for a man," the captain remarked. "But I'll tell ye a story, and mark me if it be not worse off than yer own, for if 'tis…that is a story I'd like to hear." He chuckled then to himself as if the hardships of others amused him. Edward's anger sprang up hot again, a wave of magma ready to explode.

"How can you mock the pain of others?" Edward demanded, hoping for a violent dispute. The old captain only shrugged with perfect apathy in response.

"Aye, sir, if it's a brawl yer searching for, ask Slugger O'Toole. He's down in the hold mucking shit out o' the animal stalls. No doubt he'll show you a good round or two if that be yer aim. But 'tis wiser to listen first. Won't hurt ye none," he advised.

Begrudgingly, Edward leaned on the rail next to the captain, arms crossed over his chest to keep from reaching for his sword.

"Some six years past there be a lad on board. Good lad, I s'ppose, not too bright, bit of a cabbage. He'd clever fingers, he did, only nine of them on account he lost one in a knife fight, but…the rest were right smart. Anyways, Barnaby was his name, and he came on and did his piece and never started no fights, but he was want to finish 'em when he must. A right sailor he be.

"So one week we gets a largely haul of cargo to Northern France, and they been having these terrible crop failings up there just as the Revolution started and all, people starving all over the country. Terrible times."

Of course, Edward knew. Half of France was unemployed, and the peasants were overtaking the country more out of desperation than real want to do violence. Only last month they'd forced the king into a constitutional monarchy. Edward, like many English nobles, blamed French decadence for the country's woes but, unlike many of his peers, Edward felt for the people. Although, the Woman's Circle put together nearly two thousand pounds in donations to buy the French countrymen food which was more than their government ever bothered to do. And because he'd seen much of the world and knew the pulse of different places, he did not think the bloodshed was finished in France which is why he avoided it. With barely a nod, Edward urged him to continue, intrigued by whatever tragedy the captain would spin.

"The French be dying, and we bring them grain and barley. Nearly got us killed in the doing, but the take was more than fine for the braver the seamen who could do it, and the French paid triple the going price on account of the crops failing. So we get this take, and we drive on up into the coast, and we hold off in this little Prussian seaside town that I be rather fond of for a week. And the boys go off to have their fun, see, with the money earned.

"Well, Barnaby goes into the town with the rest and finds himself a plump, li'l maid, fairer than most, I admit, with sparklers for eyes and flaxen hair and melons for breasts and all that. And he has hisself a good week and promises this little maid he'll see her again, right? So we sail up to Denmark and pick up more cargo and sails back down to Edinburgh and gets more grain and sails back ta France and gets ourselves another good prize.

"Now the tradin' in France was even tougher the second time, and I lost a good three men because the people riots on the docks. But we managed somehow, and we flash through the wind up north back to the Prussian seaside town.

"An' when a man goes through and sees Death so plain, sometimes it scrambles his head a bit. At the time, me crew were a bit more antsy than usual, and with the winter blasting us in the face, we were all in need of a good tumble and a warm fire to forget our troubles.

"Now, the men takes their leave in shifts, but Barnaby disappears the whole week he does. I sent a runner ta find him, and turns out the lad be laid up sick, he was, for a week with a fever and a dark rash cross his chest."

At this, Edward went cold, and his stomach turned.

"And when Barnaby returns, he's changed." The captain finished stuffing his pipe and paused to light himself up, inhaling the gilded smoke with pleasure and relief as he collected his thoughts. "Can't right tell ye how he was different, for there be not the words to relate it. But imagine, if ye can, a man who's lighter. S'ppose thas the closest I ken to describe it. After the week, Barnaby comes himself back, right recovered, and asks if we be returning in the next year to this town. I tells him aye. So he says next time we comes around again, he's plannin' on a marryin' the girl. So I congratulate him and thump him on the back and thinks no more of it.

"Barnaby goes about his daily fixings as before, and if his nine fingers are smarter or if his feet are lighter in the sails, who am I to blame Love?" The captain paused again and sighed mournfully as if reflecting on a fool of a son who'd stupidly shot himself in the leg.

"So we go roundabouts same as before. We be out of Edinburgh a week it was, and Barnaby's up in the riggings, and—" The captain glanced up toward the halo of sails above the ship as if his poor sight could pierce the darkness enough to see the individual ropes. Then his eyes trailed down, to the deck beside the mast.

Then the captain turned to Edward again, and in the faintness of the lamplight Edward saw a disquiet and unsettledness inside him.

"I s'ppose I shoulda known bad luck was acoming. Not no man has such good luck with takings and fine weather that some damn tragedy might not balance it out. About midday, I say, and we be goin' about the usual business of getting this old gal to port when a scream like a thousand babies dying rips into the air, it does. An' every seaman on this ship will tell ye that scream still haunts them at night. An unnatural sound it was, scared most of me men right out of their skins, and these ain't no sinking daisies these men."

"What happened?" Edward asked, fearing the captain would get too lost in the recollection and not finish.

"The lad screamed and flailed like invisible devils attacked him, and he fell, damn near thirty feet. He didna break anything on the way down…anything that we could see anyway. He hit the deck and curled into a ball with the wind knocked out of him. He stopped screaming only long enough to catch his breath, and then he didna stop. He continued like a mad siren, like he be tortured, and no one, not one man could figure out the cause. One of the men takes pity on ol' Barnaby and knocked him out with a quick blow. We didna know what to do. 'Twas no wound we could find, and he never be crazy afore. Some of the men talked of throwing him overboard and letting the sea cure all his ailments for good." The captain's eyes darkened. "But meself and old Dig was against that. I pitied the boy, but more'n that, whatever demons might be torturing him could right well fall on another man out of boredom when Barnaby was dead. So we tied him down, we did, and held him in the brig 'til we made landfall.

"He wasn't much conscious for the next week, and when he was awake, he was screaming. Then all the screaming stopped, and he slept a few days. When he woke, he begged to see me, so I goes down to talk. 'What's a happening, boy?' I asked. 'Ye seeing demons?' And he laughs bitterly and shakes his head and starts crying.

" 'I gave her my heart,' he says. 'I gave that girl my heart, and she done something with it, and I can't feel anything anymore.' He tells me he comes from a line of people from up north. A line that came in with the Saxons. Special people, he says. They have something called a Runger's heart. They grow it, right out of their chest, like a gem. They keep it secret, he says, because they're still attached to it and if any harm comes to it…" The captain waved his hand at the sea as if to imply the deepest, darkest nightmare. "Then he begs me to take him back to that little town and his girl."

The muscles in Edward's chest and stomach seized violently when the captain spoke the sailor's words. Swallowing back bile, Edward determined to listen to the remainder of the tale as it closed to an end, but he foresaw a grave end to it, worse than he first imagined.

"So we sails up the coast to the town, and I goes with him to see his girl. And around her neck on a chain is a diamond." He measured out a shape slightly smaller than his wide, flat palm. "A beautiful stone, red as blood. No stone a sailor could afford, no matter the taking. Polished real good and nice, a deep red with iridescent skin like a fish scale. And he whispers, 'I told ye to take care of it.' Well, she bursts into tears 'cause she thought he'd be happy that she got the stone he'd given her cut into a heart shape for the wedding. But the stone *was* his heart, do ye ken? And the jeweler cut away all sorts o' bits."

The captain shook his head. At this point, Edward was so ill his knees were threatening to give while his stomach violently threw itself against the inner wall of his body. He wondered why the captain was telling him this story. Had he seen Phoebe's heart? Or was it coincidence?

Either way, he couldn't prevent himself from asking what happened to the boy, his voice torn like shredded sails.

"Oh, Barnaby married her anyway. He be the town executioner. Don't need much of a heart for that," the captain added.

"Did he ever…regain feeling?" Edward asked, dreading the answer.

"Aye, a bit. The wounds, if that's what ye call it, healed, but he's not a man no more. No, ye look into Barnaby's eyes now, and all ye see is the abyss if ye take me meaning."

Edward did take his meaning. And so he leaned over the edge of the rail and violently sicked up the entire contents of his stomach and more. When he was done, the captain gave him a moment to compose himself before taking a step closer to the Edward and lowering his voice.

"Keep that gem of yers outa sight of me crew," he said. "I think there will be more consequences if it be stolen than a loss of coin."

With that he nodded once and walked away, leaving Edward stunned and silent at the rail.

Chapter Seventeen

August 11, 1789
On the Open Sea

The next day, Edward allowed Tilton to convince him into another practice bout. He knew the fencing would help take his mind from the dread and sick he'd been feeling since hearing the captain's tale. One could not brood and ponder the mythic while trying to dodge Tilton's sword. The young man was simply too skilled a fencer.

Edward ducked and found himself on the defensive again. Sucking in air, he dove into a roll and came up onto his feet, swinging with barely enough time to meet Tilton's attack. He grinned, despite the sweat rolling down his face. The ship pitched wildly, the waves bigger than they had been in days. Sailors said a storm might be rolling in, and there were several glancing between the fight on the deck and the horizon, searching for the source of the unruly waves.

Tilton overbalanced, and Edward pressed this tiny advantage. He let loose a flurry of quick movements, driving against the young man. His advantage evaporated as the ship pitched in the other direction. Usually, Edward had good balance, but the stone heart around his neck swung with his movements and then with the ship's. Suddenly, it jerked his head back a little too much, and only Tilton's swift turn of the blade saved Edward from being skewered.

Tilton grounded his sword.

"My God, Winchester," he huffed. "Are you all right?"

"Only because you are an expert with that blade," Edward said, grounding his own blade and breathing hard to recover. "Truly, you are an artist."

Tilton grinned, glowing at the praise. "My uncle insisted on it," he said. "He is a military man. I spent more time learning the sword than anything else. That is why my studies in history are appallingly behind," he added with a chuckle. He turned serious. "What is that thing around your neck? Lover's token?"

Edward straightened and ignored the question. "Perhaps we should finish for the day."

Tilton looked disappointed. "If a storm really does roll up, this will be our last opportunity to spar before we land. Let's go a little while longer."

Glancing at the sky, Edward realized Tilton was right. They were not more than a day or two outside the coast, and then a day up the river to the city. If it started raining, all their on-deck fun would be canceled.

"Very well," Edward said. "Give me a moment."

He disappeared below decks. He could not continue with the stone heart weighing him down. Over the past few days, their sparring matches had become more and more competitive as both men tested the limits of the other's skill. Edward was amazed that Tilton could outmatch him, but that only drove him to try harder against the youth. He realized he was enjoying it quite a bit. It was one of the few breaks between his periods of self-loathing and guilt, and he was not willing to give it up. Certainly not if this was the last.

Circumspectly, Edward cast an eye about before entering his room. The tiny hallway was empty though. Closing the door behind him, Edward took off the stone heart for the first time since his meeting with the count. There was hardly a place to hide it in the tiny cabin. Still, Edward stuffed it into the arm of his coat and balled that up into his bag.

When he straightened, Edward was amazed at how light he felt. For a moment, he thought that he could leave this burden behind. He could leave the heart and live his life better, perhaps travel with Tilton and all the hardship would disappear. Then the guilt found its way back in, and his cheeks burned with shame. He had done this. Did his father not always say to always strive to be the best of men? Was the best man he could be a coward who turned his back on a woman he wronged, a woman who at this moment was suffering interminably and had been for almost six months?

Edward almost reached back into the bag and took the stone heart out again. He inhaled deeply. He would step off this ship and follow the journey to save Phoebe. For now, he was fighting, and he could not do that with the weight of his crime around his neck. Not if he wanted to survive to save Phoebe. Stuffing the bag back under his bed, Edward closed and locked his door, then made his way above decks.

Tilton waited against the rail, speaking with Welfries. Whatever about, Edward could not tell, but it was the first time he saw a frown touch the dandy's fine features since they began their journey. Indeed, Tilton's cheeks were flushed even as Edward's had been moments before. At his approach, Welfries gripped Tilton's arm, almost in a warning, and then excused himself quickly.

"All well?" Edward asked.

"Of course," Tilton said, though neither of them believed him.

"Right then," Edward said. "Ready?"

For once, Tilton seemed to appreciate Edward's terseness and lack of intimacy. He drew his sword and saluted.

Hours later, Edward made it back to his room, a sweaty mass of bruises and cuts. Whatever Welfries had said had ignited quite a fire in Tilton, and he had needed working, quite like a stallion. Edward took comfort in the fact that Tilton had some bruises and cuts, though not quite as many.

As much as his pride wanted to be hurt, Edward felt relieved that this was a hurdle he knew how to face. There was an opponent he could charge. Even if he only defeated Tilton two out of every five matches, he knew this fight. Edward sat heavily on his bed and looked out the window. The storm was gathering on the horizon. Black clouds were billowing out like the chimney smoke and soot over London, with a crackle every now and then highlighting the edges.

At his feet lay his bag, and Edward reached for it and then paused. He had stuffed it under the bed before the fight. Why was it out? A cold fear gripped on him. He tore the bag open and pulled out his coat. Patting it down, he searched for the leather bag, a bump that would tell him the stone heart was safe where he'd left it. It was not there.

Swearing viciously, Edward tore out of the cabin

and back onto the deck. He looked around at the sailors going to and from and realized he had no idea where to start. Tilton was leaning against the deck rail, shockingly still in his practice clothes. He seemed unmindful of the wind picking up, the thunderous gale whipping up behind them, watching the sailors. He had an odd expression on his face, but Edward could not take that in. Edward, himself, was torn between livid and terrified.

Tilton caught his mood. "By God, Winchester," he said, "what is the matter?"

Edward strode up to him. "Someone took it," he said breathless.

"What?" Tilton asked.

"My…Phoebe's…the leather thong I carried around my neck," Edward said. "Someone stole it from my room."

"Ballocks," Tilton swore. "It's very important, I suppose?"

"Irreplaceable," Edward said.

"All right," Tilton said, casting a glance around. "Well, it is certainly not Dig. He is not wearing anything that could hide a pouch that size. O'Toole, Wells, and Thompson have been up on deck all afternoon, so it's not them."

To Edward's astonishment, Tilton began a surgical dissection of the crew as suspects. Who had not been below decks, who had during the afternoon, who was more than likely to be a pickpocket as well as a sailor.

"Although, they all are rather swarmy," Tilton added. His expression was appraising as he watched one climbing the ropes overhead. "Oh, I forgot about the captain."

"It is not him," Edward said, discounting that idea immediately. Tilton did not waste time asking Edward how he knew. He simply trusted his judgment. "When I find who did this, I am going to take out the man's eyes and throw him overboard."

"First, we have to figure out who," Tilton said. "And soon." He nodded toward the storm.

"I will go to the captain," Edward said. "Call roll before the gale hits."

But it was nearly too late for that. The ship was already rolling even as they spoke, and more men were coming topside to help out, trimming sail and securing anything that might go loose.

"No," Tilton said, eyes wide. "The storm will be our cover. Look at it," he gestured. "It will take all the men to keep this bucket on track."

"I will not skulk like a thief to recover my own property," Edward swore.

"Winchester, even if you were to call the roll and question these men, they will not turn on their own. Nor, I believe, would the captain whatever your thoughts on the man. This must be done quietly. Let me handle it."

Edward sized Tilton up. "Is there a past of reprehensible deeds I need know about?"

"Only if you count the stealing of women's undergarments and such youthful pranks reprehensible," Tilton shot back.

Edward had naught to say to that. And then Dig was pushing them both toward the hatch as the wind whipped up, ordering them down below.

Once below, more crew members squeezed by them in the tight hallway to get up top. Tilton motioned for Edward to follow him, and together they made their way farther down. They started in the officers' cabins, the whole three that there were. As Tilton predicted, neither Dig, the cook, nor the helmsman were the guilty party. They also knocked on Ole Todd's door. He opened it, and Tilton engaged him in a totally airy and thoughtless conversation about the impending gale. Ole Todd had a peculiar role on board. His leg had been broken so many times he could predict the weather with the precision of a sea god. So he had his own room.

Edward took some time running his gaze around, but found nothing that might indicate Ole Todd was their perpetrator. After two minutes of Tilton, the sea dog grew frustrated and yelled at them to get out while he rubbed fish oil into his aching leg.

The two retreated back into the hall and moved away, careful to hold on to the walls as the ship pitched in the waves around them. They had to talk quietly, between shattering rumbles of thunder overhead.

"I say, I am not fond of this weather," Tilton said, looking more pale as they made their way down to the common area where most of the rest of the crew had hammocks slung. It was empty now, with every hand being topside to make sure they survived.

"Hang out near the window and look outside," Edward said.

"Why?"

"Because otherwise you will lose your lunch."

"I will." Tilton grabbed his stomach and closed his eyes a moment. "Keep watch," he said raggedly, positioning himself next to a window but in full view of the hallway leading into the common room.

The room smelled of old sweat, salt, urine, and bad

rum. Edward wrinkled his nose as he began picking through the discarded pieces of clothing, thread-worn blankets, and sparse possessions about the room. There were a few bags and trunks. None of them yielded the stone. Edward was getting more frustrated, and fearful, by the minute.

As he tossed aside the last bag, he looked at Tilton with real worry. Of course the thief would not be so foolish to merely make Edward's own mistake and stash the diamond in the common room where anyone might stumble across it. There were a thousand tiny places on board, and Edward surely only had a day or so before he lost track of the sailors entirely. That was assuming they survived the storm.

"It is not here," he said.

Tilton nodded, having guessed that. He was turning an ugly shade of green, and Edward kicked over a mess pot for him to throw up in. Afterward, Tilton wiped his mouth with his handkerchief and declared that was the most disgusting thing he had ever done in his life. Blackly, Edward thought, *I have done far worse, and one of those things is losing that stone.*

Chapter Eighteen

August 1, 1789
Earl of Huntley London Townhouse

"Auntie darling," Ann said bursting into the room without permission. "He is gone. I have just come from the Winchester manor, and Edward has left without even so much as a goodbye note."

"Ann Theresa Gordon," Lady Eleanor snapped. "Are you a peasant?"

Ann straightened. "No."

" 'No, Aunt Eleanor,' " Lady Eleanor corrected. In response, Ann curtsied meekly and repeated the words. "Does a lady charge into a room like a bovine?"

"No, Aunt Eleanor," Ann replied.

"There is no situation, however full of strife, when a lady may behave in such a way," Lady Eleanor said firmly. "If the marquess has left, perhaps it is this behavior that drove him away."

Her words stung, and tears sprang to Ann's eyes. She did not sniffle or reply but bowed her head.

"Come, child, dry your eyes," Lady Eleanor said taking out her handkerchief and offering it. Ann came over and took it with a muffled "thank you." She dabbed delicately, which Lady Eleanor approved, then made to sit, but a look from her auntie kept her on her feet.

Lady Eleanor straightened and reached for her tea. It soothed her temper.

"Now then," she said setting it back down without the whisper of a sound. "I am aware that the marquess has left."

"Why did you not tell me?" Ann asked wretchedly.

"Because your reaction to the news needed to be genuine," Lady Eleanor said. "What did"—her mouth twisted—"the marchioness have to say?"

"She was clearly embarrassed. She said that Edward had rushed out on this trip to the Continent with no time for any social niceties and apologized profusely. She said it was a matter of grave importance."

"Did she elaborate?"

"No," Ann said. "I pressed as politely as I could. I do not think she knows, Auntie."

"That is well enough," Lady Eleanor said with a nod. "You will continue your association with her. Seek her out at social engagements, visit her often, continue to play the adoring young lady."

"But what about Edward?" Ann wailed.

"He has headed to win back his old paramour," Lady Eleanor said quite calmly.

"And I am to remain here *visiting* his mother," Ann demanded, "while he goes off to some foreign chit."

"Oh, do not worry over about that, my dear," Lady Eleanor said. "Edward will meet such bad luck, he will come home faster than the moon changes face. That's why you will continue to visit his mother because when he comes limping home, you need to be well-placed to comfort him on his return."

For the first time, Ann saw just how determined

her Auntie Eleanor was and how dangerous that made her. She wondered why Auntie Eleanor had pushed her in the direction of the Marquess of Winchester and why her mouth twisted every time she spoke of the dowager marchioness. But Ann wasn't stupid enough to ask her aunt that. No, she'd have to find someone else to ask about this particular history.

In the meantime, she nodded to her aunt and quietly took her leave, ever the obedient niece.

Chapter Nineteen

August 12, 1789
On the Open Sea

The storm raged for the rest of the day and night and did not clear again until nearly mid-morning the following day. Edward and Tilton continued their search in the hold until the rocking became too violent for them. Tilton, poor thing, was ill again, and Edward had to carry him back to his room. Then Edward retreated to his own room where he paced for a solid hour as best he could with the frolicking of the ship knocking him into walls and bed. Finally, he retreated to a corner to pray.

At some point, Edward fell asleep, though he could not tell when or how. He woke to faint light from the window and a crick in his neck from being huddled in the corner. He felt exhausted still, as if every muscle in his body ached from being beaten, which, judging by the state of his room, was not far off the mark. His belongings were scattered, the storm having tossed and tumbled everything loose.

Standing, Edward cautiously rotated his head and winced when he could not turn it well to the left. A stabbing pain prevented further movement in that direction. Squeezing the muscle, hoping for some relief, Edward walked to the small port window. The sea outside was a blazing blue, the sky two shades lighter, and the waves gentle against the side of the ship. They had survived.

God, make it so that Phoebe's heart is safe, he thought, and strode out the door.

He found Tilton asleep under his bed. Two quick shakes brought the younger man awake, and then Tilton accidentally knocked his head against the bed frame.

"Are you all right?" Edward asked.

Tilton groaned. "I feel as though I have been drinking for a week and then trampled by my father's race horses."

Edward thought about this. "Well," he said offering his friend a hand, "it cannot be that bad, then. Your father's horses are not that fast."

Tilton chuckled weakly. "Do you know how frustrated he is by that fact?" he asked taking the hand and letting Edward slide him out from under the bed.

Despite a tightness of pain about his eyes and his skin having the pallor of immature mint leaves, there was a twinkle there.

"How in God's name did you get under there?" Edward asked.

The younger man blushed and shrugged. "My older brother and I did not get on," he said. "I spent many years hiding under the bed." He paused and thought about it. "He was never smart enough to look there."

Edward snorted. "I always knew I was lucky to be an only child," he said.

"Did you find the stone?" Tilton asked.

Edward shook his head. "No," he said. "I was going to seek it after checking in on you."

"Well, I am alive, apparently," Tilton said. "If

you'll break fast with me, we can both go at it renewed."

Edward was reluctant to delay the search any longer, but he also realized he had more chance with an extra set of eyes than not. With a short nod, he assented. Tilton clapped him on the shoulder.

"It will be a fast meal," Tilton promised. "Mostly because I am not certain I can eat much." Edward chuckled despite himself, and Tilton squeezed his shoulder. "We will *find* it."

His friend's confidence boosted Edward's own, and he nodded feeling like, perhaps, they would succeed. Then he realized they *were* friends. Despite his dread and fear over the stone, Edward felt a rush of happiness at that realization. It struck Edward then that Tilton didn't even know what they were searching for. He'd seen the leather satchel around Edward's neck during their fights enough to know that was their goal, but not what was in it. He hadn't asked after the contents. *He's a good man,* Edward thought.

Tilton headed for the door if a little unsteadily. "Remember," he said. "It cannot have gotten off the ship."

Edward's stomach dropped. "Unless it was washed overboard with whatever miscreant stole it," he said softly.

"No," Tilton said fiercely. "It *is* here, and we *will* find it. Have faith, my friend."

Edward prayed Tilton was right and followed him out the door. They reached the galley in short time, only to find Cook passed out drunk in the corner. Tilton sighed and grabbed an apple from a satchel. He offered one to Edward, who shook his head.

"All right," Tilton said, taking a bite. "Let us find your stone."

The newly freed sun was doing its best to compensate for a half day and full night of being absent. It blinded both men as they climbed onto the deck. Around them, exhausted sailors were tidying up the ship's deck, tying off ropes and going about the business of getting back on course.

"Let's look around up here," Tilton suggested. "We start from the top and work our way down."

It was a sensible plan, and Edward agreed to it. They split up and both headed toward opposite decks to explore. Edward searched up one end and down the other. He glanced up in the rigging but there were only two men he could see climbing upward. He made a note to check them later. Edward was just coming back to the middle when he passed a man that caught his eye.

Edward had seen the man a few times. He had a long scar horizontal across his forehead, along the crease of his brow. It marked him out well enough. What marked him out this morning was the addition of a leather thong to his neck.

"You," Edward called storming over.

The man glanced up and then away quickly. He tried to hurry toward the stairs leading down to the hold, but Edward's long legs caught up before he could make it. Roughly, Edward grabbed the man's collar and spun him around.

"What is this?" he screamed, grabbing the leather pouch and pulling on it.

The sailor stumbled forward and then used the momentum to throw his shoulder into Edward's stomach. They tumbled to the deck with the sailor rolling deftly on top. The man got in a good two punches before Edward realized what had happened. He tried to turn his head, but pain lanced through his neck, and he couldn't turn it. Instead, he threw his forearms up to block the blows as a ring of rowdy sailors formed around them.

The sailor continued to rain blows down but quickly tired. Hours working at the storm had left him with little energy for a fight. After a few moments, he paused to catch his breath. Edward reached up and snaked his arm around the sailor's neck, bringing him close and throwing his hips up at the same time. They rolled. Sour breath and the crust of the storm from on his opponent's skin filled Edward's nostrils. He wanted to gag, but there was no time. He landed on top and raised his fist. The blow was a solid, good one. The sailor's eyes rolled back into his head, and he lay still.

Breathing hard, Edward stared down at his opponent and realized the leather pouch was gone. He glanced around wildly and spotted it amongst the crowd's feet. He stood, wiping sweat, and blood trickled from his face. Grimly, he advanced on the sailors who, muttering darkly, dispersed in front of him. He stooped to pick up the bag, but one sailor kicked it out of reach.

The leather pouch slid across the deck, between the railings, and over the edge into the sea. Edward didn't think. He followed. There was the hoarse cries of surprise and fear before the ocean crashed around him. Edward kicked hard, searching the water—still misty with bubbles and foam from the storm, the salt stinging his eyes. He saw a glint in his peripheral vision and angled left. He kicked harder, but it was naught but bubbles rising and catching the light.

Edward cursed silently and spun all around. Searching, praying, seeking that tiny tug within himself for a sense of where the stone might be drifting. The ship was cutting along, and as he glanced up, he saw the stone, caught in a circular tide. Edward pushed hard, his lungs burning, but he ignored it. He reached out, his fingers clasping around the leather thong even as a riptide caught hold of him.

He was jerked down and around, his vision spinning. Precious air escaped his mouth as he automatically tried crying out in surprise. Sea water hit his stomach and lungs. Edward snapped his mouth shut and threw his body sideways, kicking and pumping his arms as hard as he could. His fist remained clenched around the leather thong. After the fight, he was exhausted, and yet all he could think was, *if fire killed Nancy Storace, Phoebe must be drowning.*

His efforts were rewarded, and he somehow pulled free of the tide. For a half a second, he hung there suspended, shocked even at his luck, before all his instincts bore down on him, and he pushed the last of his reserves to break the surface. He held the diamond aloft, and a rousing victory cry went up from the ship which was now some distance in front of him.

It turned, creaking slowly out of the wind as sailors trimmed the white sails down. A longboat was already being lowered. Edward tread water a few minutes to catch his breath, holding the leather pouch above his head as best he could. Then, clutching it gently between his teeth, he began to swim to the longboat.

Two rough sailors, one of them Dig, pulled him in. Edward spit the pouch out of his mouth and clutched it to his chest.

"I hope that is worth risking yer life over, m'lord," Dig said.

Edward did not know whether to be insulted or relieved that the sailors believed his motivations were mere greed. He decided it hardly mattered, as long as the stone was safe.

By the time they made it back on deck, the captain was tapping out old ash. Edward was freezing, dripping wet, and more exhausted than he had ever felt in his life. The captain eyed him, then the leather thong, then nodded.

"Hamm has been put in the brig," he said.

"He should be hung up the mast," Edward snapped.

"Well, you did knock him senseless." The captain shrugged. "If ye killed him, that'd be the end of the affair. Likes now, I will hand him over to the harbormaster when we reach port."

Edward scowled, but before he could make known his extreme distaste, Tilton was thanking the captain and shoving Edward toward the hatch below. Welfries, too, was there suddenly going on about how Edward needed to get out of his wet clothes, fussing like a nursemaid.

Once at his cabin, Tilton shoved Edward in and told Welfries to stand guard.

"Tilton, that man—"

"He did not have to turn back for you, Winchester," Tilton said.

"What?"

"The crew was half about to leave you behind," Tilton said. "They certainly did not want to trim sail and turn about for you, but the captain started snapping at them like Beelzebub himself. Truly, Winchester, the captain is the only reason you are alive."

Edward started to sit down on the bed, but Tilton pulled him up.

"No, no, we need to get you out of those clothes first."

Tilton helped Edward undress and into some dry clothes. When that was done, Edward finally sat down on his bed.

"You look right exhausted," Tilton said. "Get some rest. Later, I will hear why one of the richest men in England felt need to dive into the ocean after a leather pouch. Until then…"

"Wait," Edward said. "Tilton, please. Take this," Edward handed him the leather satchel. Tilton's eyes widened in disbelief. "Please. If the crew really does want me gone, then this is safer with you. I am done for. If a man walks through that door, I do not have it in me to stop him. If that is my fate, make sure it gets to Lady Phoebe von Croy. It is a matter of the soul, Tilton."

"A woman," Tilton said. "I should have guessed. Fear not. You will survive the night. I will stay here and make certain of it." He handed Edward back the stone heart. "Now rest, Winchester, before you fall over."

Tilton opened the door and spoke quietly with Welfries while Edward slipped under the blankets. He was asleep before the door closed again.

Chapter Twenty

August 9, 1789
The von Croy Mansion, Vienna

Phoebe waited for Mary, her maid, to finish her hair. It looked wonderful. It really did, but she found she cared less about her appearance other than that it was enough. Enough to fool people into thinking she cared. She reached for her perfume, an expensive, delicate scent of jasmine and marigolds, imported from India. A gift from Edward. She paused and considered smashing it against the wall, as she had done a thousand times since she'd left England.

Then a tendril of spite filled her, and she sprayed it on her wrists. She touched some to the side of her neck. Frederick thought it made her smell exotic. It had been one of the first things that had caught Frederick's attention. It was fitting, then, that this gift from Edward should help her find a new husband. The spite fizzled out to be replaced, momentarily, by loss and rage.

Phoebe closed her eyes. No, she would not think about him anymore. He was dead to her. That part of the world was dead to her. All save for Rhys, and she had not been able to bring herself to reply to her cousin's missive all for the memories.

"Are you all right, my lady?" Mary asked, pulling the last curl from the hot iron.

Mary asked it often. Too often.

"I am well, Mary," Phoebe said, her voice sharp. "Please tell Frederick I will be down shortly."

Mary curtsied and left quietly leaving Phoebe alone with the smell of jasmine and marigolds filling the room. Phoebe regarded her reflection. The sage green dress suited well with her strawberry blonde locks. Her makeup was simple, and she required no powder to her skin. The diamond drop necklace emphasized her bosom to perfect effect, a gift from her mother.

Her mother had warned Phoebe not to fall in love.

"It never ends well for one of our blood, dear," her mother had said the night before Phoebe married her first husband.

Then, Phoebe had not responded or protested. She did not say that her mother's marriage to her father was all but a sham and that he beat his wife regularly. There was clearly no love there, and it had not saved her mother from heartache.

As if reading her thoughts, her mother said, "Duke von Croy is a good man. He will treat you well, and you will be set up for life."

She had been right about that. Lukas, the Duke von Croy, had been especially kind to Phoebe, and she had learned to love him. But then he was taken from her by consumption too soon. Now, she was alone. She had never intended to fall in love with Edward. She had only wanted to get away from the happy memories of her life with Lukas. She had gone to England to visit her cousins and spend a holiday there as a distraction.

Then Edward and heartache. Phoebe's mother had been right about falling in love. Unbidden, Phoebe's eyes moved to the box on her vanity beside the bottle of perfume. It was made of a cool marble, flecked with black and lined with blue velvet. In it lay the other half of her heart. Phoebe took the key from her bracelet and unlocked the box. Lifting the lid, she stared at the ragged edge of the red diamond where her heart had broken. Her eyes filled with tears.

Shaking the memories off, Phoebe scolded herself once more. *I will not mourn the loss of that fool,* she thought. And yet, the hurt did not dissipate. It was not as bad as it had been. Over the past six months, slowly, her feelings had cooled. Now, only a few topics made her feel anything more than tepid. She had previously been such a spitfire. Edward had always teased her on it. That life felt a million years in the past. So much had changed in the past six months.

Before she could reflect on this change, she could not breathe. Phoebe gasped, her hand flying to her chest. She struggled to suck in air and felt water begin to fill her lungs. She could only manage half a breath.

Oh God, she thought. *Oh God, I am drowning. He is going to kill me. He has thrown my heart into a lake or a pond or something. Edward has thrown me away!*

Terror filled her as she struggled to breathe. She slid off the chair and onto her knees. Eyes squeezed shut, she reached blindly for her stone heart. Knocking down bottles and glass, she found the edges of the marble box and reached inside, withdrawing the warm gem. Holding it against her chest, she concentrated on breathing.

Please, Hrungnir, she thought. *My ancestor, don't let him kill me.*

She felt the weight of moving water all around her, black and salty. The crushing lack of oxygen made her dizzy. She gasped for air. And then warmth seized her. It spread through her chest, and though she struggled to breathe, she felt safe. The weight of the water disappeared. She could almost hear the echoes of someone breaking through the surface of the water, a cry of victory on their lips.

Phoebe wavered, expecting to be plunged back into that dark, horrid place, but it did not happen. The vision faded. The feeling of drowning faded. It took another ten minutes for Phoebe to fully recover. All the while she held on to her half of the stone heart. She was sure it was Edward who had taken her heart out of the water. Which didn't make any sense.

He had never believed her. He did not believe in things he could not see. And whatever chance she might have had at convincing him was lost when he decided that her loving her first husband was a breach of trust. And yet, that feeling of safety, that feeling that engulfed her when the water retreated felt like it would surely crush her, it had felt like Edward's arms around her.

"My lady," Mary cried out, rushing to her side.

Phoebe had not heard her enter.

"I am fine," she said and was glad her voice was steady, though hoarse. "Just a fainting spell."

Mary helped her to her feet. Phoebe realized the vanity was a mess. Broken glass was everywhere, and the scents of half a dozen oils and creams used for her daily toilet were mixing in unappealing ways. The strongest was the aroma of jasmine and marigolds, which enveloped Phoebe in a thick cloud. She had ended up smashing the perfume after all.

"Please clean this up, Mary," she said, placing the stone heart in its box. She locked it up and walked out.

Downstairs in the drawing room, Frederick waited for her.

"Are you all right, my *schatzi*?" Frederick asked, teasing her.

"Of course, my dear," she said, allowing him to kiss her hand. As she glided on his arm out the door, all her feelings flowed away.

Chapter Twenty-One

August 11, 1789
Hamburg

The next time Edward's eyes opened, the window showed blue sky mixed with emerald trees. He sat up, rubbing salt crust out his eye and groaning at the deep ache in his muscles. The room was empty. Edward glanced around for the diamond and panicked at not finding it at his side. Rolling clumsily out of bed, he fell hard on the floor, tangled in blankets. A soft *thud* alerted him, and the glint of sunlight off a red facet drew Edward's eyes.

The diamond lay half out of its leather thong on his blanket, but safe, whole, well as whole as it had been before he'd slept. His entire body unclenched with relief, and he sat up, drawing it to his chest. It was still warm, not hot by any means, but he thought it might be warmer than when he'd left London. Was that a sign? He could not be sure. Hopefully, his quarry would have answers.

Edward found his clothes washed and folded neatly in his knapsack. The clothes still smelled of the sea, though, and the memories of the riptide and the fear were not ones he wished to relive. Edward supposed he could not expect his clothes to be washed with clean water, not on a ship. He pulled out his good suit, instead. He took his time cleaning as much of the salt off his skin with what was left in the basin and brushed out his hair. He tied it back and dressed slowly, making note of every bruise, bump, scrape, and cut from his tangle with the thief Hamm, plus the days of sparring with Tilton.

Thinking of Tilton, Edward made his way out to find his friend. He paused outside his door. In a short amount of time, Tilton had, indeed, become quite the friend. Beyond distracting him from the fearful future and his shame, Tilton had helped him search for the stone, and saved Edward from the captain's wrath after his narrow escape with death. He had, unthinkingly, in pure, blind trust offered Tilton the stone, and the dandy had opted, instead, to stand guard.

Edward shook his head. Tilton was a good man. With those thoughts in mind, Edward went searching the ship. He found Tilton on the mid-deck, watching the land roll by.

"Ah," he said happily. "The sleeper awakens at last. I was afraid I might need to fetch a princess or a witch or something to wake you from the spell." Tilton grinned at his own cleverness, but Edward frowned at the reminder of his errand. The smile faltered. "I am only teasing, Winchester."

"I know," Edward said, nodding to put Tilton at ease. "My thoughts were on another matter. I owe you a great deal, Tilton."

"Not at all—"

"I do," Edward said quietly. "I know it."

The dandy shifted and patted Edward on the shoulder. "I do not have many friends," Tilton said, and a shadow crossed his face as he said it. Edward could not imagine this. *He* was the one who disliked the company of people. Tilton was a fun young man, mischievous and easy-going. How could he not have friends? "I would simply enjoy the pleasure of naming you amongst them."

"If that is how we are going to continue," Edward said. "Then you should call me by my given name, Edward."

Tilton's eyes widened, and he flushed. "It would be my honor. And I, Walter." He blushed harder. "Although only my mother really calls me that."

Edward laughed and slapped him on the back. "I'll stick with Tilton then," Edward said.

Tilton told him he had slept through a day and a night and into the morning after. They were hours away from pulling into port at Hamburg. Edward could see the curiosity of the leather thong in Tilton's expression when he glanced at it hanging, once more, around Edward's neck.

"Perhaps in another place," Edward said, glancing about.

The sailors had been circumspectly eying the two as they caught up. Edward was not sure if he saw respect, greed, fear, or a mixture across their tanned and leathery faces. He was glad he had survived the crossing, and gladder still that this journey would end before night fell once more.

Before they could continue their conversation, however, the captain emerged from his quarters. He walked over without invitation.

"I am told I have you to thank for my rescue," Edward said. Captain nodded as if thanks was his given due, and Edward supposed it was.

"I told ye to keep that diamond out of sight," he said harshly. Tilton's eyes widened at mention of a diamond.

"I did," Edward said stiffly.

"Not enough," the captain said. "Makes no diffrence now, I s'ppose. We be at port this afternoon. I spect payment afore ye make off."

"Of course," Edward said.

The captain only nodded again, his expectation of payment as good as law. Both peers returned to their rooms to gather their belongings. They met, along with Welfries, on the prow and kept out of the way of the scurrying sailors. As they stood, Hamburg unfolded before them, and they took in their destination.

Hamburg was a beautiful, large city as yet untainted by the soot stains of the steam industry. It sat cradled between the River Elbe and the River Alster. Rising stone towers from churches and castles alike dotted the skyline of an ancient town with bones buried deep in the earth. The houses were of fair size, two or three stories high, whitewashed walls with exposed beams of wood in X's across the facings. These beams were painted to match the shutters in all manner of color as suited the inhabitants giving the city a cheerful, pastel countenance. The roofs were tiled with pale clay and sloped making the eye of the observer jump from place to place as in a game.

The city had been conquered and burned more times than most, and the original castle for which it was named, Hamma, no longer stood. But the city had merely grown up on top of it. That was the kind of city Hamburg was, a city of resilience and austerity. It had an old soul filled with tradition and culture but smart enough to take in the world, with all its splendor, and evolve with it.

"It's a fine place to start your tour," Edward commented.

"I hope so," Tilton said. "With half the world mad and in pieces, I have few options."

"Still, it's a city with history and class."

A towboat came in to lead them to their dock. Once the mooring lines were thrown and caught, Edward sought out the captain to finish his payment. He added a few extra in and thanked the captain again.

"Whatever ye journey, sir, I hope it ends well," the captain said.

"And I hope yours brings riches and fine women," Edward said. "You are a man of unexpected honor."

The captain laughed. "Don' ye go ruinin' my reputation."

At long last, the gangplank was brought to bear and the passengers released. Edward breathed a long sigh of relief once his feet touched to ground. At the moment, the weight of the stone around his neck was comforting rather than dragging. He still had it. By the will of God and Fate, he had survived the sea voyage. Now, he had to make arrangements to find the Comte de Saint Germaine.

Edward passed on the docks, wondering at the wave of regret that he and Tilton would be parting so quickly. He turned to his friend who was gawking at all the sights, and said, "I am staying at the Hotel Bergedorf, if you are inclined to join me."

"Sounds lovely," Tilton said, nodding. "Lead the way."

For his part, Welfries seemed just as intent to allow

Edward to do the leading, although his grasp of German was more on point than Edward's. Several hours later, Edward, Tilton, and Welfries, plus their combined luggage, pulled into the circle in front of the Bergedorf. Edward had only his one duffel bag, while Tilton had come with quite a bit more than that. His luggage took the entire top of the carriage. Edward supposed for a tour, it made sense. He was not so inclined, given his urgent errand.

The hotel was in the more expensive part of town, boasting four floors, two wings, and a restaurant all its own. The building itself stood like a large manor off the main avenue. A spectacular fountain with marbled rearing horses stood before the palatial rest stop. Flowers in this high season, daffodils and tulips, a very expensive flower indeed, sprang up in carefully planned patterns about the fountain. Tilton and Welfries took in the beauty with high appreciation, probably believing before now that no one outside of England could garden properly.

As they disembarked from the carriage, the concierge met them at the door.

"My Lord Marquess," he said in a heavily accent tone, "we have been expecting your arrival. Your man sent a message ahead."

Edward blinked, surprised that Halkerstone had taken such initiative, especially after Edward had taken such pains to hide his true destination. Then he shook himself. Of course, Halkerstone had been the one to find the transport ship. He had known Edward was coming this far at least. It was not that he distrusted Halkerstone. He simply did not want the man's judgment on him. Halkerstone was far too upright to believe in fairy stories. Hell, Edward hardly believed.

"The Honorable Tilton will also be needing a suite," Edward said. "Next to mine, if you please."

The concierge bowed low and waved at one of the footmen discreetly. Several moved to begin unloading the luggage, while another ran inside to prepare another suite.

"We have fresh baths prepared, my Lord Marquess."

"Excellent." Edward nodded. "Reserve a table at the restaurant in an hour," Edward said. "We have eaten nothing but jerky and boat food."

The concierge murmured assent and led them inside. From there, a footman guided them through hallways of marble and gilded ceilings, past murals and tapestries hundreds of years old. They came to a corner part of the eastern wing, and the footman led Welfries and Tilton off to a door across from where Edward was directed.

Inside, Edward found a sprawling set of rooms where warm water and hot cloths had been prepared. The hotel valet laid out Edward's only dinner suit, one of fine navy blue wool with matching breeches, a navy silk waistcoat, white stockings, and a silk cravat of pale gold. The valet began brushing it down. Edward complimented the man's efforts. Considering how salty and wrinkled everything had been, he looked rather dashing afterward.

His preparations were done quickly enough, and Edward found himself suddenly alone with time to spare before he need go downstairs. It was odd to go from such cramped quarters to open space. The suite was lavish—a small mansion in a set of three rooms—a calling room, a private bath, and a bedroom. Despite the heat in the fireplaces, there was a chill to the air. The city, sitting on the river, did not hold the summer heat as much as London had, and there was less humidity.

Edward picked up the leather pouch from where he'd laid it on the dresser as he dressed and went back to the fire. It had always been in his sight. The events of the ship far too fresh in his mind to leave the satchel unattended even for a moment. He loosened the strings and rolled out the stone. Sitting down in front of the fire, Edward took the stone and held it against his chest. It was probably silly, but he was hoping between his body heat and the fire, he could keep whatever heat the stone might have gained stoked.

When his bones were warmed, Edward went and sat at the writing desk. He placed the stone carefully on the desk in front of him and wrote to Rhys of the journey. Then he penned a quick note to his mother. Like Mr. Halkerstone, he had not disclosed to her his purpose or true destination for the trip, only that it was pressing business on the Continent. She had seen the look in his eye and remarked how much like his father he was when he had prey in sight.

"You are a raptor, my son," she said, but there was a note of concern in her voice that he attempted to alleviate. It was that note of concern that drove his hand as he wrote, perhaps over-ebulliently, of the journey. Although, when it came time to mention the food on the ship, Edward could not find the words to lie graciously. Instead, he mentioned Tilton and their burgeoning friendship. Having a peer on the journey would make his mother happy. She was ever pushing him to be more social.

Edward was powdering the letters when there was a knock on his door. He bade them enter.

Tilton walked in, resplendent in a fine pin-striped green and white silk jacket. He had a matching green vest and breeches, pure white stockings, and his shoes, somehow, were spit shined. Edward felt momentarily embarrassed to have so little on hand in terms of clothing, but then reprimanded himself. He was not staying here for pleasure. His mission was all that mattered, and in light of that, he did not need trunks full of luggage.

"You look very well," he said, folding the letters into envelopes.

"Why thank you, Winchester," Tilton said. Edward chided him gently and Tilton, with a flush, said, "Edward."

Tilton came full in the room and glanced about, openly admiring the suite while Edward sealed the letters.

"Writing your lover?" he asked, eyes glimmering with interest. It reminded Edward of the expressions worn by his mother's friends as they sat around and gossiped. Then he silently chastised himself. Tilton did not have the look of a viper as the ladies of the ton did.

"My mother," Edward said shortly. "And my good friend. Do you know the Duke of Brey?"

"Only by sight," Tilton said. "We have never been properly introduced. Although the duchess has the most lovely taste in fashion, I must say."

Edward nodded. That did not surprise him. Tilton was only eighteen. He had not even come into his inheritance yet. His social standing and experience in the ton would be limited. That Tilton may have noticed

Cecilia, also did not surprise him. She was a beautiful woman and lit up any room she entered. Besides, Tilton obviously relished fashion. He would take note of anyone that did the same, and Cecilia *loved* shopping.

"The next time we are in London together," Edward said, "I shall introduce you. You would like Rhys."

Tilton did not answer to that, and Edward interpreted his silence as assent. They walked down together, and Edward handed the letters off to the concierge to post. Dinner consisted of rollmops, a pickled herring fillet rolled with pickled gherkin, dark beer, spargel or white turnips as a side dish, and abendbrot, an evening bread. The food was superb, well seasoned, and a welcome change from the watery stew and stale fare on the ship.

Tilton ordered doughnuts for dessert, but Edward declined, feeling full and satisfied for the first time since before leaving London. He realized he could not remember when last he had gone out to eat with a friend and done nothing more than chat about the opera or shared interests. He supposed it would have been before he cut off Phoebe and that friend was Rhys.

At a lull in the conversation, he shifted and felt the weight of the leather pouch on his belt, reminding him why he had not had this particular pleasure in so long. It shot an arrow through his heart.

"Edward"—Tilton was getting used to calling him by his given name—"are you quite well? You look pale all of a sudden."

Edward murmured that he was quite fine and stood before the dessert was brought out. He made his excuses, saying he wanted fresh air, and promised to meet Tilton back at the rooms. With little options on places to go, Edward headed outside to the gardens.

The air amongst the verdant garden was perfect for a summer night, with a breeze blowing off the Elbe smelling like an odd mix of salt and flowers. Wandering amongst the tall, sculpted shrubs and neat beds with the expensive tulip in a rainbow of colors, Edward found a moment of calm. He took the heart out, and in the dim light of the garden, it seemed to glow. Phoebe liked gardens. She was wild in that way, fey even, for though they had courted in the middle of winter, she was always going outside and talking to the icy plants, promising to see them in spring.

She had told him come spring she would weave him a flower crown of daisies and pick lavender for the house. Edward used to tease her about it asking if she was really a woman of two and twenty?

"Come catch me and see?" she taunted, running off in the snow. And Edward had been pulled into a game of tag for the first time in twenty years. He had kissed her on the lips when he caught her, as scandalous as it was. He had not regretted it. It had felt like a fairy tale then. She'd been so beautiful with her cheeks red from the cold and her eyes wide in surprise and then delight.

He wondered if she still smiled the same. Having her heart broken, how much had it changed her?

She's still the same woman, he thought. *She's probably in a garden right now or plunking away badly at a piano.* He smiled to think of how poorly she played. *Or out with a gentleman—*

He didn't think a mere supposition could cause so much agony, but fire spread through his chest, squeezing the air out of his lungs. Panting, he fought to breathe, and as his breath wavered, his vision went dark.

What happened next, Edward could not explain. Instead of the garden at sunset in Hamburg, a scene unfolded before his eyes. It was a hallway, all gilt and done out in the baroque style with murals of cherubs and angels flitting about maidens in forests and on beaches. Phoebe walked on the arm of a gentleman. Her expression was enigmatic. There was a loftiness to her that had never been there before, a detached sort of calm. No blush across her apple cheeks, no tossing of her fine strawberry curls. Just a dispassionate regard and a murmured reply to her escort, a man of eminent bearing with an impressive mustache.

Before Edward could do more than clutch his chest and gape, the vision was gone. He collapsed to the grass, sucking in air. Edward did not fathom how long he lay there recovering. Around him, the garden remained quiet save for the soft buzz of insects and rustle of leaves. By the time Edward picked himself up and returned to the rooms, he was more certain than ever that this fairy tale was real and, what's more, he was running short on time.

****

As Edward approached Tilton's room, Welfries stepped out of a side hall. Edward paused. He had not seen the tutor all night, though it made sense as Welfries would be staying in a smaller, side room as part of Tilton's suite. Still, Edward wondered why the man was waiting for him, as it was obvious that was Welfries' intention.

Edward had had little contact with the tutor and had no particular opinion of him as anything more than hired help who, in his opinion, strove to do the best he could with a rather willful student.

"Ah, my Lord Marquess," the man said jovially. "Might I have a word?"

Edward did not want, in point of fact, to have a word with the man. He wanted to pack his things and leave that very night, but he knew that was not possible. Besides, it would not do to be rude to his friend's tutor. So he nodded and waved for Welfries to continue.

Instead of answering, Welfries glanced around the hallway nervously. He cleared his throat but did not meet Edward's eyes.

"It is, of course, none of my concern nor business as to what my lord does at night," he said carefully. "However, he is at a young age and on such a journey as this might do with better instruction in certain gentlemanly pastimes from a peer of the realm such as yourself. It would provide better, uh, guidance on the appropriate decorum and destinations than a lowly tutor as I could provide."

Edward studied the man. "Of what pastimes do you speak?" he asked, annoyed. He understood that Welfries may not possess a notion of Edward's intentions, but he was irritated nonetheless. He was not here for pleasure, and his experience in the garden had driven that point home.

Welfries cleared his throat again, even more uncomfortable. "Er, the, uh, manly arts, my Lord Marquess."

"I am not going to attend any gentlemanly events this night or any other. I have business to attend that leaves little time for distractions. Either attend to this yourself, or I suggest you leave off. If Tilton wants to find sport, he is clever and capable enough to do so on his own."

Welfries bowed low and left quickly. Edward eyed the man's retreating form. He had a feeling that Welfries was trying to get Edward to take Tilton to a whorehouse. While fun, it seemed an odd and inappropriate request for a servant to ask *for* his master. Edward shook his head and dismissed it. He did not have time to puzzle out the queerness of Welfries. He had other things to concern himself over. Like finding the Comte de Saint Germaine. He could only hope that Count Cagliostro was correct and Saint Germaine was not deceased, as rumored. For both his sake and Phoebe's, he prayed it was so.

Edward entered his room and found Tilton lounging on a sofa indolently with a sherry in hand already.

"I thought perhaps you had wandered off without me," Tilton said with a grin.

Edward frowned. "I hope you do not expect us to go out upon the town tonight," he said.

Tilton blinked. "Well…not tonight. I inquired with the concierge. Mozart's *Don Juan* is playing at the opera. I could easily procure us some tickets for tomorrow night."

"Usually, I would enjoy that very much," Edward said, pouring himself a glass and sitting across from Tilton. "However, I have already informed the concierge that I will not be staying another night."

Tilton frowned but waited for an explanation.

"You asked me on the ship about this." Edward removed the pouch from his neck and untied it. He took out the diamond and held it to the light so that the red facets gleamed.

"I imagine it is very valuable, but not for obvious reasons," Tilton said. "Although a red diamond is rare, is it not?"

Edward nodded. "You must understand, I am not the type of man to believe in the arcane."

Tilton chuckled. "Edward, you are not the type of man to use the word 'arcane.' "

Five days ago, the comment would have irritated Edward, but he had become used to Tilton's teasing manner. There was nothing hurtful in its play. More like the affection of a puppy. Frankly, Tilton was correct. He was much sharper than his dandified wardrobe implied.

Tilton turned serious. "So what is it? Really?"

"It is a heart," Edward said, then shook himself. "Half of a heart. Of a woman I cared about."

"This Phoebe you mentioned?"

Edward nodded. Tilton took the stone from Edward and studied it, commenting on its weight and warmth before carefully handing it back. Then he asked Edward's intentions. Edward had been waiting for this question, and he worried over how much to share. Now, searching Tilton's face, he realized he trusted the younger man. So he told him everything about his quest. He did not divulge his past with Phoebe, only that he had hurt her. Some aches were too painful, and that particular subject had cost him twice over, first with Phoebe herself and then with Rhys. The reminder in the garden was enough to make him never want to mention it again.

Despite his youth and his bouts of silliness, Tilton was a good listener. He did not laugh or mock

Edward's story, but listened intently, asking questions when a particular point was unclear to him. All the while, Tilton swirled the sherry in his glass absently. When Edward was finished, there was a flash of emotion across Tilton's face, which he covered by draining his glass. Edward first thought it was longing, but dismissed that notion. More than likely, it was Tilton's disbelief playing against his respect for Edward and his position. So the marquess was surprised when Tilton asked, "Do you love her?"

Edward pursed his lips. "I did," he said. "It does not matter, though. She has moved on."

"How do you know?" Tilton asked, curiously.

It would be so simple to lie—to say he knew from rumor or a letter or whatnot. But Edward could not, so he told Tilton about the garden.

It was Tilton's turn to study him. He did not say anything more on it, and his face did not betray whatever he thought, nor elaborate on his emotions— disbelief or otherwise. Instead, he stood, poured them both another drink, and sat back down, his face set.

"This is why I cannot go out upon the town with you," Edward said. "Tomorrow, I will take a private coach to Berlin to find Saint Germaine. Then, if all goes well, Vienna. I have already made the arrangements."

Tilton nodded. "Then I hope your coach can fit my luggage as well," he said. "For I am going with you." Although he said the first bit playfully, Tilton's voice was steady and solemn on the ending. Edward was caught off guard.

"I appreciate your sentiment, Tilton. However, this is my errand."

"You will need a friend, Edward," Tilton said.

"Besides, I am on a trip to see the world. Berlin and Vienna are vast metropolises, and I would be pleased to visit them."

"I will not be lingering," Edward said. "There will be no fun, no games, no opera. More's the pity."

"You cannot expect to travel across Europe without meeting conflict," Tilton said, waving his hands to dismiss Edward's points. "You will need someone to watch your back, and I am a better swordsman than you."

"And I am a better shot," Edward said stiffly. "And a better boxer."

Tilton smiled. "Says who? We did not practice those on the ship."

"Tilton—"

"It is a matter of honor," Tilton said, shaking his head stubbornly. "You will not do this alone."

"And what of Welfries?" Edward asked.

Tilton laughed. "Well, we could sneak out and leave him behind," he said. "I will not protest."

Edward sighed. "If he slows me down, I *will* leave him behind."

"Cheers to that," Tilton said, raising his glass.

It was on the tip of Edward's tongue to ask what the strife was between them, but he did not. It was not any of his business. Besides, more than likely, no more than the expected tension between a student and tutor, when the tutor is hired by parents and forced to deal with a man, not a child.

Part of the Marquess of Winchester wanted to deny that he needed any aid or person to help him with so solemn a mission. But, then, the part of Edward that realized perhaps there was more to the world than he had first supposed, that perhaps things were not as they seemed, welcomed the idea of a trusted companion. Besides, Tilton was irritating in a way that Edward thought a younger brother might be, but he found himself enjoying the younger man's presence more and more.

"Very well, Tilton, I am glad to have you," Edward said smiling. They shook on it, and it felt, at least for Edward, as if this was the actual beginning of his journey. For the first time, despite his concerns, he also felt like perhaps he had met with good luck. He went to sleep that night and slept deeply without dreaming.

Chapter Twenty-Two

August 13, 1789
Hotel Bergedorf, Hamburg

The feeling of optimism did not last. As Edward broke fast the next morning with Tilton and a very subdued Welfries, the concierge came in to inform him that the carriage that had been hired for him was now broken and would not be repaired for several days. When Edward asked if there was an alternative, the concierge assured him they were contacting others.

Tilton remarked over the table that perhaps this minor setback was a good thing.

"I believe the servants are still packing my things," he remarked. "It might take a bit longer."

Edward glanced at him in bemusement. "We only just arrived. Did they unpack all your belongings yesterday?"

Tilton nodded. "Well, we only decided to travel together late last night. The poor valet tried his best not to look aghast when I advised him this morning that we were leaving."

Tilton was obviously amused, and Edward smiled despite himself. He'd seen the mountain of luggage Tilton was toting. He could not imagine the vast amount of work involved in repacking it all effectively and quickly. Despite the joke, Welfries remained quiet.

Edward was not certain if the tutor was uncomfortable because of their interaction the night before or another issue. He suddenly feared Tilton had spoken more than he should have about their purpose and searched for a diplomatic way of testing the water.

"Are you amenable to the changes in your tour, Mr. Welfries?" Edward asked.

The tutor glanced up almost fearfully at Edward, who decided it must have been their interaction indeed.

"Of course, my Lord Marquess," he said.

Welfries' disquiet, however, was making Edward's teeth ache. Either the man sensed Edward's growing unease, or simply too uncomfortable himself, stood and made his excuses.

"What did you tell him?" Edward asked quietly as soon as Welfries had left. Tilton shrugged.

"Only that we were changing plans," Tilton said. At Edward's raised eyebrow, Tilton sighed and put his cup aside. "He attempted to bully me into not joining you. Technically, he is my guardian on this journey, and my father has rather strict ideas on how I should be handled."

"What did you say?" Edward asked, truly curious.

Tilton shrugged and did not reply. This ventured into the area between Tilton and Welfries and their strange struggle against one another. Apparently, in this bout, Tilton had won, and Welfries was unhappy about it.

Edward was going to push the issue when the concierge approached their table. His face was remorseful.

"I apologize, my Lord Marquess, but it appears all the other reputable carriages have been hired out for the next few days. I have booked one to leave Friday. It was the earliest I could manage." He held up his hands apologetically.

"That is three days from now," Edward protested. "Are you telling me there is not one damn carriage available in the whole of the city?"

Rather than answer, the concierge spread his hands helplessly. Edward swore.

"Edward, perhaps three days is not so bad—" Tilton began.

"My business is pressing," Edward snapped, his eyes flashing to Tilton. Then he softened a mite at Tilton's expression. "It is not something that can wait," Edward added, placing careful meaning onto the words so Tilton would understand.

The lordling nodded in understanding. The concierge looked between the two men and then bowed his way back. He had nothing more to add to the conversation. Edward's mind flitted through possibilities. He could buy fast horses and go that way. It would certainly save on time, but then he would have to leave Tilton behind. That did not sit well, not after Tilton's pledge to him.

Edward wanted to curse the luggage, silently he did, but it was not Tilton's fault really. Standing, Edward straightened his jacket.

"Where are you going?" Tilton asked.

"To find us a damn carriage," Edward said. "I refuse to believe there is no one in this damn city that cannot help."

And with that, he strode off, leaving a concerned Tilton behind.

Chapter Twenty-Three

August 19, 1789
Winchester London Townhouse

Linus Halkerstone nodded at the Winchester butler, Mr. Nevin, in a familiar way at the door. They had known each other many years, many more than Edward had been alive. The butler swung it wide without prompting and invited him in.

"I am here to see Lady Winchester," Halkerstone said, although Mr. Nevin already knew that. Halkerstone's monthly meetings with the Lady Winchester had been consistent since the family, including the late marquess, returned from Denmark years ago. More than that, however, Mr. Nevin, being in the service of the Winchesters most of his life, had known Linus Halkerstone since he was a child.

"She is out in the garden today, Mr. Halkerstone, entertaining Miss Gordon," he said. Then Mr. Nevin raised an eyebrow. "Miss Gordon showed up unannounced," he added in a soft voice that carried no farther than Mr. Halkerstone's ears. It was full of fluff and disapproval that tone.

Mr. Halkerstone was in a peculiar position. He was not in service, and yet, he was not of the nobility. He had been connected to the Marquess of Winchester publicly for over ten years and privately to the family itself, the Pierce family, his entire life. How much the butler knew of that connection, Halkerstone could not say. It was not something people spoke of in polite company. Nor did it concern him overmuch, as Mr. Nevin would never do anything to hurt his master or the family. The report, if that's what Halkerstone could call it, said that Nevin did not like Miss Gordon and that Halkerstone, at the moment, was the only one he could relate that to, besides the staff downstairs.

"How very brash of her," Halkerstone said softly.

The butler nodded once, firmly, his chin so sharp it could cut steak. Halkerstone wanted to ask more, to see if the rest of the staff shared Mr. Nevin's feelings. He also wanted to know what Edward really felt about this woman he had been publicly courting, if only in passing, for a few weeks now, before his mysterious departure. And then there was the departure… Halkerstone very much wanted to know what that was about.

"I wonder about her and Edward," Halkerstone commented casually. "His abrupt departure, was that to do with her, do you think?" He watched Mr. Nevin for signs of deception, but the old man's face screwed up with genuine worry. He glanced around and then stepped back, away from the front door toward the parlor which was empty.

"My Lord Marquess was acting most distressed before he left," Mr. Nevin said. "He was even injured. I do not believe it had to do with Miss Gordon though. He did not so much as see her the last week. I was wondering if you had word from him?"

Halkerstone shook his head. He did not expect to hear word, either, at least not from Edward. He had put

164

out a few letters to his contacts in Hamburg to keep an eye out. His stomach tightened at the thought of whatever mischief Edward had gotten himself into. Edward was not the type of man to do a thing lightly, which meant whatever was driving him was serious business. And dangerous if Halkerstone's gut was right.

"I will show you to her ladyship," Mr. Nevin said.

"I know the way," Halkerstone said, waving him off. Again, any other man and Mr. Nevin might have been affronted with the casual nature of Mr. Halkerstone walking through the house unattended. But Halkerstone was different, and the butler nodded, relieved perhaps to be free to attend to other duties.

"Ring the bell if you require anything," he said in farewell before passing into a wall that at once became a door and then a wall again.

Halkerstone, his mind flitting from thought to thought, headed into the interior of the house. The swiftest way to the garden was straight through to the back and out the dining room doors. However, Halkerstone wanted to be able to take in the scene and gage it before the participants were aware of his presence, which meant coming around the side of the hedges, where he might spy on conversation.

And so, bearing this in mind, Halkerstone walked through the house and turned right down the hallway behind the stairs. He passed the servants' stairwell leading down and nodded at a maid and then a footman, all on their way to the late lunch the servants kept. They all knew him and made no comment, nor even blinked, at his passing. He had run these hallways as a child, and even if the younger servants did not know this, they took their cues from the older staff and never questioned. Besides, his monthly visits were like the moon—predictable and therefore comforting.

Halkerstone passed into the east wing, his end goal to take the door out of the library and into the garden that way. He passed by the woman's solar, where Lady Winchester kept a variety of indoor plants and sometimes took tea. It was also where her writing desk was placed and, incidentally, as he passed by, where Miss Gordon was bending over Lady Winchester's desk. Halkerstone full stopped, at first too shocked to do more than stare.

For here was Miss Gordon in a quiet part of the house, when all the servants were attending lunch, and Lady Winchester no doubt out in the garden. And, as Halkerstone watched, Miss Gordon was going through Lady Winchester's letters. Halkerstone stepped into the room quietly, making no sound, and then cleared his throat very loudly.

Miss Gordon's eyes flew wide, and she straightened in a gesture of startlement. At the sight of him, her cheeks flushed with guilt and then anger. He saw the emotions playing across her beautiful green eyes, like lightning in a storm striking once, twice, then settling on a coolly preserved rage. He understood, more and more, Mr. Nevin's disapproval. There was a serpentine quality about her, moreso than the usual amount in husband-seeking ladies of quality. Although they had never been formally introduced, he saw her take in his clothing and manner and make a decision.

"Are you a new servant?" she asked haughtily. "It is rude to sneak up on someone so. I shall have to report you to the housekeeper."

"Miss Gordon," he said, taking pleasure in seeing

her discomfited that he knew her name. "I am Lord Winchester's business manager, and I do not believe you have any right to be going through Lady Winchester's private letters."

More shame tinged her cheeks. Somehow she managed to remain composed despite it. And beautiful. Halkerstone thought he understood a little of why Edward had chosen her. In a distant way, her beauty was not unlike his mother's—all blonde hair and porcelain skin. She was the type of woman that filled the part of princess in a fairy tale. Halkerstone saw beyond that superfluous metaphor. She was from a fairy tale—but the nasty kind from the depths of the Black Forest. She was the fairy queen, all haughty, inhuman disdain. Her cheekbones were hard as glass, the lips full of venom, the eyes remote.

"You have caught me, uh…"

She played up the social stumble, appealing to his protective side with a look of embarrassed helplessness, her anger diving under this new pretense.

"Mr. Halkerstone," he provided.

"Mr. Halkerstone." She nodded politely. "I confess, I was looking for a letter from Ed—Lord Winchester."

The slipup on Edward's name was on purpose, he was sure of it. They were not, as far as he knew, on such intimate terms. It was a reminder, carefully placed, to make him understand her relation to the absent master of the house. If Halkerstone was not so wary of her, he would admire the way she moved the pieces of the chessboard and used all the tools at her disposal.

"I have not heard from him since he left so suddenly and I…" She fanned herself, twice, the right amount for it to seem genuine without it actually being so. "I find myself missing him more than I can describe. I was only looking for a...a word of his well-being."

Halkerstone saw her one hand flutter to her breast and the other, the one he was not meant to be watching, try and slip a piece of paper toward her dress. He walked forward so suddenly Miss Gordon startled again. The paper fluttered back to the desk.

"I suggest you attend to Lady Winchester," he said firmly. He loomed over her, forcing her to retreat toward the door and away from the desk. "I am sure she will be wondering where you are by now."

There was another flash of lightning in her eyes, and Halkerstone knew he had made an enemy. That concerned him more for Edward's sake than his own. Who was this woman? What were her true intentions here?

As Miss Gordon fled the room in a flurry of maroon silk and cream lace, Halkerstone wondered what was really going on. When her footsteps were done retreating, he skimmed the contents of the letter she had tried to steal. It was from Edward, posted a week out from Hamburg telling his mother he was well and safe, and very little else. He was traveling with the Honorable Tilton, the son of the Viscount Marsey. Halkerstone paused. Where had he heard that name recently? He would need to check.

Whatever Edward's intentions, he had not shared them with his mother. That did not surprise Halkerstone. Edward was more protective of his mother than his late father had been, and the former Lord Winchester had been a sandstorm, large, looming, suffocating, *and* blinding. Halkerstone tidied the desk up and locked it, noting that Miss Gordon had managed, from the scratches around the ornate keyhole, to pick the lock. Certainly not a skill she learned in finishing school. She would need to be watched. What's more, she would need to be studied.

That done, Halkerstone went back out and closed the door firmly behind him. Before seeking out the garden, he went downstairs in search of Mr. Nevin. The situation would have to be handled carefully, but given the butler's feelings on the subject, Halkerstone had no doubt he would willingly help. For Halkerstone could not have Miss Gordon walking around the manor by herself any longer.

Chapter Twenty-Four

August 13, 1789
Outside Hotel Bergedorf, Hamburg

"There he is," Aishe said, nudging his brother. "The Marquess of Winchester."

The two brothers watched as a fierce-looking man with a strong jaw and a glare that cut the rain in front of him strode down the street. Dearg snorted and spat.

"A doshman if I've ever seen one," Dearg said. "We're supposed to rob him?"

Aishe nodded. "Supposed to take everything he owns, but not kill him. Maybe rough him up a bit."

"What's the point? Nobody's going to miss a doshman like that. I bet I can do it, one shot through the heart. Probably beats his servants, he does," Dearg muttered.

"We ain't paid for that," Aishe said sharply. "Just to rob him and rough him up. No killing. The instructions were specific. Besides, we're keeping everything we take."

Dearg snorted and spat again but did not argue. "Let's go then."

"There are too many people," Aishe said, glancing about. "And it's daylight. Let's follow him for a bit and see what he does."

It became apparent after a few hours that the

marquess was searching for conveyance outside the city. He cast a wider and wider net until he was in one of the lesser neighborhoods and found a small, local carriage house that was well below his station.

"He's a determined one, isn't he?" Aishe asked, after Edward's fifth attempt.

"Amazing he managed to get this far," Dearg commented. It was true. The Englishman's German was limited, but Aishe and his brother had managed to sneak very close a few times, and he'd yet to hear the Englishman raise his voice to the carriage men he'd spoken to thus far.

Indeed, as the two brothers loitered in the alley beside the carriage house, under the window where the deal was being finalized, Aishe could only hear relief in the Englishman's voice as the driver promised to show up at the hotel tomorrow and convey them to Berlin.

The marquess paid in advance, a handsome sum, and left. Dearg moved to follow, but Aishe restrained him. Instead, he gestured his brother down the opposite side of the alley. They broke free of the piss-smelling place and out onto the street.

"We got orders," Dearg objected.

Aishe nodded. "And now we can get him alone with *all* his belongings," Aishe said with a grin. "Come on, let's get a few more boys together. We can get ahead of the good marquess and take 'em right near the camp. Easy pickings."

Chapter Twenty-Five

August 13, 1789
Hotel Bergedorf, Hamburg

Edward found Tilton in the hotel's music room, enjoying a pianist with no small amount of skill. He took a seat next to his friend and politely waited until the concert reached a natural break. He applauded with the rest, impressed despite himself with the way the musician generated such silky music from the keys.

"Isn't he beautiful?" Tilton asked, admiration clear in his voice.

Blinking, Edward considered. He'd never thought of a man as beautiful, but he understood Tilton's meaning. The pianist was youthful, his hair like burnished red-gold, his features soft and supple.

"I mean his music, of course," Tilton corrected a moment later.

"Ah," Edward said. "Yes, he is very talented. Very good-looking as well. No doubt a rake if this crowd is an indication."

For the first time, Tilton tore his eyes off the pianist and to the crowd. Besides himself and Edward, it was entirely compromised of women of a variety of ages.

"Yes, no doubt," Tilton murmured. He studied the youth for a moment from under his lashes. Then, with a shake of his head, he turned fully to Edward. "Did you find us a carriage?"

"Yes." Edward nodded. "We cannot leave until the morning, but—"

"Excellent!" Tilton said. Then looked abashed. "I mean, it is a damn shame about the delay, but I mentioned to the concierge about that opera, and he assured me an hour ago that he had procured us tickets."

"Tilton," Edward said pulling a face. "I do not have a suit to go out to the opera."

His young friend waved his hand. "I am sure the concierge can help with that too. Do you know they have an in-house tailor? Come, let's go see him straightway, and we will get it all sorted."

Edward wanted to argue but found himself swept up in his young friend's enthusiasm. He supposed if Tilton was willing to go along on his quest and they were stuck for another day anyway, he could hardly hold Tilton hostage in the hotel.

"I'll tell my valet to pack all but the essentials so tomorrow morning will be a swift departure," Tilton said as they walked. "Of course, I doubt we will get much sleep."

With a rueful laugh, Edward shook his head. "You're beginning to sound more and more like my friend Rhys every day."

"Excellent," Tilton said. "I knew he was a man of taste."

Chapter Twenty-Six

August 13, 1789
Hotel Bergdorf, Hamburg

Edward glanced at himself in the mirror once again with a grimace. The hotel tailor was good. The man had suits ready for sizing in many styles, but Edward had proved to be a challenge due to his height. The only suit available had a dark green jacket with large flowers embroidered along the front and cuffs. It was not a short dinner jacket in the English style he was used to either, but rather long down the front. The matching vest was cream and also embroidered in brown and green silk thread. At least the vest was silk, not the Chinese silk he was used to, but it would pass. The cravat was large and ruffled nearly blocking his chin with its impressive height. It was all so…French.

"You look absolutely dashing," Tilton exclaimed coming in.

Edward glanced over and saw his friend was in, if possible, a more outrageous suit. It sported a greater amount of embroidery in ferns along the front and cuffs. Tilton's suit was a deep burnished brown with gold spots, and his pants were spotted as well. At least Edward's pants were a solid green.

"It is not my usual taste," Edward said dryly.

"No, it has colors other than black and blue,"

Tilton teased. "But still, it makes you look less imposing."

"I am not sure that is good," Edward said.

"Edward," Tilton objected. "It is the opera, not a funeral. Come now, or we will be late."

They went out to the hotel's carriage. As they rode, Tilton pointed out some of the architecture that Welfries had taught him about that afternoon while Edward was being fitted. Edward listened quietly, his mind elsewhere. He did not want to bring up the memory of his last opera, where Nancy Storace had burned to death, but he could not shake it either.

The Hamburgische Oper was an elegant stone building in the Greco-Roman style. Its walls were a stately gray, and columns out front were lit by large braziers where the carriages were pulling up, expelling gentry and nobles like a parade of flashy silk.

As they disembarked, Edward could feel Tilton's excitement vibrating through the younger man.

"Steady," he cautioned. "The night is young."

Tilton flashed him a grin, and they joined the throng entering the opera house.

It was a good opera, *Don Juan*. Edward usually would have enjoyed himself more. But he could not shake the death of Nancy Storace from the stage or the flight that her death had set upon him.

When they emerged hours later, Tilton gushed enthusiastically about it. When Edward did not join in, Tilton wilted.

"Oh come now, Edward," he said, nudging his friend. "I know things are, well, serious in your world, but it was lovely. Did you see the actor play Don Juan? The muscles on that man!"

Edward allowed himself a small smile. "You are right, of course," he said. "It was very good. I just..." He paused. Tilton nudged him again giving him a puppy dog face that Edward realized was his way of encouraging people. "The last opera I went to, the star died quite dramatically."

"Oh." Tilton frowned. Then understanding bloomed on his face, and he blushed bright red. "Oh!"

"Yes." Edward nodded.

It took Tilton a moment to recover himself. Edward wondered if Tilton had been there that night. His family was certainly ranked enough to attend the opening night, and he did love fashion. Instead of confirming this theory, though, Tilton said, "I understand. The last opera I went to, afterward my father and I fought." He gave Edward a tight smile. "We have not spoken since."

Edward felt a surge of sympathy for his friend. He had never really spoken of his family, but that in itself had told Edward things were not harmonious. He cleared his throat.

"Well, we have one night in Hamburg," he said. "There must be some fun to be had."

Tilton's eyes lit up. "Are you sure?" he asked. "We will be in hell tomorrow."

"We will be locked in a carriage anyway. That *is* hell," Edward said. "Listen, the only thing is..."

How did he explain to Tilton that he had no interest in a whorehouse? Tilton was young and hot-blooded. Edward had found himself less interested since his break with Phoebe. Yet, if he phrased it incorrectly, Tilton might think ill of him.

"Never mind," Edward said. "What would you like

to do?"

"Get a drink first off," Tilton said. "And then perhaps find a fair or a match. Shall we?"

Edward could barely refrain from showing his relief that Tilton had not mentioned a bawdy house.

"Let us away, then," Edward said with a smile.

Chapter Twenty-Seven

August 14, 1789
On the road to Berlin

The next morning despite all attempts to wake up early for the carriage, Edward found it nearly impossible. Only the thought of Phoebe got him from bed despite the headache and the rolling of his stomach. And only the valet's strong arms along with Edward's voice got Tilton out of bed. At least the valet had made good use of his time, getting half of Tilton's luggage down while the lordling slept.

By the time they made it to breakfast, Edward's stomach had stopped rolling, but one look at the hard-boiled eggs and it flipped three times. He waved away the food and took strong coffee instead, wincing at the bitterness.

"We need to push off soon," he said, voice rough with little sleep and less clarity.

Tilton had given up on both food and drink, even the thyme water they brought him, and sat half slumped in his chair looking entirely miserable.

"I cannot make it all the way to the carriage," he stated. "I shall die."

Edward grunted. "Well, then perhaps you should not have taken that acrobat's bet on who could finish their *bowle* more quickly. And you should perhaps have stopped after the third one."

Tilton took this advice into account and nodded, wincing at the bob of his head. "Maybe," he allowed. "But at least I did not finish an entire bottle of Kräuterlikör on my own," he said, his eyebrows rising.

Edward grimaced and then smiled slightly at the acknowledged hit.

"I will settle our bill," he said. "You try and make it to the carriage. Perhaps Welfries will help you. Where is he, by the way?"

"Gloating," Tilton said and rolled his eyes, then put a hand to his forehead. "He has already broken fast and is reading in the parlor, I believe."

"Rather smug of him," Edward commented. Tilton made a noise of assent but did not move. "Tilton, we must go."

Tilton groaned but stood after Edward did. Together they slowly made their way from the dining room.

It was beastly bright by the time they stumbled outside. The carriage stood waiting, a beat-up old conveyance, so sun-bleached it was a pale gray, and the two nags that were leading it made it look, if possible, more sad. Tilton's luggage was strapped to the top and back like heaps of hay, and nearly as precariously perched. The coachman was respectful, at least, and did not mention the hour when the two gentlemen stumbled inside. Welfries rode with the driver in front, much to Tilton's relief. Their voices muffled in comfortable conversation showed they enjoyed the ride even if the occupants of the carriage did not.

The interior of the carriage was dark at least, but the constant bumps and bumbling only made Edward feel worse. They stopped in a little village tavern mid-afternoon for lunch and to rest the horses. By then, both his and Tilton's appetites were large. The food was simple but hearty. Honestly, Edward was grateful for the repast and ate with fervor. By the time they returned to the road, they were both well enough to speak and spent no small amount of time recalling the evening's activities.

After finding a fair on the outskirts of the city, they had somehow ended up drinking at the tables with the plebeians. And, after a while, the artists and performers worked into the crowds. Then there had been too much alcohol, laughter, and ridiculousness, most of it bleary around the edges in Edward's memory.

They were getting on much better when they felt the carriage slow down and then stop. Edward glanced outside the window, saw they were surrounded by trees that threw long shadows across the road, and knew something was wrong. He heard voices raised in anger.

"Stay inside," Edward told Tilton as he opened the door.

He slipped out and was going to close the door when Tilton came out too, ignoring the glower Edward threw his way.

"What's going on?" he asked, glancing toward the front of the coach.

Edward did not waste time trying to stop his friend. Outside, Welfries was arguing with a man whose cart had a broken wheel. The carriage driver looked quite anxious, his hand sneaking under the seat toward a box. The cart was blocking the whole of the road, and there was no way to get around it. Welfries was yelling at the two men who were lounging about the broken cart.

Neither man seemed concerned about the broken wheel or the contents, a mixed combination of cauliflower, asparagus, and brussels sprouts, scattered across the road.

One of the men had a bottle in his hand and was taking sips periodically, while the other was answering Welfries' shouts with slurred answers. Edward had lived in a lot of countries. He'd seen numerous farmers and peddlers and merchants. And while he didn't make a study of them, he did not know any that carried small hand muskets. A shotgun, perhaps, to ward off robbers. But these two were not worried about being robbed of their livelihood. Intuition piqued, Edward's hand strayed to his own weapon.

Not fast enough.

The woods poured forth more men, and suddenly they were surrounded. It was a trap then.

"Villains," Tilton said, though his voice betrayed excitement instead of fear. This would excite him.

Edward decided to try another route. "What is this?" he demanded, his voice strong and sharp across the whole area betraying no fear. No, in his voice was command. Every man stilled. Even the drunkards seemed to take new stock. The one stood. Before he could take control though, Edward continued. "Why is the road blocked?"

Although he knew the reason, he wanted them off-balance as his mind raced to find a solution out of this. Tilton might be keen on fighting, and the Lord knew he knew how, but Edward still did not like their odds. They were outnumbered four to one, not counting Welfries and the driver who Edward doubted had any fighting training, and some of these men had muskets as well as swords.

The men shifted uncertainly. Edward's lack of fear coupled with his authoritative manner had them suddenly doubting their own advantage. The seemingly drunk one who was standing pulled his musket, though he did not raise it.

"This is a rob'ry, clear an' easy, doshman," he said, though his expression was flinty. He wanted violence.

Tilton opened his mouth, but Edward stepped forward and distracted him. Although anger burned hot in him, now was not the time to lose his temper. He had bigger concerns, and his life was not the only one on the line. Much as he would like to take all these blackguards on himself, it was not possible.

"Fine, then," Edward said. He removed his money pouch and tossed it between them. "Take it and go."

The men loosely surrounding them eyed the pouch, but then eyed Edward more warily. The maybe drunk leader swaggered over, the bottle in one hand, his musket in the other.

"Thas not gonna be enough, doshman," he said, leaning into Edward's space insolently.

Edward could smell the liquor on his breath and see loathing, no, hatred flickering in his eyes.

"Is gonna cost ya more than tha," he said. "Much mo—"

Edward knocked him right in the teeth, the shot sending the robber down. For a moment, there was utter silence as the whole lot of them stood in stunned amazement both at the force of the strike and its speed. It was a viper's strike. Even Edward was surprised by himself. He had not intended it consciously but moved entirely by some inner spirit. Then Tilton raised a cry and rushed the closest man with a musket, barely dodging his shot before running him straight through.

The road erupted into chaos then. The driver succeeded in reaching his box and pulled out two muskets. His aim was truer than Edward gave initial credit, and he took down one of the robbers before tossing both muskets and running in the break of the ring into the woods. With little choice, Edward dove at two men, whipping out his sword and slashing as one brought up his sword arm. He dropped the musket even as Edward ran the other through. The man recovered quickly and drew his sword but was no match for Edward's skill. He fell only for two more to take his place.

The battle was hot and fast. It seemed as Edward dodged another musket ball that between them, he and Tilton may come out on top. Then he heard an agonized cry. He parried a sword and punched with enough force to send his opponent flying backward. When he glanced around, he found Tilton swinging wildly trying to get his two away, and the drunk leader back on his feet with a smoking pistol. Over by the carriage, lay Welfries, a red bloom across his chest.

With a scream of rage, Tilton rushed forward and tackled the leader. They rolled like two dogs in the dirt. Edward moved to help but at the same time, the two Tilton had been fighting recovered. He'd only put them off and now they were reloading muskets. Edward could no more rush in to help Tilton than leave both their backs open to shots. And he knew Tilton to be a solid fighter. So, Edward went after them. He managed to take them down without much fuss, even grabbing a loaded musket before it could be shot.

His decision proved a mistake. When Edward was at last done with the lot, the leader had gotten the upper hand. He was either more wily or more skilled than either gave him credit. With blood running out his mouth and his lips already swollen, missing at least one tooth on the bottom from Edward's blow, the leader looked a mite insane as he held his musket, presumably reloaded, under Tilton's throat.

Tilton looked dazed, and his cheek was red and already swelling into other colors. Edward guessed the man got off a good punch for him.

"Hold yurself, or the youngin dies," the Roma said.

His musket was aimed under Tilton's throat. Edward could see Tilton's Adam's apple bobbed as he swallowed. He looked at Edward, and Edward was surprised to see fury there but also acceptance. Tilton nodded as if to say, "Shoot him." For all his claims he was a better shot, Edward would not take the chance that he might hit his friend.

"He's a mere boy," Edward said, trying another tactic. "Let him go."

"He's a rich boy," the Roma said.

"Then take the luggage and go," Edward said, gesturing at the carriage. It was a moot point. Another one of the robbers was already taking the reins. The Roma holding Tilton smiled darkly.

"If you kill him or me, there will be soldiers on you like maggots to shit," Edward warned. "You know this."

The robber narrowed his eyes. "Empty your pockets," he said.

Edward glared at the scum but turned out his pockets, yielding a silver cigarette case and some spare change. He threw it.

"That's all the money I have and more than you've ever seen. Take it and be gone."

"Your watch," the Roma said, gesturing to the chain.

"No," Edward said.

The Roma dug the barrel into Tilton's throat, and the lordling grimaced.

Edward ground his teeth and threw over the watch. The Roma demanded his jacket and his cufflinks next. With each demand, Edward grew more infuriated but obliged. When he'd been stripped of all valuables, he gestured to the pile of booty between them.

"Now let him go," he said.

The Roma lowered the gun but paused as he noticed the bump in Edward's vest. He pointed the musket it at.

"What is that?" he demanded.

"A worthless trinket," Edward said.

"Let me see it."

Edward took the leather pouch from his pocket, stuffing his silk handkerchief back in. Inside the stone heart was warm, even through the thick leather. In that moment, Edward wished he knew some sleight of hand, for he understood the moment that the diamond was revealed it would be taken from him. But Tilton's life was on the line. So Edward undid the ties and let the stone roll out of his hand. The Roma told him to put it on the ground.

"No," he said. "You have plenty of wealth, and you better take it and run, Roma, for I will come for you. Now, let the boy go and let us be done with this business."

"Give me the gem," the man demanded.

"No."

"I will kill him," the robber said, shoving the gun back into Tilton's throat.

Edward looked from the Roma to Tilton and back again. He wanted to kill, Edward realized. There was hatred in his eyes. He hated them, and they had never met. Edward took the handkerchief from his pocket, rubbed the stone clean, and then folded the handkerchief neatly into squares. He tucked it inside his front vest pocket as he bent down and added the stone to the pile. A spasm of pain crossed his face as he carefully set it down, one he could not subdue or hide.

"There," he said standing and stepping back. "I have nothing left."

A wild joy overtook the Roma's eyes. He grinned, pointed the gun at Edward, and shot. Tilton cried out as he was shoved forward. The Roma scooped up his booty, then made a run for the carriage, his friend clicking the horses into motion before Tilton even reached Edward's side.

"Edward, oh God, Edward," Tilton screamed.

He picked up his friend's head and cradled it, staring at the blackened hole in Edward's vest above his heart where just a bit of smoke still curled. The carriage disappeared around a bend.

"Edward," Tilton sobbed, as he shoved the vest open and his fingers brushed something burning. He gasped, retracting his hand automatically, and Edward's eyes flew open.

Edward coughed and winced, as Tilton let out a sound of happy surprise.

"By God, man," he said and hugged Edward close.

"But how?"

Edward pulled out the silk handkerchief folded tightly with the bullet lodged in the lower corner.

"I was betting on him being a good shot," he said, wincing.

"I don't understand," Tilton said, helping Edward sit up.

A sweat broke out over Edward's brow. He abruptly turned and vomited on the road.

"Damn," he said after. Tilton took out his flask and handed it to Edward who took a swig and spit it out again.

"How did a handkerchief save you?" Tilton asked.

Edward opened the buttons of his silk shirt. The bruise expanding across where the force of the bullet hit was turning an ugly shade of purple and blue.

"Chinese silk," Edward said around a grimace. "I wear it in layers," he said, gesturing at the vest, which was also silk. "My father saw it stop a bullet once in Hong Kong. It's damn expensive, but we have worn silk ever since. If the Red Coats had been made of silk…"

Edward did not finish the sentence. Tilton's eyes widened, and then he let out an explosive breath. "God, Edward, you saved my life. I'm obliged to you. My life, sir—"

Edward ignored this and stood.

"There's no need," he said, wincing. He faltered on his feet, and Tilton popped up, supporting him.

"We must get you to a doctor. I think the closest town is only a few miles up the road. Can you make it?"

"No," Edward said, gently pushing Tilton away.

He focused his eyes on one spot on the road and forced his breath to steady, sucking in large amounts of air through his mouth and expelling through his nose. When the world stopped spinning, he straightened to his full height.

"I do not care what you say, Edward. You were just shot."

"I will be fine in a few moments. Go to town. If there is any military presence, tell them what happened. If not, send a runner as fast as it can travel to the closest squadron. The horses will not get far, not with all your luggage to bog them down." Tilton flushed, but Edward did not notice. "They will need to rest them tonight, and I bet their campsite is in this valley somewhere."

"Edward, you are mad," Tilton said.

"Go, Tilton," Edward said, standing his full height.

"No—"

"I do not want to have to repeat myself," Edward said firmly.

"I know you are concerned about the stone," Tilton said, "but you should not be running off by yourself. I came along to help."

"Welfries deserves more than just lying by the roadside," Edward said gently.

Tilton's gaze sped to the place where his tutor had fallen. Tears sprang to his eyes, and he looked helplessly at Edward. Edward gripped his shoulder.

"Have them bring an undertaker and a cart," he said. "We will bury him when I get back."

Chapter Twenty-Eight

August 20, 1789
Roma Camp

Aishe drove the carriage into the camp, a ratty, gray thing that looked more like a funeral transport with a pall over the men. Dearg hopped out as a crowd gathered, his arms full of swag.

"Where are the others?" his father asked coming over.

"The doshmen were good fighters," Dearg replied. "We need to go back for the bodies." His father looked about ready to burst, but Dearg took out the leather satchel and opened it. "They were these kind of men," he said, showing off the broken diamond. His father opened his mouth and closed it again. He knew what his son held.

"Bulibasha is in her wagon," he said with a jerk of his head.

Both Aishe and Dearg's father watched the younger man walk off.

"What happened?" his father growled when the night had swallowed him up.

"Dearg shot him," Aishe said. "He shot the mark. An' if the garrison doesn't get us, that man who hired us will, you can be sure. He ain't the type to cross," he added.

"How could you let him—"

"They fought back," Aishe said. "Like demons they did. In the scuffle, I couldn't keep track of 'im. He got the young doshman dead to rights but shot the other. The mark. An' we was told not to kill 'im by any means. It's a right mess."

The father swore and then began shouting orders. The Roma scattered, making ready to go.

"Take two or three and get the bodies," the father instructed. "I'll take care of my son."

Aishe nodded and went to go as ordered.

****

Dearg knew he was in trouble, sure as he knew he was going to lose at least another tooth. But it was worth it to kill that bastard. He had wanted to, right sure, but after seeing the broken heart. Did that prig really expect Dearg to believe he didn't know what this was? He'd even dared to call it a worthless trinket. Dearg said a prayer for whoever the heart came from. Dirty doshman, killing some poor innocent, like they killed his brother.

He knocked at the door of the Bulibasha, and a moment later it opened. The old woman was shrunk in on herself, and her face was screwed in pain. She did not say it, merely asked him what he needed. Dearg thrust the diamond at the old woman.

"Bulibasha," he said, "we came across some doshman on the road. They had this." No need to go into the story. She'd hear of it, no doubt, from his father, but if Dearg could avoid a cuffing, he would.

"Where is the rest of it?" she asked.

Dearg glared at the heart, angry at its fate. "Probably broke it in half and set it in jewelry."

190

Bulibasha frowned and studied the young man. He'd lost teeth, and there was dried blood on his chin. His lips were swollen and bruised. Then the stone twitched in her hand drawing her attention. Was it warm, or was that from the fire? Her hands tingled, the nerves firing more often now. And always afterward, the pain. But this was too important to put off.

"I must read," she said. She ambled to the back of her wagon.

Lighting a stick of incense, Bulibasha laid the broken diamond gently onto a small card table. She cleared away the dishes from her tea and spread out a bit of silk. It barely reached the edges of the table, and it was worn in places, the pattern of flowers faded into blobs of color. She placed the diamond in the center and fetched her tarot deck from its secret compartment under the bed.

The tingling had indeed turned to pain, but Bulibasha ignored it. She shuffled the oversized cards with the practice and ease of a lifetime. The edges knew the nooks of her fingers, and her skin knew the surface of every picture, every word, every symbol painted on them. The pain spiked, and she stopped, inhaling sharply.

When it passed, she cut the deck and drew four cards. She placed them in a loose circle around the stone. She inhaled again and held it, not from pain this time but from what the cards said. She picked up the diamond and pressed it to her cheek. It *was* warm. Then she was off her seat and out the door, nearly crashing into Dearg who was loitering.

"Bulibasha." He caught and steadied her.

"Stupid lad." She pinched his ear hard, and he cried

out. "Who did you steal this from?"

"A toff," he stammered, bent low to avoid more pain.

"Fool," she said. "This heart is still alive. Who's to say he's not the rightful owner?"

"But…it's broken," he said.

"Have you no sense? It's warm," she cried, shaking her fist, which held the stone, in front of his face.

Before she could yell further, there was a crack in the night. The bullet hit the dirt several feet away. Dearg threw his shoulder into Bulibasha, and they both fell to the earth. She lost her grip on his ear and the stone heart. Hands grabbed her and dragged her behind a water barrel. The stone heart lay on the ground in the open. Another shot pierced the night, and this one found its mark. There was a cry. And then another shot. Whoever was shooting was either a quick reload or had multiple muskets on hand.

Bulibasha levered herself up and crawled out from behind the barrels. She began waving her arms.

"Enough, enough," she screamed.

The bullets paused.

"I want my property returned," a voice declared. "Now."

"We will give you the heart," Bulibasha said.

Dearg tried to grab her again with a protest, but she whacked him hard in the head. There was a swift movement from the bushes as a fierce looking man in a dirtied and ripped silk suit emerged. He strode forward, his gun unwaveringly pointed at Dearg's head, his eyes furious. Dearg made a choking sound, and from his pallid expression, he was shocked this man was alive. Bulibasha sat up, effectively interceding between gun and Dearg. She thought the young man was stupid, but she did not want another one of her people dead.

"Please," she pleaded with the fierce man. "You are running out of time."

The man hesitated and examined her. The other Roma, mostly her family, surrounded him. There was not an ounce of fear in him, though. He was composed entirely of determination, and had he been attacked, Bulibasha was not sure he would not win despite the numbers.

"He was foolish," she tried speaking of Dearg.

"He and his friends killed one of my companions and stole everything we had," the noble spat. "And he will pay for his crimes."

Bulibasha bent over and picked up the heart. "I cannot return the dead to you," she said, holding it carefully. "And you are not the only one that lost this day."

"Because of *him*," the man roared.

All the Roma reached for weapons, but no one dared attack. It was like they faced one of the Aesir. Bulibasha offered the heart again.

"This is far more precious than revenge, I think. And it is what you came here for. Please take it and go."

The nobleman's gaze fell on the stone, and, though his gun arm did not waver, his expression intensified. He met her stare, and Bulibasha felt power there, power and fear in equal measure.

"You know what this is," she said. It was a statement, and he did not answer, but his stare was answer enough. "Dying here will not save your love."

"Give it back," he said softly. There was a promise

of death in his voice should she not obey. Bulibasha was an old woman, and death was a far-back friend. Still, she stepped forward carefully and handed him the stone heart. He immediately enveloped it in his free hand and held it against his chest, as if one called to the other. Bulibasha suspected they did.

"You must hurry," she said. "There is little time left. A carriage full of luggage will get you dead before this journey is through. Time to ride the wind."

The man's eyes focused on her and then slid back to Dearg, over her shoulder.

"He will be punished. I can assure you. Here, Bartram." She tossed her head at a man at Edward's seven o'clock. "Fetch a fast horse."

"Two," the man said softly.

Bulibasha stared at him and then nodded. "Two horses then. And feed. Stay there," she said and hurried back into her wagon. When she emerged, she was wearing gloves and carrying a bundle of tiny yellow flowers. She put the bundle into a small sack and then in the saddle bag of one of the horses they brought around. The man's expression was wholly distrustful.

"If the heart gets too cold, you must cut the stem of this flower and pour the milk-sap onto it. This will give it heat again," she said. "But beware, both flower and sap are poisonous to you. Do not touch them with your hands."

"You know what this is and expect me to pour poison all over it?" he demanded furious.

"It is not poisonous for the stone," she said softly. "It will give it heat."

The toff looked like he wanted to argue. He was full of fury still, that was for sure. But her words about losing time had unnerved him. He slipped the stone heart into his jacket pocket and swung up into the saddle. Taking the reins of the second horse, he holstered his musket. He turned back to study Bulibasha, but whatever his thoughts, he did not voice them. Instead, he kicked the flanks of his horse, disappearing back into the night.

****

Edward could no more explain his retreat than he could explain how the old Romani knew what the stone heart was. He wanted to swear and curse them all. He wanted to kill for vengeance of Welfries, and he wanted to demand full retribution.

The instant she said he was running out of time, he knew she knew. And that had unnerved him. That she might also know he was the cause, that he was to blame, upset him. And then, of course, she was right about the carriage and the luggage. They were never going to cover enough ground to complete this with Tilton's entire wardrobe. A part of him was grateful to the Roma for taking the luggage off his hands, and that made him feel like an ass.

It had been her eyes that had settled it. She had not been afraid of him. She had been afraid *for* him. It was a furrow of the brow, a tightening in the corners of her eyes that he'd seen on his own mother's face. Edward could no more explain or justify what had just happened than he could explain how a person grew a heart through their own chest. And yet here he was, plunging through the night, hoping the horses they'd given him were, indeed, fast. Hoping that one of the horses did not break an ankle in the dark forest, hoping to find the road again, hoping for what? Redemption? A second chance?

As he told himself the thousandth time, Phoebe had misrepresented her marriage. He had fallen for her and she for him. Yes, that he could accept. He certainly could not deny it. But when certain facts came to light, it was clear they were not meant for each other, and Edward had taken steps. Perhaps he had handled it indelicately, but it was not the worst of fallouts. He had not publicly decried her. Hell, he had not said a word in either direction.

At worst, her reputation took a fall from his cutting ties. But every rumor presented to him, every ill-word toward her following that March, he had denied. He had told the truth. They were different people and did not get on as he thought they might. The heart in his coat pocket seemed to pulse against his chest calling out his deception. They had gotten on very well. And seeing her in that vision on the arm of that man had caused an agony Edward did not think he could feel again. Seeing the Roma steal the heart was even worse, worse than the physical pain of getting shot.

The horse blew out a steam of air, and Edward echoed the sound. By instinct or some higher calling, the horse under him found the road. Edward nudged it right, toward the town, praying Tilton was well and safe. He found him soon enough, with a few men, seemingly late of the tavern by the smell of beer wafting around them. They were carrying a wrapped body onto a farmer's wagon when he came up to the scene of the robbery.

"Edward," Tilton cried coming upon him.

Edward swung down and was instantly enveloped in a tight embrace by his companion. Awkwardly, he patted his back, wincing at his bruised chest where the bullet had hit.

"I am well enough," he said gruffly.

One of the men detached himself from the group and approached cautiously.

"This is the *friedensricter*," Tilton said. Edward did the translation sloppily. The local law man.

The man's accent was thick but he spoke piecemeal English. Edward's German was not great, but he conveyed the story that corroborated with Tilton's and also the location of the Romani camp as best he could. When the *friedensricter* asked Edward how he came by the two horses, Edward simply said he took what was owed him.

Whether his look or his bearing, the *friedensricter* asked no more questions. He escorted Tilton and Edward back to the tiny village and then gathered more men to search for the camp. It was too late, by then. Edward knew that if they found the camp before dark, the Romani would be gone.

There was one inn, which was little more than a hostel in the village. Tilton and Edward took the only two rooms available. When the sun rose the next morning, Edward had still not slept at all.

Chapter Twenty-Nine

August 21, 1789
Hamlet of Amt Neuhaus

Tilton did not say anything when he appeared at breakfast and found Edward by the fire, poking the ashes. It was a testament to his emotional state that he did not say anything. The small dining room was set for them, and the old innkeeper served them stew, dark bread, and ale for breakfast.

Tilton picked at his food. Edward ignored it.

"Tilton," Edward started and then frowned at the fire.

"Do not start an argument so early," Tilton said. The comment caused Edward's head to swivel and stare at Tilton in confusion. "I will not be diverted from our course, Edward," he said wearily. "We will bury Mr. Welfries and be on our way." He glanced around. "Do you think they have stationery? I should post a note to Mr. Welfries' sister. And my father."

Edward thought about indeed starting the argument Tilton seemed steadfast in avoiding, but the words would not loosen from his tongue. He had come to the conclusion overnight that Mr. Welfries' death was his fault. He was more concerned than ever that this journey was far too dangerous for Tilton. More, that he did not want his friend hurt. But Tilton had made a pledge, and it was against honor and decorum to try and dissuade him from that pledge now. So Edward remained silent.

The women of the village had cleaned and wrapped Welfries' body. Edward went to pay, but Tilton insisted on paying for the small service and burial in the churchyard. It was more luck and the Roma's hatred that had spared them Tilton's purse in the ruckus.

The priest said his prayers, and the grave diggers covered the grave. When it was done, Tilton remained.

"I did not treat him well," he said.

"You treated him better than many treat their tutors," Edward said. "He genuinely cared for you."

"In his way," Tilton said, which again made Edward wonder about the tension between the two men. "The truth is, he did not treat me well either. We so wanted to be friends. I think he attempted to do what he thought was best, but he was just so damnable annoying."

Edward squeezed Tilton's shoulder.

"God is going to strike me down," Tilton said.

"Why?" Edward asked. "You brought him to burial. You honored him."

"I am cursing his name as he sits underneath the good earth," Tilton said.

"You are being honest," Edward said. "My father always said 'honesty cannot be a sin.' "

"But it can be painful," Tilton said. "Devastating. We just never understood each other. I so wished we had."

"Tilton." Edward turned him around. "He is with God now. I think he finally understands you at last. Leave him to his peace knowing you strived to save him from those heathens. If anything, God will strike me down, for it is my fault Mr. Welfries is in the grave."

"This is not your fault, Edward."

"If I had not been so damn impatient..." Edward shook his head. "It is past, I suppose."

The *friedensricter* visited Edward and Tilton in the inn and reported they had found the remnants of the Romani campsite, but the Roma had already moved on. Edward was not surprised. Tilton was livid. After the *friedensricter* left, Tilton turned to his friend.

"They got away with it," he spat.

Edward could not explain the events of the night before any more than he could ease Tilton's rage.

"Come on," Edward said. "If we leave now, we may make it to Ludwigslust tonight. There, at least, we can get some decent clothes and reserves."

"I have no money left, Edward," Tilton admitted. "Most of it was in the luggage."

"I have enough to cover us to Berlin." When Tilton gave him a confused look, Edward shrugged. "I had a small stash in my boot. My father taught me tricks, you see. From Ludwigslust, I can make contact with the bank, and we shall be set."

Tilton followed Edward out where the stable boy had saddled the two horses. Edward had looked at them in the sunlight and found, in this at least, the Romani had not lied. The horses were fine beasts, leggy and strong. They both swung into the saddle and took off. As they passed the graveyard, Tilton raised his fist in the air in one last salute.

Chapter Thirty

August 23, 1789
Brey House, London

"My lord, there's a Mr. Linus Halkerstone here to see you," the butler announced. "He says he works for the Marquess of Winchester."

"Yes, I know who he is," Rhys said with a frown. "Send him in."

A moment later, a fair-haired man of about thirty and five years strode in. He bowed quite correctly, and Rhys, though not surprised, approved.

"Mr. Halkerstone, how goes it?" he asked.

"Well enough, Your Grace," he said, eying the butler who had not yet left. Rhys nodded, and the man circumspectly shut the door behind himself.

"What brings you here?" Rhys asked bluntly.

"I'm hoping you can shed some light on my Lord Winchester's final destination," Halkerstone said.

"He did not tell you?" Rhys asked. Halkerstone shook his head and waited. Rhys considered this as he sat down behind his desk. In truth, Edward had probably feared revealing too much in case Halkerstone thought him mad. Rhys understood the caution, but Mr. Halkerstone's circumstances and how they related to Edward were quite astray from normal.

"Did you need to get into touch with him for a

particular reason?" Rhys asked.

At this, Halkerstone eyed Rhys shrewdly. Halkerstone had spent the last four days investigating and gathering information. He had learned that Edward had spent a great deal of time with the Duke of Brey before he left, where they had not spoken a word for months before. He had learned some disturbing news about Miss Gordon's connections, and even more reports of Edward at the university and St. Giles. None of it made much sense to Halkerstone, but he had a notion that it went back to Phoebe, the Lady von Croy.

Still, it was all just supposition and notions. Nothing concrete, except the news on Miss Gordon. And that did not bode well on any front. Edward needed to be warned. Which meant Halkerstone needed to find him, which was why he was calling on the formidable Duke of Brey.

"Permission to ask a personal question, my lord?" Halkerstone said. Rhys nodded. "How did things leave off between yourself and my lord?"

Rhys blanched, shocked at the man's gall. "That *is* personal," he said. "And for certain requires a drink. Pour." Rhys nodded at the sideboard and Halkerstone went to obey. "As for my side, I never stopped being Edward's friend. I rather think things were in a better light than they have been for some months."

Halkerstone nodded. "I understand you perfectly," he said. He handed Rhys a tumbler and took one up himself. "My goal in finding out my lordship's destination is to protect his interests," he said. "To speak candidly, I believe Miss Gordon is involved in a plot that seeks to disrupt his lordship's journey. I would warn him."

Rhys sipped his scotch. Rather than be surprised, some niggling instinct of his own felt vindicated.

"You seem unsurprised, Your Grace," Halkerstone noted. He took a sip and hummed in appreciation.

"I am, though I have no notion as to why I have never quite trusted Miss Gordon. Frankly, I know little about her outside of her breeding. We only were introduced the once. And yet…" he said with a frown. "What is your evidence?"

"I went to the manor some days ago to go over the house expenses with her ladyship," Halkerstone said. At Rhys's questioning expression, Halkerstone shrugged. "It is not customary, but Lady Winchester has always insisted on knowing firsthand how the money is spent and where."

"And this does not have anything to do at all with your lineage, I suppose?" Rhys asked.

Halkerstone blinked in surprise. "I was not aware that you knew," he said softly. "Does Edward?"

"*Lord Winchester,*" Rhys emphasized his title, "has never mentioned it to me. I do not think he is aware of your connection. His father told mine, as comrades and dear friends were wont to share such intimacies, and my father told me. I think perhaps the late marquess might have told Edward in time."

"But he never had the chance," Halkerstone said with a sigh.

For a moment, he stared off into nothingness. Rhys took that moment to study the man. He must have taken after his mother for there was no visible trace of the aristocratic blood that coursed through him. He was fair-haired, sturdy, his face thin and jaw square. His eyes were a pale brown, the color not unlike the scotch forgotten in his hands. Edward and his late father, on the other hand, were hawkish, their faces and jaws angular, their hair dark, their visages fierce. Halkerstone had the look of a peasant, Edward the look of a prince.

Halkerstone abruptly drank the rest of his scotch and went back for another shot. Under the circumstances, Rhys did not begrudge him more.

"The Dowager Lady Winchester does know," Halkerstone said. "The late Lord Winchester brought her to meet me and my sister while they were still engaged. She has always known. I would like to think that our monthly visits have less to do with my handling the finances, and more to do with how she was raised." Halkerstone met Rhys's eyes dead straight as he continued. "Her father squandered his inheritance, and her dowry was very small. From what I can tell, she was managing the accounts of what little they had left from a tender age."

Rhys nodded. There had been rumors of the late Winchester's romance. Edward spoke of it as if it were a fairy tale, and he supposed his father and mother had presented it to him that way. It did not alter the fact that Edward's mother *had* to marry well, and she had.

"Any road," Halkerstone said, waving his hand as if he could wave away a ghost. "Ed—Lord Winchester asked me to watch out for his mother while he was away. My monthly visits afford me a viable excuse to call on her. The other day, as I went to see her, I found Miss Gordon snooping around Lady Winchester's writing desk. Specifically, she was looking at a letter Edward sent from Hamburg. She excused it off as merely missing him, for she has not received similar missives, but I did not believe her. I did a little digging, and it seems Miss Gordon is niece to Lady Eleanor Argent."

"I have heard of her," Rhys admitted. "She had the ladies all in a twitter last year after surviving a trek across war-torn France. Apparently, her husband did not survive the trip." Rhys frowned. He had not paid much attention to a low-level aristocrat refugee from France. Now he wondered if he should. "What does she have to do with this?"

"Lady Eleanor's maiden name is Coventry," Halkerstone said. Rhys sucked in his breath.

"*The* Lady Coventry?"

"That the late Marquess Winchester threw aside in favor of his wife," Halkerstone said, nodding.

"Damnation," Rhys cursed. He immediately wondered if the French peasants were truly responsible for her husband's death.

"Unfortunately, yes," Halkerstone agreed. "She managed to escape the Revolution and somehow got the majority of her husband's wealth back to England." Halkerstone raised an eyebrow at that. "Many of the ladies you speak of think that was her husband's forethought. Given what I know of Lady Argent, I doubt it."

"I see," Rhys said, standing. And he did.

This bit of news changed everything. Edward's parents had spun stories and tales and taken him around the world as a child. Rhys's parents had been quite strict in teaching history, specifically the history of the nobility. They believed knowing the ins and outs of society was the only way of survival, and it had kept his name, Brey, a powerhouse for many centuries. Edward may not know the backstory of the other houses, and Rhys doubted he cared. Rhys, on the other hand, was well-versed in each one and how they played off each other.

He studied Halkerstone once more. The late marquess had been careful in handling his other son, but also tender from all accounts. Halkerstone had been educated and set up for success. There was no trace of anything on the man's face in the moment. He would have done very well at court. Still, Rhys believed his intentions were true.

"Edward's destination is to find the Lady von Croy." There was a flash of satisfaction in Halkerstone's eyes. So he suspected. Rhys was not surprised. The late marquess has been a shrewd man, and he apparently had raised two astute sons. "Last we communicated, she was in Vienna, which is what I told Edward. He was going by way of Hamburg to avoid France."

"I am not sure what they are planning, Your Grace. At present, I am more concerned that their ire may be focused on Lady Phoebe, herself. Remember, Edward has no idea who Miss Gordon is, and I do not know if his father ever told him that end of the story."

"Probably not," Rhys said. "Edward worships your father. I doubt he knows any of this. And if he finds Phoebe already dead."

"He may come looking for solace in Miss Gordon's arms," Halkerstone said grimly.

"Damnation, that *will* not happen," Rhys said slamming the desk with his fist.

"That is my hope, Your Grace," Halkerstone said. "And I intend to see that it does not. If you would write to him? He may take a warning from you more seriously than myself. I will catch the next boat out."

"You intend to follow him?"

"Of course," Halkerstone said. "I have a feeling he will need someone to watch his back. Whether he knows it or not, he is my little brother, and it is my responsibility to look after him."

Rhys was not a little surprised by this revelation, but he saw the sincerity and concern in Halkerstone's face. He nodded himself.

"I will write to Edward and send warning," he said. "And I will also endeavor to check in on the Lady Winchester regularly."

Halkerstone's features relaxed. "My gratitude, Your Grace. I have some, er, reliable men of the, well, lower class type that I have set to watching Miss Gordon and Lady Argent. I will have them report to you any relevant findings. I have also set one or two to watching the Winchester house. They're not overly bright, but they are solid lads, if you take my meaning."

Rhys nodded. "Forward me a list of their names that I will know them if one approaches my people. You should know, Edward intends to go first to Berlin before moving on to Vienna."

Halkerstone pursed his mouth. To his credit, he did not ask why. Then he looked at Rhys. "Perhaps I will beat him to Vienna then. I will head there straight away and stand in the way of anyone who comes after the lady directly."

"I would be grateful," Rhys said. "She is my cousin. I will write you a letter of introduction and send it tomorrow, that she accept your protection," Rhys said. "Good luck, Mr. Halkerstone."

After the other man left, Rhys poured himself another drink. He could feel the alcohol humming through his veins. It had been a long while since he had gotten good and pissed, and contemplated being that way again. Lady Coventry. He shook his head, thinking that Edward's father, God rest his soul, had truly and well set his son up for pain on more than one account. Not on purpose, of course, but then he had never really helped his son either. Edward was in love with his father's memory. Rhys's vision of the man was incredibly different. He thought of the first time he had seen Edward, when the funerary barge had arrived back to England. What a shit of a day that had been.

Chapter Thirty-One

June 13, 1781 - Eight years ago
Dockside, London

Rhys's stomach clenched, and he felt his mother's hand tighten on his arm simultaneously. Not for the first time, he wondered if bringing her had been a sound idea, but then there was no way he could stop the Duchess of Brey. She was a woman of formidable character. Rhys knew that well. Growing up, Rhys's bottom knew that well.

As the ship sailed toward the harbor, Rhys ran his eyes along the crowd. There were families of red coats lining the docks, hoping for a safe return. He felt a wave of bitterness at these people that they might find joy in this arrival. He knew it was low of him and did not care. Then there were the ones in black, like him, with news of the worst already in hand. There were less of those in black. Few soldiers could afford to come back in barrels of rum or in urns of ashes.

Ashes. His bitterness increased that he could not even bury his father's body. He knew he should be lucky at all that the other officers had regarded his father's wishes he be burned and brought back to England instead of buried in that heathen, savage land where the rebels had taken his life. He wished they had gone against those wishes and brought him back whole, but it was too much to ask for.

Around him, families were already waving at men hanging over the railing as they threw ropes to the dockmen and tied the ship off. Women with new ribbons in their hair and bonnets, in their Sunday best with twice-turned dresses and faded colors, smiling happily because they were going to a party after this while Rhys and his mother were going to a funeral.

His eyes stopped at a splash of black deeper, even, than the velvet coat making Rhys sweat. The man and woman stood under a white canopy with an Indian servant a step behind, shading them from the sun. House Winchester, if Rhys was right. The servant had to hold the umbrella quite high, as the man was taller than most on the dock. Rhys glanced at the older lady, and even as he did, his mother confirmed his suspicions with a soft whisper.

"Lord Winchester fell in the same battle as your father," his mother added. "His son has taken the title, although he will not come into his majority for another two years." Rhys was a year younger than Edward then. "Not very sociable, is young Edward," she added, clucking in disapproval.

His mother had opinions on how young men should act and was probably more upset that Edward had not noticed Rhys's younger sister Jane.

"Your father and Lord Winchester used to be quite good friends in their youth," Lady Brey added. "I believe they still corresponded while Lord Winchester was abroad."

Ah, that explained the servant, Rhys thought. His eyes moved to study the new Lord Winchester, because he was stoutly avoiding the ship.

Edward Pierce, Marquess of Winchester was a

dour-looking young man. He was dressed smartly, perfectly in accordance with his station, though instead of wool or velvet, he favored silk. He forbore the fashionable wig of the day, opting instead to wear his dark brown hair pulled back in a tail, and wrapped in ebony ribbon. He had the look of a black prince, the Black Prince, Rhys mused.

Lord Winchester's eyes swung around to meet Rhys's, prickled by the watching of the other. Lord Winchester's face was blank, but he had the eyes of a Welshman, pale and gray. In them, Rhys saw overwhelming grief and agony and, if he was not mistaken, rage. Rhys nodded once, in silent understanding, and they simultaneously broke contact at the sound of the gangplank being brought out.

Rhys let out a breath he did not know he was holding, and suddenly, he was not so very bitter at the stream of soldiers coming down to meet their loved ones. Someone else was grieving. Someone else was angry. He was not alone.

****

Later that afternoon, Rhys moved amongst the other mourners accepting well-wishes and condolences alike. There was tea and cake, whiskey and sherry abounded, and the gentry were talking in quiet circles throughout the mansion. Rhys was exhausted from the receiving line, as much from the friends who genuinely expressed their sorrow, as from the enemies who had simpered and offered false sympathy in the form of barely concealed barbs.

It made him sick, and only his mother's dignified demeanor and unflinching resolve in the face of such indecency had kept him from losing his temper. Rhys did not typically lose his temper. He believed anger was for the lower classes. Dignity was for the refined. And yet, as the afternoon had worn on, so had his patience. He sought out a drink to soothe his temper and a friendly face to calm his worn nerves.

The butler nodded from the side of the room, and a footman appeared with his favorite scotch. Rhys nodded a thank you and sipped it to find balance. It burned going down. Robbie, the son of the Viscount Gage, clapped Rhys on the back.

"So sorry for your loss, my friend," he said quickly.

Robbie always spoke quickly, a symptom of being outnumbered at home by the fairer sex. He had seven sisters all of whom enjoyed talking quite a bit. Rhys was glad none of them were in attendance today. "Dark days with this war," he added, trying to sound wise. Robbie also had a habit of making generalized statements in the hope of sounding smarter than he was. Rhys suspected it had something to do with wanting to be taken seriously since, at home, despite being the heir, he was rather disregarded.

It did not change the fact Robbie had no real idea about the war and was not affected by it in any genuine way. His father was too old for military service, and Robbie had opted to go into university instead of soldiering, although he spent a good deal of his time chasing skirts rather than studying. His comment irritated Rhys, which was uncommon. Usually Rhys would laugh or make conversation back. There was no harm in what Robbie said, only that in this instance, he had no grounds from which to speak. And Rhys was quite done with empty conviction.

Unknowing, Robbie launched into a retake of yesterday's races and whose horses were now the highest rated amongst the gentry. Rhys half-listened, eyes searching for his sister. She was surrounded by ladies many of whom, he was relieved, were actual friends. He sought out his mother and found her talking to Lady Winchester.

So the lady had come late. Rhys imagined the Winchesters holding their own funeral for the ashes. He was about to search for the son when he appeared, seemingly out of nowhere, and handed his mother a glass of wine. Rhys blinked. It was almost servile the way the Marquess of Winchester hovered at his mother's elbow, aloof and polite. He answered Rhys's mother's question, but his expression was closed, guarded. Rhys could see his mother's nostrils flare from here, a sign she was vexed. Perhaps her patience was running thin as well.

Rhys excused himself abruptly from Robbie's presence, not caring a whit that it was in the middle of a story, and headed toward the clustered party. His arrival made his mother straighten and regain her mantle of dignity. He loved her a little more then.

"Duke Brey." Lady Winchester curtsied gracefully. She was still beautiful, enough to attract the attention of more than a few of the widowed men and older bachelors amongst the crowd. And Rhys noticed that she had. "My son, Edward, the Marquess of Winchester," she said bravely, her voice catching on the title.

The marquess inclined his head respectfully, and Rhys returned it.

"We saw you on the docks," Rhys said. "I share

your grief," he said, meeting Edward's eyes again. Up close, it was easier to see the rage there, boiling under the surface.

"Yes," Lady Winchester said, managing a polite smile despite the circumstances. "Please excuse us for not greeting you. It has been a difficult time."

The Duchess Brey reached out and took Lady Winchester's hands and clasped them.

"Yes," she said simply.

There was a moment where the four of them, just the four of them, allowed the real and deep sadness that they all felt, the loss and the heartache to permeate the air. And then it was over. One of the ladies from the Duchess Brey's circle came over to greet Lady Winchester. The other ladies drifted forward and began closing ranks.

"Drink?" Rhys asked the marquess.

Edward inclined his head again but did not speak. For a fleeting moment, Rhys wondered if the other man ever spoke. He had an image of Edward dressed in an Indian turban but still all in black, stomping around London, a dark giant causing demonic destruction, and the image struck him as amusing. *Nerves,* he told himself.

Before they could get far, Robbie accosted them.

"What ho, who is this?" he asked.

Rhys introduced them, and Edward nodded, his eyes more remote than when he was introduced to Rhys.

"Bad business all around," Robbie said. "So your father killed as well?" he asked, missing the lightning in Edward's eyes at the mention. "Terrible. So, Rhys, as I was saying," and without a beat, Robbie launched back into his account of the races, down to the bets won and lost. Rhys could see Edward stiffen and set his jaw. Once more, he felt a sort of relief. He realized he was less irritated with Robbie only because Edward was obviously so bothered, as if Edward's anger somehow lanced his own.

When the account was done, as Robbie was drawing a breath but before he could launch into another inane story, Rhys cut him off. "Thank you so much for coming, Robbie. The marquess and I have business to discuss."

It was a clear dismissal, and Rhys got away with it because he was now the Duke of Brey. Robbie was off balance but a moment, in which his eyes passed between the two men, before laughing nervously and stepping out of their presence. Rhys saw more than a few eyes note him and Edward standing together, noted Edward noticing as well. What was more, he saw many of his enemies searching for an opportunity to speak with him, but the hesitation despite that Robbie was gone, to approach Rhys with the stern figure of Edward beside him. Rhys smiled. He gestured for Edward to follow him and felt, rather than saw, Edward's thundercloud mood keeping the raptors at bay. If Rhys had not been so damn upset, he would have been delighted.

Instead of staying in the outer rooms, Rhys led Edward down a hall and into his father's study. No, his study. Edward closed the door behind them as Rhys went to the sideboard and poured himself another scotch. He poured one for Edward and handed it over, before sitting in one of the leather armchairs by the fire. Edward sat as well and stared into the flames quietly, sipping his drink.

"I apologize for Robbie," Rhys said. "He has no sense of propriety, and no connection to the war, so he does not understand."

"I highly doubt he is smart enough to understand even if he did have a connection," Edward said.

Rhys blinked at the cutting remark, and the smooth baritone that spoke it.

Edward sighed. "I apologize. That was exceptionally rude."

Rhys threw back his head and laughed, the first genuine laugh that had bubbled up from his stomach since the greasy, salt-stained message bearing the morbid news had arrived.

Edward eyed Rhys, uncertain what the laughter meant. It struck Rhys that Edward was not particularly good at reading people.

"It is amusing, because it is true," Rhys said and finished off his glass.

Edward smiled, a slight upshoot of one corner of his mouth, and took another sip. Rhys watched him roll it around his mouth, savoring the flavor. The duke stood to pour himself another and brought the decanter back to the chair with him.

"I have not laughed since I got the news," he admitted. "Thank you for that." Edward studied Rhys but remained silent. "It is like a piece of my innards has been gored out of me," Rhys said. "Like there's been a hallowing inside."

"A bullet wound that tore through you," Edward added.

Rhys nodded. "Were you close with your father?"

"Closer than some," Edward said, swirling the last

sip of amber liquid in his glass. "Closer when I was younger. The older I became, the more his position grew, and it took him away from us often."

Rhys understood. His father had been a man of not inconsiderable power in the House of Lords, a place Rhys had inherited.

"Our fathers were friends," Rhys said.

Edward nodded. He knew. "They met again on the battlefield," Edward said. "In his letters, my father spoke very highly of the duke." Edward met his eyes. Rhys acknowledged the compliment. "Neither of them should have been there."

"What you mean to say is we should not have lost the battle," Rhys said.

And there it was again, that intense rage in Edward's eyes. Nearly spilling out. Rhys saw Edward inhale a large breath through his hawk nose and then release it slowly from his mouth as he searched for steadiness. He took the tumbler from Edward's hands and stood.

"Come, Winchester, we need to get good and soused," he said.

"I must accompany my mother back home," Edward said quietly.

"I will ensure that Lady Winchester is escorted properly. You," Rhys said, "need a drink. A drink and more."

An hour later, Rhys and Edward stepped out of the Brey coach and onto the street in front of a magnificent graystone with torches well lit along the front. Footmen opened the doors for the two aristocrats, and Rhys led the way in.

"Do you have a membership?" he asked Edward as

they passed through the portal.

"I do," Edward said in a tone that said he had never set foot in this place before.

Like most things, Edward's membership to the exclusive club was inherited. His business manager paid the yearly dues and would until told otherwise. Rhys nodded. His situation was the same, though his father had brought him here the first time before he left for America. It was not the only club Rhys had membership to, but it was his favorite.

"Duke Brey." Mr. White the proprietor was out tonight and bowed respectfully. "And Lord Marquess, we have not had the opportunity of an introduction yet. My name is Mr. White, and I am the owner of this club."

"How do you do," Edward said respectfully.

"Shall I prepare a table for you?" Mr. White asked, reading Edward's silence and glancing at Rhys.

"No, Mr. White, we have eaten already. Are there any matches going on downstairs?"

"I believe there are," he said, gesturing a footman over. "William, show our guests downstairs and make sure they are taken care of."

The footman led the two men downstairs where a crowd of raucous men were shouting and betting at the side of a ring. Inside a square of ropes, two men were boxing. Rhys sent the footman scurrying for drinks and led Edward ringside.

"Do you gamble?" he asked. Edward shook his head. No surprise there. Edward was far too serious for games of chance. "How about pugilism?" At this, Edward looked interested.

"Can anyone enter the ring?" he asked. Rhys

nodded.

"You seem like you need to exorcise some demons," Rhys said.

Their eyes met again, and Rhys's eyebrow quirked in challenge.

"Indeed," Edward said, all stone serious.

"I shall put your name on the slates," Rhys said. "I expect you to do well, as I intend to bet a hefty amount."

Rhys grinned, as Edward eyed him trying to discern whether he was being mocked or not. In truth, Rhys was teasing him, but he felt excited to see Edward box. He wanted to know what this solitary, black prince was made of. Rhys called over a footman and sent him scurrying with instructions.

Together, they watched the next two matches, Rhys commenting every now and then on the opponents and Edward studying them intently. When it was his turn, he removed his jacket and cravat, his vest and shirt, and accepted two gloves from the ringside master.

Rhys was surprised by the amount of musculature Edward displayed. It wasn't just that he was fit, his skin was tan from sun exposure. Edward's skin had yet to pale in the English winter, making Rhys wonder what the other man did on his country estate.

One of the servants tied the wrists of the gloves, and Edward entered the ring. He touched gloves with his opponent, a common boxer the club hired for sport, and the two began circling. The fight did not last long. Despite the professional being the favorite, Edward downed him in the second round. Another opponent entered the ring, and Edward downed him in the fourth. When the ringside master asked Edward if he wanted to go a third round, Rhys was not surprised when Edward nodded.

There was a confident, menacing stalk to him as he circled his opponent. He was not only trying to best them, he was hunting them. Rhys doubled his bet on the first match. He did not bet the second, but the third, when the crowd was clamoring for Edward's defeat, when they expected him to go down from fatigue, Rhys laid the double winnings on his new friend.

Edward was covered in a sheen of sweat. He bled from a cut on his lip and his left cheek, plus his ribs were darkening with bruises. There was nothing fatigued about him, though. He seemed more sure, as if by now he had caught the rhythm, and as he dodged and danced around the ring, Rhys felt a sort of release. Edward was throwing his anger with every strike to skin. Rhys was losing his anger with every blow his friend delivered.

It took five rounds, but Edward defeated this new contender and raised his hand, finished with the sport. He stepped out of the ring amongst cries of support and woe for the bet losers. Rhys collected his winnings and approached with a footman in tow carrying a warm towel. Rhys scrubbed Edward's hair affectionately.

"Feel better?" he asked.

Edward stood there. They were of a height, which was unusual. Rhys was used to being the tallest man, to command the room, but Edward was about a half an inch taller. His presence seemed to both fill a space and keep others at bay. Even now, in the middle of the shouting crowd, men gave them berth.

"I do," he said and smiled, both corners of his mouth going up.

"Good," Rhys said. "There is a washroom over here. After that, we'll find some fun."

They spent a few hours on the second-floor parlor near the window, drinking and talking. Rhys did most of the talking, but Edward said some about his life in India, his studies, his father. Rhys enjoyed sitting by the windows and watching the city outside come alive. He knew the ton and its players and pointed them out as they passed, especially if there was a naughty story to tell.

He had an efficacious way about him that Edward warmed up to. Men stopped by to pay their respects, and the Duke of Brey greeted them all but did not encourage any to stay. Edward's presence helped that, and Rhys loved it. He enjoyed the private curtain by which Edward kept the rest of the world away. It was a skill Rhys did not possess. On the contrary, people sought Rhys out.

For entertainment, Rhys made a bet with himself to get Edward to laugh, which proved a bigger challenge than he first supposed. Edward seemed to stubbornly cling to his grief, as if frightened to let it go for even a moment. Rhys realized, for Edward it was a matter of loyalty. To be happy now would be a betrayal to his father. Rhys realized up until today, up until Edward had made him laugh, he had felt a similar notion.

But it was dispelled, for him at least. And as much because he wanted to see this stern man crack, he also wanted to know Edward was capable of joy. Otherwise, they could not continue this friendship beyond the night.

The drunker Edward became, the looser his hold on his sadness, Rhys noted. So the duke kept the alcohol flowing.

"Oh, by God," Rhys said, turning away from the door.

Edward cocked his head, his back to the door.

"The Marquess of Denshire just entered," Rhys said, leaning forward. "He will come over here and say something to make himself laugh. Listen for it," he said. "Ah, my Lord Marquess," Rhys said standing. He shook the man's hand and introduced Edward who rose like a tsunami.

Every time Edward rose to his feet, Rhys noted the way other men in the room cast a glance about, as if Edward's shadow reached out and touched them. He grinned.

"Your Grace," the marquess said, leaning in. "I have just come from Lord and Lady Redgrave's, and do you know who I saw?" The marquess babbled on with gossip and, sure enough, made a disparaging comment, then laughed at his own joke. It was a curious squeal of a laugh, which ended in him emitting a strange sucking noise twice.

Edward swallowed his lips and looked outside. Rhys noticed and laughed politely, then added a comment, which made the marquess laugh again. Edward closed his eyes and cleared his throat. Across the room, someone called for the marquess's attention, and he excused himself.

When Edward nodded goodbye, his face showed no hint of his thoughts. But when the marquess was safely out of earshot and they were both seated again, Rhys leaned forward.

"What did I say? That laugh sounds like two pigs fucking," he said.

At that, Edward could not contain himself any longer. He threw back his head and laughed, and Rhys joined in.

"How do you know what sound two pigs fucking make?" Edward asked. "Have you done a study?"

"Well, many of my tenants raise pigs," Rhys said. "And I was a very curious boy," he added, wiggling his eyebrows. Edward laughed again, closing his eyes and shaking his head against it. His laugh was a good sound, pleasing and not like animals reproducing or doing anything recreational at all.

"By God, Brey," he said.

"Oh, come now," Rhys said, waving a hand. "Many an aristocrat shares more in common with their heraldic animals than they would like to admit. The Duchess Foreshore, for example, has a goose on her shield and honks like one when she has had too much sherry."

Edward smiled widely now, showing teeth. "Ah yes, that one I have heard," he said and chuckled, shaking his head again.

Lord Laughton approached, and the two young lords greeted him.

"I have yet to have the opportunity, young Winchester," he said, "but I knew your father well, and I mourn his loss."

Just like that, the merriment went out of Edward's face.

"Thank you," he said politely.

"He was one of the fiercest men I have ever known," Lord Laughton continued, unaware of the effect he had on Edward's mood or night. "Iron will, that one. A great man, and a great loss for the Empire."

"Lord Laughton, I hear your horses lost yesterday at the races," Rhys stepped in quickly.

"What? Oh yes, my son." And he twisted his mouth in displeasure. "He finds the horses more important than his duties sometimes." The older man realized he had, perhaps, spoken too frankly and excused himself quickly.

"His son is an ass," Rhys said when he had gone. "But Lord Laughton is a good man, truly."

Edward did not acknowledge the comment. He was staring down at the amber liquid in his glass, and Rhys knew he was considering leaving. All the pleasantness of a good drunkenness was gone. It was important no one provoke Edward now.

Plucking the glass from his hand, Rhys ignored the sound of protest and the flash of lightning in Edward's eyes.

"Come," he said firmly, "time to seek other pursuits."

"I should return home," Edward said.

"Like hell," Rhys said. "Go home now and you will only drink yourself into a stupor and be sorry for it on the morrow."

"I will already be sorry for it," Edward said.

"Then we should make it count. Come quickly," Rhys said leaving the parlor and not waiting for Edward's answer.

Edward followed, more slowly. It pleased Rhys in a way he could not describe in his present state that Edward refused to try and catch up with him. Rhys was at the front door while Edward strode at his own pace down the stairs to where the duke had stopped. They each paused and took each other's measure, albeit drunkenly, once more.

"Well?" Edward asked, impatiently. Rhys grinned.

Rhys gave the driver of his coach directions, and they both climbed in. After a moment of silence, where they both contemplated the wisdom of a coach ride on a stomach full of swirling liquor, Rhys asked, "So tell me, what are Indian women like in bed?"

Edward narrowed his eyes and looked across the dim space at the other man.

"Please do not tell me you have yet to bed a woman," Rhys said. "There is a better brothel for that, but I would have to tell the driver quickly if that were the case."

Edward chuckled despite himself, then looked out the window. "They are all golden satin skin and blue-black hair," he said. "The women dye designs into their hands and feet and paste jewels on their foreheads. It is like going to bed with a demigoddess."

Rhys hummed in appreciation. "Well, this brothel has some dark beauties if that is to your taste," he said.

"Actually." Edward hesitated, and Rhys could tell he was battling his own pissed state, debating on what to share and what not to share. He looked at Rhys. "I have never bedded an English woman." He said this as if confused by it, and Rhys burst into laughter. Edward looked mildly embarrassed, and Rhys clapped him on the shoulder to discard the emotion.

"Well, I have never bedded an exotic, so let us switch up for the night," he said, grinning wide. Edward smiled too and assented with the short nod of his head.

The brothel was a large house on Kings Place ran by the infamous courtesan Madame Hayes. There were many bawdy houses, but this was the richest and certainly the most high class. Madame Hayes knew Rhys on sight and kissed his cheeks in the French way. He introduced Edward, as Madame Hayes fluttered a fan against her generous chest.

"He is a hunter, this one," she said appraising Edward's tall visage. "Why the black, monsieur?"

"We have come from a funeral," Rhys said, heading off that conversation. "And are in dire need of comforting, Madame."

"Ah, say no more, gentlemen." Madame Hayes led them to a parlor where women with their assets on display mingled with men of a certain class. "My girls will drown you in a pleasure you have never known before."

Rhys nodded politely but once out of earshot murmured, "It's a pleasure I have known many times actually."

Edward chuckled, and Rhys grinned, proud to have produced another laugh, if only a small one. He had been correct in his assessment. There were beauties of multiple colors here. Several Africans mixed with a few Egyptians and others of the Mediterranean, with their olive skin. There were a few red-headed Irish girls and their freckled breasts, and most of the women were English beauties with honey curls. There were no Indian women, and Edward did feel a pang of disappointment for that, but he settled on a pretty girl named Millie while Rhys chose an Egyptian beauty with kohl lining her eyes and mystery in her swagger.

Money was exchanged, and both men retired with their mistresses for the night.

Upon the morning, Rhys woke with a naked girl across his chest and a throbbing in his temple so intense he was sure he had been struck there the night before. He removed the girl delicately and then made his way over to the chamber pot where he lost the contents of his stomach first and then his bladder.

Feeling only a whit better, he washed from the basin and donned last night's funerary wear. It seemed appropriate putting the black velvet suit back on now that his body seemed to finally mirror his emotional state. As if waking up so physically miserable was like knifing an infected wound and letting all the pus seep out. It was painful and cathartic at the same time.

He met Edward in the drawing room. Edward's face expressed a mutual misery, but, and perhaps finally, his eyes no longer held rage. Instead, they seemed to reflect the same satisfaction that Rhys felt at this physical discomfort. Rhys threw his arm around Edward's shoulder as they walked out.

"Let us do it again tonight," he suggested.

Edward agreed.

Chapter Thirty-Two

August 24, 1789
Ludwigslust

Like Rhys, Edward was thinking of their first outing. He was remembering how much better he felt after their antics. How close he felt to Rhys, but perhaps more importantly, how not alone he felt in his grief. He glanced at Tilton as their tired horses walked into the cobbled streets of the town of Ludwigslust. He so wished to do that for Tilton. He wished for the time and carelessness to go debauching about for days and weeks until the pain had leeched out somewhere along the way with the alcohol sweat, the clash of fencing blades, and a thousand kisses.

Through the long dusty day of traveling, Tilton had said nothing. No words, no sounds, not even a sigh as they dismounted in front a fair-sized inn. If not for the wary way Tilton took in the stable hands and the servants, Edward might have thought he was sleepwalking. That hard, drawn expression in itself told Edward enough about where Tilton's heart was—suffering and clouded in fury. He had no idea how to tell Tilton about what transpired at the Roma camp. Or, rather, what did not transpire there.

The innkeeper was cheerful enough in both temperament and far along enough in English to settle things quickly. Neither of them had any luggage to speak of, so they wandered in and took a table out of the way near the fire. Although only mid-August, autumn had begun to creep closer, and the nights ran cooler here. The fire was bright and comforting, yet it did not reach Tilton's eyes.

"The food is not a total travesty," Edward said.

Tilton grunted.

"Tomorrow morning, I shall visit the bank and get us some funds. Then we can get some clothes and supplies," Edward said. Tilton nodded. "And I will see how far the next village is, whether or not it is worth staying on another night."

"No," Tilton said. "Even if we have to travel by night, we should do it."

"I fear—"

"The lady's life is on the line," Tilton said. "Berlin is only a few days' ride. We should leave tomorrow after we get supplies. I believe there is a branch of my father's bank in Berlin, so I will be able to repay you then."

"There is no need," Edward said waving it away.

"It is no trouble," Tilton said. "I think I will go to bed."

Before Edward could protest, the youth was gone in a fluid motion of exhaustion and grief, leaving Edward by the fire. *I'm going to have to be like Rhys,* Edward thought. *I'm going to have to get him through this. Lord Above, I know I've been rather needy of late, but I need help. Help me get Tilton through his grief. Help me find this damnable Saint Germaine and please, by Your Grace, please help me save Phoebe's life.*

Chapter Thirty-Three

August 24, 1789
Hamlet of Amt Neuhaus

Cliff touched the damp, newly turned earth gently.
A voice in deep German behind him barked out a
question. Cliff didn't turn, but the translator quickly
relayed the message.

"This is the *friedensricter*. He wants to know what
your business here is," the translator informed Cliff
nervously. The translator was spineless, but he'd come
based on Lady Eleanor's agent in Hamburg. The same
agent who, despite specific instructions sent by pigeon
from the lady herself, sent Roma onto the road before
Cliff arrived. Now Cliff was playing catch-up.

He had written to the lady after he found out what
the idiot agent had done and also assured her he had
broken the man's arms. Lady Eleanor disliked being
disobeyed even less than she liked the poor.

"What should I tell him?" the translator asked
nervously.

Cliff would have preferred a Roma. Thieving,
drunken shadows that they were—roaming and slipping
through borders like pieces of wind. Scum, to be sure,
but Cliff paid no mind. He was only gutter trash
himself.

"Tell him we are trynna to catch up to a toff," Cliff

said. "We have news of his family. And ask him who's buried here."

The translator did his work, and the *friedensricter* replied giving a short story of a botched robbery of two noblemen on the road by Roma. The body was of a servant. Cliff swore. Could this be his quarry? Was Winchester in company? The Duke of Brey surely had not left England. So with whom, then, was Winchester traveling?

Cliff tossed money the *friedensricter's* way and nodded at the translator to remount.

"We are not staying?" the man complained.

"No, we need to make time. That body is only three days old. With good riding, we can catch up and, hopefully, prevent any more trouble. The lady don't like no trouble," he added as a warning.

The translator quivered and nodded. They remounted and headed off.

Chapter Thirty-Four

August 24, 1789
Hotel Willkommen Komfort, Berlin

Edward and Tilton rode hard for three days after Ludwigslust. Although the weather held, it was still cool at night, and they were bone-weary at the end of every day. Edward worried the hard traveling gave Tilton too much time to think. He was silent and focused.

When they arrived in Berlin, it was too late to pay a call even to a wizard *and* make contact with the bank. So Edward went for pragmatism for once, and they stopped at the bank where both men presented letters and opened their lines of credit. Edward withdrew a small ransom to pay off the hotel and the magician. Then he led Tilton to the nicest hotel in Berlin, the Hotel Willkommen Komfort, and booked them both suites.

There was a buzzing energy driving Tilton, and Edward focused on getting him taken care of. Hot baths first, then a good meal. Neither of them had clothes fit to go out, but Edward offered anyway.

"I'm sure we could find some trouble somewhere," he suggested. "A brothel or a boxing match—"

"I think I will turn in early," Tilton said.

"Tilton." Edward stopped him. "I know it hurts,

and I have no way of making it easier. But a good fight might go a long way in improving your mood."

"Good night, Edward," Tilton replied and disappeared into his rooms.

Edward brooded and worried, wondering how best to draw his friend out of his doldrums. It was late by the time he fell asleep.

The next morning, Tilton seemed in a better place. He smiled, it was a small one, but a smile nevertheless, over breakfast reading the paper of all things.

"Something amusing?" Edward asked.

"Only my terrible German. Here the headline reads 'Best Night Show in all of Berlin,' and I initially thought it read 'Best Nude Show.' Those two things are a bit different," Tilton said widening his eyes.

Edward chuckled. "Well, I suppose depending on where the show is being held, it's not much different."

Tilton's smile grew. "Good God, Winchester, I must have been very bad the last few days if *you* are making jokes."

"The last week has been difficult," Edward said instead.

Tilton nodded, and grief passed over his features for a moment before being chased by lightness. He smiled again. It was forced this time, but it was there.

"I just need some time," he said quietly.

"I know," Edward agreed.

Over breakfast, Edward filled Tilton in on what Rhys had told him of the Comte de Saint Germaine. The man's history was lurid and fanciful, clearly much of it had been constructed, but the man had convinced a Hessian prince on the strength of his magic, and that was no small feat. Rhys had suggested using wealth as a price but provided Edward with other means of extracting what he needed. Of course, Rhys had known Saint Germaine's secrets. Rhys seemed to know everyone's secrets.

Except Phoebe's, Edward thought.

After breakfast, they made for the address Count Cagliostro had given Edward. It was an inn called Zauberer, in the leather-working district of Berlin. The inn was tidy and mostly empty with two barmaids wiping down tables. One was a stunning beauty with very nice assets, who stood when they entered and propped one hand on her hip in challenge.

"*Guten tog, Fehlschlagen,* we are looking for the man of the, er, inn," Tilton said.

"And what would two lovely gentlemen like yourself need with my husband?" she asked, surprising them both with a Scandinavian accent and perfect English.

"Business," Edward said shortly. He rattled his money pouch. "Of which we are willing to pay."

She gave him a once-over before nodding to the door leading to the back.

"He's prepping dinner in the kitchen," she said.

In the kitchen, they found an olive-skinned man with a razor-sharp mustache and goatee chopping vegetables.

The Comte de Saint Germaine was dressed in the part of innkeeper, despite prepping food, wearing a stout shirt of good wool dyed navy blue with an apron over top. His lips were feminine, sculpted, his expression haughty, even as a cigarette hung negligently out of his mouth. His eyes were two different colors, one pale blue, and one dark brown. His demeanor that of a man who lied for the pleasure of it. There was something about the way he cast his eyes on both Edward and Tilton that made Edward think of the old Romani woman immediately. He was not sure if that was a good sign or bad one.

"The Comte de Saint Germaine, I presume?" Edward asked. He did not wait for an answer. His gut told him this was the right man. "I am the Marquess of Winchester, and this is the Honorable Tilton. We have come seeking your particular expertise."

"I apologize that you have been misled, Herr Winchester," the Comte said, his accent unclear in its origins. "My name is Krüger," he insisted. "I know nothing of this Saint Germaine you speak of."

"Indeed," Edward said, unconvinced. "The Count Cagliostro said you would say that."

There was a moment of fragmented silence where the sounds of the tap room on the other side of the door took over while Saint Germaine's eyes studied Edward thoughtfully, and the two English nobles pretended not to mind. Whatever lie Saint Germaine might have spun next, it was forestalled by the arrival of the fetching, curvy barmaid. This time she leaned on the table between Tilton and her husband, but Edward got the notion she was here to even the odds.

"And who are these, husband?" she asked, eyes flitting between the two noblemen. Edward singled out her accent to Danish from his time up north.

"Bella," Saint Germaine whispered, his affectionate pet name selling his French upbringing. He was not incorrect though. As she turned, Edward noted her peculiar violet eyes, the sweetness of her mouth. No one could miss the other assets she displayed to advantage although Edward found himself unaffected. His thoughts flicked to Phoebe, and the perfection of her breasts, and then he cursed himself to shame just thinking of it.

He glanced at Tilton, fearing perhaps that his young friend was easily in more danger of such influences and might be caught up in a spell. Tilton's eyes, however, were on Saint Germaine, studying him intently.

"These gentlemen are from England," he said. "They have come searching for a dead nobleman."

"Oh," she said conversationally, moving behind the cook's table. She moved several knives out onto the table and began sharpening a large one methodically.

"We intend no trouble," Edward said.

The madame's aggressive display put him off balance. He was no longer certain whether to distrust the husband or wife more. He stepped away, giving himself more room.

"We are here on mystical matters." Tilton stepped forward, seemingly unafraid. He seemed amused, even admiring of Frau Krüger's sharpening skills, if that was the name they were going with. "Of the kind, we are told, only your husband can answer."

"This is the Holy Roman Empire," Saint Germaine said. "Practices of that nature are illegal and considered witchcraft."

"It is a matter of life or death," Edward said.

"If you are dying of some disease, I suggest you go see a priest," Saint Germaine snapped.

Edward's eyes flashed, and his temper flared, but before he could draw sword or musket, Tilton had pulled out the heart. He showed it so that its facets glinted like red mirrors in the light, and then set it on the table in front of Saint Germaine. Edward made a noise in the back of his throat, one of panic and animal fear at the diamond being so exposed. He crossed the distance in two strides and made to snatch it up. Saint Germaine caught his wrist in a surprisingly strong grip before he could. Edward blinked. He had not seen the man move.

"Hold," Saint Germaine said.

Edward glared with fury. Fury at the man's manner, at this place, at the fact that he needed to be here at all. Most of all, he was angry at how much fear he felt, at the thought that Phoebe might be dying and it was his fault. He had lived with this for weeks, but at the moment, it rose up in his throat and caught him so that he could not speak, let alone bear it.

"Who?" Saint Germaine asked. His blue eye was as sharp as his mustache, while the brown one seemed oddly compassionate. He asked Edward, but Tilton answered.

"A former paramour," Tilton said.

"I broke her heart," Edward choked out. "I did not know what it meant at the time."

"And you think you understand now?" Saint Germaine asked, letting go of Edward's arm. He picked up the stone and turned it over in his hands. Closing his eyes, he used his fingers to know the stone, to seek out its crevices and edges.

"Some," Edward said cautiously.

Fingertips grazed his jaw, and Edward startled, having not heard or seen Frau Krüger approach. *Was there magic at work here that let these people move so swift and silent?* Edward had not thought that possible before Nancy Storace. So much had changed that night. He side-stepped, keeping close enough to grab the diamond should he need to but out of her range.

Frau Krüger clucked at him like one would an uneasy stallion.

"You still love her," she said.

"No," Edward denied, his anger rising again.

"Then why are you here?" Saint Germaine asked, opening his eyes.

"To right the wrong," Edward said.

"What did Cagliostro tell you?"

And so Edward recounted their conversation. He hesitated before adding what the Romani woman had said. He had yet to use the poison plant she'd given him, but he had not thrown it away either. He could feel Tilton's intense gaze on him. Edward had not gone into detail of that night and his encounter with the Romani woman. He did not know how to explain it to his friend, especially after so soon their loss of Mr. Welfries. He would have to now, but Phoebe's life was at stake, and he could not hold back if there was even a chance this magician would help him.

Saint Germaine asked what the flower looked like, and Edward told him.

"Euphorbias," he said, seemingly amused. They all looked at him confused. "That's what the flower is called, euphorbias. That's an old trick. You mistrust this Sinti?" Edward stirred. He did not know that word either. "The Roma," Saint Germaine clarified. "Sinti is what we call them here, though they call themselves other names. The Sinti is right, however. The flower will bring heat, if only temporarily."

"You seem to know a lot about these Roma,"

238

Tilton observed shrewdly.

"I have known a few in my time," Saint Germaine said, though he seemed distinctly uncomfortable with this line of questioning. Edward did not care a fig. His only priority was the heart.

"How do I fix the heart permanently?" Edward asked.

"You cannot," Saint Germaine said, sitting back.

Edward blanched.

Tilton made a noise of disbelief. "We did not make this journey to be told such a fallacy," he said. "There must be a way."

"You broke her heart," Saint Germaine said. "It is not like a real stone, Herr Winchester. It is not glue or mortar that one can simply apply and repair. This is an injury. It may look like a diamond, but this is a living, breathing organ. It grows and contracts. It is like a bone and muscle break in one. It needs time, attention, room to heal."

"Then that is what we will give it," Tilton said.

"It is too late," Saint Germaine said. "If the halves had been joined and nurtured in the beginning, perhaps, but now…it is like a frostbite. This part of the organ has lost feeling, and soon, it will die completely."

"No," Tilton said. "Edward, tell him about the garden."

Edward said nothing. There was a roaring in his ears, the same roar that occurred when his body prepared itself to fight. His blood was up, and he grasped his hands behind his back so hard they shook. For all his striving, this was not a physical fight he could win. And yet, to hear the words insist that all his machinations up until now meant nothing, that he was powerless in the face of this invisible enemy, made his body fill with fire. He so desperately wanted to punch the look of bored apathy from Saint Germaine's face.

"Have a drink before you spout smoke," Frau Krüger said, offering a mug of foaming dark beer at Edward. He looked at it and then her, violent intention all over his face.

"What about a garden?" Saint Germaine asked.

Edward glared at Tilton who gestured in a "go on" manner. After grinding his teeth for a moment, Edward relented and explained the vision he'd had.

Despite himself, Saint Germaine leaned forward. "So you've had a vision of this woman while holding her heart, but you do not love her?"

"Yes," Edward growled.

Saint Germaine smoothed his mustache in thought. "I would say her feelings for you are still strong except you saw her with another man. One or both of you is lying," he said bluntly.

"Enough of your games," he snarled. "There must be a cure. I will accept nothing less, so consult your cards or your bones or what have you and find one, before I send the letter I have prepared to a certain Hessian prince of your whereabouts and that of his favorite mistress."

At his threat, Frau Krüger sucked in air between her teeth in a hiss not unlike a cornered snake. Edward was surprised he did not hear a dry rattle in the room. Herr Krüger's eyes hardened.

"You make a convincing argument," Herr Krüger said standing. "However, threatening a man who is familiar with the unseen arts is unwise. Threatening *his* love is a far greater display of stupidity."

Rhys had told him the backstory of these two, which is how he knew that Saint Germaine was supposedly dead, though Rhys kept track of the comings and goings of nobility. Edward hated the politics. He remembered some of his Danish friends writing to him of the scandal when it broke several years ago, and he knew the prince they hid from. But he hated having to threaten like this. He would gladly pay a man any sum to get what he needed. Blackmailing was a terrible way of going about things.

"I do not like being threatened," Frau Krüger said.

Edward wanted to stay angry, but the woman was right. He was lowering himself to the basest level by threatening her and her husband. He did not want to be this man. He lowered his eyes and bowed. "I apologize," he said stiffly. "I…I am sorry. It is not my way to threaten. I do not want to hurt anyone. I just *need* to fix this."

Frau Krüger's eyes softened, and she nodded.

"My dear," Frau Krüger chided. Saint Germaine looked at her. "I like being threatened less than you, but I've seen the look on his face before. You remember the night I speak of. You remember what we did, what we were prepared to do."

"What we had to do," Saint Germaine snapped.

Frau Krüger did not rise to the bait. She nodded and stepped closer, gripping his arms. "What we had to do," she agreed. "He is prepared to do the same. Can you not see?"

Saint Germaine opened his mouth to argue, Edward was sure, but Frau Krüger lifted herself onto her tiptoes and kissed him lightly on his lower lip. The fight went out of his face, and he sighed.

"Is there not some spell that will set things right? Can you wave your hands and—" Tilton wiggled his fingers.

"No," Saint Germaine said. "This is not a simple thing you ask. Most people think that magic is instantaneous," Saint Germaine said, giving Tilton a look. "That I can wiggle my fingers and shoot fireballs. The truth is, gentlemen, that magic is a natural force, and while there are some very small cases of instant results, most magic takes time to grow and build like the plants and the earth and even the force of the waves. So, no, there is no spell."

"There must be something," Edward begged. Yes, he would beg if he had to.

"We have brought great payment to compensate for your trouble," Tilton said. "That doesn't involve threats," he added dryly. Edward began to pace instead, his long stride taking him from one side of the room to the other too quickly.

Saint Germaine followed Edward's frustrated movements. The blue eye seemed to be cataloging every detail, while the brown eye hid all the man's secrets. "There may be a way," he said slowly. "A ritual, but I need to consult the spirits first." Tilton breathed audibly with relief. "Come back tomorrow, and we will see what we will see."

Chapter Thirty-Five

August 24, 1789
Hotel Willkommen Komfort, Berlin

Neither of them spoke on the way back to the hotel.
Tilton did not make eye contact, while Edward
searched for the right words. By unspoken agreement,
they passed through the lobby and went back up into
Edward's suite. Tilton took off his jacket, sat on the
couch, crossed one ankle over his knee, and waited.
Edward was not sure if that was to the good or ill.

Taking a deep breath, Edward sat across from him.

"When I got to the Romani camp, I started
shooting immediately. I wounded two, perhaps killed—
I don't know. An old woman stood screaming for me to
stop. She came out unarmed." Edward checked Tilton's
face to see if he was listening. His expression was
devoid, but his eyes were so familiar to Edward. So
familiar. It was the same emotion that had plagued him
after his father's death. Rage mixed with grief and
anguish. They were going to fight, he knew.

"She knew what the stone was, Tilton. She *knew*.
And she said I didn't have much time, and then she
offered me fast horses and the stone back. She gave me
these flowers. What did Germaine call them?
Euphorbias. She gave them in case it got too cold and
told me to hurry and I…"

"You just left," Tilton said. "You let them get away with murdering Welfries."

"No, yes." Edward shook his head. "She unnerved me. I believed her."

"So you believed her and just let them go," Tilton said quietly.

He was preparing himself for a fight. It went against his nature. Tilton liked to fence, to dance, but there was no real bloodthirst in him. Now, though, it shone in his eyes. He wanted to fight. It might have been better if Edward could have taken Tilton out the night before and worked some of this grief rage from him. But apparently, unlike him and Rhys, Tilton would not find salvation in a boxing ring.

Edward wasn't sociable. He didn't understand people like Rhys. He couldn't ease people like his mother. He couldn't lead like his father. He was just himself. But this part he knew and understood, and this part he could do. So he stood and removed his coat, his waistcoat, and his shirt.

Tilton's eyes widened.

"What are you doing?" he demanded, torn between anger and discomfort.

"Well, if we're going to fight, I'd rather not get these clothes roughed up. Come on. Stand up."

"Edward, I—"

"You need to hit something," Edward said. "You need to hit someone. I failed Welfries. I know it. My reasoning was that he was already dead and Phoebe is not, and so I made the decision. It was not honorable. Come. Hit me."

At this Tilton became angry, slamming the table with a sharp *crack*, and then he threw a pillow at

Edward.

"I'm not going to bloody well hit you," he snapped.

"That's assuming you can," Edward said calmly.

"What?" Tilton demanded.

"You are a better swordsman, my friend, but I doubt you can hit with your fists."

"If you'd hit that damn gypsy hard enough, Welfries wouldn't be dead! We'd have made it here sooner, together, and—" At this point he did stand and stormed forward. "I. Would Not. Be So Angry." He punctuated his words with swings of his fists.

Edward dodged and wove easily, dancing out of reach even as Tilton tried chasing him. His young counterpart was very swift and graceful on his feet, which Edward knew, but he was not a pugilist. He was a swordsman, and there was a difference.

Edward could have killed the Roma with a punch. He'd known that and had chosen not to. When he'd struck the man, it had been without a conscious decision, but up until that point, it had never occurred to him to kill anyone. It wasn't that he was incapable, obviously, it was that Edward liked fighting but he did not like killing.

Tilton continued to chase him around the sitting room, throwing swings and kicks, connecting every now and then. Never directly. When Edward couldn't dodge, he blocked. When he couldn't weave, he pushed back. They would have continued like this indefinitely had Tilton not screamed in frustration and thrown a wild punch. Edward had folded himself neatly out of the way. Tilton's swing put him off balance, and his heeled shoes caught on the tasseled edge of the carpet, twisting enough to trip him. He went down hard.

"Tilton!" Edward went to help him up and had his feet swept from underneath him.

Then Tilton was on top, not punching, no, but yelling and shaking Edward by the shoulders.

"Why didn't you just kill him? Why couldn't you end this? Why did you let me LIVE?"

When the last word was uttered, Tilton froze, shock rounding his eyes. The rage drained out of him, but the realization of his words filled him back up with unacknowledged pain.

"What?" Edward asked, thoroughly confused.

"Why did you give it all up for me?" Tilton asked. "You could have let him kill me. You wouldn't have lost it all then or had to go back after the heart." Tears welled up in his eyes. "So why?"

"Because you're my friend," Edward stuttered. "Because I care about you, and I was not going to let some two-faced blackguard hurt you unduly when I could prevent it."

Tears seeped down Tilton's cheeks uncontrollably.

"Tilton," Edward said, feeling awkward. "You're one of the best men I've ever met. I can only count five people that can handle my moods. And my own mother is one of them. I'm not sure that technically counts."

Instead of getting a smile, Tilton wailed and threw himself down on Edward's chest. Edward froze. He did not know what to do. He was not equipped to handle a situation like this.

"Look," he said, squirming on the ground, "it's going to be fine." He searched for words, the right words. *Damnation, what did Phoebe used to tell him?* "The worst day only lasts twenty-four hours, my friend. It will get better, I promise."

"No," Tilton said. "Not for me."

"Why?" Edward asked.

"My father hates me," he hiccupped. "He wishes I died in my brother's stead. My mother drinks herself into a stupor every night because she doesn't want to deal with either of us. None of my former friends will talk to me after I got in trouble. And my lover…left me. I thought Welfries, at least, would understand. He was so like me, but no." His voice turned bitter. "Turned out he was just another heartless fool who told me I'm going to Hell." He hiccupped again. "I'm going to Hell, Edward."

Edward's first response was, *we both are*, but that did not seem helpful in the least. Besides, Edward was damned for what he had done to Phoebe. Tilton had only ever shown himself to be a good man.

He patted Tilton on the back, trying to ignore the tears now matting his chest hair, and gently pushed Tilton back and himself up.

"Come on, old boy," he said helplessly and a mite embarrassed. "You cannot listen to foolish people."

"That's the problem," Tilton said sadly. "For all he's a cunt, my father is one of the smartest men in England. And Welfries was a genius, really, when he was not being a complete prat. See? Now, I'm speaking ill of the dead. Sometimes I just want to die."

"Tilton." Edward squeezed his shoulder. "You can be smart and a fool at the same time. Take me for example," he said sardonically. Then he turned serious. "You have to trust your heart and not others."

"My heart is always leading me into trouble, Edward," Tilton whispered. "I try to be good, I do—"

"Hey," Edward said forcefully, making him meet

his eyes. "You *are* a good man. I was not exaggerating when I said that. And if you cannot trust your own judgment in this matter, trust mine. You matter. You matter to me, and I am sure there are plenty of others you are not even aware of to whom you matter. You're a light, my friend. You shine, and there are so precious few people like you, this world cannot afford to lose another.

"Besides, I do not associate with bad men, and I certainly do not travel with them." Edward made his voice teasing. It appeared to have no effect. "I cannot imagine any reason for you to go to Hell, but if you go, I will go with you. And then we will fight our way out again."

That brought a chuckle at last from his friend's lips.

"There is no one I'd rather go through Hell with," Tilton admitted.

Edward was surprised to realize he felt the same. Rhys, certainly, he would have at his side, but Tilton on his other side to be sure. For some reason, Halkerstone popped into his mind. Yes, he could see Halkerstone being very useful in a fight. And trustworthy, covering the rear.

"I am a mess," Tilton declared looking at his suit which was torn at the shoulder and quite mussed. He picked himself up from where he straddled Edward and fished a handkerchief from his pocket. "I am sorry, Edward," he said offering it.

"It's quite all right," Edward said, taking the offered cloth and using it to wipe down his chest. He got to his feet and began redressing, his back to his friend. He could hear Tilton sniffling and trying to recompose himself. "I am sorry about the Roma camp and not telling you."

"No." Tilton waved it off. "I understand why. I just…" He sighed. "I wish…" He sighed again. "Do you ever wish you understood it all? Why you were here? Why any of us are here? What the bloody hell the plan is?"

Edward snorted. "Every damn day," he admitted.

They shared a look, and Tilton's shoulders slumped with relief. "Thank God I am not the only one," he said.

"Come on," Edward said. "Let's go out. We are stuck here until tomorrow, and if we are going to continue to speak philosophy, I need to be properly soused."

Tilton chuckled weakly and nodded. "Me too," he declared. "Absolutely me too."

Chapter Thirty-Six

August 25, 1789
Zauberer Inn, Berlin

The next day, Edward and Tilton returned to the Zauberer Inn a little worse for wear. Edward had a few bruises from their tussle that decorated on top of older ones from their travels. His thighs and ass ached from days of hard riding, and not even the down feather mattress had worked the kinks out of his back. He was beginning to feel the ill effects of their journey, and with no clear end in sight, he kept imagining coming to the end of it an old man.

The front of the tavern was busy today, and Frau Krüger was hopping with a few other bar maids. She sent them into the back with a nod. They pushed through the doors into the kitchen where Saint Germaine was ordering around kitchen staff. Once he was satisfied his staff had everything under control, he led them up the back stairs into a small private drawing room that doubled as a study.

There was a small fainting couch in front of a fireplace. One wall was lined with books. The cauldron on the fire bubbled with something foul-smelling. The desk was scattered with bones, phials, and powders along with a massive leather-bound book opened with an eagle's feather marking the page.

Neither Edward nor Tilton could make hide nor hair of the text. The faint reddish-brown color marked its age, and Edward wasn't certain whether it was iron-gall, blood, or walnut ink. He was not certain which would make him feel better given they were dealing with a warlock.

When he turned to face them, he was more grim-faced than usual. Edward braced himself for bad news.

"Have you figured out a way?" Edward asked, terrified of the answer.

"I have," Saint Germaine confirmed. "It will not be easy."

"That does not matter," Edward said, swiping his hands to push the difficulty away. Taking out a very hefty pouch, Edward offered it to the man.

"I do not want money from you," Saint Germaine said. "However, there is a far more valuable item you may procure for me."

"Just take the money," Edward growled.

"I cannot," Saint Germaine said, his dichromatic eyes flashing in sync for once. Edward paused, wondering at the words. Why could he not? Was this some strange wizard custom? Edward opened his mouth to demand his reasoning, but Tilton headed him off with a touch on the arm.

"We will not be drawn into anything illegal," Tilton said.

"Not exactly illegal," Saint Germaine said. "Exceedingly dangerous though. But I am certain men of your martial talents may prevail."

"How dangerous?" Tilton asked.

The Comte Saint Germaine smiled grimly. "There is a rare magical flower called a farnblume that needs to be plucked in the cemetery at the height of the full moon."

"Full moon." Tilton frowned, his brain hurting from the hangover as he tried to remember where they were in their calculations. "That's a few nights from now."

"Two," Saint Germaine said.

"Can we not just pay you?" Edward asked aggravated.

"We need the plant for the ritual, my lord. There is no other way," Saint Germaine said. Edward huffed and ground his teeth. "Now, let me tell you the details because it is not exactly straightforward, and this plant is not unguarded."

Chapter Thirty-Seven

August 26, 1789
Inn of the Zauberer, Berlin

Cliff waited until the marquess and his companion left before entering the Inn of the Zauberer. Frau Krüger threw a towel down at the sight of him, glaring at his back as he climbed the stairs. He didn't care much for that kind of woman. A woman should be calm, respectful. He would rather like to hit the foul language out of that one's mouth.

He found Herr Krüger in the study, staring off out the window.

"Smells like the dead in here," Cliff observed, wrinkling his nose. "You cooking a dead cat?"

"I delayed them. The errand I sent them on must wait until the full moon," Saint Germaine said. "That's two nights from now. Is that enough for you?"

"Very good," Cliff said. "Them's really believe in all this magic stuff, eh? Thought toffs were smarter than that," Cliff observed. To this Saint Germaine said nothing. Cliff shrugged. Some people just weren't hospitable. "And this little errand you sent them on. Not too dangerous, I hope?"

Saint Germaine glanced at him over his shoulder. "Nothing they can't handle between the two of them," he said.

"Good," Cliff agreed. He took out a knife and made a great show of examining its finely honed edge. "Now, my mistress's agent is awaiting my answer. Your plan works, an' I write 'im and tell 'im all is well. Your plan don't work, and I tell him to let that Hessian prince know where you are." He dug the knife into Saint Germaine's chest above where his heart should have been. "Then I break you and your lady so that when your prince comes looking, there won't be any running for ya. Understand?"

"Perfectly," Saint Germaine said. He kept his eyes lowered down at the desk. His eyes might give his lack of fear away. A blade to the chest would hurt, but it would not kill him. His heart was not in his chest to stab. "I wonder, shall we drink on it?" Saint Germaine asked, pushing the knife away and grabbing the whiskey bottle from the corner of his desk. He poured two glasses.

"You wouldn't be tryna poison me, would you, Comte?" Cliff asked, eyes narrowed.

Saint Germaine snorted, took his own glass, and drained it in proof. "No, I was trying to be a gentleman," he said, placing his tumbler carefully onto the desk.

"Well, I ain't a toff," Cliff said, but he picked up the glass and threw the drink back. "It's not bad," he said, before setting the glass back down and swaggering out.

Saint Germaine waited until Cliff's steps had retreated all the way down and faded into the noise of the tavern below. Too many people knew who he was again. Too many knew about him *and* his wife's history. The Winchester fellow had threatened him out of desperation, and when his wife had called him out on it, he'd been ashamed. This new threat, however, would need to be handled.

Saint Germaine opened a drawer, took out a pair of fine kid gloves, and slipped them on. Next, he picked up the other man's glass, studying it.

"The thing about masters of the arcane arts," he said to no one as he glinted at where the odious man's lips had left a mark on the glass, "is that we don't need poison to get revenge."

Saint Germaine took the glass and dropped it into the boiling cauldron. The color of the liquid turned from a pea green to a rabid orange.

"Let's find out who you work for," he said. "And what their plan is."

Chapter Thirty-Eight

August 28, 1789
Dorotheenstädtischer Cemetery, Berlin

Two days. Two bloody days of waiting, but they were finally at it. Saint Germaine's demands had Edward chomping at the bit, but he tried not to be a moody bastard about it. Tilton had been more than gracious, more a good friend than Edward deserved, and this was, technically, his Grand Tour. So even though they took time over the last two days in preparation, Edward also allowed Tilton to drag him to Brandenburg Gate as it was still under construction, and to the Theater des Westens for an afternoon show.

Truly, Berlin was a beautiful, cosmopolitan city, and were he here for pleasure, Edward would have liked to linger and wander. For a very brief moment while he and Tilton were walking along the Spree River, Edward thought how nice it would be to take Phoebe here. And then quickly banished the thought, blaming Frau Krüger and her insistence that he loved Phoebe for these rebellious ideas.

Still, Edward heaved a sigh of relief when the two days had passed into the night of the full moon. He was in such a hurry to get this done that when the concierge tried to deliver a message, Edward almost bit the man's head off. He said he'd pick it up later and followed

Tilton into the carriage.

The coach ride was long and tedious, stopping a little ways before the side entrance of the cemetery. Neither he nor Tilton moved to disembark. Edward would rather not be heading into a cemetery near midnight to do what most would undoubtedly consider to be witchcraft, but there was no point in hesitating. He stepped down, and Tilton followed. The carriage horses stomped against the cold and nickered uneasily. The driver was paid to wait an hour. Edward was mostly sure they would be done by then. If they had not accomplished their task, then they were most assuredly done for, and he did not want to consider that possibility.

As they headed toward the tiny side gatehouse, Edward put a hand on Tilton's arm for one more attempt to dissuade his friend. "You do not have to participate in this…sacrilegiousness," Edward said, twisting his mouth around the word. "I would understand if you waited with the carriage. Nothing against your honor," he added hurriedly.

"Edward," Tilton said patiently. "This trip is meant to teach me about different cultures." Tilton glanced at him, his eyebrow nearly in his hairline, while one corner quirked in a sardonic smile. "I am certainly learning new things," he said dryly.

Despite the late hour, the illegality of what they were doing, the knowledge that they were, most assuredly, tampering in the dark arts, and the suspicion that Saint Germaine was trying to get them killed, Edward smiled. He had no reason to, and yet with this danger looming over him and Tilton grinning like they were going into a boxing match with the odds in their favor, made the night seem less daunting.

He had been calmer since their argument. The grief and pain lay under the surface, but more of the Tilton Edward knew had returned in the last few days.

"I do not know where you get your sense of immortality, Tilton," Edward said. "But I think I would like to drink from that cup myself."

"Here they call it absinthe," Tilton said, and Edward chuckled throatily.

It was a comment Rhys would have liked, and Edward was reminded of the many, many nights they spent searching out trouble on the streets together.

"Shall we?" he asked.

Tilton wiggled his eyebrows in response, and they both headed toward the dimly lit side street as Saint Germaine had directed them. As the mystic said, there was a tiny gate here. The graveyard shift here was only one man, smoking a pipe and peering out of one eye, the other being blind and milky as the moon.

Edward greeted the man in German, telling him who sent them. The man grunted and opened the gate. Before Edward and Tilton pierced the dark trails, Edward asked if there was a particular path to avoid other graveyard shifters. In response, the gatekeeper spat at his feet.

"'Tis an evil in here," the man told them in his tongue. "I am the only guard."

Edward blinked at that and exchanged an uneasy look with Tilton. Graveyards were prime places for robbery of both bodies and goods. The richer the cemetery, like this one which housed a number of wealthy patrons, the more guardians hired to keep the rabble out at night. That did not include the additional, personalized guard hired to stand over fresh graves for the first week or so until they were no longer prime targets for the body trade.

"No one?" Tilton asked.

The guardian shook his head. "And don' be thinking I'll come a running if I hear you scream."

The two men moved deeper onto the path, the shine on their overwhelming self-confidence dimmed.

"Well," Tilton said. "I am happy we confessed today." Edward hissed at him. "In case things take a downward haul."

"My father would rise from the grave before Judgment Day if I end up dead in a Prussian cemetery, and I will feel the same if you die here. So put it from your head. We retrieve this devil plant and leave."

Tilton smiled. "Now who has the towering self-confidence?"

Instead of answering, Edward turned left down the path and headed toward their quarry. They had walked this path in the daylight several times over the past few days to become familiar with it. The added delay chafed at Edward, but Saint Germaine insisted their task could only be performed at the height of the full moon, and that was tonight. He promised wisdom afterward. Edward thought if he did not come through, he might be driven to kill the man, and he really did not want to.

The Dorotheenstädtischer Cemetery was more woods than graveyard with towering monolithic trees on either side, like vegetative sentries to guard the dead at their rest. *Or keep the dead from rising,* Edward thought.

The air was cold, too cold for an August day, more winter even than a shadow of the approaching fall. The air in the cemetery was thick with the smell of bodies though none were above ground as they could see. Both men held their lanterns high, but the darkness seemed to swell around them until…both lanterns went out simultaneously.

The moon hung above in her black mantle, gorgeous and bright lighting the path so they were not thrust into darkness. Still, Tilton and Edward exchanged silent looks, suddenly glad of Saint Germaine's insistence that they wait for the pregnant moon. Edward set his lantern down on one side of the path. He drew a sword in one hand and a musket in the other. Tilton asked how much farther as he used flint to relight his lantern. Then turned to work on Edward's.

"Just around that mausoleum," Edward whispered. The wind seemed to snatch up his voice and carry it toward their destination. The temperature dropped a few more degrees, and suddenly both men were breathing clouds of icy mist. Tilton finally managed to get both lights back and shuttered the lanterns quickly from the wind.

The mausoleum in question was a magnificent stone artifice with Corinthian pillars and three rooms to accommodate a large, wealthy family of Berlin. Out front, on a bench, sat the statue of a woman draped in robes, kissing her daughter's head. On the other side, a simulacra of the archangel Michael stood ready to contest with any demons that might approach, at his feet the serpent writhed.

Edward's eyes drifted over these things and above to the roof. Behind the mausoleum, an angry red glow seemed to wash out the moon's pale glow. That was their destination.

"What are our instructions again?" Tilton asked.

"At midnight, we pull the root and try not to die in the process," Edward said.

Tilton checked his watch. "A quarter hour to midnight. Shall we see what this evil spirit is and send it back to Hell?"

This part of Edward's plan had not really formulated in his mind. He had no notion how to sneak up on a supernatural creature, nor if it were even possible. He was also not the type to be skulking about in any way, preferring to face his foes head on. Saint Germaine had warned him that the revenant would suck the life out of him and that sneaking, along with fire, was perhaps the best weapon in his arsenal.

Edward, however, had not traveled the world and not learned a few tricks of his own. He preferred to go up against a supernatural creature with as many options in weaponry as possible and prayed that a few modern ones would help send the creature to its doomed permanent death. Dropping the bag he'd brought with him, he took out two medium sized ball-like containers painted in the shape of fish. It was naught but papier mâché, gun powder, and wicks sticking out the top. Absently, Edward hoped the revenant had never experienced fireworks before. He handed both fish to Tilton who set them next to the lantern.

"I do hope that priest we saw was reliable," Tilton muttered.

The priest had thought them insane Englishmen for asking that their fireworks be blessed, but the donations Edward had put in his hands stemmed his protests. Edward ignored Tilton's comment. He had to believe the priest was a holy man in his holy rites, or their lives were pretty much forfeit.

"Remember," Edward said. "I will distract it, and you will snatch the plant."

Tilton nodded. "No touching it." Then he pulled a face. "You know, the only plant I want on my person is a boutonniere, and somehow I doubt this will do."

Edward smiled. "I have all the faith in the world *you*, Tilton, could make this mythic farnblume work with at least one suit."

"Edward," Tilton said shocked. "Did you just tease me?"

"I admit to nothing," Edward said, with a perfectly straight face.

Tilton snorted. "Let us kill the dead then."

At Edward's signal, Tilton swung around to the left of the mausoleum, his lantern and a papier mâché carp in his hand. Edward carried the other along with his lantern. They reached either side of the mausoleum, the red glow and its source just out of sight. As quietly as he could manage, Edward opened the lantern and lit the wick. Both were trimmed to ten seconds, so without another hesitation, Edward stepped out from his hiding place and with a war cry threw it at the revenant.

He ducked back again just as a brilliant flash of color followed by a second bomb lit the night. Breathing hard, Edward counted to ten and then peeked out from his hiding place.

In the ground, a triangular black stone glowed with a menacing light that had not been there the past two days they'd come and scouted out the scene. Smoke and embers burned around the stone, but nothing else. And then a billow of black smoke erupted from the stone followed by dancing lights of magic in red and blue.

They had struck too soon!

The revenant took form before them, its face distorted and inhuman. It looked more like a plague mask, with an elongated beak and dark pits where its eyes should have been. The fingers were tipped with two inch claws, black and curved like a cat's, and it glowed with a dull luminescence, an ill-seeming green. It was hard to imagine this damned creature as human, but Saint Germaine had said it was once a man.

Edward's breath came hard and burst from him in a thick, icy cloud every few seconds. The temperature was even colder here, attacking his very skin and muscles, making it difficult to move. The revenant screamed, a high-pitched sound that wrenched and echoed painfully in Edward's inner ear, making him instinctively cover them and close his eyes against the sound.

It was a mistake, and one he recognized just before the creature's claws slashed across his chest, sending him stumbling backward. Edward opened his eyes, saw the creature looming over him, and heard Tilton cry out his name. There was a movement from the corner of his eyes, and Edward rolled out of the way as Tilton struck.

The creature screamed again, its cry this time in irritation as it whipped around toward Tilton and sent the younger man flying back. Edward regained his feet and shot the revenant in the head. It seemed to fall a few inches, crying out in pain. A curl of smoke erupted from the bullet wound, and Edward grinned. He'd had the musket balls blessed along with all their weapons. He'd even gone so far as to rub holy water into both his and Tilton's blades. As he reloaded, he heard Tilton shoot and saw another bullet strike it in the chest. He finished reloading and shot once more, this time aiming for its heart. It folded over itself, crying pathetically it seemed.

All three shots spat smoke now, and Edward congratulated himself on a job well done. Drawing his sword, he went to deliver the ending blow. Tilton stood and approached as well, sword at the ready. Then the air froze around them. Edward felt his muscles seize and stop. Pain exploded across his chest.

The revenant began to glow brighter. Edward felt his energy leaking out of him. Across the scattered tombstones, he saw Tilton's eyes wide and frightened. The blood drained from his face, and the clouds of breath coming from his open mouth became smaller and smaller. Then, quite suddenly, Tilton pitched to the right and collapsed.

Edward tried to scream, tried to cry out, but only a faint moan erupted from his mouth, and even that cost him. He felt his muscles burning and weakening, his spirit fading. He could not breathe, and his heart was pounding, trying to keep him alive. It was like drowning standing up. His sight began to blacken. He fought to stay conscious, realizing that he had been too arrogant. He had failed, not only Phoebe, but Tilton. This was his fault.

He did not know he had fallen to his knees until he blinked and the ground was closer. *I am so sorry,* he thought. *I have been the biggest of fools.*

As the blackness enclosed, his mind pictured Phoebe just as she'd been the first moment he saw her.

Chapter Thirty-Nine

December 29, 1788 - Eight Months ago
Sterling Country Estate

Edward staunchly did not believe in love at first sight. His father had always spun meeting his mother as such a tale, but Edward did not believe that part of the story. Such notions were for the ill-educated, the gullible, and those with shallow character. Edward was none of these. He was the tenth Lord Marquess of Winchester, the seed of the Pierce family line—one of good, old blood—and a man of intense education. He had been abroad most of his life, knew much about culture and the world, and he was so far from foolish as to seem diamondlike in his firmness.

That was not to say Edward did not believe in love. He believed strongly. He had witnessed it in his parents and his friend Rhys. He had seen lowly commoners taken with it, and knew that the smallest child was capable of feeling beyond what their tiny bodies could contain. What was more, Edward believed that love required action and investment. It was not for the faint of heart, but rather for the emotional hardy, the men and women who understood that love was like a plant that needed constant tending.

He had thought about this throughout most of his journey to Lord Sterling's country estate where he was meeting Rhys at a party to welcome the New Year. His mother had been "suggesting" new possible brides again. The carriage ride was long and uncomfortable. When Edward unfolded his long frame from the cramped interior, he was greeted by a weak late December sun and no less than six footmen. Rhys's carriage pulled up not a minute after Edward's, and the latter sighed with relief. At least Rhys wouldn't barrage him about love and marriage.

The butler directed men this way and that as they began unloading the carriages. Rhys followed and reached up and gave a hand down to Cecilia. Edward realized there was another carriage pulling away. Edward caught a quick glance of a red crest with a greyhound on it.

"Ah," Rhys said with a pleased smile. "They have arrived. Excellent."

Edward glanced inquiringly at his friend.

"My cousin, Phoebe, recently of Austria, and her sister Theresa who will come out next year, I believe."

Edward wondered why his friend had not mentioned cousins before but dismissed it nearly as soon as it entered his mind. Rhys and he had been separated for nearly two weeks during the Christmas holiday, as Edward had spent it in his country estate with his mother while Rhys had stayed in London.

The three aristocrats followed a footman into the estate where the butler took their cards and greeted them. Lady Sterling was on hand, efficiently welcoming her guests and directing the servants with the luggage. Walking up the stairs ahead of them were two well-dressed ladies who stopped as Rhys called out in a cheerful manner.

They turned and both smiled at their cousin coming back down halfway to exchange kisses of real affection. Edward's eyes fixated on the one, a beauty of soft curves and a playful smile. Then his eyes moved on, and he studied the older sister. The two women shared strawberry-colored hair and warm eyes, but it was the younger one, who was the prettier of the two, Edward reflected in a clinical way.

"Edward, come meet my cousins," Rhys insisted.

Edward climbed the stairs to the first landing and bent over the younger sister's hand, then did the same for the older sister.

"When we were younger, Phoebe and I used to chase each other through the gardens," he said, kissing Phoebe on the cheek. "And little Theresa used to pull my hair when I did not let her play in our games," he teased.

"To be fair," Theresa said, "you pulled my hair right back."

Everyone chuckled at that, and then Rhys introduced Cecilia and Edward.

"How do you do?" Edward greeted with a bow.

"My Lord Marquess, how stern you seem," Lady Phoebe commented. "I think I will make it my mission this holiday to get you to laugh."

She smiled to temper her words, and the sight made Edward a little light-headed. The smile was playful, teasing, and inviting all at once. It transformed her, and it seemed, temporarily, that Lady Phoebe actually glowed with some sort of inner light. Which was obviously impossible. Yet blinking did not dispel the sight from Edward's eyes. He did *not* believe in love at first sight, but as he stood there stymied by her, he wondered about love at second sight. Or perhaps love at first spoken words? Or maybe, simply, love at first smile.

Edward cleared his throat. "Please, excuse me," he said and followed the footman up the stairs. He heard Phoebe murmur an apology to Rhys and his friend laugh it off. He glanced back once before turning the corner, and an overwhelming urge to smile back grabbed hold of him. Phoebe glanced up before he disappeared, and Edward schooled his features. He could not give in. If she was going to try and make him laugh, he would need to hold out at least a few days. He could not give in, because he wanted all her attention for his own.

Chapter Forty

August 27, 1789
Dorotheenstädtischer Cemetery, Berlin

A scream interrupted the memory. Edward blinked, and black spots cleared from his vision. He shook his head trying to regain his bearings. He searched the area. He was in a cemetery. A blood-curdling scream again. Edward's eyes snapped to the source.

The revenant was tilted full back, howling in agony, its hand blackened and on fire. Something flashed on top of Tilton's chest. The young dandy remained unmoving. But the spell was broken. Edward did not think. He charged.

The revenant was still distracted by its hand and only managed to half-turn as Edward slashed his sword at it. Smoke erupted from the wound across its chest, and it shrieked, but Edward did not give it time to react. He pressed forward, slicing his sword across the undead creature, hacking at the arm it threw up in defense, trying to get to its head.

There was a moment where panic crossed its face, and Edward, the blood pounding in his ears, a war cry on his lips, stabbed the creature in the chest. A blast of white exploded from the creature, and Edward was thrown backward again. He struck a sarcophagus and tumbled over the other side.

Pain wracked his arm and back where he had struck the marble, but he grabbed the edge and staggered up. He thought he heard Tilton shout, and then a black flapping was the only warning he got before he was bodily lifted again by the enraged revenant and thrown once more. Edward landed on the grass and rolled until a toppled tombstone stopped his advancement. He looked up as the revenant hovered, his sword stuck in its chest, smoke curling from the wound.

There were other wounds, its one arm blackened, the other smoking from many cuts where he'd hacked at it, but the damn thing was far from permanent death. He'd only managed to enrage it. A red glowing erupted from behind the revenant, and Edward's hopes dimmed. By God, there were two of them. He was going to die here.

The revenant itself began to glow again, that unnatural green, and Edward's muscles seized once more. He felt his heart rate rise, and the burning began again. He saw a flicker of movement and Tilton scrambling in the background.

"Run," Edward gasped.

His breath weakened. The black spots reappeared. He was losing consciousness again, the pain from his wounds mixing with the revenant's spell, making it so difficult to stay awake. He glared up at the creature, even as his vision tunneled. He saw two shapes come around it.

This time the spell shattered. Instead of screaming, the revenant made a strangely human cry of fear and then disappeared. Edward shook his head to clear it. Above him, the statue of St. Michael stood, its metallic surface gleaming with fire. It regarded him for a moment before walking away.

Stunned, Edward watched it walk over to where it had thrown the revenant. St. Michael bent down and grabbed the creature, one hand on the head, the other on the body, and plainly ripped the head off. The body of the revenant fell, twitching several times before hissing and melting into the ground like unholy steam. St. Michael dropped the head, which also seemed to melt into the grass, and walked back over to the sarcophagus he had been protecting. He took up his position once more. Before the fire on his skin died, he looked at Edward dead in the eye and then down at his feet.

Then the flames flickered out, and he was still.

The resounding silence was thicker than water. Edward did not even realize he was holding his breath until there were more black spots and he gulped in air. It was quiet. It was too quiet. *Tilton!*

Edward lurched to his feet, pain exploding in every part of his body, but he stumbled anyway to where his friend lay on the ground. There was no color in Tilton's face. He looked like a corpse.

"Tilton!" Edward shook the young man. "Tilton? Please!"

Tilton gasped, and his eyes fluttered open. Edward pulled him into a sitting position. Fumbling in his pockets, Edward freed his flask from his jacket and unscrewed the lid. "Here," he said, shoving it under Tilton's nose.

Tilton coughed and opened his eyes blearily. One eye was red and swollen. There were scorched marks through his jacket, cravat, and shirt where the revenant had touched him.

"Drink," Edward insisted, and Tilton took a sip of strong whiskey. He coughed and choked. That wasn't a good sign.

"Are you well?" Edward asked, although it was quite clear he was not.

"I am alive," Tilton muttered. He shifted until he was sitting properly and closed his eyes, trying to get his bearings.

Meanwhile, Edward struggled to recover his breath, ignoring the screaming in every muscle where he ached. It was certain there were even more bruises dotting his body than before. Lord, when had he last been in this much pain?

It wasn't important. Tilton almost dying. Tilton injured. The revenant's hand on fire. The revenant surviving a sword through its heart. St. Michael. "How did you get that thing away?" he asked, opening his eyes. Tilton put a hand to his neck and nodded.

"I didn't," Tilton said. "My aunt."

Edward stared at him. "What?" he asked, totally confused.

With a moan of agony, Tilton pulled his ruined shirt away from his chest to reveal a massive burn where the revenant had gotten to his flesh. In the middle, perfectly surrounded by unaltered flesh, was a medallion.

"St. Benedict," Edward said, studying the impression. "Protector against evil."

"Not exactly what a man wants for his eighteenth birthday," Tilton said softly. His face looked paler in the moonlight. "Edward, I think I'm going to—" And his eyes rolled back into his head, and he went limp. Lunging forward, Edward jammed his knee but managed to catch Tilton before he could smash his head into the gravestone behind him.

"Come on, old man," Edward said, though he felt ancient himself. "We need to get you to a doctor."

Somehow, Edward pulled Tilton over his shoulder and managed to stand with the weight. His legs held. As he began walking back toward the gate, he looked over his shoulder, remembering why they'd come. The farnblume. The spot was empty, and glancing at the moon, Edward realized he'd missed the time anyway. It had been at least half an hour. The moon was sinking from its zenith.

Despair and anger rose in him, but he pushed them away. Tilton needed him, and the coach would only wait so long.

Chapter Forty-One

August 28, 1789
The von Croy Mansion, Vienna

Phoebe had declined dinner again with Frederick, the Duke of Styria, tonight. She did not feel like going. She did not feel much of anything recently. No, she felt...muted. She supposed when one had half a heart, that was better than to be expected. Mary had made more comments on it of late. Phoebe could not even care that her maid was worried.

A part of her missed feeling, but that was also the foolish part, the part that had gone ahead and fallen in love. And Phoebe would *never* trust that part of herself again. In the last six months, she had ruthlessly squashed any feelings toward *him.* Until it became habit. Until that part of her had at long last started to fade. As it faded, she felt herself fading into something lesser.

Frederick did not seem to mind. He seemed to appreciate her cool facade. He called her his little Schneekönigin, his snow queen. To be sure, he would be an easy husband. Even that Phoebe was uncertain she wanted. Lukas, her first husband, God rest his soul, had left her plenty of money to be comfortable. She did not need a second marriage, yet she allowed Frederick to continue his attentions.

Maybe it was because, of late, Frederick seemed the only excuse or motivation for her to leave the house. Maybe because he was so easy. Maybe because he was so very much the opposite of *him.* Frederick was carefree, and jolly, and stupid. He was round about the middle from too much rich food, and he had a thinning hairline only to be beaten out by an outrageously large mustache. *He* would hate him, if only because Frederick was so damn plucky.

But Phoebe no longer was. Ironic that she was turning more into the man she hated every day. Yet, it was the only solution she could see to her broken heart. To let it die. To let that piece of herself go entirely. She could not live with that kind of pain anymore.

I do not have to lose myself entirely, she thought. And so, with determination, she sat in her solar, curled up by the fire with one of her favorite romance novels. It had made her laugh and cry in equal measure, and she just wanted to lose herself in someone else's story while forgetting her own tragedy.

She was just coming to the meet cute, where the bright-eyed young maid first encounters her handsome beau, when a sharp flash of pain sliced through her chest. It made her cry out. Her first thought was, *Oh God, he's trying to kill me again,* and then her vision tunneled. Everything went black, and a scene erupted around her. There *he* was. Edward splayed out in the grass, his back against a toppled tombstone. Above him floated a horror made of nightmares, a creature so evil Phoebe could feel it through the vision.

It was going to kill him. Edward was going to die. Phoebe's first instinct was to reach out to him. *No,* she thought. *He cannot die. He cannot! He has not apologized yet.* Just like that, all her anger, her passion, her fury rose up like a roaring fire. She felt more than saw the vessel nearby. It did not matter what it was. She took hold of it and moved.

Phoebe had no real idea what she was doing, what magic was moving through her, and she did not care. She hurried forward, grabbed the creature, and tossed it away. For a split second, her eyes met Edward's. She had never seen him so astonished. Or dirty. By the light of the full moon, she could see he was absolutely filthy like he'd been rolling around in mud and soot all afternoon.

As much as she wanted to gloat at his sad state, Phoebe's fury was hardly spent, and the evil was not vanquished. She felt it behind her, and so she broke eye contact and grabbed the thing. Whatever it was, it was no match for her rage. She tore it in half, enjoying the satisfying sizzle as it melted into the ground.

As then her strength began to ebb. She felt it draining out of her. Felt the vessel return to its rightful place. She looked up once at Edward. He had not moved. He still had a slack-jawed astonished expression which only irritated her. He had changed. Even in that instant, in the quick flash of this vision, she saw how much he'd changed without her. Where was her serious scholar? Where was the man always so presentable, so polished? Was he as faded as she?

What would he say when this was over? This stupid man who did not believe in anything past what his hands could hold. He was a fool.

Her expression went down to the stone heart. Ah, so that is why she could be here. That is why she had seen his danger. But why had she saved him?

God, she wanted to tell him how much he did not deserve her or her help. But then the last of her energy faded and blackness took her.

****

Halkerstone regarded the von Croy residence in Vienna, torn between relief and anxiety. It was a fine home. In the Landstrasse neighborhood, not far from the palace. The house itself was a grand dame in the classicist style, a corner property with white-washed walls that stood six stories high. Ornate, black iron gates surrounded the building with the von Croy coat of arms in stone above the front door.

Why had Edward turned Lady Phoebe over? Halkerstone had only met her once in their courtship, and yet he had been struck by how well they got on. Some couples, well, some couples just fit together. There was a natural rhythm to their love. Halkerstone had never felt that way, himself, but he had seen it. He had seen it with the Dowager Marchioness and his father. His own sister and her husband had the same. Lady Phoebe and Edward had seemed natural together. She had brought out his joy and best humor. He had steadied her, providing a foundation for her to mature. He wondered, not for the first time, what had happened. And he had more than a sneaking suspicion of who was to blame.

None of that, however, helped him in the moment. He only prayed the duke's letter of introduction had made it ahead of him. For a moment, he hesitated. It was nearly midnight, and no one, however fashionable times they kept, would want a visitor at this hour unless they were hosting a party. The house was quiet. To be sure, there were plenty of lights on but still. *She might not even be home,* he thought, weighing his options.

Halkerstone may not have looked like his father, but he possessed the same ungodly determination that the late marquess had passed on to all his children. Halkerstone had come with a purpose, and he would not feel easy until the Lady Phoebe was secured. Straightening his back, Halkerstone knocked firmly on the door.

It was but a few moments before a butler opened the door. Like Edward, Halkerstone had needed to brush up on his German along the way.

"My name is Herr Linus Halkerstone. The Duke of Brey wrote to your mistress, Lady von Croy of my arrival?" He handed off his card, hoping the butler couldn't read English. His title as business manager would not be opening any doors.

The butler seemed genuinely confused.

"I am unaware of any visitors from the duke, particularly at this late hour," he said unimpressed and made to slam the door in Halkerstone's face.

Halkerstone was fast, putting a booted foot in the crack to prevent such a thing.

"*Mein Herr,*" he said more firmly. "Apologies, but I cannot leave. I was sent by the duke to secure her ladyship. She may be in danger."

"I assure you, her ladyship is quite saf—"

And then a scream rent the night. The butler startled, the door opening as he half turned toward the stairs. Halkerstone didn't wait. He shoved hard, letting himself in, and took the stairs two at a time. He had no idea where he was going. He hit the second-floor landing, and it branched off in opposite directions. He hesitated, listening, hoping for some indication, and then he saw a frantic maid appear from a servant's stairwell and dash into another door on the right. Halkerstone ran after her, aware of the butler's shouts and protests and other running feet as the house aroused.

The room was a woman's solar, with large windows overlooking a dark garden. The maid gently shook Lady Phoebe who was unconscious on the ground beside a couch. A book lay discarded on the floor, and a glass of sherry sat on a side table. Halkerstone knelt next to the maid and felt at her ladyship's wrist. Lady Phoebe's pulse was wild, but strong. Behind him, the butler along with a few others crowded the door.

"Call a doctor," Halkerstone instructed shortly. He lifted Lady Phoebe easily. She was no lightweight, but he was none either. "Her bedroom?" he asked the maid.

"This way," she answered and led him out through the crowd and down the hall into another room. Halkerstone laid her out gently.

"Will she be all right?" The concern of her lady's maid spoke well of Lady Phoebe.

"I do not know," Halkerstone said. "What did she eat tonight? Was there anything strange or out of place?"

The maid shook her head.

"Anything new? Any gifts or new servants?" he pressed. The maid shook her head, tears now welling in her eyes.

"No one would hurt her," she said. "She's a good mistress. We all love her."

Halkerstone held out a hand to soothe her. "Get her in more comfortable clothes." He turned to the door where the staff had followed them and looked in. "Has the doctor been sent for?" The butler nodded.

"Good. You." He pointed at another maid. "Help her with her ladyship. You." He pointed at the butler. "We need to talk."

****

Halkerstone spent the better part of an hour combing through Lady Phoebe's effects. He tested the sherry out on the house cat, checked the food she'd been served for tampering, and interviewed the staff. The cat gave him a disgusted look at the offering before sauntering off, perfectly intact. The food seemed safe and the staff understandably confused. They followed his orders without question.

Mary, the maid, had found the duke's letter of introduction, and the butler had been understandably cowed after his mistress fell ill under mysterious circumstances. Halkerstone had the servants throw out anything acquired in the last few weeks by unknown sources—wine, there was a new bottle of perfume, a rather large wheel of cheese that the cook was most perturbed to be rid of but agreed after the butler agreed to get her a new wheel.

Halkerstone thought he might be having an extreme reaction, but he did not know in the manner in which Lady Coventry would come at them. And he was too practical to take a risk. Lady von Croy obviously lived comfortably. She could afford another wheel of cheese.

Eventually, the doctor appeared. He proclaimed Lady Phoebe fit and resting and blamed the scream on hysteria. Mary confirmed that Lady Phoebe had been acting odd recently, more detached. The doctor thought it was a case of nerves brought on by too much excitement. Halkerstone didn't not think the two aligned—one did not get a case of hysteria and nerves after acting cold and detached for a prolonged period of time. But he was not a doctor, and the diagnosis brought the staff some relief. A hysterical lady they could handle. Anything more serious was to be a concern, something that, after losing their master two years ago to consumption, no one wanted to consider.

Halkerstone did not feel the need to dash their hopes. He guessed that whatever had sent Edward on his journey had to do with Lady Phoebe. Though the duke had been more than vague in his confirmations, Halkerstone was smart enough to realize that there may be forces at work they did not see. He set the footman and stable lads on guard in a rotating schedule for the remainder of the night.

"Tomorrow, I'll consult with her ladyship, if she is up for it, on other measures," he told the butler.

"Do you really think someone is trying to harm her ladyship?" he asked worriedly.

"Yes," Halkerstone said honestly. "Trust me, I would love to be wrong in this." He took a deep breath and peered out the darkened window on the city beyond. "But I really don't think I am."

Chapter Forty-Two

August 28, 1789
Hotel Willkommen Komfort, Berlin

The nearest hospital was farther away than the damn hotel, so Edward directed the coachman to take them back and paid him extra to fetch the nearest doctor. It took two stable hands to carry Tilton up to his suite. Only pride prevented Edward from asking for one himself.

It was almost one in the morning by the time the doctor arrived. They had a woman on staff who was trained as a midwife, and they roused her to tending the room. Edward paced. He was beyond exhausted, frightened, and if he did not pace, he would surely collapse. When the doctor did arrive, he surveyed the wound clinically, raising his eyebrows at Edward.

"How did he receive this?" he asked.

"Fireworks," Edward lied. "Can you help him?"

"Yes," he said shortly and began mixing a salve which he slathered across Tilton's chest.

There was color in his cheeks at least. The midwife assured Edward she would stay with Tilton and alert him if there was any change. With nothing else to do, Edward retreated to his own rooms and began stripping out of his dirty clothes. He finished undressing, washed, and then flung the blankets back to sink into the welcome comfort of the bed, thinking of how heavy and achy he felt, when he froze. *He* felt heavy, but he did not feel the familiar weight of the stone.

Scrambling to the pile of clothes he'd left on the floor, Edward tore through them like a madman. Finally, he found the leather satchel, but it was empty! The corner had torn loose in the fight. Clenching his fists, Edward threw back his head and howled.

****

Edward didn't sleep. He did not know why he bothered to try. When dawn broke through the windows of his hotel suite, he was already up and dressed. He stopped in to check on Tilton, and found the room empty except for his still friend. The midwife was gone. Frowning, Edward hurried over and felt Tilton's head. It was hot with fever.

Cursing, Edward practically ran down to the concierge desk.

"Where in all of damnation is the midwife?" he demanded.

"Uh, my Lord Marquess, we're so sorry," the concierge apologized. "Unfortunately, Lord Tilton's line of credit has been, uh, cut off," he said delicately.

"What?" Edward demanded.

"We have just received word from, uh, his father that he is not to be, uh, treated here any longer but to return home to England promptly. There is a letter here for him." The concierge offered a thick piece of folded parchment, but Edward grabbed the man's cravat and yanked it forward, dragging him eye to eye.

"If you do not *attend* the viscount's son, he will die in this hotel," Edward snarled. "So if there is a bill to pay, I will pay it. But you do not EVER disobey me

283

again, do you hear? I want staff up there in his room immediately, or I will be calling the town watch. And you had better get that doctor back presently. Have I made myself clear?"

The concierge nodded, the whites of his eyes showing in his terror. Edward shoved him back, furious with himself for losing his temper and even more so with this man for his behavior. He snatched the letter meant for Tilton, making the concierge jump, turned on his heel, and stormed back upstairs. Within moments of his re-entering Tilton's room, there was suddenly staff present to dab his forehead and clean up the place.

Half of Edward's heart longed to rush out and go find the heart, but he could not, would not leave Tilton alone. Lord Above only knew what the concierge would do if Edward left even for a little bit. He prayed the heart was safe, but he could not abandon his friend. He did not trust the concierge nor any man now.

The doctor returned to treat the fever, bloodletting from Tilton's arm, leaving him looking even paler. It was midmorning when the doctor left again. Tilton's fever broke, but he still had not regained consciousness. The doctor and his nurses had moved Tilton long enough to change the sheets and his clothes. Edward removed himself from the room and sat at the writing desk in the front room.

Saint Germaine would be expecting them. It took all of Edward's self-control not to curse the man in his letter. But making an enemy now would serve nothing. They had failed. They had failed to retrieve the farnblume, and Edward had lost the stone. He wanted to howl again. Instead, he composed a short note, reporting Tilton's injury and asking Saint Germaine to come to the hotel instead of Edward going to him. Edward only prayed he could convince the man to take money instead of the damned flower. Once he saw Tilton, he *had* to take pity on them.

He gave the note to a messenger and sent it off. Brooding, he waited for Saint Germaine to come, staring off into the window. It was well into the afternoon when the messenger returned to tell Edward that the man who ran the Zauberer Inn had disappeared two days ago. The messenger had asked around, but no one knew where he or his wife had gone. He returned the note to Edward unopened.

Edward didn't move, at least not outwardly. Inwardly his walls crumbled, his fear and shame, anguish and frustration raging like a gale.

This is what I get, he thought. *I failed.*

The sky outside was gray and reflected his mood. The temperature was cold, and a sleeting rain afflicted the streets with icy water.

"Perfect day for one's world to end," Edward muttered.

"My lord, he is awake," the doctor said, coming into the room.

****

Tilton was a sad sight indeed. His usually bright face was pale where it was not bruised an ugly rainbow. His eyes were heavy with pain and weariness.

"Edward," he called, holding out a hand.

Obliging, Edward took the seat by his side and gripped the hand gently.

"I assume we won," he said softly.

For a moment, Edward saw Mr. Storace again. He could not tell the man the truth, that he'd failed Phoebe.

Just as he could not tell Tilton now.

"We did," he said, forcing levity into his voice and a grim smile on his face. "Twice over when you are better," he added.

Tilton blinked slowly, like a cat and sighed. "Then why do you seem as though the world has ended?" he asked. "Did you not find the farnblume in my jacket?"

The room was almost too quiet as Edward tried to comprehend those words.

"Wha—what are you talking about?" he stuttered.

Tilton's eyes opened slowly, exhaustion heavy on him. "The farnblume. Blast it, man, the damned magic flower. I pulled it while you were keeping the monster busy."

At this, tears sprang to Edward's eyes. "Tilton, you…" He shook his head in utter disbelief. "You are the best of men."

"Tell that to my father," Tilton whispered, closing his eyes again. Before Edward could respond, Tilton fell asleep, snoring softly.

Edward sighed and stood. He fetched the discarded jacket from the laundry pile the servants had yet to take. Inside the inner pocket, tucked safely in a handkerchief, was the farnblume. It was a lovely little purple flower with a deeply red pollen and pistils.

The despairing part of Edward wanted to throw the farnblume away or crush it under heel as if such an act could rinse off his failure. It had cost him so much. But he could not. Tilton had pulled it. It now belonged to him. And so Edward tucked the farnblume between the leaves of the book by Tilton's bed and sat back down to wait.

****

Cliff leaned back in his chair, picking his teeth with a dagger as long as his forearm. It made the beggar in front of him nervous which was the point. Also, he had a bit of steak stuck in his teeth.

"They havet bin back at all?" he demanded.

The beggar shook his head. "They left on foot. Couldna gotten very far," the man offered.

Cliff grunted. He was willing to bet Saint Germaine had horses and supplies stashed around the city. He was a slippery fella that one. Cliff could almost admire him if he had not gotten away. Now, the toff was holed up in his hotel. The lady wanted the toff to get to Vienna, just late. Cliff reckoned it was getting on too late. The toff's lover was sure to be dead by now. Which meant Cliff's plan to delay had been overly successful. He needed to get the toff moving.

"Nothing else to report?" Cliff demanded.

"No, sir, only that a messenger came from the hotel inquiring after Herr Krüger but they sent him away."

Cliff grunted again and tossed the man a coin, then kicked him out the door. He was musing by the fire when one of the stable lads from the hotel came round.

"Got something good for you," he said, handing over a letter.

"What's this?" Cliff asked.

"A letter from Herr Krüger to the Winchester fellow," the stable lad said. "Nicked it from the front desk."

"You stupid," he said. "The concierge will know, and then there will be an investigation."

The stable lad shook his head. "Winchester strapped the concierge up one side and down the other this morning before he could mention the message.

Ain't no way he's going to tell Winchester he lost something now."

Cliff smiled, impressed, and handed over a few coins for his trouble. Then he cracked the wax seal and read it. Most of it Cliff did not understand. His reading was not high level and there were a lot of large words. Besides, to Cliff it looked like more of that magic rot. How could the toffs believe in this shit? He shook his head. It was all bollocks. *If magic really existed, them what knew it would have overthrown the toffs a long time ago*, Cliff thought.

However, this presented a problem. The Comte was definitely in the wind, and her ladyship would not be happy. How was Cliff supposed to get the toff moving and still make sure he was unsuccessful? An idea formed in the back of Cliff's skull, and he grinned.

"Can you write fancy?" he asked.

"I've a fair hand," the lad said.

"I'll give you a bag of gold to write what I say and deliver it back to the concierge."

"All right then," the man agreed readily. Cliff smiled. This would get the toff moving and kill his hope all at once.

Chapter Forty-Three

August 29, 1789
Hotel Willkommen Komfort, Berlin

Tilton woke again the next morning. Edward had managed to catch a few hours of sleep at night, his body protesting the ill treatment of the last few weeks. But he did not sleep well or long. And he was afraid the instant he let his guard down, something would happen to Tilton, so he was up every few hours checking.

When the sun streamed over the windows, Tilton opened his eyes and yawned, wincing at the pain in his chest. He looked a little better today. More color in his cheeks, but he was still pale and weak. A breakfast of porridge with strawberries and thyme water seemed to help. Edward joined him with a tray by his bedside, picking at his tomatoes and eggs.

After the footman cleared the plates, Edward took out the letter.

"I do not want to upset you," he said, "but your father has written. Do you want me to hold onto it for a bit?"

Tilton eyed the letter like it was poison but shook his head, and Edward handed it off. After tearing the seal, the young lordling scanned the contents. As he did, he seemed to sink into the bed farther, as if pushing away from the words written on the paper.

"What does it say?" Edward asked curiously.

Tilton looked at Edward, and he seemed so vulnerable, so *young,* Edward reached out and took his hand.

"Whatever it is, we will face it head on," Edward insisted.

Tilton closed his eyes as if in pain. "You can read it," he said. "You should read it, to see what kind of man has cost you everything."

It was such an odd thing to say. Tilton had only done his absolute best, helping Edward, accompanying him. He took up the letter and scanned the contents. It was written in anger, and yet the language that this man used was appalling. A line stuck out to Edward:

If you think I am going to finance you and your new lover sleazing around the Continent, buggering everything in sight, I'll hang you myself.

"What does this mean?" Edward asked, confused. "*Who* does he mean?"

"He thinks you and I are lovers," Tilton said with a sigh.

Edward chuckled. "That is preposterous," he said immediately. "Not to mention unnatural."

The heavy silence from Tilton caused Edward to study his friend. "Tilton?"

Tilton smiled with so much sorrow and pain one might think he was dying. "I told you I was a monster," he said softly. "I was not exaggerating."

Edward froze. "Wait," he said. "Do you mean—"

Tilton plucked at the embroidered flowers on the coverlet. "That night at the opera. When Mrs. Storace died? I missed that part because"—he glanced up at the ceiling, and Edward saw tears gathering in his eyes—"I had been thrown out. I was caught with my former lover, Bran. We were…" He did not finish.

Stunned. Gobsmacked, Edward stared at him. It came back in a rush then. The Baroness Ravensworth gossiping in his mother's parlor about a peer being caught with a same-sex lover. That had not been just some random scandal. That had been Tilton. And Edward had been carousing through half of Europe with the man!

"I—how—" Edward chuckled grimly and stood, turning away. Pain pierced him as sharply as if he'd been stabbed. "How could you not tell me?"

"It is not something one brings up in polite conversation," Tilton said softly.

"Polite conversation," Edward snapped, spinning around. "I told you about Phoebe. I shared my fears, my travel, my *name* with you, and you bring me this?" he asked furiously.

Ceasing his densely plucking, Tilton closed his eyes. "It was selfish," he said, "but it was easier to help you tackle your problems than to address my own. Fear not. I shall do the correct thing soon enough."

"The correct thing," Edward snarled. "Tilton, you cannot *love a man,"* he hissed.

"Yes, Edward, yes, you can," Tilton said softly, meeting his eyes.

Edward was struck at how mirror-like they were, at seeing his own grief of losing love in Tilton's eyes. How Edward understood exactly what Tilton was feeling, the dull ache behind the eyes, the clenching stomach, the hurt that crawled under the skin and would not leave.

"I loved him," Tilton said. "Natural or not, I did."

Edward had no response to this. Because he knew it was true. He turned and stormed out into the hallway, slamming the door hard enough to rattle the crystals of the chandeliers above. He was tearing halfway through his suite, throwing pillows, chairs, anything he could easily grab when a thought struck him, stopping him in his tracks. *Welfries.*

Turning on his heel, he stormed back into Tilton's room only to cry out and dive onto the bed to wrestle a musket out of Tilton's hand. Luckily, Tilton was too weak to strive much against Edward.

"Are you mad?" Edward shouted as he rolled off the bed, musket firmly in his right hand.

"I told you I was going to do the correct thing," Tilton shouted back.

"You think suicide is the correct thing?" Edward screamed.

"I'm going to Hell anyway. Might as well be on my terms," Tilton snapped, eyes narrowing.

Edward opened his mouth to argue and realized he would have made the same choice.

"No," he growled.

"No, I'm not going to Hell, or no, I'm not allowed to do it myself? Are you going to shoot me, Edward?"

"Of course not," Edward refused.

"Why not?" Tilton demanded.

Why not indeed? What Tilton admitted to was more than illegal, it was revolting. It was wrong. It was untenable. And yet, Edward could claim no better. Had he not acted callously and hurt a woman he claimed to love out of jealousy? Had he not fully broken her heart in the most physical and emotional of senses and then failed to repair or even atone for this sin?

"No," Edward growled again because he could not voice all this.

Tilton sighed. "Please, Edward, please give me the musket back." Edward shook his head stubbornly. "Please, if you had any affection for me at any time, please let me do this myself. I cannot bring honor to my family name, Edward." He sighed again, and it seemed as though all the weight that Edward felt when he carried Phoebe's heart had quadrupled and settled over Tilton. "I cannot go on like this."

Edward straightened, walked out, hid the gun under some couch cushions, loudly made a show of opening and closing every door and closet and drawer in the outer room to confuse his friend, then returned empty-handed. He closed the bedroom door behind him and took up the seat by Tilton's bed once more.

"Welfries knew," he said without preamble.

At this announcement, Tilton looked faintly surprised and then nodded.

"How? Did he...oh, God, he did not blackmail you, did he?" Edward asked, horrified.

"No," Tilton said. "I blackmailed him. Or I tried." His mouth twisted, and then he met Edward's eyes. "Welfries was like me. He preferred male company. We both knew what we were."

Edward could not wrap his mind around this. "Then he was—" Before the crash of guilt could come, Tilton shook his head.

"God, no," he said. "Welfries preferred his men big and hairy. I caught him fu—" A strangled sound escaped Edward's mouth, and his eyes almost popped out of his head. "Uh, I caught him with one of the stable hands," Tilton remedied. "I did not tell my father, obviously. After the scandal at the opera, Welfries was assigned to be my tutor. I thought as broken as my heart was, at least someone who understood me was accompanying me. Maybe, you know, we wouldn't go chasing skirts but chasing other things together."

Tilton paused to gather himself, then shook his head. "But apparently, my father had given one of his speeches. Though he did not know Welfries was like-minded, he railed about my condition anyway, enough to guilt Welfries into taking all the fun out of the trip. The only way I could get him to let us travel with you was to blackmail him into it."

Edward was shocked. He did not know what to say to this.

"How did you know Welfries knew?" Tilton asked.

"He, uh, stopped me in Hamburg and urged me to take you to a brothel," Edward said.

Tilton snorted hard, but his mirth did not last. "You should have let the Roma kill me," Tilton said. "So much could have been avoided. Least of all my inheriting the title," he said bitterly.

"No," Edward said, surprising himself with his vehemence. "You are still a good man, and suicide is a cardinal sin."

"So is fucking other men, Edward," Tilton said.

Edward flinched and stood. "I do not…understand that." He stared at the floor angrily. "But that is between you and God, and I cannot imagine that He put you on this Earth this way to…to just be a sinner. It makes no sense," he added.

"So you think it a disease?" Tilton said sadly.

"What? No," Edward snapped. "That is also ridiculous."

"Then what am I, Edward?" Tilton asked.

The question was earnest. This is what had been plaguing Tilton from the beginning. Edward had seen hints of it in passing, an expression here, a tone there. The sobbing demand to know why Edward had saved his life. Edward had little skill in hiding his moods particularly when he was conflicted. For better or worse, people responded to that and helped him. Tilton, however, had been chased into hiding all his fears and shame, burying it under a mask of good-nature and optimism. How difficult must that have been?

To pretend constantly. Edward shook his head. He could not do it. And he realized he'd been trying for near on six months now. Trying to convince himself that he did not love Phoebe, that his feelings were not still as strong as sunlight on a clear day. He had been miserable and done a piss-poor job. Tilton had been excellent and gotten caught.

Edward stared at him. He thought of Rhys and how when he'd gone to Rhys with his mad story about Nancy Storace and a stone heart, Rhys had believed him, not just because it was Edward but because he had touched something ephemeral. Or perhaps the ephemeral had touched him via his dreams.

Edward thought about his journey so far. He'd been more than touched by the supernatural, the mythical, magic. Stories from the captain and Mr. Storace, a revenant in a graveyard, a living statue of St. Michael, a magic flower that could ignite. A diamond that was a heart. Even beyond the mystical realm, Edward had been faced time and again to reconsider what he knew for sure, to expand his borders and reconcile his prejudices. He was beginning to understand that the world was vast, far larger than he first imagined. He did not and could not know what all it encapsulated.

At the base of it, Edward did not have an answer for Tilton. He could not fathom in any respect an attraction to a man. They were so hairy for one. And also lacked all the delicate softness Edward found alluring in women. But had he not already seen different kinds of love in his life? Loving someone like yourself so often came up in the myths and folklore he studied it was synonymous with the purist kind of love. Even on this journey, from Saint Germaine and his wife, their odd relationship, to Roma protecting their own, even to Welfries. Maybe love was bigger than he first took it for, and it was not Tilton that needed to change.

What was Tilton? He was a good man. He did his best, and he put his best face forward. He teased and risked his life for Edward, and it mattered little whether he did it for selfish reasons or not. He'd given his word and stuck by that. Edward had given his word too and not followed through.

"When I went to Rhys with my madcap story of Phoebe and a broken red diamond, he said: 'I cannot say with any real certainty what is possible or impossible in this world. And since I cannot say, I am therefore willing to take possibilities however improbable under due consideration.' I do not have an answer for you, Tilton," Edward said. "But I have read more stories than I can remember, and I know you are not alone in your tastes."

He paused, gathering his thoughts. "I have acted poorly toward you. Even if you say it was selfish helping me, you did more than I could ever ask for. You kept me going. You gave me hope, and you helped me stay the course when I was feeling lost. I have told you before, and I meant it. You are a good man. One of the best, in fact. And I am sorry I left your side. Right now, you are in Hell. Together, we will come out of it."

Something broke inside the younger man. A dam of repressed emotion gave way, and with a cry, he threw himself at Edward and held on, sobbing. Edward patted him awkwardly until the cries had subsided, until he was ready to let go and sit on his own again.

"I have ruined your vest, Edward. I'm sorry," Tilton sniffled.

"Think nothing of it," Edward said. "One does not need to dress well in Hell."

Finally, Tilton laughed for real.

Chapter Forty-Four

August 30, 1789
Hotel Willkommen Komfort, Berlin

The next day, Edward came back to check on his friend. The doctor was finishing replacing the bandages.

"How does it look, Herr Doctor?" Edward asked.

"Better," he said. "It is a good thing his lordship is young. I have seen older patients with burns not survive. But he is strong." He nodded firmly. "A few more weeks in bed and he shall be fit as rain."

"Weeks," Tilton complained. "We do not have time to wait weeks. Edward, you must go on without me."

"We will speak of it later," Edward told him softly. He nodded at the doctor and waited until he had left. Servants came in and out, fluffing pillows, straightening, and carting away the laundry at last. Edward was going to have several words with the concierge.

When they were finally alone again, Edward took up his post by the bed. He had not had the opportunity to tell Tilton about Saint Germaine's treachery or his failure. He searched for a way to begin now.

"Oh, good God, what has happened? You never told me what Saint Germaine said," Tilton pointed out, seemingly reading his mind.

"Because he said nothing," Edward told him. "He was gone, Tilton. I sent a messenger after you were injured for him to come here. Apparently, the innkeeper of the Zauberer Inn fled the city with his wife several days ago. He sent us on a fool's errand and disappeared."

"But that makes no sense," Tilton said. "Why? He refused our money. He genuinely seemed as though he wanted that farnblume."

"My guess is the threat of revealing his identity was too much and he sent us on the errand to give himself time to flee," Edward replied.

Tilton wilted under this news. "But we almost died," he whined.

Edward chuckled, but it was short-lived. It was more than they almost died. He'd lost the heart.

"Still, you must go on," Tilton was saying.

"I cannot leave you here by yourself," Edward said. "The concierge will have you on the next boat to England, I daresay, the instant my back is turned. And besides…I lost the heart." At Tilton's concerned expression, Edward told him about the torn satchel.

"Well, did you go back and search for it?"

"I could not leave you," Edward said. "By now—" He gestured at the window as if putting on display an entire city of thieves.

"You must go back and look for it," Tilton said firmly.

"It's a red diamond, Tilton, I do not think—"

"Go, Edward," Tilton insisted. "Have faith and go check."

"The concierge—"

"Will find a musket pointed at his nose should he come bother me," Tilton said, pulling the gun from under his pillow. "By the way, your hiding place was abominable." Edward opened his mouth to argue, but Tilton's expression became mulish, and he cocked the musket. "Go, or I will shoot you myself, Winchester. You're not wearing silk today."

Tugging his vest straight, Edward stood. "That's because you snuffled all over it."

A smile tugged at Tilton's mouth. "Damn right I did."

Chapter Forty-Five

August 30, 1789
Hotel Willkommen Komfort, Berlin

Edward made sure to stop and have more words with the concierge expressing his expectations for when he got back. He left the man sweating and pale. Usually, Edward hated being rough with the staff, but the instant that man had taken care away from Tilton, he'd made Edward's blacklist. Besides, a good tongue-lashing made sure that Tilton would be cared for while Edward made this journey. He also felt better that Tilton had the musket for he'd no doubt the younger man would use it.

The carriage ride in the late afternoon out toward the cemetery felt like it took weeks. As it plodded along, Edward considered other options. A red diamond, even a broken one, would garner some interest. Perhaps he could put out feelers with the local jewelers. Maybe he could locate some of those in the body trade. He should probably report it stolen to the local authorities and get some sort of people moving. Tilton, as always, was right. He could not lose hope now. He had to persevere.

The carriage slowed to a stop, and the horses danced uneasily. The sun would not set for hours, yet the cemetery felt darker than the rest of the world. The shadows crawled longer across the ground creating spaces of cold and dreariness. Edward tipped the driver enough to wait for him and entered by the side gate.

Walking the now familiar path, Edward kept his eyes alert on the ground for any sign or hint of the diamond. Every step made his stomach twist tighter and his guilt heavier. He suspected he would never feel light again but by thirty be a stooped old man under the gravity of his sins.

As he rounded the hill that hid the scene where the battle had been, Edward slowed. Despite the sunlight filtering in through a patch of clouds, Edward listened for the sounds of the revenant, stretching his senses for that hint of evil on the air. By the time the spot came into sight, he was wound tight. The area bore signs of their struggle, but no monster waited for him.

Blackened soot and scorch marks burned the ground and several stones where their fireworks had struck. The grass was torn up in a variety of places, and one gravestone lay flat from where the revenant had thrown Edward into it. He made a note to donate funds for its repair and whispered a silent prayer of apology to the poor deceased against whom he may have trespassed. Edward walked the site twice, going over inch by inch, frustrated, and angrier at himself by the second. The stone heart was not here.

Slumping against the wall of a crypt, he gazed about feeling very lost. His eyes fell on the statue of St. Michael. He'd been avoiding looking at it, for fear he would find it looking back at him. No, the statue was looking down at his opponent, the serpent underneath. Edward pushed himself off the wall and walked over, reaching out a hesitant hand to touch the smooth metal.

Just metal, cool and slightly verdigrised in the sunlight.

"I saw you walk," he said softly, letting his hand fall. A sharp pain raced up his hand as two fingers were sliced open by a ragged edge. Edward swore and looked down at the source, his pain immediately forgotten. There, nestled in the coils of the metal serpent, hidden in the afternoon shadow of the statue, was the stone heart.

Edward reached out and plucked it from the statue, glancing up in awe at St. Michael. Then he remembered: before going back to sleep, the statue had given him a meaningful look and then *looked down* as if to direct Edward's attention to where the stone heart lay. Edward had been so preoccupied with the fact that the statue had come to life, he had not even considered that it was trying to help him further.

"Thank you," he whispered. "I—thank you."

Edward held the stone heart against his body and felt it was barely giving off any warmth itself. There was no time to lose. He needed to get the heart warm now.

****

The Comte de Saint Germaine pulled his wife off the road and into a little copse of trees hidden from view. Frau Krüger wanted to protest, but she knew better than to question her husband at times like this. He had been born on the road. There was magic, silt, river water, and starlight in his veins. She also was not entirely certain the man was not part animal. And not just from his bedroom sport.

Where she had seen nothing, no hint that there might be another traveler or more nearby, he had read the signs correctly. Ten minutes passed, and a farmer's wagon ambled by, a farm wife pestering her poor husband who looked about as exhausted as the mule that pulled them. Their wagon was filled with turnips, and as the wagon hit a rut as wide as a ravine, it bounced a few out.

Frau Krüger leaned into her husband, enjoying his spicy scent, and waited patiently. Three days on the road with nary a sign of pursuit but she did not doubt him when he said it was time to leave. He was a survivor. They both were, and his mystical arts had never failed them. It was his arts that had gotten her out of a forced relationship with a Hessian prince. Some women would have quailed at the idea of being in proximity of a man who used what most regarded as the dark arts. But Frau Krüger had been raised in the streets of Altona before gracing the beds of powerful men. She had seen real evil, and she did not think what her husband practiced was evil. Besides, he had grown her a diamond. How many women could claim that about their husband?

His body relaxed a moment before he said, "Come, love," and pulled her back onto the road. Frau Krüger paused long enough to collect the abandoned turnips before following him.

"How much farther do you think?" she asked.

"I have seen several recent markings," he told her. "I imagine the family cannot be more than a week ahead of us."

She tried not to groan but a small sound of complaint escaped anyway. Saint Germaine glanced at her, a teasing smile at his lips.

"Not as comfortable as the inn, huh?" he asked.

"I just wish you had let us get horses before we

left," she said.

He shook his head. "I could not. They were watching us. Frank will sell the inn and send the money to us in Vienna. But first we have to find the family."

"Because of the Englishman?" she asked. "I do feel bad just leaving him."

"We will settle that debt," he promised her. "He has a powerful enemy, one bent on the destruction of his love. Had we stayed, the cards said we would have perished. But I left him a note that should help."

The catch in his voice gave him away. He used to be a better liar when he was performing his mysticisms at court. The years of parochial living had settled him into a satisfied laziness. She did not mind it. In fact, Frau Krüger hoped they were able to open a new inn and settle once more into a simple life after this.

"You mean I would have perished," she said softly.

Her husband glanced back at her and sighed. "I could not take the risk," he said quietly. "I have the proper spell, but it is complicated, and you know magic."

"Magic works in its own time," she said, parroting what he had told her a thousand times. He nodded.

"My grandmother will know, and she will help," he said.

"Yes," Frau Krüger agreed. "The question is how much will she criticize my cooking?"

****

When Edward got back to his hotel, he grabbed his fine kid gloves and the yellow flowers or euphorbias that the Roma had given him. Then he went to Tilton's rooms. Tilton was sitting up with a book spread across his lap staring at the farnblume, the magic flower dried and flattened now from a few days between its pages. *When did my life become all about magic flowers?* Edward wondered.

"Did you find it?" Tilton asked, snapping the book shut and enclosing the farnblume once more. Edward held up the diamond, and Tilton's face relaxed into a smile.

"I told you," he said.

"You did," Edward agreed, grabbing an empty wash basin and bringing it over to the bed. "Now, I need your help."

Carefully, Edward placed the diamond into the bowl and handed the bowl off to Tilton, who moved his book onto the bed beside him. Meanwhile, Edward put on his gloves and took out the euphorbias from the bag he'd kept them in since the Roma camp. In the forefront of his mind, he was very aware of the Roma's warning about how poisonous the little flowers were and careful not to let any part of the plant touch his skin. Then he unsheathed his dagger.

"What should I do?" Tilton asked, holding the bowl.

"Make sure I cover the entire heart," Edward said, putting his blade to the stem.

Tilton held out his hand. "Edward, wait! Are you sure? Are you sure we can trust this?"

Edward hesitated, thinking back to that night, to the old Roma woman's face. The grandmother, frightened but knowing. Could he trust her?

"Do I have a choice?" he asked out loud. "If I do not warm her heart…"

Grimacing, Tilton nodded. "Do it," he urged.

Carefully, Edward sliced along the stem of the

plant while holding it over the bowl. A thick milk erupted like white blood from the flower. Edward directed the stream of liquid as best he could while holding the flower just below the bud, almost daintily, aware of its poisonous nature. Tilton tilted the basin in different directions, making sure the milky sap trickling down covered the diamond completely. In the end, the red diamond sat in a shallow pool with more dribbling down like liquid lace around its edges.

"Now what?" Tilton asked, as Edward carefully wrapped the remnants of the flower in a handkerchief for disposal.

"I do not know," Edward said.

As the last word escaped his mouth, the white liquid abruptly burst in a flash of flames. Pink smoke curled from the bowl as both men reared back. Another instant and it was gone. Edward crept forward. The liquid had vanished, and the heart seemed shiny and new. Hesitantly, he plucked the heart from the bowl and even through his gloves felt a steady warmth.

Eyes wide he stared at Tilton. "It's almost hot," he said.

Tilton studied it and then met Edward's eyes. "She said it would not last though, correct? Edward, we need to leave as soon as possible."

Chapter Forty-Six

August 30, 1789
The von Croy Mansion, Vienna

Phoebe fanned herself, but it was entirely an affectation. She was not sweating, and the evening was refreshingly cool. No, she was simply bored. Everyone kept making such a fuss, but she was *fine*. And Edward's man, Halkerstone was making much of a spectacle of a fainting spell. That is what Phoebe had decided had happened. She had not told the doctor of the vision, because that would be foolhardy indeed. She had certainly not shared her experience with Halkerstone. No, Phoebe understood that verbalizing her experience would merely put her in the category of histrionic women, and she had no interest in that.

Honestly, though, Phoebe pondered that her vision sounded more probable than Halkerstone's. Assassins! She had half a mind to send him away. She did not know what to make of such assertions. Either Edward had gone mad or the world had. If not for Rhys's letter insisting that she keep Halkerstone around, she would have dismissed him immediately.

Meanwhile, Frederick, the one person who was supposed to be her steady and consistent foundation in all this, was acting incredibly dense. It was frustrating. Phoebe had half a mind to send him away as well, and he was royalty.

"Are you sure you are well, my dear?" he asked for the third time.

"Quite well," she lied, flapping her fan in agitation. If he asked her one more time, she was going to hit him over the head with it.

Phoebe paused. She hadn't felt this, well, anything in a long while. Not angry, not sad…other than those moments when *himself* had exposed part of her heart to some insane danger. Tonight, however, she had experienced the strangest sensation of *heat* earlier as she prepared for her evening out. Mary had noticed Phoebe had even become flushed and needed a bit of powdering. Now, Phoebe was irritated, nay, angry and frustrated and fidgety.

What could be causing these sensations?

Her mind, entirely of its own accord, skittered to Edward. Was he…doing something?

No, she decided eventually. Edward might believe she was in danger, but he did not believe in the supernatural. And yet he had been attacked by an evil spirit. She had seen his face. He'd been gobsmacked. Phoebe snorted inelegantly and then blushed when Frederick turned to her.

"You know," she said. "I *am* feeling not quite myself. Please excuse me?"

He half stood, offering to escort her, but she belayed his fears and slipped out quietly.

Phoebe left the box seat of the performance and wandered down to the lobby. She ordered a footman to bring the carriage around. It was hours before the performance would be over, so she had no doubt there was enough time for it to drop her off at home and come back for Frederick.

A few moments later, the footman escorted her outside to the carriage and helped her ascend inside. Once safely ensconced, the carriage lurched into motion. All the while, Phoebe considered her current predicament. Or, rather, Edward's.

Could he believe now? He'd leapt into the sea to retrieve her heart. At the time, she suppositioned he'd acted more out of sentimentality than proactive fear. Edward may have claimed he felt nothing for her, but Phoebe knew that she hadn't been misled in his feelings. His reasoning for letting her go was, of course, absurd, but also extremely English and oh so Edward. It showcased that sentimentality did not really align with his personality. And yet his face. The fact that Edward, somehow and for reasons unexplained, had been in mortal danger in a cemetery at night battling an evil spirit of some sort seemed to disprove Phoebe's assertion that Edward did not believe. And Halkerstone's presence? Obviously, Edward believed something was afoot.

Could there be a world where Edward Pierce, tenth Marquess of Winchester, actually believed in myth? And, if that was the case, should Phoebe care? He had cast her off for feeling. He had striven to make her feel guilty for actually adoring her first husband who had treated her so tenderly. No, she and Lukas had not been a love match, but he had been a wonderful man, and Phoebe owed no one, least of all Edward Pierce, the stupid, inane, arrogant tenth Marquess of Winchester, an explanation for her romantic past!

Nor did she owe him any fealty or affection though she had saved his life. *But only to rub it in his face later,* she told herself. *I can do whatever I please,* she determined.

As if response, the carriage lurched to a halt. There were shouts and then gunfire. Phoebe jumped in terror and dove to the floor in between the benches. She grabbed the tiny dagger that was most assuredly *not* supposed to be part of her hair decorations and brandished it in front of her while holding her breath. The door opened a moment later, and Mr. Halkerstone poked his head in.

"Milady? You all right?" he asked. He took in her position and the dagger held out in front of her and wisely chose not to comment.

Phoebe cleared her throat to work moisture back down into it. When was the last time she felt such fear? Oh, that's right, when Edward had almost drowned her. "Well enough, Mr. Halkerstone," she said, sitting up. "Trouble, I take it?"

"Nothing that couldn't be handled," he said.

"I do not remember you coming as escort to the theater," she said, reprove in her voice.

"And yet I'm here," he said, grinning. He was almost handsome when he smiled, and he reminded her of Edward for some reason. "Do you need a hand back up? We should get you home." He didn't say it, but the unspoken, "home to safety" was there.

Phoebe took his offered hand and managed to regain the bench despite her many layers.

"Thank you, Mr. Halkerstone," she said, trying for the calm and cool temperament that had seemed so easy before tonight.

He nodded and shut the door. A moment later, the carriage was in motion again, and Phoebe let out a long breath. Perhaps assassins were not so outrageous a concern as she first supposed. Phoebe rearranged her skirts and decided to blame Edward for everything. If she could blame him and regain her icy composure, then life would surely return to normal. By the time the carriage arrived back home, however, Phoebe only felt warmer.

Chapter Forty-Seven

September 1, 1789
Hotel Willkommen Komfort

The next morning, Tilton was already awake and directing the servants to see to his packing by the time Edward made an appearance. The young lordling was dressed and standing, well, leaning on the bureau. His vest was unbuttoned, and Edward could see the bulk of bandages disrupting Tilton's usual slim silhouette.

"We have to get on the road, Edward," Tilton said. "I've already ordered the carriage."

"You can barely move out of that bed," Edward answered chagrined.

"Luckily, I will not be moving, the horses will," Tilton said amiably.

Before Edward could argue the point further, a servant appeared with two letters on a tray.

"God, please tell me one of those is not from my father nagging again," Tilton said darkly.

"No," Edward said, studying the handwriting. He tore open the first, scanning the contents. It was perhaps the oddest piece of correspondence Edward had ever received, so it suited the journey admirably in this regard, and it was from Rhys.

The contents caused Edward to see Miss Gordon in a new light. He could not imagine the young lady, so prim and proper, organizing an attack, nor anyone she was related to. *But I have seen more from any number of husband-hunting females over the years.* Yes, the ton had driven home the point that husband-seeking women were very dangerous predators. Besides, Rhys had mentioned he'd sent someone to Phoebe. If his friend was that concerned, Rhys must have had real evidence of a betrayal. Edward handed Tilton the letter after he was done.

"Bad news?" Tilton prompted taking it.

"I do not even know how to qualify it," Edward said.

As he did, Edward took up the second letter and opened it. It was a quick note from Saint Germaine with apologies for the hasty disappearance. Oddly, it seemed to back up Rhys's claims that Edward's quest was in danger of being derailed by aggressive forces. Another piece of paper folded inward detailed the ritual for bringing the heart back to life, and Edward sat down heavily as he read over it.

The servants finished their packing, as both Tilton and Edward carried so little with them at this point, and scurried out.

"Well, this is barmy," Tilton said, finishing up Rhys's letters. "Ex-lover's vengeance, ancient family scandals, and now sabotage? My, my, Winchester, I'm not sure I could write a more thrilling adventure than the one we find ourselves in."

"It gets worse," Edward said softly, handing over Saint Germaine's letter.

Tilton glanced over it and then the ritual.

"But this says you have to cut open your own chest," he protested. "Who survives that?" he demanded.

Edward stared at the floor. It was a sacrifice. And it made sense that the only way to prove love was through sacrifice. It made a keen and macabre sense. To warm a heart, one must risk their own heart. Just as Phoebe had risked her heart by offering it to him and in turn been irrevocably damaged from it, he must risk an equal amount of damage and, quite possibly, death.

"It balances the scales," Edward said, softly.

"It's hogwash," Tilton said disgustedly, throwing the ritual away. "Don't tell me you believe this madman? There's not even anything here about the damn flower."

"Maybe he lied about the farnblume to give himself time to get away," Edward said. "He did mention someone threatened him and his wife. Who knows, Tilton? But he sent us the ritual anyway. What choice do I have?"

"A lot of choices," Tilton exclaimed. "The first of which is to go speak with Lady von Croy. Listen, we do not know anything of her feelings as yet. We may arrive in Austria, and your fair maiden may set her eyes upon you and fall madly in love again."

Edward shook his head. "I hurt her, Tilton. And I meant to."

"Yes, and you owe her an apology for that, not your life," Tilton argued. "None of this." He gestured disgustedly at the ritual. "This does not sit right with me, Edward. It doesn't fit. Besides, you did not even pay Saint Germaine. What man sends a ritual without payment?" Edward did not answer. Tilton bit his lip and reread Rhys's letter. "Do you really think this Miss Gordon and her family are capable of setting up the attack on the road from Hamburg?"

Edward considered all the facts given. If it was a plot by Miss Gordon's family, they would have had to have acted swiftly and decisively. And they'd have had to know where he was going. Only a few had known: Halkerstone, Rhys. These were two men Edward trusted with his life. He frowned. *Count Cagliostro knew*. Edward did not trust the man.

"Maybe," he said in answer to Tilton's question and explained about the count.

For once, Tilton glanced around suspiciously. He hobbled over to the door leading out to the sitting room, checking for ears, and then firmly closed it.

"Well," he said, "we have two advantages."

"What, pray tell, are they?" Edward asked feeling, not for the first time, entirely out of his depth.

"The first is that these people do not know that we know something is afoot," Tilton said quietly. "Which means we have an element of surprise to counteract their plans."

"The second?" Edward prompted.

"Me and my years of experience sneaking around," he said.

Any other time Edward would have chuckled, but he was overwhelmed.

"Do not worry, Edward, we will make it to Austria," Tilton promised.

"Oh, we will make it if I have to kill every person who steps in my way," Edward said evenly. "I just feel as if…as if the entire world is conspiring against me. Is that insane?"

"Well, you are walking around with a piece of your former paramour's heart tucked into your waistcoat,"

Tilton pointed out.

Edward had no reply to the truth in that statement.

"You're going to have to follow my lead, even if it sounds ludicrous. Can you do that?" Tilton asked, quirking an eyebrow in challenge.

"Of course," Edward said with a firm nod. "I trust you with my life."

"Out of Hell?" Tilton asked.

Taking a deep breath, Edward threw back his shoulders and nodded firmly. "Out of Hell it is," he replied.

****

It turned out, Tilton was serious about the ludicrousness of his plan, but Edward could not fault its effectiveness in confusing whoever might be trying to sabotage him. It certainly confused him.

After settling the bill with the hotel and a quick breakfast, Edward and Tilton loaded into the coach they'd hired for the long journey to Vienna. But halfway to the city limits in Berlin, Tilton stopped the driver, and they disembarked. They waited until the carriage was out of sight, and then Tilton hailed a hackney, which brought them to the docks. This was made far easier now that Tilton's luggage consisted of a single bag. Edward cringed to think if they were still doing this with a carriage full of trunks. From there, they boarded a small fishing vessel, Edward carrying both their luggage since Tilton's injuries prevented him. The captain ferried them downriver as far southeast as he could manage.

As the water passed, Edward spent his time trying to compose a speech for when he was once again in Phoebe's presence. Tilton passed the time equally between reading from the book he'd brought and staring at the farnblume pressed into its pages. Edward had noticed Tilton kept the book on his person, though he'd no notion why. Neither of them knew what power, if any, the flower contained. And neither of them could properly manipulate it even if they did. Edward reasoned Tilton kept the flower nearby because it had physically cost him.

His perfectly unblemished looks were now blemished by a massive scar across his chest. True, his face was as fine as before, but a scar was a scar, and Tilton's had not even healed yet.

"Edward," Tilton said quietly. "I have been contemplating the situation."

"How do you ever have the energy?" Edward drolled.

"I'm younger and more handsome," Tilton replied back immediately. Edward snorted. "So it has occurred to me part of the problem may be in your name."

"My name?" Edward asked, not following.

Tilton glanced at him. "Yes, Edward, your name. The Winchester name. It *is* fairly heavy and catches a lot of attention. Perhaps you should shed it until this errand is done."

There was cold logic in Tilton's thinking, and Edward nodded.

"I'll be the Earl of Hereford's son," Edward decided. "His name is also Edward, so no worries there. But he's on the Continent looking for new ventures for his father. It's plausible and somewhat truthful."

Tilton nodded with approval. "I'm going to take on the role of Lord Ashby," Tilton said grinning. Ashby was a dandy of the top order, well-known for getting into all kinds of scrapes.

"It suits you a little too well," Edward said.

The boat dropped them off at a tiny village on the edge of Lake Krüpelsee. It didn't take them long to find a farmer willing to take them on to the next town, and in this way, they leapfrogged for a few days, changing modes of transportation often. Five days later, dirty, exhausted, and looking very much the worse for wear, the two noblemen arrived in Vienna looking not like noblemen at all. And so their entrance into the city escaped the notice of those watching the gates.

Part Three

Chapter Forty-Eight

September 4, 1789
On the border of the Holy Roman Empire

The Comte de Saint Germaine held very still and listened. He was always surprised when people failed to listen. So many people lacked that basic skill and missed so much of the world because of it. Sound was the first giveaway for someone sneaking up on you. It was the sense that told him where to hunt and who to trust. It was what had made him love the forest and city in equal measure. It was what had introduced him to the spirit world. He tilted his head straining.

Beside him, his wife breathed slowly and waited. Saint Germaine had never thought he'd fall in love. That had never been part of the plan. It had always been to lie and cheat his way through Europe, duping the doshmen and taking more than he gave away. And then he'd met her, his Bella, his love. What a smart, challenging, infuriating woman. Her instincts had not been honed in the forest, but she was a survivor. She was blessed with the skills on whom to woo, to manipulate, to act, and most importantly, to be still. Now she held his heart in a hidden pocket in the fold of her skirts, close to her juncture of her legs. It was a fitting place.

Finally, the sound reached Saint Germaine's ears.

Bells tinkling, but a particular set of chimes. It was his grandmother's favorite wind sprite dancing nearby, protecting the campsite. They were close.

"A mile maybe," Saint Germaine whispered, pointing. "We should hit scouts soon."

Less than a mile of walking and the sound of dogs barking greeted them. Two huge mastiffs broke through the forest snarling and growling until Saint Germaine crouched and held out his hand. They whined and nuzzled at him. He scratched behind their ears. The big softies both fell over, exposing their bellies for more rubs.

"Didn't expect to see you two so soon," Dearg stated, slipping through the trees like a shadow.

"Ran into a bit of trouble in Berlin," Saint Germaine said with a shrug. "Had to slip away fast."

"She was expecting someone," Dearg said, nodding. "Come on. Food's almost ready."

Despite the years since Saint Germaine had seen the wagons, little had changed. The campsite was set up as usual, a circle of wagons with a bonfire in the middle. Break out fires were placed at the perimeter. Children ran free, giggling and playing with the dogs or practicing different skills from magic to music.

The shadows of the trees slanted with the afternoon sun across the campsite, and Saint Germaine realized he'd forgotten how beautiful it was. This freedom, this way of life. It wasn't easy, by any means, but there was comfort in belonging.

"So, it's you," his grandmother, the Bulibasha, said with a grunt. "Come inside. Have some stew."

The stew was a delicious venison with root vegetables and spices from lands farther than most had ever traveled. His Bella drank copious amounts of water, unused to the level of heat while his grandmother grumbled about unseasoned crud that outsiders ate. Saint Germaine actually loved Bella's cooking. It wasn't bad; it was just different. But that was not something he could tell his family. They thought everyone else's food was too salty or dull to even consider.

"What brings you home?" Bulibasha asked finally.

Saint Germaine didn't hold back. He told the story, all of it, while Bella curled up on the bed drowsy with food and exhausted from the trip. When he was done, his grandmother pursed her lips.

"We met this outsider," she said. "On the road near Hamburg. Dearg, stupid boy that he is, killed one of his companions and stole the stone heart."

Saint Germaine sucked in a breath. "How did he get it back then?"

"He stormed the camp," she said. "He wants to fix it badly."

"I'm not sure he can," Saint Germaine said. "It was cold, Grandmother, but he has had at least one vision of her holding it close. There is a strong connection there, though he denies it."

She nodded. "I gave him spurge flowers to add some heat, and you gave him the ritual. He must figure out his own way now." Saint Germaine nodded. The toff had mentioned the flowers, but had he used them?

"The forces against him are powerful," Saint Germaine said. "This bitter revenge has grown black over thirty years. The spirits tell me her name is Lady Eleanor Argent. She has attacked our people twice now. Her man threatened me and my wife, and this stone

322

heart lover of the toff's."

"Argent?" Bulibasha asked, perking up. "Then it is three times," she said. "She was a lady in France. Threw the Doe family off her land with men on horseback and guns. Killed two of theirs. Blamed her husband's death on them while she ran away with his gold. This one needs attending."

"I will do whatever you need," Saint Germaine promised. "But we must continue on to Vienna in a few days."

"Why?"

Saint Germaine hesitated. "He pulls at me, this man. Or maybe it's the lover." Saint Germaine sounded puzzled. "They have been pulling at me since the day he walked into my inn. You told me to trust my instincts."

Bulibasha nodded. "Well, she has the giant's blood same as us," she said. "We made promises to protect our people, so we will help these two and balance the scales. Let us divine a fitting punishment for this Argent before you go."

"She is in England," he said. "What kind of magic will reach over that distance and still strike her?"

"You must trust in the magic, grandson," she snapped. "Here, we will start with dreams, and then we will build some nightmares."

Chapter Forty-Nine

September 7, 1789
Earl of Huntley Townhouse, London

Ann found her Auntie Eleanor lounging on a divan in the reading room, staring out the window at the puffy clouds running across the sky. It was one of those uncommonly beautiful days with the sun shining, the temperature at the perfect pitch between autumn crisp and summer warmth. An open letter sat quite forgotten on her lap. Ann studied the letter circumspectly. Cheap, thin rice paper with sloppy handwriting in brown ink.

"News, Auntie?" Ann inquired, unable to keep her curiosity at bay.

Auntie Eleanor turned, a pleased smile dancing across her pouty lips. She made a humming noise of assent. "Yes, darling. I do believe the Lord Marquess will be returned to you within the month. Any day now, the Lord Marquess will quit the Continent and come home quite heartbroken. I trust you can take him in hand from there?"

There was an underlying threat in that, and Ann swallowed around a sudden dryness in her mouth. She nodded. Her aunt studied her.

"You look tired, my dear," Auntie Eleanor said. "Are you feeling quite well?"

"Quite well," Ann lied, putting on her best smile.

In truth, she had not slept in some time. It was like a demon haunted her dreams. For the last few nights, she'd had nothing but nightmares about her future, and with every terrible event that unfolded before her sleeping mind, her auntie dearest was to blame. In one, all of Ann's hair fell out, and it was after her auntie forced some horrid new French soap on her that they later found to be laced with poison from the horrible French peasants. In another, they lost all their money after her auntie dearest gambled it away. In yet another, a scandal of epic proportions unfolded as Auntie was accused of murdering the Marchioness of Winchester and caught!

The last one struck a particular nerve as Ann woke feeling quite certain that Auntie Eleanor was capable of such grotesquerie. Three nights in a row as if some terrible cloud followed her. And for three days, Ann had tried her best to dispel the dreams. After that last one, she felt driven, *driven* to find the truth. A truth. Any truth as to what her aunt was up to.

Ann cast about for an opportunity. "I was going to take a stroll about the garden," she said. "Did you want to join me?"

"No, darling, I have an appointment at the modiste," Auntie Eleanor said. "We're all going to need new clothes for your wedding," she said, a triumphant smile on her lips.

A maid appeared in the door carrying a shawl and bonnet. Lady Eleanor rose gracefully, setting aside the letter to affix the shawl around her. Then she took up the letter again, folded it, clearly intending to put it away before she left. Ann knew her aunt would lock it in her writing desk in the corner of the room. She curtsied and made her excuses, gliding toward the back of the house where the door let out to the gardens. As soon as she turned a corner, she ducked into the servant's staircase and waited until she heard the front door open and close.

Steps coming down the stairs above her drove Ann out of her hiding place, but she set her shoulders back, took a steadying breath, and glided back to her aunt's reading room in case a servant caught a glimpse of her. At the door, she glanced back, but whoever it was had continued down into the kitchen. There were no servants to witness her slip inside the reading room. She closed the door quietly behind her, and mindful of being caught in Lady Winchester's household by that dreadful man, she locked the door.

Turning around, she slowly glided to the window and peered out, catching sight of her aunt's carriage as it turned the corner. Reassured, Ann went over to the writing desk.

Ann, of course, was a very proper young lady, and she had always striven to maintain the image of English perfection. She'd become quite good at it. But when she was at finishing school, she'd met a few girls who were from lesser families. One, in particular, had had a special skill set involving locks and stealing. For Ann, finishing school was boring. She'd the type of body and manner that pleased people, and the teachers there were no different. So the introduction of learning to pick locks had been mostly to abort boredom and see the consequences should she ever get caught. She had gotten through all of finishing school and two years afterward without any mistakes. Up until a few weeks ago, she had never been caught.

It was a skill she rarely used. Being the daughter of an earl simply afforded her everything she wanted, let alone needed. But every now and then, Ann had found it useful. And since she could still find no one to explain to her *why* her auntie was so hellbent on this marriage, Ann decided it was time to go to the source.

Auntie Eleanor's desk was a beautiful mahogany piece with a top that came down over the writing space and locked as well as four drawers underneath, two on the left and two on the right. First, Ann opened the top. Here she found the desk organized and neat. There were six smaller drawers tucked behind the writing space. These drawers held materials: fresh red wax, twine, dried lavender to decorate correspondence, a small perfume bottle to mist the page, ebony India ink, and a beautifully carved pen with an extra sharp nib.

Four slots sat next to these tiny drawers. Two of the slots were occupied by sheaves of unused paper the color of fresh cream. The other two held household bills. Nothing of consequence here. She closed the top and locked it. Next, she searched the drawers.

The two on the left were unlocked. One held playbills as auntie was a fan of the stage. Another held her aunt's latest embroidery loop and extra floss. The top drawer on the right took a few minutes to pick. Once opened, Ann found a collection of letters in neat bundles, all bound by twine and piece of heavy parchment on top indicating the year.

Choosing the last year, Ann untied it and shuffled through finding mostly letters from acquaintances, some from Ann's cousin Peter at Eton. Near the bottom she found a very lurid letter from a married earl here in England addressed to Auntie right before she fled

France. It was clear that this wasn't the first exchange between them. *And her husband still alive at that point,* Ann thought. She tucked that letter into the front of her corset and retied the twine. She browsed the other stacks but none of the paper or handwriting matched the one she'd seen on her aunt's lap. Closing the drawer, she regarded the bottom drawer.

The lock gave way after a bit of wiggling, but inside, she only found bank notes and a pouch of spare coins. Ann stared at the drawer in consternation. *I know it's in here,* she thought. Sitting back, she stared at the drawer, then the desk, eyes combing the details for a sign of where her aunt might have hidden the note. Her eyes returned to the drawer, speculatively. She picked up the bag of coins and the bank notes and put them on the floor. Sticking her hand in, she felt along the top of the drawer above for a catch or lever but found nothing. She stared into the empty drawer, and it occurred to her how shallow the inside of the drawer was compared to how deep its facade implied.

She felt along the velvet-lined bottom until her fingers found a stray piece of ribbon in the exact color as the velvet, perfectly camouflaged from eyes. Tugging it, the bottom of the drawer lifted out and revealed an entire stack of *other* letters. On top, of course, was the cheap rice paper with messy brown handwriting.

It was a short note from a man named Cliff promising that he'd successfully delayed Edward and killed his hope. He also pointed out that a man named Saint Germaine had slipped through his fingers, but he sent the letter that would end his life anyway. Ann's eyes widened. Killing a man seemed a bit overdramatic.

She put that down and took out another note. This was from the same writer, explaining how some of the men he'd hired had almost killed Edward. Ann's stomach sank. She did not want Edward to die. She did not want to marry him *that* much. Setting that aside, she picked up another note. This was from someone else in Vienna, illustrating that they'd attempted to kill a Lady von Croy in her carriage but had been foiled. At this point, Ann's hands began to shake. She read every letter, all more serious than the last.

One outlined success in killing her uncle, Peter's father and Auntie Eleanor's husband, and demanded payment for the job. Another described success at stealing letters from Lady von Croy and planting them in the marquess's house. There were older notes, older crimes. Correspondence with unsavory types for any number of unpardonable offences.

Ann had always known her aunt to be a woman of means and ambition. She had never guessed she was so cruel and tactical in her methods. *A lady does not rely on savage miscreants and physical violence to get her way,* Ann thought. *She relies on her feminine beauty and subtle maneuvering. What's worse is she risks us all in a scandal by her heavy-handed tactics!*

Ann could only imagine the gossip rags if they got wind of this. Why, if someone found out even a portion of this, the entire family would be ruined. Ann would never marry. Her sisters would never marry. Her mother and father would be turned out of every drawing room in the whole of England.

And to go up against the Marquess of Winchester? What would he do if he found out? Ann did not know Edward very well, but she knew him well enough to know he'd hunt down any who transgressed against his family. Besides, his best friend was the Duke of Brey! They had made better before Edward left, or so the rumormongers said. What would he do?

Images of a gibbet floated to mind. Brey was wily and politically connected. He would certainly have her father killed.

Ann paused.

Edward *was* best friends with the renowned Duke of Brey, a man lauded for his savvy political maneuverings. And if Edward's horrible Mr. Halkerstone had informed him or the Duke of Brey of Ann's faux paus, why they could be on to them already. She had not told her aunt that she'd been caught snooping—she'd have to explain why. Now, she realized how fortuitous that had been. This might still be salvageable, but she needed to get *ahead* of it.

Gathering the letters up, Ann bound them with some twine. She fixed the velvet bottom back into place and restored the bank notes and coins into the drawer. Then, gripping her lettered package, she quietly exited the reading room. Glancing about, she found herself alone. She returned to her rooms and stuffed the letters into a large reticule, then pulled the rope to summon a maid.

"Send my card around to the Duchess of Brey, please," she ordered.

Then Ann set about selecting a suitable gown for an afternoon assignation with the man who might save her future, or destroy it entirely.

Chapter Fifty

September 7, 1789
Brey House, London

Rhys, the Duke of Brey, was enjoying a quiet lunch with his wife, when his butler brought a card round.

"Who is it from, darling?" he asked lightly.

Cecilia broke the seal and scanned the contents. "Miss Gordon," she said, frowning. "I know the name, but I cannot remember when we were introduced."

At the name, Rhys's senses came into sharp focus. He did not blink out of place, but his mind caught fire, wondering at the possibilities.

"We were introduced at the opera, I think," he reminded her. "She was on Edward's arm."

"Ah yes." Cecilia smiled and then frowned again. She had an adorable frown. Rhys had always loved it on her. Of course, he preferred her smile, but he did like her frown. "But, Rhys, that was a very awkward interaction."

"It was indeed," Rhys agreed, thinking back. "Dearest, I wonder if I might sit with you when Miss Gordon comes to call. I feel it will be…illuminating."

Cecilia, who knew her husband's moods and smiles and the assorted twinkles he kept carefully banked in his eyes, spied one of indulgence and mischief.

"Darling, you may, of course, stay to greet Miss Gordon with me, but if you make her cry or, I don't know, have her arrested, I shall be cross."

Rhys's smile grew, and he winked.

****

When Miss Gordon was shown into the sitting room, Rhys was full to the top with curiosity. It did not show. He would not be so droll as to display his interest. Instead, he stood from the couch beside his wife and bowed.

"Your Graces." She curtsied. She was, Rhys reflected, very pretty. There was a classic quality to her beauty that he could not deny. It made his distrust of her grow.

"Miss Gordon, so good of you to call upon us," Cecilia said, ever attempting to put people at their ease.

"It is my pleasure," she said demurely.

Miss Gordon then proceeded to engage Cecilia in a clever if superficial conversation on the news of the ton. The two ladies went back and forth for a quarter of an hour while Rhys lounged. He made agreeable noises and nodded at the appropriate places, but what took up most of his attention was her reticule. It sat on the couch beside her, something poking against the fabric sides in a way that suggested a stack of papers.

As the conversation came to a natural lull, Miss Gordon turned to Rhys directly.

"I confess, Your Grace, I have other reasons for calling on you," she said. "I was wondering if you have word from the marquess? I worry about him."

Rhys kept his smile in place, but there was something about the way she tilted her head at him that he decided to indulge.

"Indeed, I received a letter today," he lied easily. "Would you like to see? There is a most amusing tale of the hotel staff mixing up his luggage."

"I would love to read it," she agreed.

"Darling, we will not be but a minute," he promised.

As he led Miss Gordon out of the receiving room, he threw another wink over his shoulder at his wife. He signaled one of the footmen to follow at a discreet pace and stand guard. His staff were trained in more than service and compensated accordingly. Rhys also left the door to his study open. One could never be too careful with a gentlewoman's reputation.

"Now, Miss Gordon," Rhys said, gesturing for her to take a seat. "Do tell me why you have really come."

For the first time, she seemed uncertain. Rhys couldn't tell if it was a talent for acting or genuine. She plucked at invisible lint on her skirt, shifting on the leather chair in front of him.

"You must understand," she said, keeping her voice pitched low, "my only desire is to secure a good match and uphold my family's name."

"As is the desire for any well-bred woman," Rhys agreed.

"Yes," she said and continued, "but perhaps I have come to discover certain family members have been, shall we say, too ambitious to help me meet this goal. I was unaware of the…" She hesitated. "Lengths to which some people went. Lines were crossed."

"And yet you seem to cross some lines quite willingly," he said, narrowing his eyes at her.

Her cheeks blushed. "He left without a word to me," she said, eyes hardening. "A shrug off from a man in his position is not a small thing, even for a woman of my breeding. I only wanted to know where and why but I would never—" She cut off abruptly.

Rhys considered. She was taking a chance coming to him. She knew his reputation and his friendship with Edward, and she must know he could use her misstep against her. But apparently, there was a line that Ann Gordon *would* not cross. She was somewhat brave. He had to give her credit there.

"I assume you have brought me proof," he said, eyes straying to the reticule she clutched in her lap.

Miss Gordon's chin rose haughtily. "Perhaps," she said. "You are a man of means and guile, Your Grace. If *anyone* can handle this quietly and, perhaps"—she wet her lips—"acknowledge our friendship at a party, I would be willing to provide quite a bit of evidence."

Brave and clever, he amended. She was asking for a step stool in society. And she was correct. Some people had taken Edward's leaving of her without blinking as Miss Gordon continued her attentions at the Winchester house, it seemed all was still well. However, there were rumors. Edward's reputation was turning to rake, and Miss Gordon, it was rumored, was his latest conquest. But if Rhys as the Duke of Brey acknowledged her, then whether or not she was on Edward's arm, Miss Gordon would be a woman to know. And she was asking him to keep scandal away from her family name. That would take quite a bit of maneuvering if she had real evidence against Lady Eleanor.

"I can commit to those stipulations," he agreed. "As long as your evidence is compelling."

Miss Gordon studied his face and then nodded

firmly. She opened the clasp on her reticule and withdrew a stack of letters bound by twine.

"I found these in a secret compartment in her desk," she said. "They detail quite a few sins."

Rhys took the stack of letters, untied the twine, and picked up the top one. He scanned the contents with a frown. Putting that aside, he picked up another, and his eyes narrowed. When he looked up, there was rage in his eyes.

"Swear on the Lord God that you did *not* know what she ordered," he demanded.

"I did not," Miss Gordon said, eyes wide. "I swear. She kept pushing me to visit the marchioness and insisted Edward would come home soon heartbroken. She never said how or why. I could not, for the life of me, figure out *why* she was so obsessed with him. Why did it have to be Edward?"

"Because twenty years ago Edward's father cut her off abruptly to marry the marchioness," Rhys said. "It was quite a scandal and ruined her chances at a match. She was the pearl of the season, but by the end no one wanted her. She went to the Continent to find a foreign nobleman to wed, which she did. I will not say the late marquess handled things well, because he did not. But that does not justify the ruination of another woman, especially my cousin!"

Rhys slammed his fist down on the desk.

Miss Gordon jumped. "I did not know," she said, terrified.

Rhys studied her and believed her. Her actions in Lady Winchester's study were too amateurish. Besides, Lady Eleanor would never put her niece in a position to be caught when she clearly could pay off a peasant or person in service. Miss Gordon was trying to buy her way out of the scandal, and Rhys could not blame her. In her shoes, he would do the same.

"Very well," he said reining in his temper. "I will take care of this quietly. Do not tell your aunt we have spoken, and do not alert her that things have changed. I am sure you are quite good at playing the perfect niece."

"Thank you, Your Grace," Miss Gordon said, standing hurriedly and dipping a curtsy. Even in a hasty rush, it was perfect. She was gone in the next moment. The footman glanced in, and Rhys signaled him to follow her out. Then he stood and went back to the receiving room.

"Is everything all right?" Cecilia asked. "Miss Gordon said a quick goodbye and then disappeared with unseemly haste."

"No, my darling, things are decidedly not fine," he said, leaning down and kissing her gently. "I am going to have to have a woman killed."

"Oh dear," she said. "Miss Gordon?" she whispered.

"No," he said. "Her aunt. We will see Miss Gordon in social situations in the future and treat her with respect."

"A bargain?" Cecilia asked. "What did she bring?"

"Evidence that Lady Eleanor is behind Phoebe's ruination amongst other things."

Cecilia thought on that a moment and nodded. "Well," she said, picking up her embroidery loop. "It would be better if it were not done in London. Perhaps, she should take a journey back to France? Terrible things are happening there I've heard."

Rhys turned the idea over in his mind and nodded slowly. "An accident would be an elegant solution," he agreed.

Chapter Fifty-One

September 7, 1789
Vienna

They had made it at long last. It had taken them almost a week, but they finally arrived on a crisp day with blue skies and bright clouds. The air was starting to turn toward autumn, the day's heat dropping off to a cool twilight sooner.

The instant they set foot beyond the city's gates, Edward wanted to go straight to Phoebe's house, but Tilton stopped him.

"You smell like a four-day-old cow pad, and your suit, honestly, is in a state, Edward," he said. "No woman, no matter how handsome or rich you are, is going to take you in like that. Come on. We must recover."

Edward wanted to move forward now that they were *here* at last but did not argue. The travel had been hard on Tilton, but he was bearing up well. They had taken wagons and hired second-rate coaches, trying to stay hidden from their enemies. Despite the lack of riding, the constant jolting of their conveyances had not been especially restful. Tilton was still pale and weak. His burn wound was slowly healing over, but it pained him a great deal. A good rest in a comfortable bed would do wonders for him.

Like a bloodhound on the scent, Tilton found them a nice hotel, not the nicest, but nice nevertheless. They rented a suite again with two rooms, ordered hot baths, hotter meals, and sent a card around for a tailor. As sunset painted the whitewashed buildings outside orange and then red, Tilton sighed back into a couch looking well pleased with the world.

For all the struggle and hardship he'd encountered, there had been a subtle change in Tilton since Berlin. In those quiet moments when no one was watching, his guard went down. Instead of melancholy, he seemed more at peace, relieved even. Edward was grateful to God that he felt it. Tilton's situation was complicated, moreso than anything Edward had encountered, and while he was still trying to puzzle that out, he felt it unfair that Tilton should be in such a position.

To be honest, Edward was surprised at how quickly his disgust and dismay evaporated. The first day out of Berlin, on the boat, he'd asked a couple of tentative questions about Tilton's, well, preferences.

"Edward," Tilton had said. "I am *not* interested in you. You are not my type."

"Well, fine then," Edward said, highly offended. At which point, Tilton laughed at him.

"Are you more angry that you're not my type or that I'm not attracted to you?" he asked unable to hide his mirth.

Which had irritated Edward and he'd said, "I am quite a catch in most circles."

To which Tilton had laughed harder. And then Edward, realizing what he sounded like, starting laughing as well.

Edward found himself academically fascinated.

Once he realized that so many references in his books were referring to men like Tilton, a lot of things made more sense. He could not help his curiosity. He did not realize he was pestering until Tilton had flat out asked if Edward was going to help him catch his next love while they rode in the back of a turnip wagon drawn by a deaf farmer and his deafer wife.

"I...could," Edward said, surprised at the query. Tilton laughed so hard tears started streaming down his face, and Edward, red faced, couldn't help but join in. Few people made him laugh. Fewer still made Edward laugh at himself. Honestly, it was difficult to stay mad at the younger man. He was just so cheerful.

Now that they had made it, that they were *in* Vienna on the cusp of success, Edward wanted to spoil his friend a little.

"Listen," he said. "I have no intuition on how things with Phoebe will turn out. But I know that you are still on your tour, and I have diverted you from quite enough fun. How about I procure us some tickets to the opera for later this week?"

"Oh, you know I love opera! That sounds wonderful," Tilton said.

Edward handed him a glass of wine, and they saluted. "Out of Hell," he said.

"Out of Hell," Tilton repeated the toast and drank.

The tailor showed up early the next morning and took their measurements. There were a number of nearly finished pre-made suits near Tilton's size but nothing in the patterns he wanted. Nothing quite as colorful as Tilton preferred. Nothing was made to fit Edward who was too damnable tall, and so Edward paid extra for some fast work and sent the man on his way.

He just needed one good suit to see Phoebe. He tried not to pace knowing it would take at least another day.

Edward was preparing himself for some serious brooding when a knock at their suite interrupted him. A servant came in followed by Halkerstone.

"Good God, man," Edward said. "What are you doing here?"

Halkerstone seemed to take Edward in in his travel suit, worn and scuffed about the edges despite the laundering. He took in Tilton lounging on the couch, eyes half-lidded almost as if he were falling asleep, but pale and his arm stiff across his injury. And then Halkerstone did a perfunctory bow.

"The Duke of Brey sent me ahead to ensure his cousin's safety," Halkerstone said, eyes flicking back to Tilton.

Edward made quick introductions and told Halkerstone he could speak freely in front of Tilton.

"How did you find me?" Edward asked. "We only just got in last night."

"I had the bank manager notify me when you began drawing on your credit," Halkerstone said. "Going under pseudonyms was smart."

"We've been plagued every leg of our journey," Tilton said. "It seemed the best way to throw off the scent."

"How is Phoebe?" Edward asked, coming forward. "Is she okay?"

"There have been attempts," Halkerstone said darkly. "She's had fainting fits, and I was concerned about poison, but we've found no evidence, and the lady recovered. I hired some local muscle for about the place, but there are disturbing rumors, milord."

"What rumors?"

"There's a price on her head," Halkerstone said bluntly. "A pretty one too."

"Christ," Tilton said, blanching.

"I've got to go see her," Edward said, heading to the door. Halkerstone blocked him.

"She's going out tonight, milord," he said. "With Lord Frederick, the Duke of Styria." Halkerstone stared hard at the floor.

Edward straightened. He knew this was a possibility of course. Phoebe was a beautiful woman with good breeding and plenty of money. Any one of those reasons would attract other suitors. He was sure this Frederick fellow was whom he'd seen in his vision in the garden in Hamburg. It still hurt to hear it spoken out loud.

"Is it serious?" Edward asked.

Halkerstone hesitated. "I don't know," he admitted. "The duke is serious, but Lady von Croy…her heart is not in it, I think."

Tilton shared a meaningful look with Edward that Halkerstone didn't miss.

"That does not mean she won't marry him if he asks," Halkerstone added reluctantly.

"No, I suppose it does not," Edward said softly.

"Calling on her in the afternoon when you"—Halkerstone ran his eyes over Edward's suit again—"are more up to your usual snuff will be best, milord."

A flush crept over Edward's skin. Even his business manager thought he looked a mess. Good Lord, the world had certainly changed.

"You're injured," Halkerstone said to Tilton. It was not a question, but Tilton nodded. "What has happened on your journey?" Halkerstone pressed.

Edward wasn't sure if he was trying to distract them or genuinely curious. But another exchange with Tilton spoke volumes about what they could *not* tell him. Stone hearts, cursed flowers, haunted graveyards, and, oh yes, an insane woman bent on Edward's destruction. At least Halkerstone knew that last part. Still, Edward did his best to relate their misadventures.

Halkerstone listened closely. What Edward did not say, he seemed to read between the lines. Halkerstone did not question the inconsistencies, but he did not miss them either, Edward thought.

At the end, Halkerstone shook his head. "That's quite a tale," he said. "Given who your enemy is, I'm not surprised."

"You don't seem the type of man to be surprised by much, Mr. Halkerstone," Tilton noted.

The business manager grinned at him, and Edward realized Tilton was right. Halkerstone was never surprised, or if he was, he hid it like a well-schooled courtesan. He was decisive and a quick-thinker. In matters of business, he always gave his opinion, and there was always sense, but he never batted an eye if Edward disagreed with him. Edward rarely did. He was not a master of finances, and he bowed to a mind more trained than his in such matters. His father had trusted Halkerstone implicitly. Even his mother went over the finances with the man once a month.

The man's loyalty was a credit, but for the first time Edward realized it was also a little overzealous. Would he have traveled hundreds of miles for another client? He frowned, not liking the idea of questioning Halkerstone's motives, but after the trip he'd had,

Edward was questioning Halkerstone's intentions.

"Mr. Halkerstone," he said, "why are you here?"

"As I said, the Duke of Brey—"

"The Duke of Brey could have sent his own man," Edward said. "Why are *you* here? It is not that I am ungrateful—"

"But you've been chased about long enough to want to know a man's reasons," Halkerstone finished for him. Edward nodded. For the first time ever in his memory, Edward saw Halkerstone hesitate.

"Truth is," he said, "your father, the late marquess, took care of me and my family when we were younger. When he left for the War with the Colonies, I promised to take care of you and your mother. I keep my promises, milord."

Edward nodded slowly. His father had had that effect on people.

"Very well," he said. "Thank you, Mr. Halkerstone. I trust that you will continue to protect her ladyship until tomorrow for me?"

"Of course," Halkerstone said, nodding. "Until tomorrow then."

When he left, Tilton's eyes stared at the door. "Well, he's an interesting chap," he commented.

"Yes," Edward agreed.

"Do you trust him?" Tilton asked.

Edward considered for a few moments. "Up until a few weeks ago, I trusted everyone in my life. That might be a bad habit, but I think Halkerstone is a good man."

"I do not think he said what he wanted to say," Tilton said.

"What do you mean?" Edward asked.

Tilton frowned and chewed his lip with his teeth. "It's just a feeling, but from one person who has hidden his truth for so long, I do not think he answered your question with the answer he wanted to say. Not that he lied, only that…he evaded."

It was something to consider. If Halkerstone had secrets, Rhys would know them. And Rhys would not send a man he did not trust, certainly not with Phoebe's safety. If he was certain of nothing else—and honestly he was not—Edward could trust Rhys's instinct. For now, Edward would trust Halkerstone. Anything else could be solved at a later period. At the moment, he needed to prepare himself.

As if reading his mind, Tilton asked, "What are you going to say to her?"

"I've no damned idea," Edward admitted. He sat down heavily on the couch, considered drinking himself into a stupor, and discarded it immediately. He needed to be sharp tomorrow, to look his best, and the face of a man fighting a hangover was not going to win fair maiden back. But was that what he wanted? Was that what he hoped for? He glanced at his bag where the ritual Saint Germaine had sent sat tucked up amongst his other correspondence. One heart for another.

"Well," Tilton said, drawing his attention back. "Perhaps we should practice. I'm sure someone can go out to fetch a wig for us."

"A wig?" Edward asked, thoroughly confused.

Tilton blinked. "Edward, I cannot play the part of Phoebe without the right wig. Honestly, man, what's wrong with you?"

At that, Edward buried his head in his hands, shoulders heaving with laughter. Tilton grinned on the couch.

When he could speak again, Edward wiped tears from his eyes and held up a beseeching hand. "Tilton, you must promise me something tomorrow: when I go to speak to Phoebe, you *cannot* be in the room. Making me laugh is not what I want to do in the middle of pouring my damned heart out."

"Oh good," Tilton said, relaxing back into the couch. "You've finally admitted you still love her. I was worried I was going to have to beat it out of you tonight. What would happen to your reputation, Winchester, if an injured man beat you near to death?"

But Edward's good humor had fallen away to be replaced by anxiety and fear.

"I thought love had to be perfect," he admitted. "Easy and soft and fitting." He wove his fingers together. "Like a well-tailored suit. My parents seemed to have lived this fairy tale—that perfect love, two souls joining to make one." Edward studied the floral patterns in the carpet. It was Turkish, if he wasn't mistaken, and beautiful if well-worn. "When I found out she'd loved her first husband, I was devastated. I just thought—" He struggled.

"That it should be you and only you in her heart?" Tilton asked.

"Yes!" Edward said, leaping up. "She was the only one for me."

"It's not a contest, Edward," Tilton said with reproach. "I've been in love a dozen times before Bran."

"But was it really love?" Edward challenged.

"A form of it," Tilton said, calmly. "You're right though. There was something easy about Bran. His

346

presence was so restful. It felt deeper, more tangible than the others," Tilton said softly, his eyes faraway. He shook himself before the sadness took over. "Perhaps it was one-sided, or perhaps the purse my father held up was too great for him to turn down."

"Oh, Tilton," Edward said, wincing.

Tilton waved a hand to dismiss the memory of his erstwhile lover. "The point is, you were selfish, Edward. You condemned her for loving, which is the most natural thing in the world, just because she dared love more than you. Despite the very strange circumstances we find ourselves in, this is not a fairy tale."

Edward snorted. "No, it's more like a Scandinavian epic more and more."

"The point is, do not punish her for adding more love to this world, even if, in the end—" Tilton took a deep breath. "—she does not choose you."

They both fell silent after that, lost in memories of love and heartache, loss and grief. Tilton retired early, and Edward followed soon after. As he lay staring at the crescent moon outside, he prayed for guidance before sleep took him.

Chapter Fifty-Two

September 8, 1789
The von Croy Mansion, Vienna

The morning seemed a month long. Breakfast was years. The tailor took eons to complete the last fitting. The only thing Edward took his time in and did not feel it a waste was carefully wrapping Phoebe's broken heart stone in a swath of black velvet and tucking it oh so carefully in his jacket pocket by his own heart. It had cooled over the week it took them to get to Vienna. He could not tell if it was colder than when he first began his journey back on the docks of the Thames in London. There remained a flicker of heat, a tongue in protest or rebellion or, he dared hope, lingering affection.

I do love her, he thought, amazed by this thought. Amazed by his feelings and the insecurities that had kept them locked up for so long because, he realized, that's what they were: fears and insecurities. He had been a fool. Worse than a fool, he had been cruel and ignorant. Not even he was sure he was worthy of redemption.

By the time Edward and Tilton had climbed into the carriage, it was nearing two o'clock and Edward was nearly ready to tear his hair out. With the carriage making pacing impossible, Edward's knee jumped in an uneasy rhythm.

"Be easy, Edward," Tilton murmured as they drew up in front of an elegant white-stoned town home.

"Impossible," he replied.

"Very well, then be honest," Tilton suggested.

They climbed out of the carriage, and Edward rapped firmly on the door. A moment later, a butler answered, and Edward presented his card.

They must have been expected, because the butler moved aside to let them into the front hall.

"Her ladyship waits in the parlor," he said gesturing.

Mr. Halkerstone was in there staring out the window, along with Mary who worked on an embroidery in the corner. Edward's eyes fixated on Phoebe. She looked just as stunning as the first time he saw her, but there was no smile this time. Her face was devoid of emotion, a statue. She watched him, her eyes darker than he remembered. Her strawberry hair fell around her in soft, loose curls, her graceful hands folded on her lap. He wanted to reach out and take one of those hands. Instead, he bowed low.

"Lady von Croy," he murmured. He managed to introduce Tilton without stumbling over his words, though his throat was suddenly very dry.

"Marquess Winchester," she greeted coolly. She studied Tilton for a moment before her eyes once more slid to Edward. They stared at each other while Edward panicked. His mind went utterly blank, and he quite forgot how to speak. Tilton cleared his throat and nudged Edward helpfully.

"I, uh, I have recently come from England, uh…" He glanced at Halkerstone who had not turned toward the speakers, thank God, but was clearly listening. How the hell was he supposed to say what he needed to say? And Mary? Edward's eyes slid to the maid, his doubts stemming his words.

"I believe you have come to return something of mine," she said and held out a hand.

At this, Halkerstone did turn around for Edward had never mentioned the diamond to him. Mary paused in her embroidery, but when she saw him looking, she went back to it.

"Perhaps you might give me a moment alone?" he said his voice rough from dryness.

"Mary stays," she said but waved a hand at the other two.

Tilton bowed to Phoebe and nodded encouragement at Edward. As if he did not work for Edward himself, Halkerstone took directions from Phoebe and left. It occurred to Edward as the door closed behind him that Mary had been with Phoebe all through her sickness when she grew the heart. She must know about it.

Silence fell again between them, interrupted only by the soft hiss of embroidery floss through cloth.

"Well?" Phoebe asked, holding out her hand once more.

Inhaling deeply, Edward took out the bundle of black velvet from his pocket and handed it over.

"Do you have the other half?" he asked, kneeling beside her.

"Of course," she said. "Not down here." She frowned at him, the first exhibit of emotions. "Why would I ever show you the rest of my heart when you nearly killed me a dozen times since I gave it to you?"

"I swear to you, Phoebe—"

"You do *not* get to use my name anymore, my lord," she hissed.

Edward closed his eyes and nodded, acknowledging the point. He cleared his throat, working moisture into his mouth. "I swear I did not understand what you had given to me last winter—"

"Clearly," she said softly. "You threw it away. You threw me away."

"And it was the most foolish thing I have ever done. Ph—Lady von Croy, I did not understand our love, but more than that I did not understand love. I was selfish and ignorant, and I am so regretful of the cruel way in which I treated you. I apologize."

He paused to give her a chance to respond or, at worst, cast him away as he'd done to her. Instead, Phoebe stared at him, clutching the velvet-wrapped bundle until her knuckles were white. Edward jumped into the silence.

"I never intended any harm to come to you. There was a…a tragedy which led me to investigate the heart and find out the truth of it. Once I realized, I sought out a magician to help me heal it."

"You? Sought out a magician?" she asked, eyes widened in disbelief.

Edward shrugged. "I did not know what else to do."

"Is that why you were in the cemetery?" she asked softly.

"No, well, yes partially. We were to fetch this magic flower. It did not turn out well. The magician…disappeared," he said embarrassed. "The times that you were in danger are entirely my fault, but

I did my best to keep you safe."

"The water?" she asked.

"A sailor kicked the stone overboard during a fight. I jumped in to get it," he admitted. Edward stared at his hands, searching for something else to say, something to convey the depths of his feelings now.

"My Lord Marquess, I appreciate that you have brought my heart back to me safely, but now you should go. Take your man with you. I am quite done with love," she said softly.

From the corner came a noise, and they both glanced over to see Mary duck her head. Edward noted tears falling onto the embroidery hoop.

"I know I do not deserve—"

"No, you do not," Phoebe cut him off.

Edward hesitated. "Do you know a way to fix your heart?" he asked. "If it is within my power, I will do it."

"I just asked you to leave."

"And I will," Edward said. "Even if fixing your heart means I am no longer in it, I would do it. I owe you that much at least."

Phoebe stared at him, and he saw tears gather in her eyes. He wanted to cup her cheek and smooth the tears away, but he did not reach out for her. He had lost that right.

"I do not think there is," she said quietly. "It will die, but at least it will be safe. I will be safe, so take comfort in that." She stood, smoothing down the front of her dress. "Now if you will please leave."

Edward stood and turned to go but paused. He looked back at her, memorizing her face. "Will you tell me that you do not love me?" he asked. Phoebe looked away and out the window. "If your broken heart is really cold, then tell me. I need to hear the words."

"Leave, Edward," she said. "I do not owe you anything."

Before he could obey, though, Phoebe swept out of the room through another door.

****

A numbness spread over Edward, and he imagined this was how Phoebe must feel. He left the parlor and found Halkerstone and Tilton trading stories in the foyer. They both cast him pitying glances, but even that did not signify. Edward understood what a broken heart was now. He thought he'd been brokenhearted when he read Phoebe's letters. No, that had been foolish pride masquerading as betrayal.

His heart was beating, but there seemed a hole in his chest.

"She wants you to leave with us," Edward said softly to Halkerstone. Oddly, the butler standing in the shadows made a noise of protest and stepped forward, casting a worried glance at Halkerstone.

"I will convince her to let me stay on for a bit, my lord," he said softly. "Until I hear word from the duke that things are taken care of on that end."

"Of course," Edward said nodding. "I thank you. I'm sure Rhys will be grateful as well."

Tilton put a supportive hand on Edward's shoulder. "Edward, I—"

"Tilton and I are going to the opera later this week," Edward interrupted. "I promised him. You are welcome to join us."

Halkerstone paused at that and then nodded. "I love the opera," he said.

Edward nodded. "Good. That's sorted. We should

go," he said to Tilton.

He left then because he did not know what else to do. The world had muted itself into tones of gray. Everything felt fuzzy. Was this what a cold heart felt like? He would never see colors again? Is this what Phoebe saw now? He hated himself a little more.

Edward did not remember the carriage ride or passing through the front of the inn. By the time he came back to himself, Tilton was shoving a beverage in his hand.

"There's some laudanum in it," Tilton said. "Drink."

Edward obeyed without thinking and afterward let Tilton take off his jacket and waistcoat and push him into bed. Tilton brought the covers up and tucked him in.

"Go to sleep, Edward," he said softly. "It will be better later, I promise."

They both knew he was lying.

****

The laudanum made its way through his body, numbing his heart and mind enough for Edward to slip into a deep sleep. He awoke sometime after midnight to the city draped in black shadows. There was no moon, and the sky was a glittering ceiling of a thousand stars. He opened the window, welcoming the cool breeze into his room and into his head. The cobwebs left by the drugs were swept out leaving Edward free to think. And feel.

The sadness crashed over him like a downpour. For a few minutes, Edward closed his eyes and allowed himself to really feel the heartache. It hurt. It was hard to breathe. Pressure on his chest. Tears stinging his eyes. Edward gasped. He shook as if a freeze had taken over, and for a while that is all he could do: tremble and cry and hurt.

Finally, finally it passed out of him. The heartache remained but the tears stopped. The shaking ceased. His breath returned. The hollow in his chest remained. Opening his eyes, Edward walked back to his bags and took out the ritual Saint Germaine had sent him. A heart for a heart. All he had to do was get Phoebe's heart back. This time, he needed both pieces. And he knew just the man to help him.

Chapter Fifty-Three

September 9, 1789
Gates of Vienna

Amongst the steady trickle of pilgrims and farmers, the Comte de Saint Germaine and his wife Bella walked their horses to the great gate outside Vienna. They wore nondescript clothing and would have blended in unnoticed had Saint Germaine not pulled his mare to the side just outside the gate. A guard from inside the house poked his head out and walked over.

"*Guten Nachmittag*," Saint Germaine greeted the guard who murmured back. "My wife and I are hoping to visit some friends here in the city." As he said it he made a peculiar gesture with his hand.

The guard's eyes narrowed, and he nodded. "What friends were you seeking?"

"Two English doshmen. One like an eagle and the other a dandy," Saint Germaine told him.

A nod and the guard spit. "There are many travelers who pass this way. I've not seen or heard of two English doshmen."

Germaine sighed and tossed him a bag of coins. He knew the Englishman was in the city. The cards and the pull had brought him here. Apparently, it would take a bit longer to find him. As Saint Germaine moved to guide the horse into the city, the guard held up a hand.

"You should know, though, another man, an English tough, came by asking about a similar pair yesterday," he told Saint Germaine.

Saint Germaine exchanged a look with Bella, before nodding at the guard.

The two moved their horses along, joining the ingress crowd of travelers until Saint Germaine found an inn on the outskirts of the city with a family symbol carved into the sign. Roma were welcome here. They took a small room on the second floor, Bella dropping her saddlebags by the bed and letting out a long sigh of relief.

"Before you go about your planning, love, know that the English tough is mine," she said. Reaching down to the saddlebag, she pulled out a blade shaped almost in a U. "Bulibasha gave me a *special* gift for him," she said, eying the blade. There was the faintest trace of oil on the surface. Saint Germaine's guess was that it would be fast-acting.

"Anything for you, my love," he said. They both knew he'd consulted the cards every single night since they left the Roma camp. If the cards had given a warning, he would have trussed her up and been about this business on his own. But the cards had revealed the imbalance tipping back in their favor. Besides, Bella was a survivor.

She grinned at him. "So, the Englishmen or the tough first?"

Saint Germaine considered. He went to the window and threw it open, inviting the outside air in. Tilting his head and filtering out the sounds and smells of the city around them, he listened for the wind. It blew in through the streets from the Danube River, reeking of trash and detritus and warning him to take care of the dirty work first.

"The wind says your present comes first, darling," he said.

She sighed with satisfaction. "I love the wind," she said. "Now ask it where the hell he is."

****

Halkerstone was enjoying breakfast in the downstairs servant's hall when the butler delivered a note. He knew immediately who it was from given the bold, firm strokes of the handwriting. But he put the note aside for the moment until he finished his breakfast. It wasn't that he didn't want to help or obey Edward; he simply expected it to be a goodbye note explaining a quick departure.

From the little interaction with his brother in Vienna, Halkerstone knew that Edward's journey had wrought fierce changes. The rough edges had been worn down, he was bringing people like Tilton into arm's length, and he was thinking about his actions. His ability to accept had grown. Even his kindness thrived. So it had killed Halkerstone to see Edward's heartbreak all over his face when he left Phoebe yesterday, although Halkerstone had not been surprised by the outcome.

However strenuously that Lady von Croy insisted she felt nothing for Edward, her ladyship had gone up to her room right after speaking with him and not come down. They were both suffering, and Halkerstone wished he could do more to help. He had made a promise to the Duke of Brey, and he would keep it as best he could. He'd sent a message back already detailing what had transpired, both of the attempts on

Phoebe's life and the outcome of her interaction with Edward. He hoped that the duke could stop Lady Argent before Edward returned home. He did not want Edward traveling by himself, but he could not leave Lady von Croy either.

Once he'd finished his breakfast, Halkerstone pushed aside his plate and broke the seal of the letter. He was already trying to organize a reply in his mind that might convince Edward not to quit Vienna until Phoebe was protected. Halkerstone was certain he could persuade Edward to stay a bit longer using that angle. Then the words on the page broke through his mental composition. Twice in as many days and Halkerstone was shocked. He reread the note, turned it over, searching for an indication that might prove this note was falsified or in code. Nothing.

No, Edward wanted him to steal not one, but *two* red diamonds from Lady von Croy. And his reasoning was that her life depended on it.

****

Edward tried not to allow himself to sink into despair. He got up the next morning and wrote a note off to Mr. Halkerstone. He only hoped it sufficiently impressed upon the other man the importance of gaining custody of both diamonds. If Halkerstone did not or could not go through with the theft, Edward was already trying to figure out an alternative plan. Perhaps he could find Roma in the city to help. They were certainly for hire, and, it seemed, they understood what the stone hearts were. They would understand his reasoning.

Luckily, Tilton took Edward's distraction for heartache and did not push him. After breaking fast, the dandy put on another new suit and went for a stroll about town. With Tilton away, Edward formulated his plan. He tasked the concierge with procuring tickets to the opera and other events, one for each night. He wrote the tailor requesting suits enough to cover both himself and Tilton for at least two weeks. He just needed to keep up appearances for a few more days. Squaring his shoulders, Edward closed his eyes and fortified his purpose. He'd come this far. He would finish what he started.

****

Phoebe stared out the window of her bedroom and sighed. She felt…lost. Her heart was no warmer nor colder than it had been yesterday when Edward had finally returned it. There was a time right after she'd left England, that Phoebe had dreamed if she ever received her broken heart back—she would feel free again. Light and silly and everything that she'd felt before he'd crushed her. As if repossessing her heart could erase the foul play that had been enacted against it.

Then she'd imagined that her heart would shrivel up and become dust as her feelings turned from love to bitterness and finally to nothing. When she had saved him in the cemetery, Phoebe remembered her anger and the injustice done against her from Edward. That had felt good; it had felt powerful. It was perhaps then that she realized Edward was coming closer *with* her heart, and Phoebe reveled in the idea of hurting him the way he'd hurt her.

When Mr. Halkerstone had advised her of Edward's imminent arrival, Phoebe found the anger difficult to manifest. Honestly, anxiety and fear warred within her more than her anger. She feared that in this final confrontation, her heart would betray her again. When Edward walked into the room…

That changes had occurred were plain and obvious. He appeared as lost as she felt. His eyes were haunted. His usually well turned out appearance was less than cavalier. Had he left his valet in England? He was traveling with a dandy who, from all appearances, was fond of smiling, and Phoebe knew how much those things irritated Edward.

As infuriating as it was to admit, Edward was just as handsome as she remembered. Maybe more so because for all his inherent fierceness, there was a vulnerability to him that Edward had never displayed before. It was like a wolf showing its belly. And then the bastard had the gall to apologize.

Well, Phoebe had felt the anger then. It had swarmed upon her like angry bees, and she just wanted him to understand what he had done. The problem was he seemed to. Or he was trying, and for all she had loved him, Edward had never been particularly good at empathy before this. He'd needed a translator, and she had been good at that for him. When they were together, it had simply worked. Now he was trying on his own, and still incredibly bad at it, but he was trying. So Phoebe felt guilty about turning him away. She! Who'd suffered and cried and nearly drowned. The memory of his face asking her to tell him she did not love him made her stomach curdle.

I cannot afford to love him again, she told herself for the thousandth time that morning, pressing a hand to her middle, ordering it to behave. *If I do and he breaks my heart again, I will not feel anything.*

Phoebe held both pieces of her heart on her lap and stared out the window at the treetops swaying in the wind. There were hints of autumn—a yellow leaf here and there. The morning was still cool, though it would grow warmer in the afternoon. Sunlight sparkled across both broken diamonds, but it did not warm them. One was heavy and nearly spent, though a stubborn flicker of heat held on. The other was lighter and hotter. The intense movements showcasing her changing emotions. The broken edge of this one was smoothed by months of handling, months of easing and petting and rubbing. Months of self-nurturing and care.

The two pieces no longer fit together. Too much time had passed. The lighter part of her was ready to let the heavier piece go. She was broken. It was not comfortable but it was tolerable. There were other people in this world far more broken and still able to find happiness. So she would be a little less of the person she'd been nine months ago. So she had lost a piece of her innocence and her youth. Time and life did that. She could still be happy.

The idea of happiness made her think of Frederick. She was never going to love him. There was safety in this, but now with both pieces of her heart back, Phoebe balked at the idea of marrying a second time without love. *I do not need a partner,* she thought. *I do not need anyone. I am capable of taking care of myself. I do not need Edward or Frederick or Halkerstone.* She paused. Halkerstone had proven useful. Not that she wanted to marry him but if he could get whoever wanted her dead off her back, well, she would pay him a handsome sum. So maybe she needed him a bit longer. The man seemed as stubborn as Edward. He refused to leave her household, and she was too tired to argue with him.

"Here's a nice cup of tea for you, milady," Mary said, setting a tray down. "It'll perk you right up."

Mary glanced at the two heart pieces in Phoebe's lap. She knew what they were. She was from a family that had served Phoebe's from a time before their families were English. When they'd been Saxon conquerors.

"Thank you, Mary." Phoebe set the stones aside on the swath of black velvet Edward had given her. They winked and sparkled pink in the sunlight as she took her tea.

"I've never seen his lordship look such a mess," Mary said softly.

"I do not want to talk about him," Phoebe said.

"Of course, milady," Mary murmured.

Phoebe drank her tea in silence while Mary straightened and made the bed.

"Lord Frederick has sent an invitation for tomorrow night," Mary said. Phoebe wrinkled her nose. No, she could not play this game any longer.

"I think I will have to break things off with him," she admitted.

"Oh?" Mary paused.

Phoebe spared her a withering glance. "Do not act as if this does not make you happy," she said. "I know you don't like him."

"It's not my place, milady," Mary protested.

"And, no, this does not mean I have any inclination on getting back with Edward."

"Course not," Mary said, though she was clearly disappointed.

Phoebe sighed again and finished her tea. "Lay out

the blue water-silk dress," she said. "Send Frederick back a reply agreeing to his little concert tomorrow."

"Yes, my lady," Mary said. "Anything else?"

"Clear my schedule," she said. "After tomorrow evening, I do not want to see anyone else."

Chapter Fifty-Four

September 11, 1789
Wanderin Inn, Vienna

Saint Germaine and Bella had spent the better part of two days reconnecting with contacts and the underground, searching for both parties of Englishmen. Word of two foreign toffs in a middle-class neighborhood inn had reached them finally. The English tough who had threatened them, Cliff, proved a more difficult prey to find.

"A rat, that one," Bella said spitting. "Probably holed up somewhere."

Saint Germaine agreed. "With enough coin to shut most wagging tongues. No matter. We know what he wants."

"The doshman," she said. Her husband nodded.

"And if he sees me going for a visit, it might just flush him out," Saint Germaine said.

****

The sun was setting, and the inn was growing noisy with the workers stopping in for a bite or a drink on their way home. Edward's room was in the back corner and overlooked the stable yard which was quiet and empty. He managed to go out the night before with Tilton and then showed his young friend all his plans for the next week. But after Halkerstone arrived with the diamonds, Edward knew he could not wait any longer. Phoebe would realize they were gone soon.

So he pretended to feel ill and urged Tilton and Halkerstone to take the tickets to the opera. He hated not keeping his word, but he had made a promise to Phoebe first. If he lived, he would make it up to Tilton. If not, well… *That's what the letters are for.*

Edward finished powdering the last letter. He held the paper up and tapped it gently, letting the additional powder fall away, and blew at the wet spots until the ink dried. Satisfied, he folded the parchment and then held the sealing wax in the flame of the candle on his desk. Three smart drops and he pressed his signet ring into the bright red wax.

On the front of the letter, he wrote Tilton's name and laid it against the others. Six letters sat neatly on the desk. Edward stared at them but not for long. His eyes were, inevitably, drawn to the black velvet bundle which held Phoebe's heart. Despite serious misgivings, Halkerstone had brought him the diamonds this afternoon, after Phoebe had left for a concert. His business manager had not been happy to be thieving from a grieving woman. Edward applauded his honor and reassured him it was not for the wealth of the diamonds, but to save her.

He was certain Halkerstone had misconstrued and thought Edward was going to use the diamonds to buy the price off Phoebe's head. That wasn't the case. Instead, Edward had put out feelers with the innkeeper on contacting the Roma. One of the letters was addressed to them and left instructions along with a banknote for payment to eliminate whoever Lady Eleanor's agents were. The Roma would do this,

Edward was certain.

The other letters were addressed to Rhys, his mother, Halkerstone, and Phoebe. *Six letters to the most important people in my life. Six letters is all I have to give.* Sighing, he set the letters aside and pulled out the Saint Germaine's ritual.

The Roma had said only one heart could warm another. He'd thought by bringing the two pieces together, it would mend things. As if Phoebe's heart was a broken piece of pottery and gluing the two ends together would work. It hadn't of course. It was a silly idea but Edward had been desperate. The coldness in Phoebe's eyes when she looked at him. Edward sighed and smiled bitterly.

Now he understood why. When he'd studied the larger piece of Phoebe's heart, the part she'd held onto, he found its edges softer and worn. The broken piece no longer fit. She'd taken care of her piece. He had neglected his. But he could tread one more path to try and fix what he'd broken.

Shucking off his jacket, Edward unbuttoned his shirt and folded both neatly on the chair. He pulled out his dagger, the dagger that had tried to take his life once already, and the heart pieces and went into the bedroom. He closed the door behind him and rolled the carpet out of the way. Really, no reason to ruin a good rug.

Kneeling in front of the fireplace, Edward took a deep, deep breath. Then he undid his belt and folded it into fours, then bit down hard. Only one heart could warm another, and if Phoebe's heart could not warm itself, it was left up to him. He reread the ritual and, trying not to feel like a total moron, read the magic words. Taking the dagger in one hand, he placed the tip under his sternum and to the left. Saying a quick prayer to his father for guidance, he plunged the blade in.

****

Tilton stared up at the Wiener Staatsoper, the Renaissance style opera house. It was a grand old building with two levels of archways in the front, a bronze roof, and pale gray stone. And as much as he wanted to, Tilton could not make himself go in.

"Are you ready, Tilton?" Halkerstone asked.

Tilton knew he was lucky to be in such company. The fact that Halkerstone was a very good-looking man did not hurt. Not that Halkerstone displayed any interest in that avenue, but still Tilton enjoyed the company of good-looking men, if only to be able to look at them. Besides, Mr. Halkerstone had fallen quickly into calling him Tilton, and even though their rank did not match, Tilton understood this to be a sign of trust and friendship. The lordling found that was much more important to him than observing social normalcies.

"This feels wrong without Edward," he said.

His friend had put on a brave face. Even after Lady von Croy had dashed all hopes of reconciliation, Edward had tried to shift the focus away from his obviously bleeding heart. He'd bought tickets for every major event in Vienna and gone to a show last night with Tilton. Tilton thought part of it was a need for distraction, and part of it was surely a denial of said bleeding heart. So when Edward had begged off tonight, Tilton had not tried to pull him out. He knew what it was like to lose love.

"He needs some time," Halkerstone said.

"I know," Tilton agreed. "I *know*," he repeated and

368

frowned. He knew Edward staying behind was probably for the best. So why did he have this dread collecting in his gut? "I confess, I understand why she rejected him, but I thought she might not. There just seemed like this connection between them."

Halkerstone watched other gentles glide through the opera house's doors.

"Lady von Croy may change her mind," Halkerstone said. "She needs time as well." His thoughts were clearly somewhere else. Tilton got the idea he was torn in his loyalties. He was technically Edward's business manager, but he'd been in the von Croy household for two weeks.

"We have done all we can to help," Halkerstone said, more to himself than to Tilton. "They must sort it out for themselves now. I just pray his lordship is not foolish."

"Why would Edward be foolish?" Tilton asked with a frown. "You do not think he's going to try and go see her, do you?"

Mr. Halkerstone shook his head. "She's at a private performance tonight, and he knows that."

"Oh." Tilton nodded. His frown deepened. "Then what foolishness are we speaking of?"

Halkerstone did not say anything and did not meet his eyes.

"Mr. Halkerstone, of what are you thinking?" Tilton pressed.

The eyes turned, and it struck Tilton that Halkerstone's coloring was completely different from Edward but the shape of his eyes was exactly the same. There was a fierceness in his stare, not gray like Edward's, but brown and hard.

"You have his lordship's confidence," Halkerstone stated, studying Tilton.

"We've been through a lot together," Tilton said. "Edward…he is my best friend."

Halkerstone nodded and pulled Tilton away from the glittering masses entering the theater into the shadow by the side of the building.

"His lordship asked me to fetch something of Lady von Croy's for him," Halkerstone said. "He said her life depended on it. I asked him directly before we left if his plan was to fence the diamonds tonight, and he said no—"

"The diamonds!" Tilton yelped. "Fuck! We have got to get back."

Then Tilton took off at a run, waving his arms like a madman at the nearest hackney and leaving Halkerstone to catch up or be left behind.

****

Phoebe fanned herself absently as she watched the others giggling and laughing at their card games. Such things held little amusement for her now, though she was not above participating if only to pass the time. She had pulled Frederick away earlier in the evening and let him down. He had sighed and shook his head as if he'd known.

"My little ice queen," he said. "I knew I did not have the power to warm your heart."

"I am sorry, Your Grace," she said. "I find myself unable to return your feelings."

"Very well," he said and gracefully brushed his lips against her knuckles before letting her go. He had invited her to stay for the rest of the evening because he was a gentleman and not the type to seek out callous revenge. Unlike some people she knew.

"Besides, I have hired this musician just for you," he reminded her. He knew how much she liked a good violinist.

So she had stayed, gliding through the boring night until, at last, the violinist was set up in the main hall.

The musician Frederick had hired was a young man of perhaps twenty with freckles and a gap in his tooth and toyed nervously with his bow as he waited for the assembled nobles to settle. Phoebe perched on a couch to the side and signaled a footman for more wine.

Soon enough, the lad was ready, and he put bow to strings and began to play.

Phoebe closed her eyes and sat back into the couch cushions as much as her stays would allow. He was a very good musician. She felt it there, in the depths of her heart, a stirring. One song shifted into another as Phoebe listened, feeling more alive, more connected to the world than at any other point since her heart had broken. She swayed, and the music built toward a crescendo.

A wave of warmth flooded her, and Phoebe put her hand to her stomach. She felt surrounded, covered in heat.

"My lady, are you all right?"

She opened her eyes and found a footman bent over her, concern on his face. The music stopped as the violinist noticed that something was off.

"I'm fine," Phoebe snapped, annoyed at the disruption. Several people around them glanced at the source of the disruption, and Phoebe felt a wave of embarrassment. The footman straightened and made to leave.

Another wave of heat hit Phoebe, and this time, with it came pain. She uttered a small cry.

"My lady." The footman hesitated and then signaled for the butler.

Phoebe wanted to yell at the young man that she was fine, but she wasn't. More pain, this time agony but it was separate from Phoebe, outside of her. She tried to speak, but the heat overwhelmed her, and she moaned. She heard something *thump* to the ground. From far away, she heard cries and running, but in her ears, she heard someone whispering her name, whispering love words.

"Edward," she gasped.

The agony was unbearable, and it echoed inside of her, vibrating so hard that it seemed to shake off a layer of ice that had formed around her own pain.

"Phoebe, Phoebe, darling, are you all right?"

Frederick's voice, but she couldn't answer. She moaned and then realized she was sobbing. She tried to say "no," she did not want to go through this again. She did not want to feel this way ever again, but Edward's pain was so powerful, and it vibrated so hard, like music, like one string shaking back and forth until the string next to it catches on and begins to vibrate as well. Phoebe's pain began to pulsate, and she was so angry. She was so angry and hurt and—

"How dare he?" she demanded.

"Shhhh, my love, they are getting the doctor."

"I am not your love," she snapped and then moaned as another wave hit her. This time, it wasn't pain though. This time it was soothing.

Chapter Fifty-Five

September 11, 1789
Verlorene Liebe Inn, Vienna

The pain was unbearable, but Edward shoved all that aside. He did not have long, so he cut deep enough to get through the skin, a jagged hole three and a half inches wide. Biting down as hard as possible, screaming around the leather as he did, he shoved the stones inside of his body and up. Instinctively, he curled into the fetal position. His stomach clenched, and sweat burst out of his pores like raindrops from a cloud. He choked on bile, felt his entire body shudder, and shoved the heart pieces higher, under his lungs and as close to his rapidly beating heart as possible.

A wave of dizziness and nausea came over him. Distantly, he heard screaming, someone screaming his name.

"God above, Edward!"

That was definitely Tilton. What was Tilton doing back so early?

"Somebody help! Get a doctor fast!"

That was Halkerstone. They were supposed to be at the theater. Edward tried to laugh, but all that came out was bile and the little chicken he'd had at dinner. A shame, really. The chicken had been quite good.

He felt something leave his wound and realized

Tilton had pulled his hand out of his chest. Another wave of dizziness came, and this time he swore he heard Phoebe say, "I am fine."

Phoebe. How he loved her. *I love you so much, Phoebe. I was such a fool. How young and ignorant I was not to trust your sweet heart. I'm a reprobate, but I would do anything. I did do anything. God above, Phoebe, forgive me.*

"Edward, oh God, what did you do?" Tilton asked.

"Move away! Let me help," a new but familiar voice said.

"Saint Germaine? Where the hell did you come from?"

The voices filtered out. Edward had no idea what he had done or where he was. He was aware that he was bleeding a great deal and that he was probably dying. Blackness overtook him, and Edward moved deep into his own being.

He was aware of pain. Not his pain. That was all around him like fire. No, this pain was old and desperate and angry and deep. This was Phoebe's pain. He felt it inside of him as if it were his own. The shock at reading his letter. He saw his own firm handwriting and those horrid words, words written out of fear and cowardice. Words meant to wound so that he would not be hurt. They were a child's words.

Then he felt the heart break. It was not unlike the stabbing agony from the dagger, but it was more thorough, riding through his entire soul and severing a piece of it clean off. Then there was anger, fury really. A fury at the mistreatment, at the lies, at the cowardice, and finally at Phoebe herself. She was angry at herself for giving her heart to him. He clearly didn't deserve it.

Edward had thrown away the most precious thing she could ever give like it was nothing, and she couldn't even take it back.

He saw it now. Phoebe in his library, the heart in two pieces in the box. Phoebe tried to pick up both pieces, but one was too heavy, too hot. Like a coal it seared her. She cried and tried to take the whole box, but it wouldn't budge. She wept, livid at the injustice of it all, and then she heard the butler coming back. Frustrated but out of time she scooped up the half she could lift and fled.

Shame filled Edward. It was worse than he thought.

"You inherited my stubbornness," a voice said.

The memory dissolved and was replaced by the late Marquess of Winchester.

"Father?" Edward said. "Are you really here?"

"Of course. I'm with you and your mother." His father grinned and winked. "One of the advantages of being dead—I can be in two places at once."

"I'm such a reprobate," Edward said.

"You were misled by an evil woman, Edward," Lord Pierce said. "And by me as well. I should have shown you all my secrets. I thought I was doing right by you, making you a better man than myself, but if I had been honest and set you a better example, you might have been spared this."

"I do not understand," Edward said.

"We are not of small emotions, Edward. When we feel, it is always with great intensity. Let me show you."

Edward saw a vision of his father kissing another woman, not his mother. Edward studied the couple, unsettled but unable to dismiss the vision. Lord Winchester was young, younger than Edward, perhaps Tilton's age. His fashion was a good forty years old. The woman was dressed in plain clothes, twice turned out. He could see she was not of gentle birth, but pretty nonetheless. There was a familiar quality about her. Something about the color of her eyes, pale like whiskey, and the tilt of her head.

The vision shifted, and now the woman was pregnant. Edward watched his father put his hand on her swollen stomach, and started.

"Father," he said aghast.

His father's reply was a sigh. "I loved her very much," he said and appeared beside Edward. He did not look at his son, but instead at the vision before both of them. It shifted again. There was a toddler, and once more the woman was pregnant. Lord Winchester wrapped his arms around her, and she leaned back to accept a kiss over her shoulder. Edward was too stunned for words.

"Her name was Claire," Lord Winchester said. "I would have married her, but your grandfather refused me. He even went to send her out of my reach." Lord Winchester grew angry for a moment. "Before any of that came to pass, Claire died in childbirth when bringing our third child into this world."

"I have siblings," Edward whispered. He stared at his father, feeling like his whole world was falling down. "And you never told me. What about Mother?"

"I loved her too," Lord Winchester said. "We met several years after Claire's death. It was time for me to marry, and I started courting a woman named Eleanor, eldest daughter of Lord Coventry. I was so numb after

Claire's death, and Eleanor was my mother's first choice. It did not matter much to me. Then I met your mother, and she was this balm to my aching soul, Edward. She was so wonderful, and I just fell again."

Edward did not know what to say.

"I should have told you," Lord Winchester said. "It was my fault that those letters came into your hands. Eleanor, the woman you know as Lady Argent, knew what you would do once you read them."

Edward suddenly felt very lost. He did not trust himself to speak.

"I am asking your forgiveness, son," Lord Winchester said.

A lump closed Edward's throat. "I…" Where did he start? "What are their names? My siblings?"

"Halkerstone," his father replied. Edward sucked in his breath. It felt like another blow. The late Winchester put his hand on Edward's shoulder and squeezed. "I know this is a lot of truth, many secrets that you may not want to hear. But I would never abandon any of my children. I will not abandon you now even if you hate me for what I have done.

"Right now, Edward, you must fight. You must fight for your life and your love. You must show her the intensity of your feelings. You must show her what your love really feels like."

"I am frightened," Edward said. He would never have admitted it in life to his father. To admit that he was a coward would have been the ultimate insult, the ultimate shame. But Edward knew now that shunning the woman he loved was worse.

"That is because under all that intensity, your heart is tender, Edward," his father said. "She already loves

Kitty Shields

you for it. Just think. You have stabbed yourself. The easy part is over," he added dryly. "You can do this."

The image of his father faded to be replaced by moving lights in thick clouds of color. Phoebe's stone heart, the cold half. Somehow, Edward had sunk deep enough into himself to reach it. He paused there, uncertain what to do, and then felt his father's hand squeeze his shoulder again. It steadied him. *Show her,* his father said.

Edward thought of Phoebe, of her face, her laugh, her cleverness. He thought of the way she smacked him on the arm when she was irritated, the way she tilted her head when she was teasing him. He thought of the waves in her hair when it was down and the curve of her waist. He thought about the moment when he realized he was in love, and he felt an airiness come from within. He was calm now.

Whispering how he felt, Edward undid the bolts on his heart and let his love, his passion run freely out of him and over her. It was hers now, all of it. All that he had to give was hers. Edward smiled. He felt the blackness grow more dense around him. It was like walls were pressing in. The swirling lights reflected against clear, crystalline planes. Edward felt safe somehow and let oblivion take him.

Chapter Fifty-Six

September 11, 1789
Verlorene Liebe Inn, Vienna

Saint Germaine walked toward the inn casually. He did a double take on the name of the inn and snorted. Did these Englishmen have a sense of humor, or were they that lost? But he did not focus on the name long, instead scanning the street. Night had fallen, and the streetlamps were ablaze, hiding demons and monsters and ghosts in the shadows. He was somewhere close by, Saint Germaine knew. The wind sprites had told him. The toff was at the inn coming up on his left, but the thug was also close by as he'd predicted. There, across the way was Cliff, leaning against the alley wall, a hood pulled up hiding his features, but Saint Germaine knew. He lowered his eyes and pretended not to see.

With his left hand, he signaled Bella who followed some twenty feet behind. Behind her were a number of cousins and Roma from other families. Volunteers who, once they'd heard the story, had offered to help. At his signal, they scattered, casting a wide net. Saint Germaine did not look back but trusted his wife to take care of her business. She didn't like being threatened, and Cliff was going to find that out very soon.

The Englishman, however, needed help. The cards

had gotten dark this afternoon, and Saint Germaine did not like the way they were reading. If the Englishman died, the owner of the stone heart surely would as well. *Hopefully, the fool has not messed up the ritual,* he thought.

A hired cab crashed into a pothole nearly hitting Saint Germaine as the horses scrambled under the whip. It stopped in front of the inn, and the dandy as well as another man dashed out. They were through the door in a second, and Saint Germaine broke into a run. Whatever was happening wasn't good.

He followed the clatter of boots up the stairs and down the hallway to a corner bedroom. From the open door he heard, "God Above, Edward!"

And then: "Somebody help! Get a doctor fast!"

Saint Germaine darted into the room and almost ran into a knife unsheathed with frightening speed toward his chest.

"Edward, oh God, what did you do?" Tilton asked, pressing a balled-up shirt into a fountain of blood that had erupted from the doshman's chest.

"Move away! Let me help," Saint Germaine insisted, eying the man with the knife.

"Let him through!" Tilton said.

The man dropped the knife and stepped back. Saint Germaine knelt and told the dandy to keep pressure on the wound. He spied a blood-soaked paper with the title "Heart Stone Ritual" on top. Snatching it up, he scanned the contents.

"This is not what I sent you," he said. Glancing at Tilton. "This is not *real!*"

"Well, that's what we got," Tilton cried. "Please, help him. I think he put her heart inside his chest."

Cursing, Saint Germaine cast about for anything that might stop the blood.

"The flower, the farnblume," he said, grasping. "Did you get it?"

"What? Yes, it's in the book on the side table in my room. Halkerstone."

The other man darted out and returned later with a slim book. Saint Germaine took it, opened to where the farnblume had been preserved, and crushed the flower in his palms. He closed his eyes and reached out to the magic in the air around them. He felt a response, like a male voice calling from far away.

"Right now, Edward, you must fight. You must fight for your life and your love. You must show her the intensity of your feelings. You must show her what your love really feels like."

There was love there, surrounding the dying man.

Saint Germaine tugged at it, pulled like he was heaving a great weight closer. He heard: "She already loves you," echo out of the ether. Someone was communicating with this man.

She, Saint Germaine thought. *The lady is the key.* He felt the magic in the farnblume respond and awaken between his palms.

"Move your hands," he told the dandy.

"He'll bleed out."

"Either this will work or it won't," Saint Germaine said. "But you have to move your hands."

Tilton stared at him a second longer and then pulled his hands away, taking the blood-soaked shirt with him. The wound was ugly. A long, jagged cut under the sternum and to the left. It seeped blood. Saint Germaine slathered the wound with the dried flower petals, watched as a purple smoke rose up and hissed. The wound bubbled, and Edward thrashed. Both the dandy and Saint Germaine dove forward to hold him down.

A moment later and the wound was closed. The toff stopped moving.

Tilton checked his neck for a pulse. "He's alive," he said.

"But will he live?" the other man asked.

They both looked at Saint Germaine. "I think that's up to her."

Chapter Fifty-Seven

September 11, 1789
Styria Mansion, Vienna

Phoebe came to in a bed not her own. Frederick was there, holding her hand. Mary was fanning her from the other side. Her chest hurt, but it was not the familiar feeling of a heart broken. It was, instead, the feeling of affection and love and hope. Edward's emotions. Phoebe struggled to sit up. A doctor told her to rest, that she'd had another bout of hysteria but she was fine now.

Hysteria? Phoebe wanted to laugh. If they knew what was causing her "bouts", they would surely lock her up. But she dismissed the men and their stupidity.

"I want to go home," she said.

"Phoebe, stay the night and rest," Frederick urged her.

"Frederick, I'm going home," she said and threw back the blankets. Mary, knowing *that* voice, hurried to help her from the bed.

Both prince and doctor tried to argue, but Phoebe waved them away and told them quite specifically if they wanted to be of any use to call for the damn carriage. She wasn't sure what worked, her foul language or the fact that she was walking away from them while they tried to bully her. Either way, Phoebe was downstairs and inside her carriage within a quarter of an hour.

She let the carriage get far enough away from Frederick's manor before changing courses. She knew where Edward was staying from Halkerstone, of course, and as the carriage navigated closer, the feeling in her heart confirmed it. Whatever he had done, Edward had nearly sacrificed his life for her. Phoebe was aware that this had not fixed the broken pieces. Rather, they were suspended together in a safe and wonderful place.

She was also aware, oddly, that the pieces could be rejoined now. Not instantly; her heart was too out of shape. But wherever he'd put her heart, it felt like, given time and nurturing, the two pieces would grow back together. There was a chance where there had not been before.

She pulled up to an inn in a middle-class neighborhood. The driver helped her down, and she paused, gazing up at where she knew he had to be, somewhere on the second floor. There was a shout from behind them, and she glanced over her shoulder. Some kind of kerfuffle in the alley. Her driver took out the musket he'd taken to carrying and held it at a ready, but a few lads spilled back into the street laughing and carrying on. Clearly, just some drunks roughhousing.

Phoebe lifted her skirts and entered the inn with Mary on her heels. She ignored the innkeeper and the stares of the surprised patrons as she glided by in full evening gown. The staircase was narrow, but she managed to fit and down the hall to an open doorway where a few male voices were arguing.

She poked her head in. Edward was unconscious on the bed. There was a pool of blood by the fireplace.

Tilton waved his arms at a man who was probably a doctor. Halkerstone stood in the corner, his face dark and worried, arms crossed. Another man stood to the side. This one...

He looked up at her arrival, and their eyes locked. He had two different colored eyes, one blue and one brown. There was something familiar about him, a quality of his face, or the set of his shoulders. She narrowed her own gaze.

"*Herzschmerz*," he greeted softly.

Heart strings, Phoebe translated. Here was another of the small group of people that grew stone hearts. They were distantly related. Phoebe's mother had told her the Roma identified each other in this way. It was like greeting a cousin.

"He almost died for you," her distant cousin said, stepping closer.

It was on her tongue to say he was an imbecile, but the words would not come out. Edward was so pale, white as the sheets underneath him.

"The next part is up to you," her cousin said.

She looked at him again and realized he was confirming what she already knew. Phoebe could stop this. She could reach in and take back her heart, no doubt from the ugly wound on his chest, inside Edward's body. Or she could stay there, a part of him. She could choose to let herself love him again, knowing this time that he loved her.

"Everyone out," she said.

The doctor and Tilton stopped arguing at the order. Her cousin stepped past her. She wondered idly if she'd ever see him again. Halkerstone stopped to take her hand and kiss it, a pleading look on his face before he too left. The doctor shook his head and muttered, but he did not pause. Last, came Tilton.

He too took her hand.

"I know he's thick sometimes, and he's not particularly good at giving comfort." Tears gathered in the dandy's eyes as he spoke. "But he does love you. He has fought demons and magicians and the damn ocean to get here. Please, forgive him if you can."

And then he let her go and left, closing the door behind him.

Chapter Fifty-Eight

September 12, 1789
Verlorene Liebe Inn, Vienna

Edward woke to a soft hand stroking his face. He
opened his eyes, and the light that struck them caused a
groan to escape his lips and close them again. His eyes
were crusty, and his chest filled with a dull, throbbing
agony. Someone pressed a warm cloth to his cheek, and
it felt good. He focused on that. He tried licking his lips
which were dry, and a glass was pressed to them. He
tasted the contents carefully. Water. He drank greedily
and sputtered when too much splashed over his chin.

Reflexively, he tried to sit up, but more pain shot
through his body, so much so that it made him dizzy.

"Hold still," a beautiful voice said. Phoebe's voice.

Edward opened his eyes again. She sat at his side
and wiped his chin with a clean cloth. Their eyes met,
and despite the pain, he felt himself filling with joy.

"You are the biggest fool I have ever met in my
life," she said.

Edward winced. "That was not the reaction I was
praying for," he said.

"And what reaction should I give to a man that
opens his own chest?" she demanded.

"Admiration?" he hazarded. She glared at him.
"Pity," he ventured. Phoebe sighed. "Sympathy?"

"You are hopeless," she said. Edward caught her hand and pressed it to the thick layers of bandages around his chest.

"Am I?" he asked. "I am such an imbecile, Phoebe, I should never have cut you off. I love you. I was too foolish and simple to understand what that meant before, but I have learned some. I am learning. And I am so sorry."

Phoebe's eyes softened, and they were filled with warmth once more. "I know," she said. "I can feel it." She tapped his chest gently, which still hurt, and he winced. "I was planning on being done with love, but…it appears my heart isn't so heavy anymore."

****

Mr. Halkerstone sat in a back booth of a dirty tavern, waiting for his quarry. By not a miracle but magic apparently, Edward was going to live. After a long night of pacing and worrying and Phoebe's tender care, the doctor had come the next morning and proclaimed Edward would pull through.

It had taken a bit of goading, but Tilton finally gave Halkerstone an amended version of their journey including the magic flowers, revenants, magicians, and mayhem they'd experienced. Halkerstone had also lifted the suicide letters that Edward had placed on his desk and, after Tilton finally collapsed, opened and read each one. He burned the one intended for Lady Winchester. Her son would live, and she need not know about the suicide attempt unless Edward decided to tell her. He left Tilton's by the man's bedside while he snored away the morning and delivered Phoebe's to her while she waited for Edward to wake up. To which she promptly told him if he ever opened her mail again, she would see him beaten in the streets. He believed her.

He kept the one intended for the Duke of Brey. He would return it to Edward later. There were things said that perhaps Edward might still find easier to express in writing instead of in person. But he could decide that when he was up and about. The letter to himself found Halkerstone surprised. Most of it regarded ensuring that his mother was taken care of and the distant cousin who would inherit the Winchester title was treated with the same respect. But there was also an expression of gratitude for Halkerstone that was very personal and he wondered if Edward knew more about their relationship than he'd let on.

The last one puzzled Halkerstone until he'd heard Tilton's revised story. And it was this letter, to the Roma, that had him sitting in a dirty inn on the outskirts of town waiting for a man with two different colored eyes. He showed up, eventually, with a beautiful woman on his arm and seemed to sniff Halkerstone out despite his best efforts to blend in.

The man whom Tilton identified as the Comte de Saint Germaine sat down and introduced himself along with his wife.

"You work for Winchester," Saint Germaine said. "Does he live?"

"He does," Halkerstone said. "He made preparations in case he did not. I believe this letter is best addressed to you."

Saint Germaine took it and read it, his wife reading also over his shoulder. Then he stared at the bank note.

"You could have taken this," he said flicking the corner of the bank note, "if you've read this already."

"It's not my money," Halkerstone said. "And you

helped save him. This is the least he owes you. But I was also hoping, if you know who or where the agents of the Lady Argent are, that you would tell me. I'll pay a separate fee," Halkerstone offered, putting another bag of money on the table.

"No need," Saint Germaine said with a wave of his hand.

"The bastard you're looking for is dead," the wife said, a satisfied smile crossing her features. "Killed him myself."

"This is more than enough for us," Saint Germaine said, tucking the bank note into his jacket with a smile. "I will make sure the other Roma are paid for their aid. Let us consider all debts met."

Halkerstone was surprised, but he had a feeling there was more to the Roma's involvement than just money. So he nodded and gave thanks and excused himself.

That left only the Lady Argent herself to take care of, and Halkerstone hoped that the Duke of Brey already had that in hand. He headed back to the von Croy house to gather his things and pick up a change of clothes for Lady Phoebe. A letter from Rhys had arrived, and he found, to his great delight, that the Lady Argent had indeed been taken care of.

Chapter Fifty-Nine

September 17, 1879
Verlorene Liebe Inn, Vienna

Later that week, Edward dozed. His chest felt on fire, but beside the obvious pain from the healing wound, was the amazing feeling of Phoebe's heart beating next to his. He could feel it, and it gave him a sense of peace he never knew he needed. He was happily imagining their future together, going through how he would propose, the wedding they would have, the children. So he was slightly vexed when a knock at the door interrupted his musings.

Halkerstone walked in without waiting for Edward's permission. That would have annoyed Edward more than two months ago. Now, he understood a bit about why Halkerstone was so casual, had always been just a little too comfortable with him. Edward wondered if Halkerstone was even aware of it and decided, right then, that he did not mind. This was his brother.

Upon seeing him awake, Halkerstone smiled. Edward was amazed to see his father in that expression and shocked he had never noticed before.

"There is a letter here from Duke Brey," Halkerstone said, holding up a piece of parchment. "It seems the Lady Argent secretly returned to France to outrun some nasty rumors about herself. Unfortunately, the peasants found her. It also seems Miss Gordon is being courted by the son of the Viscount Gage and an engagement is imminently expected."

"Have you been reading my mail?" Edward asked.

"Well, you were unconscious, and since it was from the duke, I thought it might bear news of our enemies." Halkerstone shrugged, not in the least shamed. "I have made sure news of Lady Eleanor's demise is being spread through the lower circles here in Vienna as a precaution. However, a friend of yours, the Comte de Saint Germaine, already took care of Lady Eleanor's agent. Or rather his wife did. Apparently, the man threatened her, and she did not appreciate that."

"The lady is fond of knives," Edward said remembering.

Halkerstone grunted. "And poison too, apparently. I believe there will be no more attacks on the Lady von Croy."

Edward smiled. He did not know what was more amusing, that Halkerstone had opened his mail and not thought twice of it, or that he had gone ahead and spread rumors to prevent more attacks.

"We have a lot to discuss, you and I," Edward said softly.

"All in good time, my lord," Halkerstone said. "First, we must get you healed."

"I have nothing to do but lie here in this bed, Halkerstone," Edward said. "So while I do, sit down and tell me about you and my other sibling."

Halkerstone's expression was purely his own, then, and almost hilarious in its hangdog shock. Then his face cleared, like chalk being erased from a blackboard, all thoughts and emotions vanished. Court trained indeed.

"Where did you hear such things?" Halkerstone asked carefully.

"Do you believe in the stone heart?" Edward asked.

Halkerstone considered and then, gravely, nodded once. He'd seen the wound on Edward's chest close from crushed flower petals. Yes, he was willing to believe in diamonds that were hearts.

Edward chuckled dryly. "You come by belief so easily, brother."

"There are too many beautiful and terrible things in this world not to believe," Halkerstone replied. "God has made so many wonders, and we have only discovered a fraction of them. You have not answered my question."

Edward nodded. "If you believe in the stone heart…" Edward's hand unconsciously touched his chest, his fingers finding where Phoebe's heart lay instinctively. "Then believing in spirits should not be a far leap of faith. Our father told me, when I was unconscious."

Halkerstone sat down and made himself comfortable. "I see," he said. He considered this for a moment more in silence, then nodded sharply. "Then let me begin by saying you have a sister, and her name is Claire."

Stone Heart Historical Reference Guide

Nancy Storace

Born in London, Nancy was a child singing prodigy in England by the age of twelve. This led to further study in Italy and to a successful singing career there during the late 1770s. While in Monza (or shortly before in Milan) in 1782 she was recruited to form part of Emperor Joseph II's new Italian opera company in Vienna. (This is actually why Phoebe ends up in Vienna. I knew Mozart was there at this time period, and as I was researching opera, Vienna became the perfect place to end the story. So, in some ways, the book starts and ends with opera.)

After marrying in 1784, Nancy left Vienna in 1787 and returned to London, where she continued her career, notably singing in her brother Stephen Storace's operas one of which was *The Haunted Tower*. She remained in London, but by 1808 had retired from the stage. She died in 1817.

Stephen Storace

Stephen Storace established himself with his sister in Vienna. In the early 1780s, they moved back to London. In 1789, he moved to the Theatre Royal, Drury Lane, where he established his credentials as a young man who could quickly and competently produce good results. He also had an impresario's skill for judging what would make good box-office hits. He took to adding famous numbers from the Vienna operas to "spice up" works which needed it. Storace spotted a niche in the market for the new "romantic" style of ghost-stories, gothic horror, and romance, and his first purpose-written work for Drury Lane employed all these elements. *The Haunted Tower* (1789) was a box-office sensation, selling out for fifty nights in succession.

Drury Lane Theater

Drury Lane Theater is real, although it has been in continuous use for about 300+ years. In the story it is referenced as the "new opera house." The current iteration was actually demolished in 1791 (two years after this story took place) and wasn't rebuilt until 1794. The theater described in the book references the second iteration (1674-1791) of the opera house and its architectural features.

Bedlam Hospital

Bedlam, or Bethlem Royal Hospital, is famous for inspiring not only the word "bedlam" but also several books and movies. It is a psychiatric hospital closely associated with King's College London. It has history dating back to the 1200s. By 1789 it was as described in the book—deteriorating. The walls were buckling, the floors uneven, and financially it was nearly bankrupt. Also, Edward would not have been allowed to visit without a pass from the governor on the board of the hospital. Bedlam was a convenient place to put Mr. Storace because of his so-called mental breakdown.

The Rookery of St. Giles

Rookery is another word for "slum." The Rookery of St. Giles was famous during its heyday and written about by several people, including Charles Dickens who referenced several in *Oliver Twist*. St. Giles was torn down in the late 1800s as part of an urban redevelopment, but it would have been around during Edward's time. To be fair, the Storaces would probably have afforded to live in a better neighborhood, but I wanted Edward to very much be a fish out of water in that chapter.

Count Alessandro Cagliostro

Count Alessandro di Cagliostro was the alias of the occultist Giuseppe Balsamo. Cagliostro was an Italian adventurer and self-styled magician. He became a glamorous figure associated with the royal courts of Europe where he pursued various occult arts, including psychic healing, alchemy, and scrying. His reputation lingered for many decades after his death, but continued to deteriorate, as he came to be regarded as a charlatan and impostor, this view fortified by the savage attack of Thomas Carlyle, who pronounced him the "Quack of Quacks."

When casting for an appropriate historical magic-user that eventually fell to Saint Germaine, I stumbled across Cagliostro. He was just too interesting not to include. The admittance he makes that he shared a jail cell with a Roma (which in this case is actually Saint Germaine) was not far off from the truth. At least the jail part. He was actually involved in the famous Affair of the Necklace and jailed in the Bastille for nine months. In history, this took place in 1784, but I liked the idea of this man weaseling his way out of trouble, and Cagliostro was quite famous at the French Court pre-Revolution. By the time our story comes around, 1789-90, Cagliostro was actually captured and tried by the Spanish Inquisition. He managed to have his sentence commuted from death to life imprisonment.

Comte de Saint Germaine

The Comte de Saint Germaine was a European adventurer, with an interest in science, alchemy, and the arts. He achieved prominence in European high society of the mid-1700s. Prince Charles of Hesse-Kassel considered him to be "one of the greatest philosophers who ever lived," and he was also known as *der Wundermann* (the Wonderman).

The fact is this guy was nuts. Saint Germaine used a variety of names and titles, an accepted practice amongst royalty and nobility at the time, but no one actually knows anything about his origins. Historians *think* he was a Portuguese Jew. Either way, the more reading I did of him, the better he became for this part-spy, part-thief, magician character wending his way through Europe. The real historical figure spoke many languages, was educated in history and science, and convinced people he could transmute metals or remove flaws from diamonds.

He had so many identities, including the Marquis de Montferrat, Comte Bellamarre, Chevalier Schoening, Count Weldon, Comte Soltikoff, Graf Tzarogy, and Prinz Ragoczy. In order to deflect enquiries as to his origins, he would make far-fetched claims, such as being 500 years old. Again, he was just too good of a historical character *not* to use. It made sense to make him actually part of the Roma people. Traveling, he would pick up languages, he would learn about different cultures and how the nobility worked. I really like this character, and you'll probably see him again soon.

British Museum at Montagu Mansion

Montagu House was a late 17th-century mansion in

Great Russell Street in the Bloomsbury district of London, which became the first home of the British Museum. I know we only see this place briefly, but I wanted to clarify that this was a real space and the first British museum was essentially a house. The British Museum bought it in 1759 and demolished it in the 1840s to make way for the present larger building.

Slugger O'Toole
Is a reference in the Irish folk song *The Irish Rover* as one of the sailors on board the ship Edward takes.

Lady Coventry
The real Lady Coventry was born in Ireland, the eldest child of John Gunning of Castle Coote. Her name was Maria. She and her sister Elizabeth grew to fame after being discovered at a ball held at Dublin Castle by the Viscountess Petersham. They were the Kardashians of their time. Their beauty and charm alone managed to get them from a house party in Dublin to the drawing rooms in London, being presented at court to the king, to marriage into the English elite. Maria, who was notoriously tactless, was reported to have made a notable gaffe by telling the elderly King George II that the spectacle she would most like to see was a royal funeral. Fortunately, the king was highly amused.

In March 1752, Maria married the sixth Earl of Coventry and became the Countess of Coventry. She died at twenty-seven by lead and mercury poisoning, the toxins introduced in her beauty regimen. Obviously, her name was not Eleanor Argent, nor did she marry a French nobleman. When I was searching for inspiration for Eleanor, I wanted an ambitious beauty, and the original Lady Coventry fit the bill, so I borrowed her name.

Dorotheenstädtischer Cemetery
Established in 1760, the Dorotheenstädtischer Cemetery is a real cemetery that still exists today. It is a Protestant burial ground which hosts a number of famous inhabitants. Most notable are resistance fighters killed by the Nazi regime, some of which plotted a failed assassination attempt of Adolf Hitler. It is considered a cultural landmark, and conservation efforts to restore graves robbed and damaged during WWI and WWII have been underway since the 1990s. I liked that it both exists today and back in Edward's time. It seemed a perfect place for the graveyard fight scene.

Duchy of Styria
In the book, Phoebe is being courted by Frederick, the Duke (or Herzog) of Styria. This person is fictional. However, the Duchy of Styria is real. It's now known as the Duchy of Austria. At the time, the Duchy of Styria was filled by the House of Hapsburg nobles, who were also the Holy Roman Emperors. At this time (1789) the Holy Roman Emperor was Joseph II. I wanted Phoebe to be courted by a powerful man, a man on par (or better) than Edward whose own title, the Marquess of Winchester, is very powerful, hence matching her up with a (fictional) duke.

A word about the author…

Kitty Shields (she/her) lives outside Philadelphia, where she writes to overcome the fact that she was born a middle child with hobbit feet, vampire skin, and a tendency to daydream. In her spare time, she binds books, takes bad photos, and tries to avoid the death traps her cat sets for her. She earned an MFA in Creative Writing from Arcadia University in 2015 and has been published in several journals including *The After Happy Hour Review*, *Furious Gazelle*, and *Sick Lit* among others.